To my parents,
Dudley and Norma Delffs

DUDLEY J. DELFFS is a writer and English professor at Colorado Christian University and the former fiction editor of the literary journal *Mars Hill Review*. His essays have appeared in *Discipleship Journal*, *Inklings*, and numerous other periodicals. He is the author of *A Repentant Heart* and *The Prayer Centered Life*, as well as the novel *Forgiving August*, which was a nominee for Colorado Book of the Year, 1993. Dudley and his wife make their home in Littleton with their two daughters.

ACKNOWLEDGMENTS

So many people have helped shape Father Grif, and I'd like to thank them here. The idea for *The Martyr's Chapel* and my protagonist first emerged in Professor Jon Manchip White's Detective Fiction graduate course at the University of Tennessee. Thanks, Professor White, for your encouragement and belief in my characters ten years ago.

The advice and information provided by Sergeant Steve Curti and Sergeant Ray Torrez of the Arapahoe County Sheriff's Department proved invaluable. Matt Sutton provided great suggestions and professional support for this venture.

I'm so grateful for my community of students, colleagues, and friends at Colorado Christian University and their shared interest in my work. To my Wednesday afternoon fiction workshop—thanks for sharing the journey. My teaching assistant, Mike Mitchell, freed up time for me to spend with Father Grif. Dr. Phyllis Klein, Dr. Elaine Woodruff, and Dr. Stan Dyck have been especially kind and supportive, as well.

To my many friends who struggled, laughed, prayed, and encouraged me during this venture, a heartfelt thanks. The relationships you offer me and my family provide a rich model for the community of Avenell.

I'm indebted to the wonderful folks at Bethany House Publishers for their warmth and professionalism. David Horton and Sarah Nierman provided excellent editing and improved the manuscript. Barbara Lilland, thank you for your sustained interest and gracious commitment to this project. Your kindness and efficiency make working with you such a pleasure.

None of this would be possible without my friend Kathy Yanni and her associates at Alive Communications. Your intelligent feedback, patient guidance, rich wit, depth of support, and honest faith inspire me beyond words. Thank you, Kathy.

Finally, my family provides me with the deep love and support that makes all of this worthwhile. My wife, Dotti, and my children sacrificed time while this story came to life. Thanks for your patience, your prayers, and your reminders of what's most important to Father Grif and to me. My parents have also played a pivotal role in this project. I'm most grateful for their appreciation of education and literature. Thanks, Mom, for passing on your love of good books. My parents' support and unfailing belief in me have carried me through many writer's slumps.

CONTENTS

For whoever would save his life will lose it,
and whoever loses his life for my sake will find it.
For what will it profit a man,
if he gains the whole world and forfeits his life?
Of what shall a man give in return for his life?

Matthew 16:25–26

Chapter One

CALL IN THE NIGHT

———

I STOOD AT THE marble altar before a packed Sunday congregation in the Divine Cathedral when the shrill screams began. My homily was going well—I was rambling on and on about how we all needed to love one another more. The sharp intrusions broke through my consciousness with their regular rhythm. I realized my phone was ringing before I realized that I had been dreaming.

"Father Grif," whispered a husky voice.

"Yes," I warbled, feeling for my glasses on the nightstand. Almost three A.M. I responded instinctively, like most pastors do, the way parents awaken to comfort sick children. It had been some time since I'd had a dark-night-of-the-soul call, if, indeed, that's what this was.

"Yes, this is Father Reed. Who is this?"

"Father Grif, I need help . . . I need to talk to you. It's all over . . . please help me." The voice was barely audible, yet nonetheless familiar. I hated to ask who it was, since the caller presumed I knew him, but I couldn't pull a name or face into focus.

"Who is this? How can I help?" I asked, sitting upright now.

"It's Truman. Gentry Truman, Father. I'm . . . I'm going to die, I think . . . and I want to talk to you . . . before I do . . . before it's too late." His voice sounded metallic, full of distance and static—from a car or cell phone, perhaps.

My heart knocked on the roof of my chest in a heavy-fisted pulse. "Gentry, hold on. Where are you? Let me call an ambulance, and I'll be on my way."

My thoughts skipped through my mental map of our small town, recalling our most famous resident's address. I had been there a couple months back at the beginning of fall term. It was the old Mayfield home, beyond the soccer fields off Pine Road in a little neighborhood of restored Victorians called Grove Park. I had loved the old place since boyhood and could remember Mrs. Mayfield, the librarian from undergrad days. Ever since her death over a decade ago—until Truman's recent extensive renovations—the vacant manor house had accumulated dust, legends, and empty beer cans from fraternity hazing parties.

"No, no . . . ambulance." He struggled to get the word out. "I only want to talk to you. . . . I'm here—" The line went dead.

I impatiently drummed the phone trigger without success, then waited a moment to see if he would call back. After a laborious sixty seconds passed, I could wait no longer. A man's life and soul were in jeopardy.

I dialed the police department and got Andy McDermott.

"Andy, it's Father Grif over on campus. I just had a call from Gentry Truman—yes, that's right. Now listen, I think he's having a heart attack. He sounded weak, said something about dying. No, wanted to see me. That's right. I don't know where he was. He started to tell me, but we got cut off. Can you send an ambulance to his house? And maybe trace the call from my line? Oh, I see. Okay, well, send the ambulance right away. I'm going over there right now, too. See you there."

Fumbling for my clothes draped on the cedar chest at the foot of my bed, I heard a light tap on my door.

"Come in, Bea," I whispered and realized there was no need to, since she was obviously awake. My older sister bounded in from the dark frame.

"What's going on, Grif? Car accident? Hospital call? It's Berthy Weismuller, isn't it? I told her not to be out in that garden planting those bulbs. She just doesn't listen, does she?"

My sister's perky voice and alert demeanor betrayed our different approaches to waking. She often awoke fully coherent, expecting to complete the previous night's discussion on anything from theology to the parish picnic. I, on the other hand, could spend several hours in mute solitude before rediscovering the necessity of language. The only exceptions, thankfully, were times like now when I was urgently needed.

"No, Bea, it's Gentry Truman. It sounded like he was dying—said he wanted to see me. I've got to get over there. We got disconnected before he could tell me more." I stood with my back to my sister and pulled sweats over my T-shirt and boxers.

"Truman, eh? Here's your chance to convert him, Grif. Weren't you saying that he seemed interested in the things of God at President Milford's dinner party last weekend? I'll make some coffee and wait up. I'll pray for him. And for you."

She retied her pink flannel robe as I slipped on loafers—though instantly wishing I had grabbed my tennis shoes instead—donned my jacket, and unlocked the back door. "Be careful," Bea called out behind me. My sister's strong maternal instinct lacked natural focus, and I often resented her hovering care, but tonight I was curiously grateful.

A misty, fog-strewn night caressed me as I stepped out the door of the rectory. Usually I walked wherever I went on campus, sometimes rode my bike, and only took the late-model Buick sedan the parish provided when I drove down to the valley. Or when there was no time to waste.

I wheeled through the deserted streets impatiently, sparring with the sheets of fog, led more by familiarity than faculty. Scarecrows and percalesheet ghosts haunted empty lawns, heralding Halloween, only a day away. Turning off Pine Road, I scanned the large gingerbread houses, looking ornate and ominous in the silver strands of moonlight breaking cloud cover. There. An ambulance and a police cruiser materialized through the heavy gray veil, with the former's golden cat-eyed hazard lights winking shamelessly at the red-blue bubble lights next to it.

Gentry and Marcia Klein Truman had bought the biggest Victorian manse in Grove Park—as this little faculty enclave was called—restored it, and painted it pink. It announced their arrival and the kind of people they were louder than a trumpet from the clock tower on the quad. I scanned the small courtyard and three-story mountain before me. The wrought-iron gate hung open like an awestruck mouth, and no lights were visible except for a dimmer in the front hall. I walked through the gate and heard voices.

"I don't know what on God's earth you're talking about," a woman's voice snapped.

"Sorry, ma'am. It's just . . . well, Father Grif called, and he's not one to make prank calls," Andy McDermott replied nervously.

"Well, I don't care if the devil himself called." A man's voice this time. At first I thought it was Gentry's voice, but lower, more regal. Likely his brother's; I understood that he lived here, too.

"We checked upstairs. There's nothing here for us, so we're taking off, Andy—got a heart patient to pick up in Mumford." Two blue-shirted medics backed out of the front doorway with an empty gurney and blended into the night. I let them pass, then entered the home of the man who had called me dying only minutes before.

"I'm Griffin Reed, Rector of Avenell Parish. Mrs. Truman, I believe we've met before." She looked startled, irritated by my sudden appearance. "I'm terribly sorry for all this, but about fifteen minutes ago, your husband, Gentry, called my home. He sounded very weak and asked to see me. He mentioned that he thought he was about to die. We were disconnected before he could tell me where he was, so I called Officer McDermott here and had an ambulance sent right over."

Marcia Klein Truman drew my eyes magnetically to hers. Her angry demeanor faded as she readjusted the sash of her silk kimono-style robe and tucked one black lapel under the other.

"Mr. Truman is well, then?" I continued.

A man snorted, and the brother whose voice I had heard stepped forward from around the corner. He, too, wore a robe—thick terry cloth with a discreet monogram, *CES*, above his heart. He clenched a newly-made highball in his right hand. "*Well* is not the word I would ever use to describe Gentry's condition," he replied.

"Gentry . . . I don't . . . He's not here." The famous actress, so poised and articulate on screen, seemed disoriented. "We haven't been getting on very well lately," she lowered her voice.

"What a charming understatement," said her brother-in-law, ambling forward.

Andy McDermott looked at me impatiently and asked, "Should I call the sheriff or not?"

"No, let's hold off for now. Maybe you could wait on the porch, Andy?" My eyes telegraphed to him the discretion required for this peculiar situation. Under the circumstances, it appeared the family would be more willing to talk to me than to the law. Andy shuffled outside and braced himself against the white porch railing as I pulled the heavy door shut.

Gentry's half brother extended his hand to me as if I were a guest at a dinner party. I felt expectantly disoriented—in part, because the curtain behind our hometown worldwide celebrities was being lifted.

"Cale Sanders," the tall man interjected. "Brother of the boy-genius playwright, Gentry Truman. Half brother, actually—we had the same mother."

I shook a limp hand. Although it was the middle of the night under extraordinary circumstances, I doubted that meeting Mr. Sanders in any setting would be much different. Although a bit leaner and taller than his brother, Cale bore him an odd resemblance: what Gentry Truman would look like had he taken better care of himself. With a touch of gray on his temples, a healthy tan, and a thin mustache that reminded me of David Niven, Cale Sanders cut a dapper figure, even in his bathrobe.

"Father Reed, I'm terribly sorry to put you through this," Mrs. Truman began. "Gentry and I had a disagreement yesterday—the night before last. We were at a theater party, and, well . . . we both said some horrible things. I haven't seen him since then—he hasn't come home. Did he really say he was dying? He's been drinking quite a lot." She regained some of her composure. "Cale, have Marcella make some coffee for us all."

"Yes, your majesty," sniffed Sanders. He darted to the back of the hall and reemerged almost as quickly.

"Where do you suppose he could be? He really did sound in dire need of assistance. He wanted to talk to me before it was too late, he said. Could he be in his office or with friends from the theater?"

"Gentry's all melodrama, Father Reed," said Cale, dismissing my concern. "He pulls these little stunts every so often to get Marcia's sympathy. That's why she stays married to him."

"Cale, *please*. Father, I'll make some calls and see if I can find him," said Mrs. Truman, as if I had granted her permission. "Please, have a seat in the den." She ushered me into a large sitting room to our immediate left and turned on a matching pair of Tiffany lamps. "I'll be right back," she said and retreated up the staircase off the entryway.

Cale Sanders flipped a switch against the wall, and the gas fireplace ignited like a giant match, blazing into blue warmth. The room was exquisitely furnished in muted jewel tones, with several leather armchairs and cherry bookcases lining one wall. On the opposite wall a glass display case enshrouded golden statues and medals, Tony and Academy Awards, Pulitzer prizes, trophies that glittered even in the dim light.

"Fix you a drink while we wait, Padre?" asked Cale, opening an armoire bar.

"No, thank you," I replied.

"What? A whiskey-palian who doesn't drink? Surely not."

"Are you always this offensive to strangers, or can I attribute this to the late hour and unusual circumstances?" I asked calmly.

"Just a little joke, Father Reed. Forgive my familiarity." He lifted his second nightcap to his lips just as a frail black woman entered with a tray of steaming coffee, cream, and sweeteners. I thanked her and fixed myself a cup with extra sugar.

"I take it that you're not alarmed by your brother's call to me, Mr. Sanders," I ventured.

"No, not really. Gent and I have our little spats, just like he and Marcia do. I'm put out with him right now because he brought me here to direct this new masterpiece of his, and then he can't finish it on time. I've been waiting three weeks for him to show me the actual script—and not just the outline—for a show that's supposed to open in less than a month!"

Sipping my hot java, I recalled that Bea, in her inimitable way, had shared rumors of Truman's bout with writer's block. It was no secret that his formerly stellar career could use a success. I still marveled that a writer whose work I knew and respected so greatly had come to live here in our small college community of Avenell, let alone that I was sitting in his parlor while he might be dying.

Gentry Truman was the two-time Pulitzer-winning playwright of such American classics as *Rising Star, Breakfast in Birmingham*, and his best known, *The Ghettos of Heaven*. He had dined with presidents, gone drinking with Hemingway the day before Papa's death, and dated celebrities from Marilyn Monroe to Bianca Jagger. He had been painted by Warhol, photographed by Avedon and Leibovitz, and interviewed by his peers. He was a legend, the kind of theatrical genius who with Arthur Miller and Tennessee Williams formed the triumvirate that defined the American stage for over four decades. In the final phase of his career, Truman continued to write in order to disprove critics who whispered that his talent had peaked but that his ego hadn't yet caught up.

I had devoured his work in college and even now saw stage productions whenever I could. Gentry Truman was *the* playwright emeritus of the American theater, a catalyst of experimental realism in drama, a world celebrity; he had surprised everyone by accepting a writer-in-residence position at our secluded school. Seems he grew up with his grandmother and half brother—I guess that would be Cale—in the valley town of Mumford, about fifteen miles below, all the while observing the affluent fraternity boys and starry-eyed debutantes who attended Avenell. Despite the class hatred that clearly emerged in his plays, he still felt kindly disposed toward the tiny college.

Since he had arrived here this past August, I had managed to have several brief conversations with him. While he played the role of curmudgeoned celebrity, I sensed an authentic seeking heart underneath, the poet who could not hide his hunger for God in the characters he brought to life on the stage.

The drumbeat of Marcia Klein Truman's steps down the staircase broke my reflection. She burst into the room more upset than before. "No one's seen him—he's not in any of his usual places."

"Did you try the Tiger Bay Club?" asked Cale, referring to the bar and grill frequented by faculty and grad students.

"Yes. It was closed, but the manager said he hadn't seen Gentry since Wednesday. I tried there, I tried Mitch's house, Gent's office, the Rolling Meadows Motel, his car phone, and his cell phone. I even called that pathetic little man who drives this town's only taxi, and he hadn't seen Gentry, either." She went to the bar and retrieved a European cigarette from a carved wooden box. Her blunt chestnut hair shone beautifully in the light. Even without makeup, in the middle of the night, the actress still possessed that larger-than-life radiance that won her roles in some of the greatest films of the decade. The exotic clove-scented smoke wafted my way. "I called the New York penthouse and the beach house and left messages, although I don't think he'd go either place alone," she continued. Cale sighed and fixed her a drink.

My mind returned to Gentry, and I wondered if perhaps his desperate call had been born more out of drink than his soul's need for salvation. I finished the last of my coffee and looked at my watch. Almost four A.M.

"Is your deputy friend still outside, Father?" asked Marcia. "Maybe I should file a missing persons report."

"They make you wait until the person has been missing for forty-eight hours," Cale declared. "I'm sure he'll turn up today. Hung over and meaner than ever."

"Father, I'm sorry about all this. Sorry to involve you in our family's personal matters."

"Mr. Sanders is correct. If Gentry still hasn't turned up in another day or so, you can file a report." I struggled to find a graceful exit line. "Well, if there's anything I can do for you, or if you hear from Gentry and he would like to see me, please don't hesitate to call." I headed toward the door, and both Marcia and Cale extended their hands. We shook politely, and Marcia thanked me once more for my trouble.

Andy was sitting in his Carroll County police car sipping from a thermos of coffee.

"So what did you find out? Is Gentry Truman missing or not? Should I call Sheriff Claiborne? Has he been kidnapped? Do you think the wife killed him to marry the brother-in-law?" Andy McDermott compensated for the mundane routine of small-town law enforcement by imagining the worst offenses possible in any situation.

"Now, Andy, just hold on," I said. "Yes, he is missing, I suppose, but it appears to be a domestic dispute. They were at a party, he was drinking, they fought, and he hasn't come home yet. Mrs. Truman called friends and possible places he might go and couldn't locate him. Nonetheless, they think he'll turn up later today. No kidnapping, no murder." I juggled my glasses off and rubbed sleepy eyes with my thumb and index finger.

"Well, shoot. You mean we came out here for nothing? What about that phone call you received? Was it for real or not?" Andy's heavyset frame looked older than his twenty-five years, while the light in his hazel eyes was much younger.

"I'm not sure about the phone call, Andy. I do believe it was Gentry Truman, but he may have just had too much to drink. Let's not be disappointed that something worse didn't happen." I fished my keys out of my pocket and shivered in the predawn morning air. The fog seemed lighter and airier than before, tissue paper wrapping about to be undone by the sunrise.

"I guess you're right, Father Grif. Call me, though, if anything else happens. Otherwise, I'll see you Sunday." He returned to the police car and I to my trusty LeSabre.

As Andy sped off toward town, I looked up and saw a frail light in the third-story window. A pair of eyes peered out from behind a lace curtain. I blinked and the face was gone, whisked away by a moonlit shred of fog. The fine hairs on the back of my neck stood up, and I sensed a darkness settling over this large pink manor.

Chapter Two

ALL SOULS' DAY

―――――

THE WEEKEND PROCEEDED as usual with Saturday spent winter-proofing the car, the house, and Bea's garden. Pete Abernathy, our twenty-six-year-old curate here in the parish, came over to help, and I welcomed his company. Peter was one of my favorite people. He first came to me about five years ago during his junior year, right before Amy and I were married, asking all kinds of spiritual questions. His dirty blond cowlick and innocent green eyes enhanced his easygoing demeanor. But beneath the friendly nature was a heart grieving the divorce of his parents, the heart of a man bursting to leave adolescence behind. I was struck by his honest vitality, the urgency in his desire to know intimacy with our Father.

I became a mentor of sorts and came to view him like a son—people often mistook him as such. Next to Bea, Peter provided the most real support for me throughout Amy's ordeal and eventual death. It bonded us, and so I was delighted when Peter felt convicted in mind and heart to attend Avenell's fine little seminary here. His internship coincided with the bishop's decision to appoint a curate for this parish—someone to help me, especially with the many needs of a Generation X student body. He stayed on, and I thank the Father every day for his companionship and brotherhood.

"So will the Tigers make it to a bowl game this year?" he ventured, pouring iridescent antifreeze into the Buick's radiator. "What's their record now?"

"Pete, I received the strangest call last night." I knew I could trust my curate with such privileged information. "Gentry Truman called me at three in the morning, claimed he was dying, and said he wanted to see me before it was too late. Naturally, I called the police and an ambulance. We all showed up at his house, and he wasn't there. Seems he and Mrs. Truman had argued at a party a couple of nights ago, and he'd never returned home. I got the impression this wasn't the first time this sort of thing had happened. Nonetheless, I've had the strangest impression all day that something is terribly wrong."

"So the celebrities struggle like the rest of us, huh? You mentioned once before that you thought he was asking a lot of questions about God and stuff." Pete retrieved the dipstick, found the oil level satisfactory, and replaced it like he was threading a needle. "Have you heard whether or not he's come home today?"

"Yes, I called after lunch and spoke with their maid. Seems Mr. Truman hasn't returned, and she wasn't sure where Mrs. Truman was. Do you think it would be intrusive to call again after dinner?"

"That's our job. Right?"

We moved to the back of the house, disconnecting outside hoses and wrapping water pipes. The discussion eventually returned to the Avenell Tigers' chances of post-season play. The lingering gold of the afternoon embellished my mellow mood, and I savored the smell of burning leaves from the other side of campus. As twilight descended with the plain beauty of an Amish quilt, I talked Peter into staying for supper—Bea's famous deep-dish pizza—and *Prairie Home Companion.*

A dozen or so trick-or-treaters came hobgobling up just after dark, and we laughed at the variety of clowns, ghosts, Batmen, and Barbies. Screams and moans from the "haunted" house up the block mingled with the bacchanal sounds of various fraternity parties across campus. Peter stayed until eight before departing for his student ministry's All Hallows'

Eve party. Around nine Bea and I began eating leftover candy corn and popcorn balls, and she challenged me to a game of Scrabble. I debated a follow-up phone call to the Truman home but decided to wait until morning.

———

On Sunday Father Jackson brought his small flock of parishioners up from Mumford for possibly the last time. They were completing a building program that had replaced the sad, clapboard structure of St. Anthony's with a new redbrick facility. It was sleek and modern and would hold around three hundred if everyone came, which would only happen on Christmas Eve and Easter. It attracted the younger families with children who wanted programs and youth pastors and all the amenities of a rec center. I didn't blame them, but I continued to wrestle with what the purpose of a church should be in a community.

Philip Jackson, in his late sixties, didn't really fit in with all the new changes and the needs of the younger families. Most of the parish, including himself, knew he was about to retire and pass on the torch to a younger vessel. Personally, this made me nervous, since it was logical that the bishop would offer the post to my curate, Peter, if he wanted the job. Even though he would be only fifteen miles away, it grieved me to think of our brotherhood separated by even that short distance.

Father Jackson, Peter, and I chatted "backstage" in the vestry, donning our white cassocks and albs, the stoles which usually punctuated our vestments with color, also white this All Saints' Day. I enjoyed this ritual of dressing, the time spent with these men of common calling and purpose. It still held the kind of excitement of a bride preparing for her walk down the aisle, and I often felt some disappointment with individual churches who had abandoned vestments altogether. The symbolism of the garments had, indeed, been carried too far before, as virtually everything religious has, but it added a sense of ritual that never ceased to enrich the worship service for me.

I helped Father Jackson with his chasuble, content to allow him to conduct the service since it was his last turn with us. I would deliver the homily and dispense communion; Peter would read the gospel and distribute the bread and wine, as well. The theatrical anxiety I felt before each service never went away. I secretly believed that all ministers have something of the actor's ego. We have to in order to go in front of a group of people and perform not entertainment, not our own story, but the greatest story of humankind: the story of divinity made flesh.

My mind associated acting with Gentry Truman, and I drifted back to his voice on the phone early yesterday morning and the expression of need that, assisted by alcohol or not, sounded deeper than just a spat with his wife. I chided myself for forgetting to phone. Wouldn't it be wonderful to see his face this morning there in that back-row spot where he sat when he came once before?

With Philip and Peter in front of me, I checked myself in the small gilt-framed mirror beside the door and smoothed the waves of my dark blond hair. More gray hairs in the sideburns, it seemed; I still wasn't used to having turned fifty last month. My hairline seemed to recede more than usual, my full face and clean-shaven chin seemed pale. Even my crisp blue eyes—secretly my favorite feature—appeared older. "You've got that Robert Redford look, all handsome and golden, that makes all the parishioners swoon," Amy had often teased. I had always laughed it off, but I was as vain as the next man and treasured her attention. My poor, sweet Amy.

"Grif, you coming?" Peter's terse whisper broke my reverie. The organ bellowed out "The Church's One Foundation," and Father Jackson was already halfway down the aisle. The sanctuary was packed this Sunday, mostly because we were forcing two congregations into one sanctuary, but also because a lot of students were in attendance—a good sign, with credit going to my curate for his rich, relevant ministry to the college population.

As I made my way to the front of the church, I was once again struck by its neo-Gothic presence—the central archway, the narthex, the solid carved oak pews, the stained-glass windows of Miracles and Deeds of Christ shining rainbow hues into our gray-stoned walls. If one didn't know better, the Cathedral of the Divine could transport one to England with its octagon tower just above the altar, between the choir and the apse, and its ancient pipe organ acting as royal sentry. Although it felt ancient and timeless, the Divine had only been completed a few decades prior. Its predecessor, the Church of the Divine, had been expanded and rechristened as a cathedral in the late '60s. Despite the splendor of my present surroundings, my favorite church on campus remained the original little chapel dedicated back in 1867, St. Xavier the Martyr's Chapel. However, when it was clear that the university would flourish, the trustees declared the Martyr's Chapel too small and rustic for a school with such a glorious future ahead. Nonetheless, the dormant chapel remained a lovely, intimate sanctuary.

Realizing that much of the service had passed while I daydreamed, I made a mental note to visit the Martyr's Chapel tomorrow, to spend my prayer time there in the morning, perhaps after my jog.

Tugging discreetly at my amice, I tried to focus my thoughts on what I would say in mere moments. Peter read the gospel of Matthew, the passage exhorting us to care not about our needs such as food, shelter, and clothing. The reading concluded with, " 'But seek first his kingdom and his righteousness, and all these things shall be yours as well.' "

It was time for me to stand and inspire the community to true security and freedom from worry, to chat warmly about Matthew's words, about what it meant for us all to be saints. A cool bead of sweat trickled down my side, and I caught Bea's smiling face from the second row. Mrs. Joan Dowinger sat on the far right, fourth or fifth row. Jim and Susan Pascalini watched attentively with their two teenaged boys from the back corner. Sergeant Dan Warren and his lovely wife, Diane, and Officer McDermott loomed above me from the front row of the balcony. Henry and Martha Merritt caught my eye and smiled their warm assurance. I was a blessed man to live in such a community.

"As I reflected on Matthew's words," I began, "I thought of the time when I was in seminary and my car broke down. It was right before final exams, almost Christmas time. I had been waiting tables, and I had no money. My sister was out of the country, my father was in a retirement home on a limited budget, and my home church—St. Paul's over in Crescent—was already helping me pay tuition. I didn't know where to turn. I didn't know where the money was going to come from to pay for a new transmission.

"I prayed constantly. A week went by. I caught rides with friends and even hitchhiked once. Still my car didn't get fixed. I got angry. This was supposed to be a happy story. Here I was sacrificing to go to seminary, giving my life to the ministry, and this was how I was rewarded."

Smiles and nods, the students seeming genuinely interested in my personal connection to a familiar passage.

"You know, that old beat up VW Bug never did get fixed. I finally had it towed from the seminary parking lot the day I graduated." Warm chuckles. I continued to explain how God doesn't always give us what we want but what we need, with apologies to the Rolling Stones. I concluded, "Our Father wants us to depend on him for everything—even VW transmissions. But if we don't get what we think we need, we are to trust Him nonetheless. It's a difficult temptation to resist taking matters into our own hands and thinking that we know better than God what we need in our lives."

Now the punch line: "This is what it means to be a saint. Not someone who's perfect, who has everything together, but someone who depends on God as his or her Father virtually all the time. It takes practice to exercise our faith, but it's what makes us all saints this All Saints' Day." I elaborated with quotes from Bonhoffer and Annie Dillard and closed with a brief prayer.

Thirty minutes later, after visiting with parishioners and changing my vestments, I drove Peter, Philip, and Bea down the mountain. Lunch never tasted so good as we celebrated with a visit to our favorite spot down in the valley. Miss Percy Walker had owned and operated the Scenic Restaurant on the Mumford square next to the Carroll County Courthouse for more than twenty years. She had been written up in virtually every travel guide, *Southern Living* recipe collection, and even *Gourmet* and *Bon*

Appetit. She remained the same Miss Percy throughout the peaks and valleys of fame. She continued, as always, to cook the same green beans, clover-honey corn bread, mashed potatoes, creamed corn, and twenty-four-hour pot roast that I now feasted on for lunch. Bea had the chicken and dumplings and complained the whole meal about how thick the gravy was—hers was never that rich. Father Jackson and I just smiled. He stuck with his favorite, the cheddar cheese meat loaf, which he claimed, like our hope in Romans 5:5, "does not disappoint."

Bea rolled her eyes and muttered, "Can you believe humanity!" under her breath. I was certain to hear a lecture on my colleague's sacrilege all the way home. Pete kept the conversation lighthearted by describing costumes from his student ministry party the night before.

All around, it was an idyllic weekend, typical of our simple life in Avenell but nonetheless satisfying to the soul. I awoke Monday morning eager to face the week and tackle a meeting with Mrs. Dowinger—Bea's nemesis on the Ladies' Auxiliary committee—that I had been dreading for some time. The cool spell brought in by the tag-team trade of October for November had now tethered autumn in place. In fact, I could smell a cold front on its way. The sun was not yet up, and the campus was bathed in another swath of gray film; the temperature, gauged by my bare feet on the hardwood floor in the dining room, a nice low twenty-something.

Don't get me wrong; I took pleasure in this year's extended Indian summer, the bright treetops' sunlit reds and golds, the evergreen border of the Cumberland Ridge nestled on the horizon to the east. I had enjoyed fresh squash and tomatoes from Bea's garden well into October. But by last week, the warm clime began to feel not only unseasonable, but unnatural. I love autumn and had begun to wonder if it would ever arrive. Except for the brittle leaves under the maple grove in the field behind the rectory, it might have been August.

However, this morning offered perfect conditions for my morning jog, my ritual to start the day, my time to anchor myself in memory or prayer for the day ahead. After quickly donning my sweats, I exited silently through the kitchen door so as not to wake my sister and stretched against the back porch steps. Then I took off, winding my labyrinthine way through the small college community we call home.

In many ways Avenell is an exemplary college town, a southern Ivy-Leaguish kind of school with handmade antebellum brick and jade hedgerows parceled out on top of a mountain. Founded just before the War Between the States by the Episcopal Southern Diocese, Avenell still exudes a nostalgic air of utopian promise.

The location came first, and what an idyllic setting it was. Members of three parish churches in middle Tennessee donated over three thousand evergreen acres along the Cumberland Plateau. Foremost among them was Blanton Stewart, a shrewd, reportedly unscrupulous cotton planter and slave trader who, in an attempt to impress the young Episcopal woman he loved, donated one thousand acres, including Eaglehead Mountain. As I turned up Maryland Avenue, I smiled to myself. For some reason the skeletons in the impeccable university's closet always amused me.

But impeccable it was, right from the start. Bishops Otey and Polk called on wealthy southern planters up and down the Mississippi as well as the southern Atlantic Coast. (Cities like Charleston and Savannah smugly prided themselves on their "missions" contributions, according to Bishop Polk's journal, which we have in the Avenell Library archives.) Our founders had their own pride, as well. They refused to pass offering plates or conduct tent revivals in order to generate funds. As a result, contributing to Avenell University became a kind of status symbol for the affluent planters. By the time the war came along, the Southern Diocese had amassed a small fortune in trust. Although the Union victory disrupted the schedule for groundbreaking, the founders held fast to their extraordinary vision. During Reconstruction, while the rest of the South limped and crawled through the holocaustic aftermath, Avenell University proceeded without delay. The architectural, cultural, and even ethical aesthetic of Avenell was based upon an idealist hybrid of the best of all worlds: classical, southern, and Episcopal traditions. Practically speaking, the founders borrowed heavily from Oxford, Cambridge, and West Point.

The result, as I looked around the fog-strewn streets, was not an educational and theological utopia, but it was nonetheless charming and endearing: ivy-covered brownstones, large white Victorian houses, small redbrick cottages with porches embracing three sides in an odd angular hug, sheepdogs and spaniels lounging on flagstone walks. Despite the definite British feel, the campus retained something almost Appalachian in its ambiance, a lingering humility from the first gray clapboard classrooms and first stone structure—the original chapel, St. Xavier the Martyr's Chapel—my retreat destination at the end of my run.

I loved this community, perhaps the platonic idea of such a place, as much as the actual people and buildings. As a Carroll County native and son of a lifetime faculty member, I grew up hearing tale after tale of Avenell's founding, history, and even its ghosts. While its seclusion and snobbish image sometimes troubled me, I loved it as much as any of its founding fathers ever did. If nothing else, its striking beauty continually surprised me. I never grew tired of its sameness that was ever changing, like a favorite watercolor landscape by a master artist. The way sunlight rained through the rose window of the Divine Cathedral in spring, or the way the campus took on the dynamic personality of youthfulness with each incoming class. The way I felt as I watched my white breath billow before me as I ran through cold, crisp mountain air. Beatrice often said that I wouldn't be a minister if I weren't assigned to Avenell Mountain Parish. Perhaps she is right.

As I neared the halfway point of my run, the fog continued to unspin itself from some invisible bolt of moist, gray cloth, its fine mist ground to powder barely discernible on my face and hands. As it enveloped me even deeper, I gave myself to it and became another ghost, someone who belonged to this enchanted landscape every bit as much as Bishop Polk or Blanton Stewart.

The only other soul stirring on such a dreamy, fog-drenched morning was our current president, Franklin Milford, whom I often saw on my morning runs. There he was, fetching his *Tennessean*, not in his usual monogrammed, dark flannel robe, but already suited on this Monday morning. Probably getting ready for a board of trustees meeting or some official duty for the university. We waved as I turned the corner past his house. He disappeared into the cloud bank that had descended on the President's Manse, an imposing antebellum Georgian with whitewashed brick and green shutters.

I followed my usual course down the main line of Southern Avenue, past the lecture halls, Otey, Hammond, and Stewart, and Avenell Library, past the Memorial Gymnasium and Richmont Field, the bleachers and clubhouse, right onto State Street, and around Grove Park, the neighborhood where most faculty live. I recalled my visit to Gentry Truman's home and chastised myself for not calling again to see if he had returned. Perhaps memory loss came with turning fifty? Or maybe I didn't want to embarrass Mrs. Truman again. I certainly didn't want to deal with Cale Sanders—but I wondered about my prodigal's whereabouts, both physically and spiritually. I promised myself to call later that day.

I continued across the footbridge to the duck pond, behind Pine Woods, and onto the bridge covering the Jackson River. A scream or voice moaned from the back of the woods. I paused to run in place and listen but decided it was the wind picking up the open mouths of treetops.

The adrenaline enhanced my anticipation of my special spiritual retreat. The Martyr's Chapel, the original house of worship for the newly established Avenell University, now sat forlorn on the other side of Pine Woods near a beautiful meadow bathed in wild flowers each spring and summer—mountain laurel, delphinium, wild poppies. The chapel's locale was no longer the heart of campus, and it continued to exist more as historical edifice than as a place of worship. A few vacant cottages and former dorms, now mostly used for storage, were St. Xavier's only neighbors.

The brownstone was basically a crude version of the practical chapels of the British low country. Never holding more than a couple hundred worshipers, the tiny three-room church now served as a popular wedding site for betrothed students and alumni. I favored it as one of my sacred places, a spot where I could be alone with the Lord and enter into retreat with Him for an hour or even several days. Other than curious freshmen or fraternity initiates, no one else ever came here.

During the first week of each month, I made it a point to visit, at least for an hour or so, and pray for the various goals and needs of the church for that month. November had already shaped up as a busy one, what with the Ladies' Auxiliary Fall Festival, Homecoming, and Thanksgiving. Today had its own troubles—my meeting with Mrs. Dowinger—and I would need as much time alone with my Father as possible to stay focused on loving and serving the members of my parish. This morning was the perfect opportunity for such a retreat, with the sun just filtering through the misty spectrum lingering against the faded green mountainside.

I paused on the other side of Pine Woods and smiled at my little haven. The structure captured the diversity of Avenell University perfectly, the blend of wealth and European sophistication with the simplicity and resourcefulness of the mountain people who settled the area. Mountain stone was mixed with imported marble to form the walls. A small, uneven rose of a window bloomed at the north end, one of the first stained-glass windows in the state, stunning with its blend of vibrant reds, greens, blues, and golds. The side windows were imported lead, supposedly smuggled in by Blanton Stewart during the War Between the States.

The beautiful Chapel of St. Xavier the Martyr was an exemplary work. It was also shrouded in romantic mystery because it took its name from another artifact smuggled—or worse, stolen—by founding father Stewart. The ruby-handled Martyr's Blade, as legendary as the Shroud of Turin and just as incredible, was rumored to have been buried in the foundation of the church. Used by an Asian assassin to end the early missionary's life, the knife had not been seen for over a hundred years; it was reported missing from the British Museum during Stewart's heyday as a gunrunner.

The sacred relic had become one of the myths of campus life.

I stood and listened to the cawing of a crow in a poplar tree almost bare now. The mountain whispered "fall is here" in the solitude of the moment. But I felt ill at ease, the same feeling I recalled having outside Gentry Truman's house last Friday night. Striding toward the chapel, I noticed footprints, weeds bent and crushed from the weight of walking bodies. Probably only kids, students out over the weekend for a Halloween thrill, I told myself. If only that had been the case.

The main door at the side of the stone church opened without resistance, unlocked as usual. Inside, the metallic smell of blood assaulted my nostrils, and a stiff body slumped in the altar chair.

Chapter Three

LAST RITES

———

FLIES BUZZED INSIDE my head. I scanned the room, and nothing else seemed amiss except for the body propped in the battered mission oak chair I was accustomed to claiming as my own. Gentry Truman could have been resting in a deep slumber, save for the massive gunshot to the right side of his head exiting, presumably, through the back of his skull, the source of the dried blood plastered into the tan chair cushion.

Incredulously, I drifted toward him, trying to take it all in. His extended hand dangled toward the floor, fingertips just brushing the golden hardwood. The morning light crept through the thick windows with my same trepidation. This couldn't be happening. . . . Gentry Truman, world-renowned, prizewinning playwright, could not be dead; and of all places, he could not be dead in my sacred little Martyr's Chapel.

My mind pinballed with possibilities—a Halloween stunt, a scene rehearsal for his new play, or the cold, hard cord that kept tripping my heart. He had killed himself. He had come here to pray or meditate, to wrestle with God over his writer's block and failing marriage. Perhaps he even called me from here. And now he had taken his own life.

My empty stomach churned, prodded by the penetrating stench of stale blood. Truman's body looked ashen and impassive, one eye seared open from the bullet's exit. I closed my own eyes, as if to make the discovery return to the oblivion of my ignorance only moments ago. But the scene remained lodged in view even with my eyes shut. The odor. The sense of desecration. I swallowed hard.

I took one step toward him up to the small altar table and looked around him for the weapon. No gun in sight. I scanned the dark corners and then looked under the table and chair. Still no gun. Very odd.

Suddenly the door slammed shut and I jumped at least a foot, praying all the while. Only the wind, it turned out, but the sharp retort brought me out of my shocked state. I had to get out of there fast, without touching anything, and get Dan Warren and the police there as soon as possible.

As I backed out of the small room, grasping the simple pews for support, I had the presence of mind to lock the oaken, castlelike door from which I had entered. I jogged slowly, deliberately, conscious of my hamstrings pulsing like cut rubber bands. The nearest home was some distance away and belonged to English faculty member Caroline Barr. Just beginning her second year as assistant professor, she was a striking woman my match-making sister kept on her short list. I wasn't ready for dating again yet—wasn't sure if I ever would be—but now was not the time to worry about Bea's well-intended but misguided efforts to mend the loss of my wife.

It took me several minutes to reach the small white cottage with the smooth river stone chimney on the side. Prim blue shutters and window boxes of pale chrysanthemums graced each window beside the porch, a sharp contrast to the surreal horror I had just witnessed. I rang the doorbell and then knocked impatiently. Likely, Professor Barr would still be sleeping, but this was certainly an emergency if there ever was one.

"Yes, who's there?" came a soft voice.

"Professor Barr, it's Griffin Reed, the parish rector. There's been a terrible accident, and I need to call the police."

The locks on the door began jangling even before I could finish. Caroline Barr ushered me in quickly without a word and led me to her kitchen.

"There's the phone, Father," she said calmly. "I'll make you some tea."

I dialed 9–1–1, heard dispatcher Maria Alvarez's familiar voice, and explained my gruesome discovery. She told me to wait at Dr. Barr's until a squad car picked me up. Another would go directly to the scene.

"Father Reed, I couldn't help but hear. Are you sure it's Gentry Truman? Dead?" Caroline asked. Her appearance suddenly caught my attention: sleepy-eyed, straight auburn hair askew, white cotton robe printed with small waffles and pancakes. She was beautiful, full of life . . . the antithesis of the desecrated form in the Martyr's Chapel.

"Yes . . . Dr. Barr. I . . . thank you," I tried to focus. "Yes, I'm afraid it is Truman, and he looks to be quite dead. I'm guessing his body has been there at least a day or so."

"Please call me Caroline. I'm so sorry you had to be the one to find him . . . in the little chapel in the woods, you said? Why, that's not very far from here. Oh my . . ."

She went pale just as the teakettle whistle shrilled through our exchange. We remained silent as she handed me a cup of chamomile tea, hot and soothing. My mind still could not quite focus on what must have occurred in that "little chapel in the woods." Things like this simply did not happen in our sleepy college community. We had some characters, like any small town in the South, or any college town for that matter, and certainly curious events transpired from time to time. But murder had never been one of them since I'd been here.

A police car whirled into earshot and then screeched abruptly up the gravel drive.

"Thank you, Miss Barr—Caroline. I greatly appreciate your kindness," I said and lifted my mug.

"Perhaps we can chat again soon under less . . . well, tragic circumstances." She tried to smile, fear still in her eyes.

"Yes, that would be nice," I replied. "Thanks again." And I let myself out the door and into the squad car in one fluid motion.

Dan Warren accelerated and backed out the drive, gravel splattering like hot grease. "Father Grif, what in the world is going on? Maria said you found Gentry Truman dead?"

I felt the chill of perspiration trickle down the sides of my chest. "Yes. It's Truman all right. Shot in the head—looks like suicide. In the Martyr's Chapel of all places, Dan. I can't believe it," I said.

"You got any idea what he was doing there? Was he meeting you?" Dan braked to the shoulder of the narrow county highway. The chapel loomed on the hillside above us. "Didn't McDermott tell me something about you calling him over to Truman's house the other night? Something about Truman having a heart attack and calling you?"

"No, I didn't have an appointment with him this morning. That business the other night—peculiar, all right. He called me at three in the morning, said he needed to see me before it was too late, before he died, and then we were cut off. I called Andy and had an ambulance sent over to Grove Park to that big pink house the Trumans remodeled."

I looked up at my giant of a friend, his dark skin like mahogany in the now sharp morning sunlight. I liked his combination of authority and compassion. Dan's over six-foot frame rivaled my own, while his chest barreled out with a solid effect and his wide mustache masked an ageless face. As the only black law enforcement officer for our county, Dan had prevented racial tensions from escalating into violence more times than I could remember. People either respected him or feared him. He was easygoing, his bass voice firm and rich as molasses, yet gentle. His size intimidated many, but I liked having someone to address at eye level.

Dan regularly attended my church with his wife, Diane, and their twin girls. This past summer he had invited me fishing with him down at Falls Creek. We caught a few bream, and sitting on a mossy bank beside him that day, I knew I trusted Dan Warren not just as a police officer, but as a friend.

We strode along the hem of Pine Woods, into a rust carpet of dried needles and splintered pinecones. "Seems Gentry wasn't home. He and Mrs. Truman had a big fight the night before. He was drinking, she said."

"So Truman never called you back? You never found where he was calling from?" asked Dan.

"That's right. I trusted Marcia Truman's story and figured it was a domestic problem. I called the next day and left a message with the maid. She said Gentry still had not returned. I meant to call again yesterday."

The Martyr's Chapel came into view across the horizon. A police Jeep was already on the scene, having four-wheeled across the wooded trail I had jogged less than an hour before. Two officers waited at the door and hailed us as we approached.

"The last time I saw Gentry Truman was at Dr. Milford's dinner party two weeks ago. We had a good chat—we always did. I'm a huge fan of his work, and I think he respected me despite the fact that I'm a priest. We talked about this new play he's been working on. In some sense, we talked about faith, about what he felt like writing on a particular character who leaves the church but ironically discovers faith in God by doing so. I confess, I've been praying for Gentry's salvation since he came here a few months ago. The fact that he would argue theology with me, would challenge my beliefs and respect my opinions and my own doubts, gave me hope that eventually . . . And now this. I simply can't believe it."

Dan asked for the key, and I handed it over to him. He gingerly turned the lock, and the sensation I'd experienced half an hour before invaded me again.

He and the two other officers had their weapons ready to fire and deftly covered the entire building in less than a minute. I had not even considered that someone else might be hiding, waiting to prey on the next entrant.

I found myself sitting on the hood of Dan's cruiser while he radioed for Doc Graham, our county practitioner who doubled as coroner, and for Sheriff Claiborne. A controlled cadence of activity began, like ants covering an apple core, and did not cease for the next two hours. I was there for most of it, lost within myself, quieted by the intrusion of grief and evil into our community. The image of Gentry Truman, slumped and bloodied, lingered behind my eyes.

Finally Dan offered, "I can take you home soon. You'll need to come down to the station to give your official statement, but you can wait until after lunch. Take a shower, let some of the shock wear off."

"God have mercy on his soul," I muttered. "What would drive a man of his talent to take his own life?"

Dan shifted nervously. "We don't know that it's a suicide, Grif," he replied in a low voice. I looked him in the eye.

"What, then? Murder? Who could do something like this? Here of all places?" I stammered.

"It *looks* like suicide. There's gunpowder residue on his right hand. His cell phone was on the floor—with your number being the last he dialed—but there's no weapon. That's what's strange about all this."

I recalled my observation of the same conspicuous absence and told Dan as much. I repeated my question. "But who would want to kill Truman?"

"Maybe a vagrant. Some bum passing through who slept in the warmth of the chapel. This weekend was the first real cold spell we've had. Maybe Truman surprised him, and he snapped. We don't know." Dan shook his head and looked out over the panoramic mountain view as the sun finally penetrated the remaining scraps of fog. He took out a pack of mint gum, nervously unwrapped it with his broad hands, then offered me a stick. I knew Dan was trying to quit smoking and had been successful for several months. "Thanks, but no," I said. "So what happens now?"

"Well, we take him to the morgue. Doc Graham will run his tests, tell us what we already know. Sheriff'll hate this because of all the publicity and hype, not to mention the state boys and probably even the fibbies comin' in on this. Not every day a world-class writer gets himself shot to death in a church."

Dan propped a black-booted foot against his car's front fender. A bearded man and a blond-haired teen emerged with a body bag that contained the remains of Gentry Truman, soulful genius of language and drama.

"I want to go back inside before we leave, Dan," I said.

"What for, Grif? It's a mess in there," my friend replied.

"The Martyr's Chapel has always been one of my favorite places on campus, a private place. I came out here to pray this morning, something I do every couple of weeks or so. Now this violation . . . I can't shake the image of Truman. I just want to see my sanctuary again without a corpse in it." I struggled to explain myself and feared Dan would not understand.

"Come on," he said. "But it's going to take some time for this place to be a sanctuary again, you know."

If it ever will be, I thought to myself.

In the house of golden shadows, Harry Graham popped the back of his camera shut and began snapping the floor of the foyer. I recalled briefly nodding when he arrived over an hour ago. He stopped to make notes in a stenographer's pad before acknowledging our presence with a nod.

"Have you found the weapon yet?" I whispered. "Or know when it happened?"

"No, Grif, there's not a thing in the church that could've made that kind of wound in Truman's head," replied the bald little doctor. "It's been over twenty-four hours, maybe much longer. Hard to tell yet."

I looked around my spiritual home, my beautiful, quiet Martyr's Chapel. I genuflected and said a silent prayer as I approached the altar once more. An odd patchwork of crimson-brown smears stared up at me from the cold wooden floor and altar chair. The sun streamed through the colorful rose window above us, providing an odd spotlight, a garish illumination for the rouge stains. They shone dull and listless as red clay. The rest of the sanctuary appeared unscathed, but the presence of whatever evil had transpired here was nonetheless palpable. Would I ever be able to come here alone with the Lord again? Would the Martyr's Chapel ever recover the presence of the Spirit, snuffed out by such tragedy? I could not imagine it at the moment but had learned in my fifty years never to limit God to my own imagination.

My mind cast several scenarios as to what happened here over the weekend, tried to visualize someone waiting—perhaps a homeless man wandering through town. But my instincts told me something darker, more calculated had transpired. Maybe Truman had taken his own life. Or maybe someone he knew lured him here. Waiting . . . waiting all his or her life, perhaps, to release an accumulation of tarnished rage with no regard for this sacred place, this house of worship. Waiting, crouched in shadows, heedless of the cross on the wall or the meaning behind it. Gentry Truman enters tentatively, uncertain he wants to be here, unsure of why he's come. It's a dark night of the soul, perhaps, or a respite from his drunken binge. Truman hears movement, and before he can react, the other is upon him.

Perhaps Gentry himself was that other, darker shadow. Perhaps he came here knowing what he would do and how he would be found. Something just didn't make sense here, though, but I couldn't quite put my finger on it.

"Father Grif, you okay?" I shook my head and allowed Dan to put his big hand on my shoulder and slowly usher me back outside. I automatically took one last look at the bloodstained chair. I turned my head and a prayer rose from my lips.

"Into thy hands, O Lord, I commend thy servant, Gentry. . . . Into the hands of a faithful Creator and most merciful Savior, beseeching thee that he may be precious in thy sight. . . ." I inhaled deliberately. In some moments it was hard to hold on to faith. The small wooden cross on the wall caught my eye, however. *"Wash him, we pray thee, in the blood of that immaculate Lamb that was slain to take away the sins of the world. . . ."* I stifled the impulse to both laugh and cry at once.

In the unsympathetic morning light, Dan escorted me across the meadow, back toward his police car. Harry Graham was still scribbling copious notes in his green notebook while another officer took exterior photographs. The entire chapel was now encased in yellow police crime-scene tape.

I worked hard to regain composure. "Do you really think someone was waiting deliberately for Truman? He just happened to wander into this isolated little church?" For some reason Dan's theory about a vagrant seemed a typical product of his training, logical but implausible. I wondered, too, why Truman would come here instead of the Divine Cathedral, which in its opulent splendor was certainly more to his taste than the Shaker simplicity of the chapel.

Dan shook his head. "Don't know at this point, Father Grif. Either way, this ain't a pretty scene, especially for a church. And with the victim being a celebrity and all, every camera between here and the moon will be down here by the end of today." He took out another piece of gum and continued. "People don't have no respect nowadays. They'll murder you soon as look at you, don't matter if you're in church or in Harlem after dark."

———

By the time Dan dropped me off at the rectory it was almost eleven o'clock. My stomach rumbled, but I couldn't imagine eating. Dan assured me he'd be there when I was questioned that afternoon, and I thanked him for his kindness and support. As I sat on the porch unlacing my tennis shoes, my sister's voice rose from around the corner, and I dreaded having to recount all the details to her morbid scrutiny. Ten seconds later she appeared from the direction of the garden with Officer McDermott, whom she had taught in Vacation Bible School not so awfully long ago, she was telling him.

As Beatrice finished reminding Andy of his popsicle-stick Noah's Ark fifteen years ago in Bible school—"simply the best ark I've ever seen"— I determined that I would guard the details from my sister as best I could. Naturally, she would be working against me.

I love her, of course, not just because she's my sister, but because of the kind of friend she is, the kind and decent woman she is. But she can be rather sensational at times, and this was just the sort of thing she would relish. She's not discontent, but our lives here are rather quiet compared to her former missions work and inner-city teaching. And while she's more than ten years older than I am—which often feels like an entire generation—Beatrice is still young enough at sixty-one to enjoy life to its fullest. A suicide—or better yet, murder—was just the sort of thing for her to romanticize and enter as a puzzle to be solved. Her faith would not be as unsettled as mine, and I envied her that.

I could imagine her response. She would warmly console Gentry Truman's widow and family, would command an army of food from the Parish Ladies' Auxiliary, but she would nonetheless enjoy the excitement of it all.

"There you are!" she noticed all of a sudden. "Griffin, what in the world are we coming to? Gentry Truman—dead! And you found him. What a shock to the system!" She clutched her throat as if she were about to be ill. "I was terribly worried about you already, and then Andy here pulls up and I just knew you'd keeled over on that morning jog of yours—you're not as young as you used to be. I've told you before to cut back on the strenuous exercise."

I rolled my eyes and prayed for patience while my sister continued. "Andy told me what happened. Just unbelievable—and in the Martyr's Chapel of all places!"

Officer McDermott made a quick farewell, eager to escape a boyhood Bea would never let him forget. I stood with my shoes and socks in hand, she took my arm, and we walked up the porch steps to our home.

"Grif, what's the world coming to? Not only do we have a horrible murder here in little Avenell, but in the Lord's house of all places. Evil's afoot."

"Who said anything about murder? It's likely a suicide, Bea. And you should not be discussing it with anyone, especially the Ladies' Auxiliary. It's bad enough that Andy discussed it with you."

She sighed, and I couldn't help but notice a certain twinkle in my sister's eyes; her genuine grief over the end of a human life was being transformed into a three-dimensional puzzle. Perhaps that is how she remained so strong during painful times.

"I knew something was going to happen today as soon as I woke up,"

Bea continued. "The Spirit was trying to warn me, I think. Since you were already up and about, I made coffee and decided to have morning prayer time before breakfast at the altar rail in the Divine. I came in the side door, your door from the vestry, and immediately felt a chill down my spine. It was like entering a room and knowing someone is watching you, or knowing the furniture's been moved. I knew you were in trouble, as sure as I'm standing here."

She concluded, "I simply cannot believe this. What a tragedy. Can you believe humanity?" My sister clasped her hands as if to pray.

I stood with one hand on the door and the other holding my running shoes and socks. "Can you believe humanity?" is one of my sister's favorite expressions. It's used to question anything that doesn't square with her standard of godliness, everything from a May-December marriage to the sky-high price of a new transmission at Goodyear. In this case, it seemed that her question had finally found an appropriate focus.

I, indeed, could believe humanity and its capacity for selfishness and cruelty. Unlike Catholic clerics, who have the benefit of a specific time for confession and absolution, we Episcopalians manage to burden our ministers at every given opportunity. As a result, I've been invited to enough teas, lunches, breakfasts, and dinners to come to expect some secret sin to be unburdened. Yet I try never to give up on people. I passionately believe that the essence of faith is hope, that there's no soul soiled beyond redemption. However, the end of Gentry Truman's life tested my belief at that moment. While intellectually and theologically I could hope for his last-minute redemption, in the wake of this reality my heart questioned otherwise.

Or worse yet, what if he was murdered! Our Lord can forgive and forever change even the heart of one who takes another's life, but could I? King David came to mind, a man after God's own heart, who nevertheless managed to commit adultery and then murder to cover it up.

Fragments from the Psalmist sprang to mind: *Have mercy on me, O God, according to thy steadfast love; according to thy abundant mercy blot out my transgressions. Wash me thoroughly from my iniquity, and cleanse me from my sin. . . ."*

Whether praying for myself, Gentry Truman, or his murderer, I didn't know, but my prayer was interrupted as Bea and I stood in the hallway of the rectory with open mouths.

"Father Reed, thank heaven you're home. I must talk to you right away—it's about Gentry." Marcia Klein Truman sat on the sofa in our living room wearing a neatly tailored navy suit with a small Chanel handbag on her lap. Her puffy lids betrayed bloodshot eyes as evidence of her concern. "I have a terrible confession to make."

Chapter Four

INTERROGATION

"FORGIVE ME FOR letting myself in," began Mrs. Truman, "but your door was unlocked, and it was rather cool outside. I had that little man—Bert or Bart or whatever his name is—drive me here in that outdated taxi of his."

"That's quite all right, Mrs. Truman. You're always welcome here." Bea reacted first and, to her credit, rose to the occasion. "I'm Beatrice Reed, Griffin's sister. Can I get you some coffee—something else to drink?"

Marcia looked at Bea for the first time and seemed startled by her presence. She demurred, "No, thank you."

I apologized for my appearance and ushered her into my study. "I'm terribly sorry—" I began.

"No, don't apologize for the other night, Father Reed," she interrupted. "It's perfectly understandable—I'm glad you sent the police around to check on us. I've just returned from Nashville and—"

"Mrs. Truman, have the police reached you yet?"

It became clear that she had not yet received the news about her husband's death, which made me even more curious to hear her confession. I had delivered news of disaster and death in a variety of circumstances, and it was never easy. I began as gently as I could.

"I've just come from . . . from our little chapel over on the other side of campus, at the edge of Pine Woods. I went there to pray this morning, but I found . . ."

Marcia Truman looked at me with the kind condescension reserved for children telling a tall tale.

"I found Gentry . . . dead. I'm terribly sorry to have to be the one to tell you." My voice fell to the floor.

"What? You're not making any sense. You found Gentry inside an old church, dead? This is not a very funny joke, Father Reed. I thought I could trust you, that's why I came here." She looked as if she might become hysterical. I rose, stuck my head out the door, and asked Bea to make us some strong coffee. Returning to the widow's side, I leaned against my desk and tried to fill in more missing details.

"I'm assuming you haven't been home this morning. I know the sheriff tried to contact the house, and no one was there." I imagined how terribly unkempt I looked, especially compared to the chic, jewelry-laden diva across from me.

"No, my son and I drove down to Nashville on Saturday morning and are just now returning. I called Cale this morning, and still no sign of Gentry. That's what I wanted to see you about . . . I feel so guilty. And now, I can't believe what you're saying is true." She extracted a linen square from the small navy purse and dabbed her eyes.

Just then Bea entered and set a wooden tray on my desk. She wanted to linger, but I gave her a look that meant business. I poured Marcia Klein Truman a cup of black Kenyan roast into a mug emblazoned with the seal of the Episcopal church. She stared ahead, as if reviewing a film role in her head over and again to take in its nuances.

"What do you feel guilty about, Marcia?" I placed the cup in her hands. She lifted it to her lips, sipped daintily, and smiled.

"Gentry and I quarreled terribly Thursday night. There was a big theater party that evening at Mitch Ferrel's house on the outskirts of campus—you know Mitch, head of the theater department here? Gentry didn't wish to go, in part because Cale would be there taunting him publicly about his writer's block on this new play. On the other hand, he didn't want to go because he would see several people there that neither of us cared to see. . . ."

I nodded, encouraging her to delineate her meaning.

"It's no secret, Father, that I wasn't always happy with Gentry. He was so much older, and I often felt so confined here. Don't take offense, but I'm not quite cut out for small-town life."

Our mutual smiles broke the tension. "None taken, Marcia," I assured. "Avenell is not for everyone. I totally understand."

"In my unhappiness, Father, I've considered leaving Gentry several times. I've even had a few relationships. . . ." At this she began to weep and make a small, contained sound of distress like a kitten. I crossed to sit beside her and offer my handkerchief.

She took my shoulder instead and released the torrent of grief behind the dam. We sat in silence as she poured out the emotion of a tortured conscience. My sympathies believed fully in her sincerity, and I suddenly wished that I might share my own grief with her, that we could embrace in a mutual consolation of lost spouses and regretted opportunities. But I remained composed as usual, always intent on upholding my profession. Honestly, at times like this, I believed the Lord's work would be better accomplished if I allowed myself to be more transparent.

Marcia extracted herself from my forearm and immediately began to apologize. I shushed her and offered my finest hanky, one from an Egyptian cotton four-pack I'd had the forethought to finally open. A birthday gift from Philip Jackson, who purchased them on his last Holy Land tour just a few months ago.

"I don't know why I couldn't stay faithful to him," she sniffled. With her red eyes and feminine vulnerability, she unwound the raw pain beneath her controlled actress's facade. "Part of the problem, you see, is that Cale and I were once involved. In fact, he's the one who first introduced Gentry to me—at a cast party for *The Color of Night*. Even though my relationship with Cale was long past, my marriage to Gentry only fueled the animosity between them. Then when I became involved with . . . an actor in L.A. last year, Cale never let Gentry forget it. Then once we came here, I ran into an old friend, someone I grew up with and hadn't seen in years. One thing led to another, and before I knew it, I was considering leaving Gentry again. . . ."

"And this man was at the party last week," I inferred.

"Yes, and you might as well know. He and I were still seeing each other. On top of that, there's a young woman, a graduate student, whom Gentry took up with just to spite me. She was there, and Gentry disappeared with her for over an hour. I had Frank drive me home—"

"President Milford?"

Her eyes scanned mine. "Yes, Franklin Milford drove me home, and Gentry came in a few minutes later totally sauced. He called me every kind of horrible name he could think of. I kept my cool until he started mocking my performance in the revival of *The Color of Night*. 'No wonder you thought you could play Rachel so well—it takes a whore to know one. But she's so much beyond your range, it was pure charity to give you that role,' he said. I started crying and calling him the same kinds of names. He stormed out around midnight, and I never saw him alive again. . . . And now I never will."

I thought she might weep again, but she did not.

"Despite how much I hated him at times, I'd never harm him, Father," said Mrs. Truman. "I could no more take a life . . . than you could."

She trusted me more than I trusted myself in that regard.

"Do the police have any idea what exactly happened in your chapel?" She wrestled the words.

"No, at least not that they've told me," I replied. "Gentry was shot. That's all we know at this point."

"Oh my," Mrs. Truman whimpered, as if visualizing the scene I had discovered that morning. "Did he . . . did he do it himself?"

"It seems likely. But it's possible he was murdered. Was Gentry in the habit of going to the Martyr's Chapel, Mrs. Truman? He made it plain to me that he wasn't exactly a religious man, but perhaps he was just private about his faith."

"I appreciate your charity regarding his character, Father," she said, "but—someone could have killed him? Oh my . . ." The illumination behind her famous aqua eyes dimmed, as if her mind was overloaded with too much information to process.

We sat in silence. I realized that she needed to get home and attend to the details of the loss procedure: phone calls to Truman's daughters and friends, funeral home, cemetery arrangements, and the like. I knew the process far too well—I could at least offer to help out. Except with someone of Gentry Truman's magnitude, there would be other calls to make: press agents, PR representatives, reporters, and celebrity mourners.

"I'll be glad to drive you home," I said. "I'm sure you have a lot of details to attend to." She nodded vacantly. "I'll be glad to help out any way I can," I concluded.

She rose. "I just feel so terrible about . . . my part in all this. Gentry would never have been out alone in the first place if he and I had not quarreled." I gently guided her arm toward the door and grabbed my keys off Bea's polished cherry dining table.

In the short car ride to the gingerbread Victorian, I tried to assuage her guilt. "I appreciate what you've shared with me. I want you to know that God is more than willing to embrace us with His mercy if we only ask Him to. I'm not saying that because I'm supposed to, either. I believe it with all my heart, or else I couldn't do what I do, day in and day out."

Marcia looked up at me with admiration. "And thank God you do." A sincerity sang through her voice that I could not deny.

"I do have one favor to ask, Father," she whispered after a quiet interlude.

"Anything, of course," I said.

"I want—and I know Gentry would want—you to officiate the service."

Prepared for anything, I was nonetheless taken aback. "Yes . . . I'd be honored" stumbled from my lips. Was my momentary kindness clouding her judgment? Would Gentry really want a priest to officiate a service, a Christian burial? Could I do it in good conscience?

"We can discuss the details after I've talked with Gentry's daughters and with Cale," she stated matter-of-factly as I braked in front of the black iron gate masking the old house. "I'll call you this evening. Thank you. For everything." She let herself out of the car before I had time to kill the engine and open her door. Then she disappeared inside the massive oak door without looking back, in a way that only an actress could accomplish: quick, clean, dramatic.

I drove back home thinking aloud about the extraordinary details of the morning, a practice usually reserved for composing sermons and Bible lessons. But the parameters of this day continued to unfold like a never-ending map charting strange territories, a map that could not be refolded again.

Bea greeted me at the door. "So how is the new widow holding up?"

"You don't sound terribly sincere," I replied.

"I'm sorry, brother, but you have to admit she's a smooth one. I don't want to judge anyone, but she certainly seems to have the most to gain from Mr. Truman's death. You know, I read in *People* that—"

"That's enough," I said firmly. "You don't even know the woman, and you're already speculating on things you have no business in."

Bea pouted. "I'm just trying to protect you."

"Thank you, but the Lord and I do a pretty fair job most of the time." My annoyance subsided, and for the first time I realized that I had not eaten all day. "I'm going to get in the shower now, and I'd appreciate a sandwich for lunch when I get out. I have to be down at the police station sometime soon."

"Yes, you do. Sheriff Claiborne called and asked if we would both come down immediately after lunch."

"Both of us? Why does he want to see you?" A visit to the sheriff's office would only fuel my sister's runaway rocket of speculation.

"I suppose he knows what a shrewd judge of character I am," Bea said playfully.

"Hrrumph!" I sighed loudly. "If he only knew. I'm serious about this, sister. I don't want to hear so much as a whisper issuing from your lips about anything that cannot be verified."

" 'Righteous lips are the delight of kings, and he who speaks right is loved,' " my sister shot back.

"Listen to the proverb," I instructed. "The operative words in your case are 'he who speaks *right*.' " I then proceeded to my room and to a hot shower.

"I hear you, *Father Reed*. I hear you."

———

By one o'clock we were down at the sheriff's office, sitting on an ugly, brown-plaid loveseat talking with Dan and Sheriff Claiborne about what we knew. Or, disappointingly enough, what we didn't know.

"The only time the chapel's locked is in January, during the winter break. Other than that, it's open year round. Besides, there's a lot of keys floating around among the parishioners; anyone who wanted in could count on getting in," I explained. Gentry Truman might have been going there on a regular basis for all we knew.

"We rarely even lock our doors at home, Sheriff!" Bea interjected. "We would never want to discourage anyone—well, except a murderer— from entering God's house."

"When was the last time either of you were in the Martyr's Chapel?" Dan Warren asked.

"Let's see. I went out there for some prayer and reflection a week ago last Wednesday, so that would be the twenty-first, I think." My Daytimer was at home on my desk and could verify my mental calculations.

Dan wrote something down in his file. The sheriff turned toward my sister. "And you, Miss Reed? When was the last time you were there?"

My sister hesitated, and I found her pause odd. She went out there with Mrs. Hightower from church once a month to clean, and that was it, to my knowledge.

"Well, now, let me think. Mrs. Hightower and I were out there on the first of October to clean it good. You'd be amazed how much dust can collect in that tiny little church in just thirty days!"

"And that was the last time you were out at the Martyr's Chapel?" Sheriff Claiborne asked.

"Yes. Mrs. Hightower and I go out there the first of every month and clean the place. That was the last time." Bea smiled sweetly, and I wondered if she was lying. But I didn't know why she would be, and since I did not want to embarrass her publicly, I decided to ignore my hunch.

"Tell me about the phone call you received from Gentry Friday night, Father," the sheriff said, changing course.

I recounted, as accurately as possible, the exchange Gentry Truman and I had had just shortly before his death. As I got to the later events at the Truman home, Sheriff Claiborne nodded and murmured, "Yep, that's what McDermott said."

He stoically took in all the details before moving on to a general line of questioning. "Hear anything unusual on campus this weekend, anything at all? Voices, cars, noises of any kind?" He stroked his chin, and I noticed a small sandpaper-like spot he had missed shaving. Sam Claiborne reminded me of his old high school nickname, "Bulldog," with his small stature yet determined expression. His questions seemed sincere, not obligatory, as if he had suddenly realized that my sister might be an invaluable resource for pruning the local grapevine.

"There's a lot to hear on campus during a weekend, especially Halloween, but I don't recall hearing anything unusual. Just your typical parties. Children trick-or-treating. Fraternity boys shouting and talking, girls laughing and squealing."

Bea interjected, "Dogs barking—the Hendersons' across the street especially, their golden was terribly lonesome last night. I remember hearing a car honk about midnight Saturday as it drove by toward the state highway. Nothing out of the ordinary."

The sheriff stood from behind his desk and began pacing the narrow, well-worn strip of tan linoleum leading from his desk to the office door. On the other side of the bulletproof glass, a redheaded young woman held up a manila folder and motioned to her superior. Dan saw it, too, and said, "I got it, Chief," and was back with the file in hand before Claiborne could respond. The sheriff sifted through the file's documents while Dan looked over his shoulder.

The sheriff finally turned his gaze back on us as if no time had elapsed since his original question. "Father Grif," he directed, "did you hear anything at all before you went into the chapel this morning?"

I thought about the wind's moans I'd heard but felt silly mentioning it. "No, Sheriff, nothing but the wind."

"I've heard fraternity boys often use the chapel for hazing purposes," ventured my sister proudly. "Perhaps some were out there over the weekend and heard something. Daniel, you might want to ask around at the various houses on Fraternity Row."

Dan looked at the sheriff, who looked intently at Beatrice. They were both having a hard time knowing how to assess my sister's instruction.

Claiborne finally spoke and began rubbing his chin again. "Doc Graham just faxed over his preliminary report. It estimates time of death sometime early Saturday morning, no later than sunrise. Since you talked to Truman around three, that gives us a window of approximately four hours. Do either of you know anyone who might have been out there—other than fraternity boys?" He looked directly at Bea. "Anyone from the church maybe?"

We both thought for a moment. "I'm sorry. To my knowledge, there was no reason for anyone from our parish to be out at the Martyr's Chapel."

"I really think you should question those fraternities," Bea responded.

"Is there a specific reason that you think some frat boys were out there that night, ma'am?" asked Dan. He leaned in, and Sheriff Claiborne stood up.

"Well, no . . . but you never know." I could tell she hated to disappoint her audience.

"We are considering that maybe a drifter jumped Truman unexpectedly," replied the sheriff. "I'll have Dan and McDermott ask around at the frat houses, too."

He stood and looked out the glass wall toward the filing cabinets behind the receptionist's desk. "Tell me how you knew Gentry Truman again. Warren, you gettin' all this down?" The sheriff moved suddenly, refilled his coffee mug, and yelled out the door for more.

"I've been a fan of Gentry Truman's since I was an undergraduate. I was an English major, Sheriff, and especially enjoyed drama. As you know, Truman was a literary legend by the time he was thirty. I'll never forget the first time I saw *Rising Star* with Jimmy Stewart in the lead. When Truman came here last year and accepted the writer-in-residence position, I was ecstatic. We talked at socials, the president's dinner parties—he even came to a service once. A very sensitive man beneath that curmudgeon's exterior. He heard that I quoted from *The Ghettos of Heaven* in a sermon once and told me that if I ever did that again he'd have God fire me. And then he let out this great belly laugh."

Sheriff Claiborne nodded, waited for Bea to chirp in, but she didn't.

"What about his family? Did he get along with his wife and kids? Did they come to church with him? Ever come to you in private, anything like that?"

"Sheriff, let me remind you that the relationship between priest and parishioner is privileged, as you well know. Gentry's wife seems nice enough. I've only been around her at social occasions. She didn't attend services, either." I tried not to sound pious, as if I blamed the sheriff for asking, or as if I had been prejudiced against Marcia Klein Truman for her absences. "She's a very attractive woman, early forties, quite a bit younger than her husband. Gentry told me that they met in New York in a Broadway revival of *The Color of Night*. She had the part of Rachel, the role Vivian Leigh originated back in the early '50s. Quite a good actress, according to Gentry."

My sister raised her eyebrows, as if I liked Gentry Truman's wife, whom she had already established as her prime suspect. I had been waiting for her to cast shadows on Mrs. Truman's reputation, and now was her chance.

However, I kept speaking before she could begin. "Mr. and Mrs. Truman each have children from their previous marriages. In fact, she has a son who's a freshman here at Avenell this year. His daughters are all in New York. Or is it California? There are three daughters, I believe, all somehow involved in the entertainment business." I surprised myself by how much I knew about Gentry's private life.

The sheriff nodded and perched a hip on the corner of his oak desk. "You have anything you want to add, Miss Bea?" The sheriff returned to his sincere approach with my sister, practically begging her to unleash the gossip he suspected was there.

"Oh, I don't really think so, Sheriff. Grif knew Mr. Truman much better than I. One hears things, but you can never pay any attention to the silly gossip that floats through a Ladies' Auxiliary in a small town." I was proud of my sister's restraint.

"Well, that's true, Miss Beatrice. And I know you're not one to gossip. But often rumors lead to truth or to people who know the truth. Smoke means a match was lit somewhere. If you'd care to share anything you've heard, I'll certainly keep in mind that it's only rumor. . . ." The sheriff humbled himself like a suitor late for a first date.

My sister looked to me as if for permission, then cleared her throat dramatically. Dan handed her a paper cup of water. She sipped and said, "As a matter of fact, I did hear that Mr. and Mrs. Truman were having problems back during the spring and summer. They were supposedly on the brink of divorce. It was even printed in the 'Chatter' column of *People* magazine. Seems Mrs. Truman fell in love with someone on campus." Bea relished sharing this last revelation.

"Did you hear who this someone might be?" Dan asked.

"No, Dan. In fact, that was part of the big mystery. Seems one of the women in our Auxiliary works in the library and overheard the Trumans arguing in the stacks down in the basement. He said something to the effect that they had moved from New York to remove temptation and yet she had managed to do it again. She then accused him of seeing one of his students, which he denied. It went on and on, a terrible row."

Sheriff Claiborne was back to stroking his chin, scratching the spot his razor missed. Dan Warren was taking notes. Neither seemed certain what to ask next.

Bea broke the silence: "Marcia Klein Truman strikes me as a very demanding woman—"

"Sister, remember our little talk. You don't even know Mrs. Truman."

"True, Grif, I don't. But I do know that she's always making Mr. Spradley down at the market order special items—kosher meats, French truffles, guavas from Tahiti. Says she refuses to drive all the way to Nashville or Atlanta when he can order it for her. Seems his usual brands aren't good enough; everything has to be European, organically grown, or gourmet."

"Really, Beatrice. That's not exactly a scientific basis for a character study. Grant the woman some right to her choices. She's from the city, with exotic tastes. It doesn't make her dangerous because she likes caviar instead of sardines."

Dan turned his head, but I caught the corner of his smile. I also wondered if, despite my defense, Bea was right. Despite the fresh details from her visit that morning—which I was pleased Bea had not brought up yet—Marcia Truman had initially struck me as very demanding indeed. It was over a month ago at a reception for new faculty in Logan Hall. She and Gentry kept everyone entertained with their celebrity stories, each trying to upstage the other. Funny thing, though. It wasn't the way she treated Gentry that formed my impression, but rather the way she treated her son—Dylan, I think his name is. He practically waited on her the entire time. In fact, I had thought he was with the local caterer at first. And while I wanted to give her the benefit of the doubt—if nothing else but for Gentry's sake—I wasn't the least bit surprised when I had heard about her alleged affair. Truth be told, I was just as tempted to judge as my sister.

"You've both been very helpful. If we have further questions, we'll call you. Father Grif, we'll need to keep the church locked up for a few days, get it thoroughly searched and cleaned up. Dan, would you show these folks out, please?"

"We don't use it for regular services, so the chapel's yours as long as you need it," I replied.

Dan escorted us out of the sheriff's office and down the hall to the steel, double-doored entrance. He shook my hand and said he'd see me Sunday if not sooner.

During the short ride home, Bea sighed, "Well, we didn't learn much there."

I imagined Sheriff Claiborne making a similar statement to Dan right then.

"What do you think? Who murdered Gentry Truman?"

"How should I know? We still don't know that he didn't kill himself. The police don't even have a clue yet, and you think I would?" I tried not to sound exasperated.

"I don't buy that drifter-waiting-in-ambush theory for one minute. We simply don't have drifters in Avenell. Oh no, my bet's on Mrs. Truman's mysterious paramour."

"Bea, I thought we went through this already. . . ."

We drove in silence along the state highway leading back to campus, Bea obviously miffed that I wouldn't join her amateur sleuthing. I tried to distract myself from our new center of gravity with the sloping landscape. Most of the autumn colors were now peaking, bright crimson blushes among the roadside pines and cedars. The town of Avenell was virtually nondescript except for the presence of the university. The main street ran parallel to the Louisville and Nashville rail tracks, although the big diesel trains no longer stopped at the faded green clapboard station on the north end of town. We had the usual grocery store, gas station, all-night convenience market up near the interstate, Dairy Queen, and post office. On campus, of course, we had the university book and supply store, the Eagle's Nest Diner, as well as the Bishop's Common. No shopping malls or movie theaters (except for the theater department's screening room that showed cinema classics on weekends), and only the Tiger Bay Pub, and one liquor store with a drive-through window.

I wondered how the media would portray us. The town was southern picturesque, but now the portrait had been marred by an unwelcome intrusion. I pondered whether the murderer was someone outside our community, someone who violated us with an alien darkness. Or whether the murderer was someone we knew, someone whose volcanic heart could no longer be contained beneath a placid exterior.

I agreed with Beatrice that we didn't have real drifters in Avenell, but as we passed the tiny post office next to Spradley's Kwik-Shop, I couldn't resist trying to shake her certainty. Pointing to a grungy man in a torn flannel shirt, I said, "There's old Charlie. He's a drifter of sorts, I suppose. Maybe he finally went off the deep end." I didn't think our town drunk could be a murderer any more than Bea did, but I enjoyed breaking the tension of my previous anger.

"Oh, for the love of grace, Griffin. Charlie Baxter couldn't hurt a fly. Last Friday night he was . . . probably loaded up on cheap whiskey, I'm sure. How can you even joke about poor Charlie doing something so violent and brutal?"

Her defensive question sobered us both as I silently replayed my memory-tape of the slumped playwright blood-plastered to the altar chair in the Martyr's Chapel. I regripped the steering wheel and turned off the highway toward campus. The two-lane road was surprisingly congested. I expected the news to be out, but nothing prepared me for the deluge of traffic. News vans with mini-satellite dishes and out-of-town cars already lined the streets close to campus. At least two reporters were taping shots as we drove past, making sure to get the octagonal tower and the rose window of the Divine Cathedral into their frames. I dreaded the sensationalism that would follow, as well as the negative publicity for Avenell.

Beatrice was thinking the same thing. "Look at all these vultures. They'll crawl out of the woodwork and make it sound like Avenell is just a hotbed of sin and vice."

"Promise me right now, Bea, no interviews. I don't care if Barbara Walters agrees to be your best friend, you'll give no comment. Agreed?"

"Grif, I'm hurt. Do you think I have no respect for the dead? Of course I won't be interviewed!"

I turned into our drive and found a small collage of reporters, cameras, and lights already assembled. A mess of cables, cords, and electric wiring had practically spun itself into a web around the front of the church and parsonage.

As I switched off the ignition, my sister said, "Mark my words, though, about Gentry Truman's death. I'm not so sure the man killed himself. My intuition tells me that someone did him in. A lot of secrets will be exposed before we get to the bottom of this."

"*We* won't be getting to the bottom of anything, sister. You are not to go playing amateur detective. This is not an episode of *Murder, She Wrote* for you to solve before Jessica. This is real life, someone we actually know, with real repercussions. That includes real people's reputations, so don't be speculating about poor Mrs. Truman with anybody. And that includes your Auxiliary ladies."

My sister pouted like a little girl chastised for a good deed. I love Bea, and I didn't mind her inquisitiveness; I suppose I even enjoyed her mothering me some of the time. But I didn't like her nosing around in others' business, especially when the consequences were so grave. I knew her sulk wouldn't last long—she'd be talking about Truman's death again before supper.

As we got out of the car, a striking blond woman in a long trench coat darted from the side of our house with a cameraman in tow. She shoved a microphone in my face before I could reach the porch.

"Father Griffin Reed? Is it true that you found the body of Gentry Truman in the church known as the Martyr's Chapel here on campus?"

I found myself nodding without realizing it. "No comment," I finally mustered, pressing forward. Bea had made it to the door and was fumbling with the latch.

"One last question, Father Reed. Isn't it true that *you* are a suspect in Truman's murder?"

Chapter Five

FEAR AND PITY

"ISN'T IT TRUE that you were the last to talk to the victim alive? Isn't it also true that the two of you often argued over beliefs in God?" the reporter charged.

"No! Why, that's not the way it was at all." My anger brought me back to myself, and I squared myself before the woman's porcelain features. "You listen to me, miss. You take your sleazy allegations somewhere else. To accuse me of Gentry Truman's murder—why, you ought to be ashamed of yourself!" I bolted up the porch stairs and into the door Bea held open for me.

"It's just my job, Father! No offense!" the young woman yelled behind me. "Nothing here, Tom. Let's head back over to Truman's house and see if we can catch the wife again." Her cameraman grunted, tilted the camera down, and hitched his low-riding jeans back up the horizon of his backside.

Prime Edition adorned the back of his black jacket, and I heard my sister voice both our contempt, "I do not believe humanity! The nerve of that woman to accuse you of Gentry Truman's murder. Why, I'd never believe it if I hadn't seen it with my own eyes. That *Prime Edition* show is so sleazy—not even Roberta Montoya watches it!"

Serious sleaze, indeed, if the chief gossip of the Ladies' Auxiliary refused to watch it. The room felt cold, and I checked the thermostat and raised it a few degrees. Then I slumped into my easy chair beside the stone fireplace.

Bea busied herself in the kitchen, and I knew it was all she could do to keep from calling one of her friends to report this latest insult. Venturing to keep her distracted, I called out, "We may want to light a fire tonight. What do you think?"

"Fine, Grif."

"Should we invite Peter over? We could play the rubber game of Scrabble from the other night."

"That's fine. You know Peter's always welcome."

I peeped in the swinging saloon doors to the kitchen and saw my sister craning before the window to see the variety of reporters, celebrity anchors, and mechanical equipment each required.

"No harm in looking," she said curtly.

I smiled and headed to my study. This whole business was fueled by the same morbid curiosity that drove people to rubberneck alongside roadside accidents. The attraction/repulsion accompanies any tragedy, but with a celebrity involved, it captured public interest on a broader scale. In fact, it was probably the closest thing we had to what Aristotle defined as dramatic tragedy—the downfall of a person of renown that evokes fear and pity in the viewers. And thanks to shows like *Prime Edition* and even the evening news, for that matter, which exploited such losses, it threatened to become pure spectacle.

As I scanned my bookshelf for Aristotle's *Poetics* to check my memory, my cold, angry fear enveloped me once again. The intensity of such a private, intimate act as grief reduced to nothing but a sensational headline and a sound bite for higher ratings. Such exploitation and consumption was a tragedy all unto itself.

I knew my critical spirit was supported by more than just the events of the day, more than just my frustration with our culture's weaknesses. No, below those feelings was a current of loss that even now, four years later, I could not easily assuage. The powerlessness, the fear, the wound that only seemed to grow with time. . . .

It was the same kind of fear, the same kind of helplessness I felt when Amy first became sick and was diagnosed with cancer. It would eventually encompass the same kind of rage and doubt. We had been married only a month over a year when we decided that at our ages—I was forty-six, she thirty-seven—we should try to start a family if we ever intended to have one. We both longed for children, excited by the possibility of twins that ran in her family. While we enjoyed the satisfaction of a life of service, ministry, and teaching, each of us felt a deep reservoir of love within waiting to nurture a child. It flooded our hearts at times, especially when seeing friends with their little ones or when I officiated christenings.

I yearned for children, ached to create with Amy an image of God's blessing. A blond pixie girl with Amy's eyes. Oh, those eyes. Deep translucent green framed in hazel like some exotic gemstone. Or a son to bear the Reed name into the next generation. Neither would ever be. I couldn't even hold on to Amy, let alone create a product of our love.

When I think of our life's undoing, I always remember the beginning. She came home from the OB/GYN's office and knocked on my study door.

"Grif, we need to talk."

Before I could rise from my chair, she was in tears.

"They found a cell mass . . . inside me. I can't have kids, Grif. I can't have kids."

She melted against my chest, and I didn't have anything to say. She was so weak that I literally held her up. I remember running my hands through her honey hair, comforting her as best I could, and looking up and focusing on a book that leaned out crooked from my bookcase: C. S. Lewis's *A Grief Observed*. That's when the deep unsettling started inside me. Somehow I knew that no matter how hard I prayed or how much I hoped, it didn't matter. It was God's way of foreshadowing the loss, and perhaps He considered such a sign a kindness, but it seemed cruel at the time.

I never told Amy about that premonition—never told anyone about it. I'd like to think I read too much into things like that, but then they prove true. Amy went through two rounds of chemo and radiation, the cruel mountains of hope and anger, the loss of her beautiful gold hair, the nausea—all of it. I endured the role of a minister, but it became an automatic series of motions, like when I waited tables to put myself through seminary. I'd take orders, serve food, clear tables, all the while turning over dispensationalism or Luther's treatise on grace in my mind. While she was sick, I still preached, taught, comforted, studied Scripture, but this huge shadow floated around inside my heart and head. It expanded like an oil slick until I could not breathe without inhaling the dark, stagnant smell of loss.

Amy had been dead four years now. I would never be over her, of course.

Afterward, I went on sabbatical for six months, traveled abroad, visited Bea in her little village in southern China where she taught English to young children and loved them with her fierce, unnerving love. In fact, it was Bea who unknowingly convinced me to stay in the ministry. I was so angry then, so enraged that Amy and I both had devoted our lives to God only to be teased by such a brief time together, taunted by what might have been had she lived. It was so hard to view it the other way, the proper "Christian" way, that we were fortunate to have been given even a short time together, that I shouldn't question His will. But I couldn't *not* question it—I'm as human as Job, and I lost myself in the *why* of Amy's loss.

"You must be willing to ask why, or you'll never come out the other side," Bea explained matter-of-factly.

"And what is the other side?" I retorted.

"Why, faith, of course. The hope that we can't see right now. If you had all your questions answered, you'd still be just as sad and just as angry.

Will you love Him in the midst of your loss? That becomes the real question."

That day I just shook my head and ate my rice in silence. It wasn't some dramatic epiphany that allowed me to spring back into serving God with gladness. But it was a subtle turning point, nonetheless, a slow wrenching pivot. Despite the burning hole in my heart where my grief resonated, there was a quiet center to it, a small eye of stillness amidst the ravaging winds. Beatrice uncovered it that day, lanced the isolated pocket of despair festering inside me. I can't explain it, but a peculiar kind of faith has continued to grow from that empty hole. As angry and grieved as I still am much of the time, I discovered amid my sorrow that I still care about people. I still love God. I still believe what Julian of Norwich wrote: "All manner of things shall be well."

I prayed that Marcia Truman and Gentry's children would find a similar thread of God's hope to cling to.

———————

"Grif—telephone!" Bea called out from the dining room. While my sister screened my calls fiercely when I retreated to my study, I was still annoyed.

She stuck her head in my door. "Sorry to bother, but I think you'll want to take it. It's Marcia Truman." She extended the cordless phone from her right hand like a present.

"Thank you," I said, and then into the receiver, "Hello, this is Griffin Reed."

"Thank heavens you're home," came the sensual voice. "I need to talk to you tonight about Gentry's service." Hers was a voice whose speaker knew its effect on people and had made a career off it. "That is, if you're still willing. I heard you were assaulted by those scum reporters just as badly as we were here at the house. I'm sorry, really sorry."

"Don't apologize. Of course I'm still willing to do the service. What time would you like me to come over tonight?" I wondered if I'd still be

willing to do Gentry's service if his widow were not so charming. I hoped
that I would.

"Would eight o'clock be too late? By that time, I hope some of these
dreadful vermin will have scurried back to their holes. Gentry's two older
daughters will not have arrived yet, but we can at least go over prelimi-
naries."

"I look forward to meeting the rest of your family," I replied.

"Yes, I hope we can all agree on what Gentry would want." The
thought seemed to distract her. "Well, I won't take up any more of your
time, Father Reed. Thank you again . . . for this morning and all. I feel
much better. We'll see you at eight. Good-bye."

I stood holding the phone until the recorded operator beeped ob-
noxiously for me to please hang up the phone or dial again.

———

That night Beatrice, Pete Abernathy, and I sat over a supper of stew
and homemade bread and kept the conversation away from Gentry's
death as long as possible. As Peter dished up his second helping of Bea's
savory beef, potatoes, and carrots, she wiped the corners of her mouth
with a paper napkin and announced, "Well, I can't stand it any longer.
You two can play coy all night if you want to, but I know this situation
is on your mind just as much as mine. And I might as well tell you, I still
do not like the idea of you going over there tonight, Grif."

Peter let a slight smile unfold. I refilled my bowl and tore off another
chunk of sourdough.

"You could be walking into the black widow's parlor, for all we know.
She reminds me of a Delilah—a good actress just so she can get what she
wants. And maybe she just wants to keep a close eye on you in case you
heard or saw anything at the scene of the crime that might incriminate
her. For your own safety, Grif, don't go over there alone tonight, please."

"I suppose I should take you along as my bodyguard?" I asked playfully.

"No, no, Grif, I'm serious. Take Peter with you. Or maybe Dan Warren or one of the elders—Dwight Taylor or Jack Sheridan, perhaps. They're big men."

"I have been working out, you know," said Pete. He and I began to laugh, and I got so tickled that I had to have a drink of iced tea to compose myself. Bea, needless to say, was not amused.

"You two laugh if you want. You both deserve each other!" With that my sister rose and began to noisily clear the table.

"We'll do the dishes for penance," I offered.

"Absolutely," Pete chimed in. "As usual, a wonderful meal, Miss Bea."

A curt "thank you" was her only response. She retired to the living room and her favorite wingback, a chair that matched her character perfectly with its bold feminine swirls of botanical peonies and hollyhocks in blues and reds. She tuned in *Wheel of Fortune* but not loud enough to eclipse her muffled chatter on the phone to Roberta Montoya.

Meanwhile, Pete scraped and I rinsed and loaded the dishwasher. "Would you like to go with me tonight?" I asked. Despite my sister's melodrama, it suddenly seemed like a wise idea for many reasons.

"Seriously? Wouldn't I just be in the way?" he countered.

"I believe your presence would make the visit seem more official. Also, Gentry Truman has three daughters—and then there's Marcia's son, Dylan—who are all much closer in age to you than to me. They might be comforted more by someone they can relate to. Plus, you know what it's like to go through a divorce, which all of them have endured."

To myself, I thought, *And you might be more objective than I am concerning the Widow Truman's charming character.* Was it real or merely guile? What if Bea was right? Despite her nosiness, she was a good judge of character. Was Marcia Truman really a Delilah, waiting to cut the locks of anyone who stood in her way? The woman had won awards for being such a fine actress; she'd even been nominated for an Academy Award several years ago.

"Sure then, I'll be glad to go with you. I need all the practice I can get dealing with these kinds of situations."

"It's settled, then," I said and patted his shoulder. If nothing else, another pair of eyes inside the Truman house couldn't hurt. Peter's presence had a very calming effect on me, and the fears I had felt earlier seemed years removed.

As my curate wiped the table and stacked place mats, I gazed outside the kitchen window as a warm autumn-orange glow nestled up against Eaglehead Mountain. But the vista was broken by the net of cables, mini-satellites, trench-coated reporters, and ball-capped men and women with cameras on their backs. After Marcia's call this afternoon, the torrent of calls from producers and reporters became so unbearable that I let the machine take all calls. I returned none of them and even unplugged a thick yellow cord that some television crew had attached to our front porch outlet.

Like flies in August buzzing around Bea's kitchen as she made strawberry jam, the media hyped Gentry Truman's death as their lead story. Bea informed me that her favorite talk show had been interrupted three times with inconsequential updates. She accurately observed that if his death were ruled a murder, this might become the next "Crime of the Century," feeding the public's repugnant appetite for violence and celebrity. In fact, Bea heard from her friend Charlotte, the society editor for our local *Clarion*, who heard it from a reporter from WCHT, a Chattanooga TV station, that every major network was on site for coverage. Dozens of local affiliates from all over the South had also converged on Avenell in hopes of watching a real-life drama—as dark as any Gentry Truman ever wrote—play itself out.

"What are you thinking?" asked Pete, setting the pepper mill back in the whitewashed cupboard. "I know this must be hard for you, finding the body and all. I figure this must remind you a lot of losing Amy."

"Yes, it has," I said, appreciating the kind sensitivity of this man I loved like a son. "Right now, though, I was just wondering how this man's death is going to affect our little community here. I can't help but fear that it will have permanent repercussions."

"If it hasn't already," he said. Silence ensued, and Pete respected my cue not to talk further about Amy.

"Do I need to run home and change clothes before we go to the Trumans'? I don't want to embarrass you."

I scanned Pete's jeans and V-neck sweater. "You look fine. Even though we're going on business, I don't want it to seem too stiff or formal."

He nodded, and I looked up at the copper rooster clock above the stove. Noting it was half past seven, I said, "I guess we'd better be going soon. It may take longer since we'll have to dodge the media and clear the police guard outside the Trumans'."

"I'm ready when you are," Pete declared and let out a long sigh.

We left Bea cross-stitching Christmas ornaments for the annual Holiday Craft Bazaar that was only a month away. I heard her pick up the phone just as the door closed behind us and knew she'd be on the line to Roberta or Doris or Mary Alice again when we returned.

Peter, in his black leather jacket, and I, in a forest field jacket and wool cap, blended into the cast of the night—straggling reporters, undercover police and special agents, and the usual students and faculty out for a curiosity walk on a fine autumn night.

Andy McDermott stopped us at the corner of Pine and Princeton and then smiled sheepishly when I lifted my cap. "Can't be too careful," he warned.

As we turned the corner, a male model-turned-reporter was taping a spot in front of the library. "Avenell University, a school for the southern elite, founded in 1856 by Bishop James Otey and funded by wealthy cotton and tobacco magnate Blanton Stewart. Modeled after Oxford, with unique antebellum touches, Avenell has become an impeccable liberal arts institution and graduate seminary. This well-groomed, preppy college is nestled beautifully within the splendor of the Cumberland Mountains, if not incongruously within its rural Tennessee locale. Its standing in literary circles is especially well known thanks to the *Avenell Quarterly* and the Avenell Summer Theater Program, and most important, because of its most famous faculty member, writer-in-residence Gentry Truman. It was here this morning that the legendary playwright was found dead, shot in the head inside the rarely-used historical church, ironically known as the Martyr's Chapel. . . ."

The reporter's description of the campus was accurate enough but didn't fully capture the ambiance, the feelings of pride and nostalgia that enveloped students and residents alike in Avenell. There was a symbiotic relationship between the town and the university—each needed and enjoyed the other. There was a mutually shared superiority in the prestige of Avenell, for the school and the town. Nonetheless, it was charming, even quaint in the best sense of the word. The social class differences, while remarkably apparent, did not prevent the prevailing sense of community. Young women from aristocratic New England families, fully dressed to the nines in designer dresses, could frequently be seen sincerely conversing with the local salesgirl at the drugstore lipstick counter. Young freshmen from western prep schools would congregate in the local barbershop, talking with the regulars about hound dogs and dove hunting, dropping peanuts in their Cokes because the old men did. Locals—the "townies," as they were often called—sincerely enjoyed the air of youth, vitality, and glamour that the affluent student body brought to their unique community. It was an odd, complementary relationship that had endured for the better part of the school's existence. I grew up watching it, since my father taught mathematics here, and I experienced it firsthand as a student over thirty years ago.

"I see the tabloids are already calling it the 'Murder Chapel,' " commented Pete. I nodded and recounted the assault by the *Prime Edition* reporter that afternoon. My curate whistled incredulously and shook his head in contempt. "Anything for a story," he summed up.

Strolling down Southern Avenue past the President's Manse, my mind returned to how—or even if—a murder would complicate or fracture the community spirit. It was likely my imagination, but at the corner of Oxford the streetlights seemed brighter than usual, as if a higher wattage had been installed as a result of what could happen under cover of darkness. Despite what administrators would have the press believe, I knew Gentry

Truman's death would resonate throughout our community in irreparable ways.

Poor Dr. Milford was probably beside himself. I'd read his official press statement in the evening *Nashville Banner* and could just imagine how alumni and fund-raisers were responding. Avenell prided itself on its quiet, reserved image, its stalwart reputation as the most expensive private university south of the Mason-Dixon line. Although it provided numerous scholarships and minority recruitment programs to balance the student body, Avenell University still remained a mostly white, upper-class institution. While I appreciated it and loved the unique community spirit, my affection did not blind me to the classism Avenell perpetuated. My travels abroad, my life in Memphis and ministry there in the projects of Orange Mound, even my time in New York at Union Seminary all broadened my vision of human beings. If nothing else, Gentry Truman's death would remind Avenell's genteel administrators that even they could not prevent certain harsh thorny weeds from intruding into their carefully tended academic garden.

Approaching the Grove Park faculty neighborhood, Pete and I noticed that a police guard of a half-dozen dark coats discreetly surrounded the block. They would not permit any media within a block of Truman's pink Victorian gingerbread. I knew from Bea that a helicopter had circled all afternoon like a metallic vulture but had finally relented after dark. At the wrought-iron gate in front of the house, I identified ourselves to a black-suited man with tired eyes, and after checking a small note pad, the plainclothes officer let us pass. A simple wreath with ebony ribbons graced the door. Very tasteful.

Marcia Truman greeted me herself after the first ring of the doorbell.

"Come in, Father Reed. So good of you to come. I hope the media circus didn't give you too much trouble. I apologize for the police cage, as well. Please, come in." Then noticing Peter, she hesitated.

"Mrs. Truman, this is my curate, Peter Abernathy. Peter, this is Mrs. Marcia Klein Truman, the wife of Mr. Gentry Truman." My introduction sounded ominously formal. They shook hands politely, and then she ushered us inside. "I hope you don't mind me bringing Peter along. He'll be assisting me with the service, and I thought Gentry's children and yours might be more comfortable with someone like Peter than an old priest like me," I explained.

"Of course, Father, a splendid idea. But you're not that old, now." She smiled, lighting up the foyer at least another fifty watts. "Marcella, take the gentlemen's coats, please."

Pete shed his jacket, and I removed my cap and coat and smoothed the rumpled wave of dark blond across my forehead. In a sleek mahogany framed mirror, I quickly caught my own image and perceived myself as rather plain and disheveled compared to my lovely hostess.

Although my vanity annoyed me, especially under the present circumstances, I could not help but be self-conscious about my appearance in the presence of someone like Marcia Truman. As she ushered us into a small library to the right of the entryway, I noticed again her luminous vitality. Petite in size but large in personality, likely what a theater critic would call stage presence. She wore her straight chestnut hair bobbed at the shoulders and looked solemn, yet still appropriately glamorous, in pin-striped navy trousers and jacket. The conservative mourning clothes, however, could not conceal her penchant for jewelry; a large oval gold brooch offset her right lapel, a pearl choker above that, and below, a half-dozen rings on long, elaborately manicured fingers. Much more together than she had been at my home earlier today.

"Thank you again for coming, Fathers," she said. "May I get either of you a brandy, tea, coffee?"

Just as I was about to respond, I noticed that the room was not empty. In front of the cavernous fireplace, perched on a small settee, was Dr. Milford. Standing to his right Cale Sanders, very tall and pointed looking, gazed out a dark window with a teacup in hand. Beside him was a very young woman with short, curly brown hair. She turned to look at me curiously, and I recognized Gentry Truman's penetrating eyes. She had to be one of his three daughters. On the opposite side of the room, next to the glass display case full of gleaming awards, a short, heavyset man with a salt-and-pepper beard thumbed through an old theater program.

"Coffee would be nice, thank you."

"Father Abernathy?"

"The same, please. And call me Pete, Mrs. Truman."

She nodded, turned, and gave a silent signal to a maid who appeared from around the corner.

"Let me introduce you. You both know Dr. Milford, of course."

Franklin Milford stood erect and offered his hand, his silver hair gleaming in the window-reflected firelight. "Griffin, so good of you to come. Peter."

Did I notice a look pass between him and Mrs. Truman as I shook his hand? For some reason, it didn't surprise me to find him here, but it did seem a little unusual. Apart from the circumstances, he seemed very comfortable.

"And you remember my brother-in-law, Cale Sanders."

The thin man emerged from the dark corner of the room and extended his hand impassively. Withdrawing from Pete's hand, Cale smirked. "Well, well. Batman brought Robin with him this time. How sweet."

Pete looked confused, but I simply ignored it. "I'm terribly sorry about your brother, Mr. Sanders."

Cale Sanders nodded condescendingly and unfastened a leather button on his Irish tweed blazer. Yes, he definitely looked like a much sharper version of his brother. The resemblance seemed stronger now that Gentry was not available for the comparison.

"Cale's been here for the past few weeks," Marcia explained to Pete. "He's directing the premiere of Gentry's new play, *Chameleon*. It was to have opened in a few weeks—Homecoming weekend, I believe. If only Gentry had finished it, that is."

"We're better off that he didn't," snipped Cale. "His talent dried up years ago. He knew it as well as the rest of us did. We've been rehearsing the same five scenes for over a month. He was washed up. . . . He knew it, too. That's why he pulled the trigger."

The room held its collective breath, stifling with the heat of anger.

"But so much of his fine work lives on," I mediated. "A small concession in such a devastating loss, but a gift nonetheless." In many ways I hated moments like these, hated the perfunctory compliments and obligatory dialogue that evaded the complex web of family relationships.

The curly headed woman stepped forward. "I'm Jenna Truman. Thank you, Father. You're right about my father's work. Many people die without leaving anything behind, let alone the kind of literature Papa produced." It was not difficult to discern the crackling animosity between Jenna Truman and her uncle and stepmother. Marcia's omitted introduction was not an accident, but her slight was covered by the maid's entrance with a silver serving set. Jenna and Peter shook hands warmly, and she seemed pleased at his presence.

The short, bearded man broke the tension, as well, by extending a pudgy hand. "I'm Casey Atwood, Gentry's agent." He smiled as if I were a potential client.

A rich coffee smell laced with a hint of almond liqueur wafted through the cozy room. The maid served her mistress first and then me. Marcia led us to leather armchairs against the wall. A small Yorkie terrier drowsed before the hearth. Cale Sanders and Jenna Truman gathered across from us on a hunter green love seat while Franklin Milford loomed next to Marcia's wingback. Mr. Atwood remained across the room, engrossed in documents procured from a small leather attaché. I realized then that he was the infamous Casey "Cutthroat" Atwood, once a major power broker for stars and celebrity writers. I recalled reading an article in the dentist's office—*Vanity Fair*, I think—about how Atwood's power had diminished in the wake of talented newcomers and the amazing rate of turnover for Hollywood players. I felt a bit star-struck to be thrust into such a distinguished gathering.

"Father, you and I don't really know one another very well," Marcia Truman said. "But I must tell you that Gentry was very fond of you. He thought highly of your intellect, and he respected your faith . . . no small accomplishment. I remember him saying, 'That Reed is not your typical preacher'—his way of paying you a compliment. That's why I know he'd want you to lead the memorial service." Her eyes, a cold, shimmering mediterranean, searched intently into mine. The others unconsciously seemed to lean in toward me as they awaited my response. I began to feel claustrophobic.

"And I know how Mr. Truman would finish his statement you cited. 'That Reed is not your typical preacher; shame a mind like his sits around filled up with thoughts of God all day!' That's what he told me once." My remark brought smiles all around. Jenna looked off toward the fire, as if caught up in her own bittersweet memories. Cale Sanders remained stoic, but his eyes betrayed more condescension. Marcia smiled sadly, appropriately.

"Of course I'd be honored to conduct the service."

"It means a great deal to me, to all of us." She sipped her coffee and looked down at the small dog. He raised his head as if on cue, then resettled into the thin Persian rug.

"When would you like to schedule the service? I assume interment will be in New York?"

"Actually," she responded, "Gentry requested to be cremated and his ashes spread over Eaglehead Mountain. His final romantic gesture, I suppose. His other daughters are on their way. I thought Dylan would be back from the airport with Lisa by now. Lucy is directing a film in Eastern Europe, however, and can't arrive until late Wednesday night. I think Friday morning would be the best time."

"That's ridiculous! Why wait four more days?" bellowed Cale. "Let's get it over with as soon as possible."

Marcia remained composed and decisive. "This is no small-town affair, Cale—no offense, Fathers. Arrangements take time. Friends like Tony, Marty, and Liz have to rearrange their schedules to be here. The service will be on Friday. Let's say eleven o'clock."

Jenna fidgeted nervously.

"Franklin—Dr. Milford—has already assured me that classes will be canceled and the university closed on the day of the service," Marcia continued. "I know we all need to get this behind us."

Dr. Milford patted the widow's shoulder awkwardly, but she did not seem to mind.

"I assume we'll have the service in the Divine Cathedral?" I asked and noticed that Pete was discreetly taking notes.

"Yes, the cathedral will be just fine. Dr. Milford and I were talking earlier, and we both agreed that holding the service there might help dispel the aura this tragedy has brought to campus. Gentry secretly thought the Divine quite lovely, the irony, he said, of something so atypically tasteful in this area."

"High class in the low South, he called it," said Cale, obviously sharing his brother's temperament. "At least, he loved the way it looked on the outside. God knows if he ever stepped foot *inside* it."

I nodded and sipped my coffee. "Who will be delivering the eulogy, Mrs. Truman?"

"I'd be honored to." Cale's voice still contained a sardonic edge.

"Excuse me, please," said Jenna. She moved quickly and gracefully as a cat but was obviously upset. Casey Atwood, whose presence I had almost forgotten, rose quickly after her, exchanging a pregnant look with Marcia on his way.

"Very high-strung girl," said Cale, touching his mustache, "like her father. She and Gentry were estranged, you know. She's on medication—the shock and all."

Marcia's eyes flashed fury toward Cale's erect profile. Peter shifted uncomfortably. Avenell's distinguished president took Jenna's place on the sofa.

"There's no excuse for 'medication' like a good death in the family," Cale continued. "Who knows, she may have been the one who popped dear old dad in the noggin. She certainly had cause enough."

Chapter Six

WHISTLING IN THE DARK

"CALE, THAT'S ENOUGH!" snapped his sister-in-law.

"I believe I'll turn in for the night." He pretended to yawn. "Better fix one more for the road." I could smell the bourbon on his breath from where he stood, pouring another highball effortlessly. "Good night, all. Father Lone Ranger." He nodded toward me, then curtsied in front of Pete. "Father Tonto. I'll see you both at the service." He exited the room with a light step, as if he had just completed a ballroom dance number. Franklin Milford sank back nervously in the thick green upholstery and coughed.

I could tell Marcia wanted to try to explain the hidden drama I had just witnessed but didn't quite know where to begin. "I'm terribly sorry, Father. Everyone's a little on edge. Cale . . . Cale's just being Cale. He's really not as bad as he seems; he's just under a lot of stress like the rest of us. He and Gentry had a typical brother, love-hate kind of relationship. His sarcasm is a way of grieving."

Why was she defending him? Peter and I silently exchanged the same question between us.

Time for some acting of my own. "What did he mean that Jenna certainly had cause?" I blurted. "I'm terribly sorry. . . . Forgive me, it's none of my business."

Just then Jenna appeared from around the corner as if hearing her name. "Father Abernathy, may I see you for a moment? Alone, please." She smiled feebly.

"Of course." Pete rose wide-eyed and followed her across the hall to a room shielded behind glass French doors that I had failed to notice until then. A lamp shone through the elegant panes, and Jenna shut the door and took a seat out of my line of vision.

"Your question is understandable," Marcia replied, looking worriedly into the den where her stepdaughter was confiding something to my curate.

"It's just that Jenna has never forgiven Gentry for leaving her mother to marry me. She's very young, very naïve." She paused and sipped coffee with a perfectly manicured pinky extended, then added, "Presumably, she also stands to gain a considerable inheritance. Along with me and the other children, of course."

"I don't understand. Would Jenna be concerned about her inheritance?" I asked.

"Well, Gentry had basically cut her off this year when she turned twenty-one. He felt it was time for her to make her own way in the world. Poor thing doesn't have a head for business, so Gentry simply wanted her to learn to appreciate money without having everything given to her. He got her a good PR job here with the university. It's a miracle she's held on to it these past few months."

"So she lives here with you?" I asked.

"Yes. Gentry insisted—thought it would give them a chance to get better acquainted. But it's been a bit of a strain for both of them," explained Marcia.

"I see."

Casey Atwood reentered the room. "Has the weapon been found?" He landed his portly frame before the fireplace. The Yorkie seemed alarmed by his proximity and began to growl a low threat.

No one but the dog said a word for several moments. "Shut your yappin'," Atwood snapped back at the terrier. "Well, has it?"

"No," stated Franklin Milford. "And that's why the police are officially declaring this a homicide in tomorrow's press release. Otherwise, it has all the markings of a classic suicide."

Marcia looked at him oddly, unaffectionately.

Milford caught her look and tacked on, "Not that it would make Gentry's death any less tragic. It's just that . . . with suicide there's some immediate closure. None of this sniping with short fuses, wondering about motives and inheritances, and the like. That's all I meant."

Atwood concurred. "Well, when you're dealing with Gentry Truman, more people had reason to want him dead than those wanting him alive. He was a pain in the neck to every one of us around him. Don't deny it."

"Casey, Franklin, please," said Marcia. "He's dead, for heaven's sake. Maybe we all had our differences with Gentry, but the man is dead now. Dead. He's not coming in with that half-drunken smile of his begging forgiveness, telling us stories of where he disappeared to, making us laugh and forget our anger at him. He's not coming back. . . ." Tears cascaded down her face and into the lap of her fine knit suit.

"I'm sorry. I never meant to upset you. You know that," Milford comforted her.

Atwood picked up his black attaché and strode toward the widow. "I loved Gentry as much as we all did, Marcia. You know I'll miss him. I'm calling it a night. We can discuss business later in the week when we're all feeling better. Good night—I'll show myself out."

"Mr. Atwood," I said, shaking a firm hand.

"Pleasure, Father. Good night."

While our university president consoled his most famous faculty member's widow, I stood and looked into the den to check on Pete. He, too, was standing, smiling kindly at the bereaved daughter, his blond cowlick nodding sympathetically. She gave him a small hug and mouthed "thank you" as she moved forward to open the doors.

"Good night, Father Pete. I can't thank you enough. I'll talk to you soon, once my sisters are here," said the young woman, clearly more vibrant than she had been the entire evening. I felt like Beatrice for having such a thought, but did she have a romantic attraction to Pete or had she merely found release for her grief? Likely both, I figured.

"You're welcome, Jenna. Please call if you need someone to talk to. I can't imagine what you're going through," said my curate, noticing my presence at the edge of the hallway.

"Mrs. Truman, Dr. Milford, I should be going, too," I said and shook hands with them both. "We'll need to discuss the details of the service once Gentry's other children arrive. Perhaps Wednesday evening?"

"I hope I haven't wasted your time. I thought we could have made more concrete plans. . . . Wednesday would be fine, Father," whispered Marcia, composed but not in control. "Thank you for coming. I'm sorry about the way . . . this turned out tonight."

"Grief does strange things to us all, Mrs. Truman. No need to apologize. I hope you can get some rest. If there's anything I or my curate can do for you or your family, don't hesitate to call."

"You're very kind. I know why Gentry liked you." The widow smiled with sincerity. Her companion nodded my way.

Marcella emerged right on cue with jackets and my cap and led us to the door. A different police officer nodded our way from the yard, and we were through the iron gate and around the corner before either of us said a word.

"Well, why didn't you tell me?" Pete began.

"Tell you what?"

"That trying to console a grieving family, especially one that doesn't particularly like each other, is like trying to wrestle an alligator."

I bowed my head and smiled. "Welcome to the world of ministry," I said.

We remained silent for another block or so as the night surrounded us like a Victorian set, shawls of fog wrapping shadows beneath towering streetlights, the echoes of our footfalls muffled on the leaf-strewn sidewalk. Peter turned his collar up and shoved his hands deeper into the vented pockets of dark leather. I looked over my shoulder and tried to imagine the conversations taking place at the Truman mansion just then.

"How was your conversation with Jenna?" I didn't want to pry or ask Peter to betray anything confidential, but I was intrigued by the fragile young woman and her family's comments about her.

"She simply wanted me to know—wants *us* to know—that she and her sisters would like input for the memorial service. She's afraid Marcia and Cale will control everything, apparently like they always do, and she and her sisters will remain outsiders. I assured her that you and I would do everything we could to respect the wishes of each family member as much as possible."

"She trusted you, I could tell. I'm glad you came along. She probably views me as being too attentive to her stepmother. After you left the room, Marcia told me that Jenna's never forgiven her father for leaving her mother for Marcia. Did Jenna mention her mother at all?"

"Only that she's as flaky as Gentry was. Her mother's an actress—Gina Knowling's her name. She played the secretary on the old *Dragnet* series and has had a career of small parts, according to Jenna. She sells real estate in Beverly Hills now. Jenna said she's coming out for the service, so we'll probably get to meet her."

"Sounds like Gentry Truman was consistently attracted to dramatic women," I commented. "Anything else?"

"Well, nothing directly, Grif. But I can't help feeling like Jenna's got a secret. It's the feeling I get around the students I minister to when one of them feels guilty but doesn't know what to do with the guilt."

"Any idea what her secret might be?" I asked. The moon suddenly floated free of cloud cover but still appeared blurred through the fog banks, as if underwater. I stumbled over a flattened Coke can and it skipped forward to the curb. Pete gingerly volleyed it back in my direction like a soccer ball. I took up his game.

"No idea. I may be way off," he replied. We kicked the can for almost two blocks until we came to Hammond Dormitory, where Peter was a Resident Assistant in exchange for a student apartment and a meal pass to the cafeteria. We stopped to catch our breath before saying good-night.

"That Cale Sanders is a piece of work," Pete said. "I wouldn't trust him as far as I could throw him. If Truman was murdered, then the brother's the obvious candidate in my mind."

"Just because he drinks too much and tries to hurt others' feelings?" I asked.

"No, not just his being a jerk. I figure that he probably grew up in his famous brother's shadow. You know, professional jealousy and all that. He clearly has a theatrical streak."

"Yes, indeed," I said, mulling over the possibility. "You're really as bad as Beatrice, you know."

He chuckled and punched my shoulder softly. "And you're not? When you've got a man shot in the head in a little country chapel with a family as screwed up as his apparently is, then it's hard not to be suspicious. You can't tell me you weren't looking at these people tonight wondering if one of them murdered Gentry Truman."

"I'm as guilty of being human as the next man," I said. The bell tower rang out, and I waited to speak until I counted ten tolls echoing between us. "Well, good night. Bea will be wondering what's happened to us if I don't show up soon."

"What's on your calendar tomorrow?" the curate asked.

"I'm thinking about going to Rockmont to see John," I replied, surprised at how easily the possibility sprang forward. It had been brewing in the back of my mind all afternoon.

"I think that would be good for you. Tell him hello for me. I'll see you when you get back, then. Good night." Pete turned and jogged the short distance to the dorm entrance.

I looked up at the five-story brownstone, as distinguished as any Manhattan apartment building, and scanned the mosaic of yellow-lit windows and charcoal frames. The wind picked up and slipped its fingers through a beech tree to my right, and I watched Peter disappear into the honeycomb home of male freshmen at Avenell University. If I recalled correctly, Dylan Klein lived in that dorm—when he wasn't serving as waiter and chauffeur to his mother. Perhaps Peter could have a chat with the young man, see how he was handling the loss of his stepfather.

I turned and decided to take the long way home—five blocks round by the fraternity houses and across the intramural fields instead of the direct route four blocks behind the library. The fog continued to enshroud the campus, and soon I couldn't see more than a dozen feet in front of me. The temperature had dropped at least ten degrees since Pete and I had started out two hours before.

Fraternity Row was upon me before I recognized it amid the fog. A neat neighborhood of red and brown brick three-stories parceled out like packages beneath the fir and pines behind them. The Pike House, the Sig Eps, the Betas, the Delta Upsilon Ducks. Even through the fog, decaying jack-o'-lanterns leered toothless grins from several front porch rails, remnants of Halloween two nights ago. Ah, Fraternity Row . . . Over three decades melted away as I paused in front of the seventh and final house, home of the small, bookish tribe known as Alpha Omega Chi. I had felt instantly at home among the brothers there as a freshman back in the '60s. While radical groups protested and other Greeks partied to forget the world's turmoil, we AOChis prayed and fasted. An odd little monastic fraternity, we were often the butt of other Greek clubs' jokes, but AOChis kept a low profile and the highest GPA on campus. We never won at flag football or intramural soccer, but we led the campus in philanthrophic fund-raising, tutoring, and the number of alumni in full-time ministry positions. I continued to serve as one of a half-dozen faculty sponsors required for the club.

The sound of voices simmered over my shoulder from one of the other houses and burst my reverie. Yes, I should check up on the brothers of Alpha Omega Chi this week. The voices grew louder and a door slammed. I began walking again, slowly, and made my way to the intramural fields that would bring me back to Southern Avenue and the parish manse I called home.

Walking along the north perimeter of the athletic fields, I heard a rustling behind me, something louder and sharper than the wind. I stopped. Nothing. The fog now spilled around me like a gray-flannel soup, and my heart clamored against my rib cage. I started walking again and heard someone or something following several paces behind me, but there nonetheless. I stopped again and called out, "Who's there?" and felt very foolish for taking this route. I could've been at home by now, sipping a nice Sleepy Time tea and fending off Bea's prying questions.

I started off again and began a loose jog. My mind spun with possibilities—a late-night joker, an undercover police officer, Gentry Truman's murderer. I began trying to calm myself, reciting Scripture verses as I heard the someone behind me run to keep up. " 'The LORD is my light and my salvation,' " I whispered between my labored breaths. " 'Whom shall I fear? The Lord is the stronghold of my life; of whom shall I be afraid?' " I was now running at full speed. " 'When evildoers assail me, uttering slanders against me, my adversaries and foes, they shall stumble and fall. Though a host encamp against me—' " and just as I saw the diluted glow of the streetlight ahead of me, I fell. My glasses somersaulted across my face into the grass, my cap sprang forward, and I landed on my hands and knees like a child. The footfalls behind me sped up. Struggling to collect my faculties and ward off an impending blow, I braced and waited. A dark form sped by like a cheetah without stopping. And without my glasses I could distinguish nothing—not even height or gender.

So . . . was someone chasing me or not? If so, why didn't he stop while I was down? If not, did we just happen to be going the same way? It seemed odd and ominous to me as I collected my glasses and brushed dewy grass from my cap and jacket. I did not like someone playing games with me. Although it was probably something a frat boy would be bragging about at breakfast, I didn't find it funny in the least. I felt very foolish for my fear.

I limped home, whistling in the dark all the rest of the way.

———

After answering Bea's questions for the fourth time, I took a hot bath and perched a hot cup of tea on the edge of the tub.

"You'll catch your death of cold, Griffin Reed, as sure as I'm standing here," my sister warned from the hall outside the bath. "If someone doesn't try to kill you first! My word, out wandering across the playing fields in the middle of the night, chased down like a stray dog! I still say you should call Sheriff Claiborne this instant and tell him what happened. There's a murderer on the loose!"

"I wasn't harmed, Bea. I feel foolish enough as it is without making this a federal case," I said. "I tripped in a gopher hole, that's all. Someone just happened to be trailing behind me."

"Then why didn't they stop to help you up, like any decent person would have done?" accused my sister.

"Maybe they were afraid of me," I smiled back.

"Hrrumph," she grunted just as the teakettle whistled, beckoning her into the kitchen.

I soaked in the tub for half an hour, sipping the tea, warming body and spirit after the coldness of a day filled with death and frustration. My mind drifted between prayer and sleep, and I started when my sister rapped on the bathroom door.

"Griffin, are you okay in there?" she called.

"Bea, help! I'm drowning! Someone broke in through the window, and now they're trying to drown me!" I splashed up a miniature tidal wave and made a gurgling sound. "Help!"

I loved it when my sister was at a loss for words. After a moment, she shrieked, "I'll call the police! Grif, fight him!"

I opened the door in my worn terry-cloth robe and beamed. "It's okay. I caught him and flushed him down the drain."

My sister stood there in a long, rose-printed nightgown that seemed to cover every inch of her large torso. Her gray hair had been loosed from the back of her head and braided on either side, making her look girlish, the way she looked when I was a toddler. "You are a horrible person, Griffin Reed! Why, I thought you were seriously in danger there for a minute! What's going to happen when you cry wolf and you really do need assistance? Just tell me that!" Her eyes flashed anger with just a hint of appreciative humor for my stunt.

"You're going to give me the benefit of the doubt like you always do, sister," I said, buffing a towel against the back of my wet head.

"We'll see about that. I'm going to bed now. I'd appreciate it if there were no more pranks tonight." She turned sharply and headed for her bedroom down the hall. "Good night, you silly boy."

As I lay in bed, scanning the stack of books and magazines on my nightstand, I was struck by my own hypocrisy. I had felt anger that some fraternity boy could have been playing a joke just to scare me, and then I willingly did the same to Bea less than an hour later. I knelt bedside and said prayers and felt even more like a schoolboy than I did while being chased.

" 'Yours is the day, O God, yours also the night; you established the moon and the sun. You fixed all the boundaries of the earth; you made both summer and winter. I will bless the Lord who gives me counsel; my heart teaches me, night after night. I have set the Lord always before me; because He is at my right hand, I shall not fall. Seek Him who made the Pleiades and Orion, and turns deep darkness into morning, and darkens the day into night; who calls for the waters of the sea and pours them out upon the surface of the earth: The Lord is His name.

" 'If I say, "Let only darkness cover me, and the light about me be night," even darkness is not dark to thee, the night is as bright as the day; for darkness is as light with thee. Jesus said, "I am the light of the world; he who follows me will not walk in darkness, but will have the light of life." ' "

My prayers sobered me this night, and I went on to confess my sins, to pray for my sister, for my parish, for my friends and fellow clergy. I prayed for Gentry Truman's family and for the week ahead. Once more I felt boyish inside, humbled before the Father who loves me.

————

In my dreams that night I was to meet Amy in the cathedral, but when

I arrived I found Gentry Truman lighting a prayer candle, the center one in the petitioner's box. We talked familiarly, and he told me he wasn't happy, that he didn't know how to write his new play. He was afraid it would never be finished. Then Marcia Truman came in, only she looked like Amy. She didn't see Gentry and me and proceeded straight to the sacristy behind the altar, where she took out a gun with a gloved hand. The barrel dripped red when she pulled the trigger, and somehow Truman collapsed beside me in a bloody puddle. Marcia/Amy put a scarf over her head and ran down the center aisle with me chasing behind her. For some reason I couldn't leave the church, so when she ran out the door I was left behind, defeated and horrified, betrayed. The cathedral suddenly became the Martyr's Chapel, and Gentry Truman was now propped in the altar chair the way I had found him the day before.

The red-lined numbers of my digital clock—2:49 A.M.—brought me back to the safety of my warm bed. I sat up and shook my head as if rattling such a nightmare from the labyrinth of my mind. In the hallway the bathroom night-light cast concentric shadows toward me. Bea's door was shut, and I could hear her lightly snoring. At least one of us would get a good night's sleep.

I got up and looked out the kitchen window toward the cathedral. I saw one lone policeman huddled on the front steps. The moon shone three quarters full, risen above the fog now like an inverse sun over a silver horizon. I suddenly felt compelled to go inside the sanctuary but remembered my dream. What was I going to do once inside? Pray? Perhaps. More likely try to face the demon I had just dreamed, the one who had attempted to stain my wife's memory with Gentry Truman's blood. I stood at the window until I heard the grandfather clock that had been my mother's chime three bells.

My flannel pajamas, last year's Christmas gift from Bea, embraced me kindly. My mind wandered drowsily as I automatically filled the kettle and found the bull's-eye of the front burner. When I heard it, at first I thought I was dreaming, walking in my sleep, perhaps. But then the steam whistled harmonically through the lips of the kettle, and I assumed I had identified the tune playing in my head.

But it didn't stop when I poured my water over a tea bag and replaced the kettle on an unlit eye. My head cocked instinctively west, toward the Divine Cathedral, and I wondered if my ears were playing the same kinds of tricks my mind had played on me in my dreams. Ever so faintly I could hear someone whistling "The Church's One Foundation"—the tune I had whistled home tonight after my fall.

Now fully awake, adrenaline inflated my heart's rhythm. I stood in front of Bea's door to see if she heard it, too. Her heavy breaths continued rhythmically.

I knew I would not rest until I checked the church for myself. Grabbing my robe, I forced my feet into tennis shoes without lacing them. Outside, the night air was crisp with crystalline dew and my breath shone in front of me whiter than the fog. The whistling had stopped; only a passing car could be heard bearing down the highway toward the interstate. It seemed best to inform the patrolling officer on duty outside the dark castle, but when I approached the front entrance he was nowhere to be found. The front doors were locked, so I decided to try the side door.

Surprisingly, no reporters or photographers prowled the street or camped nearby. I deliberated on calling out. But what if I hadn't really heard anything? Maybe I had only imagined that I was whistling that hymn again. I didn't want to get a reputation like Bea for exaggeration and sensationalism. Bea's warning about my crying wolf sent her voice whispering "I told you so" through my brain.

The side vestry entrance was locked as it should have been. I stooped and lifted a small flagstone to my right, groping moist earth for the emergency spare key. Once in the lock it turned without a sound. I shivered and now heard Bea's voice chastising me for going into the night air without my coat. Inside the dark storage room, I waited for my eyes to adjust and realized just how foolish I was to be out alone, in the predawn hours, in a cavernous structure like our cathedral. Either way, it seemed foolish: If there was someone here, what was I going to do when I found him? If not, then I'd feel silly, spooked by imaginary sounds or my own dreams.

I began to feel my way around. Vestments for holy days hanging on a large freestanding iron rack. Last year's missions conference souvenirs—maracas, a poncho, a Russian bust of Stalin made of plastic, two carousels of slides. And the projector. I made my way through the mess, vowing to clean it out soon. A good Saturday project for Pete and me. My rubber-soled feet made short scuffing sounds on the floor, and I could feel the cold nipping at my bare ankles.

Now I could see the altar, the choir loft, the large organ pipes looming like black smokestacks in the shadows of Gothic arches. No one. Not a sound.

Then I saw it.

Flickering shadows. A candle flame. Cradled in the small red-glass votive, a solitary tongue of orange-and-blue flame. My neck hairs bristled, and I shivered in the coldness of my fear. Someone had just lit a candle in the Cathedral of the Divine at three o'clock in the morning and then whistled "The Church's One Foundation" on the way out. No, that couldn't be. I had seen an officer guarding the door less than half an hour ago. Dan Warren told me the campus was covered.

Suddenly it felt like I was back in my dream. Like a somnambulist I shuffled closer to the light, transfixed by the way it pierced the darkness vertically. Like a knife.

"Who's there?" I yelled. "In the name of the Lord, I demand to know who's there." My anger flared like the tiny candle.

No sound. Only shadowed silhouettes across the stone walls, the inky-dark stained glass in metallic shades of gray, silver, platinum, pewter. Then a sound—someone shuffling from behind the altar.

Chapter Seven

OFFERTORY

"Freeze or I'll shoot!" boomed a male voice. Arms formed a large tri-angle pointing a dark-barreled circle at my chest. I became the statue he commanded and tried to register the voice echoing through my church. My hands were up as far as my robe would allow. A blunt searchlight raked across my face.

"Father Grif!" barked the familiar voice.

"Officer Wilson?"

"What's going on, Father? What are you doing over here in the middle of the night?" He replaced his sidearm and shone the light at my feet.

"I couldn't sleep, Jerry. I woke up and thought I heard someone in here—I thought I heard whistling. So I looked for the officer—you—I'd seen earlier at the front entrance, but when I couldn't find you, I came around and let myself in the vestry door. I had just noticed this candle burning when you caught me."

Jerry Wilson was new to Carroll County, and Bea's verdict was still out as to whether or not he would fit in. I had met him only a couple of times with Dan.

"Sorry, Father. I heard someone in here and couldn't imagine how they got past me. Then it took me forever to find the key to unlock the front door. I must have been in the squad car looking for it when you came looking for me." He shifted uneasily, and his boots and holsters creaked like only oiled leather can. I looked back at the candle still burning gently, quietly, like any other petitioner's candle might.

"So you didn't light that candle?" Wilson inquired. An edge of suspicion bordered his voice, or perhaps it was merely weariness and the way his low, sonorous words echoed into the stone arches above us.

"No, I wish I had."

"Then there had to be somebody else in here," he concluded.

"Yes, and he was whistling on his way out."

We walked to the small metal stand with its bouquet of thirty-odd votives. Next to the candles, the donation chest guarded its secrets like a virtual Pandora's box. Impulsively I opened the heavy lid and jumped back as if expecting a snake inside. Instead, nothing. Empty. No coins, bills, or even old jewelry left as an offering like we'd found once two years ago. Only shadows, dark like deep water in the two-by-three-foot box. A sudden glint at the bottom.

"What's this?" I reached in.

"Don't! Don't touch anything, Father! I know you mean well, but the intruder's prints could be on that box."

He was right and I apologized.

Leaning into the mouth of the box with a pencil extended, Officer Wilson fished up a handgun by the loop below the trigger. "Well, well," he said. "Guess this isn't what usually turns up in the offering plate."

I shook my head, drained of energy and credibility.

The sweaty deputy became more animated. "Look, I'm gonna have to call Sheriff Claiborne on this. He wanted to know if any little thing happened. Why don't you go back home and wait till he gets here. And please don't touch anything else on the way out." I nodded and began to follow him out the front when I remembered that I had to lock the side door again.

"Do you think whoever left this is still here?" I asked before turning.

"No, I think he had enough time to catch a plane to China for as long as we been standin' here yappin'.'" He couldn't hide his frustration very well, and I felt like a teenager busted for curfew. I nodded and headed back the way I'd entered.

———————

Sheriff Claiborne went through all the stages of grief in about five minutes. First denial, then anger, then pleading with me to remember forgotten details, then acceptance. I recounted being followed on the way home from Truman's house, falling, having someone whiz past me. Feeling silly, I told the sheriff, "When I was a little boy, Daddy always told me that there was nothing to be afraid of in the dark as long as I could whistle. So after I fell, I was a little shaken up, and I began to whistle 'The Church's One Foundation' the rest of the way home. It's the same tune someone whistled on the way out of the church tonight."

He didn't know what to make of this. "Maybe Truman's murderer feels guilty and wants us to catch him," he finally surmised. "Maybe he wanted to talk to you earlier, you being a priest and all, and then got cold feet."

"Do we know for sure that Gentry was murdered?" I asked, sipping a pot of Kenyan AA that Bea kept on reserve for middle-of-the-night emergencies. It was now going on five A.M.

"We feel pretty certain," the sheriff confided. "Doc Graham says there's nothing conclusive from his autopsy, but he's waiting on a state examiner coming in tomorrow." The sheriff seemed wide awake and, like his deputy, energized by the details of the case. "Men don't shoot themselves in the head, hide the gun, then drop it off in the collection box a few days later."

My sister rattled cups and plates from the kitchen, preparing breakfast despite both our insistence that we weren't hungry. Like our mother and grandmother before her, Bea believed that food and drink could always comfort. "Nothing that a good cup of java and homemade bread won't help," she always said. I smelled cinnamon rolls, hot from the oven.

Sheriff Claiborne looked from the kitchen back to me and lowered his voice. "There's nothing to say the killer might not strike again."

"What makes you think so?" Sheer incredulity raised my voice. I heard Bea closing the oven door and dreaded having to recount our conversation later.

"I'm not at liberty to say just yet," he continued. "Father Grif, until we know why it happened the first time, we can't be sure it won't happen again." A deep soul sigh. "I don't mean to alarm you. It's just that we haven't got any solid leads so far, and I've got everybody from President Milford to the governor pressuring me to wrap this case up and tie it with a bow as soon as possible. You think I want to have this continue?"

I nodded compassionately, patted his thick shoulder.

"I'm only thinking out loud. Now you're sure you only heard one sound and you didn't see anybody? Even a moving shadow?"

"Sorry, Sheriff, nothing." I paused and took in the sensual aroma of sweet cinnamon bread that would be set before us momentarily. "Do you think the person who left the gun is the murderer? What if Gentry *did* kill himself? What if someone else found the gun but was afraid to come forward with it? They want the weapon to be found, but they don't want to be accused."

"The innocent have nothing to fear, Father. Why wouldn't an innocent person step forward and tell us where they found the gun originally?"

"I don't know, Sheriff. Maybe he or she is afraid. Afraid of the real killer."

He jumped to his feet. "I've got to be going. And this is not to go any further for now. I told Wilson to keep it zipped, too. That's all we need in the papers—'Murderer whistles while leaving gun behind.'"

He paced across the room toward the phone. "Mind?" he asked and began pushing numbers.

"No, of course not. Help yourself," I replied.

His voice lowered, and he nodded and squirmed and then turned sharply, replacing the receiver. "Father Grif, do you believe in ghosts?" Sam Claiborne's weary blue eyes searched mine. The man continued to surprise me.

"Complicated question, Sheriff. In short? Yes, I believe in supernatural forces." The kitchen was suddenly too quiet for Bea not to be listening. "Why do you ask?"

"Just curious. Numerous prints were found in the Martyr's Chapel, mostly yours and your sister's, and a few were Gentry Truman's. . . . A couple have not been identified." The sheriff walked to the window and pulled back the thin chintz drape. Two of his men now patrolled the cathedral, outlined by the first rays of sunlight illuminating the campus. "All the prints on that gun we found a couple hours ago belong to Gentry Truman. Except for one partial which matches the mystery prints in the chapel."

"Did you have Gentry's prints on file or were they taken off his corpse?"

"Doc Graham made them during the postmortem. Why?"

Now it was my turn. "Just curious. So what looked at first like the perfect suicide now looks like murder?"

"Exactly."

I couldn't resist. "Did you find anything else?"

Claiborne turned and looked at me intently. "If you'll keep it to yourself, I'll tell you another fact, as well. Truman's wristwatch was busted with the hands stopped at 2:17 A.M. Assuming that the watch was working properly—and most expensive Gucci ones do—then we have a much more precise time of death than the span Doc Graham gave us. You say Truman wasn't a particularly religious man?"

I turned over this precise timing and recalled seeing the very Gucci watch to which Sam alluded. A sleek titanium-looking model that Truman wore along with a gold-link bracelet on his left wrist. I remembered the distracting jangle the two made together when Truman had dined next to me at President Milford's dinner party. I darted back to the sheriff's question. "No, but like I said before, in his writing and beneath that grumpy persona, Gentry Truman was seeking God. I'm confident of that. Whether he found Him or not . . ." Honestly, I was as surprised at the information as I was at Sam's inquiry. If Truman were going to haunt the campus, I believed he would likely choose the Tiger Bay Pub over my church.

"I hope he found some of what he was looking for, Father. No man deserves to die like he did. No man."

Just as he was almost out the door, Bea entered bearing a platter of steaming rolls and a new pot of Kenyan AA. "Don't you dare leave this house without breakfast!" she ordered.

"Ah, Miss Bea, you shouldn't have." He smiled kindly.

"You've got to start the day with some nourishment. These are home-made rolls; I baked them myself. There's fresh juice and the last ripe cantaloupe of the season from Mr. Spradley's market. Any news?" She placed the tray on the table and directed the question to me.

"Nothing new. Just waiting to see what happens next," I replied, lifting a warm sticky bun from its cinnamon nest.

"I've really got to get back to the station. Thank you, Miss Bea." Before she could respond, the sheriff grabbed another cinnamon roll and bounded out the door.

My sister then interrogated me much more thoroughly than the sheriff had. In my retelling, I simply omitted the end of our conversation.

"I don't understand why you didn't wake me, Griffin. You have no business traipsing into the church in the middle of the night. In your robe, no doubt, without your coat."

I laughed at the irony of her statement, as if she were my protector. I could just imagine waking up my big sister and asking her to accompany me. She'd have been in heaven.

"I'm going up to see John today, so if anyone needs me and can't wait, you know the number," I said, licking my fingers.

"Ah, dear John. Are you sure you should be going alone? With next to no sleep?"

"I'll be fine. The drive will do me good   it's beautiful this time of year."

"Well, give him my best and ask him when I'll have the pleasure of seeing him at my dinner table again. Oh, Grif, I forgot to tell you. Joan Dowinger called twice yesterday. She was most upset about you not keeping her appointment."

"Good grief! A man died, and Joan can't wait another day or two to complain about something? I'll call her when I get back this afternoon."

"Well, I gave you the message now. I don't want her accusing me of not telling you when she calls." My sister began collecting coffee mugs and crumpled napkins.

"If—no, when she calls this morning, tell her that I had to go to the state prison to see a needy inmate."

"That's a hair's throw away from being a lie, dear Reverend," smiled my sister.

"No, it's just a unique arrangement of the truth."

The drive up to Rockmont State Penitentiary was a tonic itself. My tired body and weary spirit soaked in the colors from the Cumberland Plateau and surrounding hills leading into East Tennessee the way a blotter absorbs excess ink from the details of a sketch. The morning held a golden aura close to the trees and blue-framed skyline, then infused the golden light through the myriad of scarlet maples, pumpkin-orange beeches, yellow-gold tulip poplars, and toasted oaks. The interstate traffic on I–70 was light this Tuesday morning and made my connection to I–40 dissolve in a comfortable two-hour stretch.

Located halfway between Nashville and Knoxville, just north of the interstate, Rockmont housed a sobering assortment of lifetime criminals, convicted murderers, serial killers, and career felons. My friend John Greenwood had once been there himself, convicted of a murder he didn't commit—but that's another story. The result of the year's time in the maximum security institute changed John profoundly; he went from embittered bank vice-president to less embittered believer in Christ that year. After his name was cleared and he was released, he attended seminary and became a Baptist minister, of all things. It was during this time that we met, sheerly by the grace of the Lord—holy serendipity, my sister calls it—at the Samaritan's Gate retreat center over in the Smoky Mountains further east. Although retreatants were encouraged to maintain silence—if not for their own reflection and solitude, then that of the other retreatants present—John and I took several hikes together and talked for hours.

Initially, it was the odd kind of freedom that one experiences only with a kind stranger. We both felt comfortably honest about our lives, about our faiths, about why we were there and what we were hoping for.

At that first meeting ten years ago, John was wrestling with some residual anger over his imprisonment and false accusations, and lingering bitterness over the affluent businessman's lifestyle he had left behind after his wife's murder and his false imprisonment for the crime. He had accepted the calling of our Lord to the ministry and was hoping to find a nice small church in some backwoods part of Tennessee or Georgia when Warden Brown called from Rockmont and asked John if he'd be interested in being prison chaplain for the thousand inmates, guards, and staff who lived and worked there. John laughed at first and almost hung up the phone. But the Spirit nagged at him gently, unrelenting until he ended up taking the position.

John later told me that most of the peace he experienced about taking the job resulted from that week he spent in retreat when we first met. It was a pivotal time for me and my faith, as well. I had just turned forty and was going through what I now think of as my first mid-life crisis. Unmarried yet yearning for a lover and kindred spirit, I came to deal with my own dirty laundry basket of anger, fear, and bitterness. John was almost fifteen years my senior, but he felt more like an older brother than a father. When spiritual direction became a ministry trend a few years ago, I realized that John filled the role for me more than anyone else, and I felt doubly blessed because he did it so naturally, so unselfconsciously, the way I believed true spiritual nurturing and mutual accountability should happen. The support from my sister and Pete Abernathy knew no bounds when Amy died, but I would never have made it through the loss a stronger man without John.

Consequently, I saw him as often as I could, at least once or twice a quarter, and he usually came down to spend holidays and sometimes vacations with us. I knew Bea secretly had a crush on him, and I had even fantasized about such a union for them myself, but John was too dedicated to his flock there to ever settle down again. Just last year he had decided not to retire, even though, like me, he took on an assistant chaplain and delegated more responsibilities to area pastors and churches. But he was as spry as ever, eyes sparkling like a man who knows his purpose and delights in embracing it, like the man he is.

The last hour of my journey effortlessly raced by as I ended up giving God thanks for such a man and friend as John Greenwood. I especially needed him today. I wondered if he had heard of Gentry's death on the news.

I pulled off the interstate and onto the state highway that would take me to the security gate at the prison. Minutes later, a guard called for verification, checked my name off his list, and directed me to the west parking lot. Inside the compound I emptied my pockets, handed over my keys, wallet, coins, and ID. The particular guard on front desk duty, a young blond-haired woman whose name badge read *Sandra Udall*, remembered me from my last visit at the end of August and quickly checked my person for hidden weapons or contraband. "It's not every day I get welcomed like this," I joked.

She smiled back. "It's not every day I have my hands all over a priest, either."

I found myself blushing as she called another guard to lead me through the maze of locking gates and buzzing locks to the corridor where John's office and the chapel were located. My escort, a large angular guard with square shoulders and a dark flattop, remained curt and unfriendly, intent on his job. I knew his attitude from previous visits and heard many stories from John about guards, along with administrators and citizens, who viewed ministers as undeserved perks, like television or gym time, for prisoners now viewed as less than human.

A couple of inmates passed us, one with a steel gray mop and bucket, another in an orange jumpsuit with hand and ankle shackles. Seeing the white tab of my clerical collar floating above my navy blazer, the head-shaven inmate smiled a dirty yellow grin and yelled, "Pray for me!" My guard, Sergeant Flattop, remained impassive and firmly pressed my elbow forward, but I quickly called out, "I will!" The institutional smell of ammonia and urine, lemon wax and mildew assaulted me as we turned another corner in the dimly lit cinder-block corridor.

"Don't waste your breath praying for scum like that, Father," growled my escort. "They have no regard for human life."

"It's hard to believe, son, but God says it's never too late for any of us. I don't know how to say this without sounding trite, but prayer is never wasted breath." I heard myself say these words and wondered if I would still say them if I knew that the inmate I had just prayed for was Gentry Truman's murderer. As was often the case, I believed in theory, but I wanted to believe in faith.

"Whatever." The guard refused to look me in the eye. He led me to John's office, then trailed off down the hall. I knocked on John's door before entering.

"Griffin! Good to see you! How in the world are you? I'll be right with you." My friend turned his bearded chin back to the phone attached to his ear and neck. "Right . . . Yes . . . I will." I could tell he was impatient, and he puppeted his hand in a mouthy manner as if to apologize for the long-windedness on the other end of his phone. "Yes, I know. We sure will. I'll do everything I can. Yes."

I scanned the cramped office, not much bigger than a broom closet, and delighted in the diversity of books, souvenirs, prisoner files, and icons. Coming from the monochromatic grayness of the hallways and into John's office was like watching a film change from black-and-white to technicolor. A great copper crucifix dominated the largest wall space, a sculpture by a former inmate that almost didn't get made because a guard thought it was a weapon. I suppose in many ways it was. A weapon against hopelessness.

A new addition lit up the space directly above John's desk, a child's drawing of a blue family at an orange playground, and I knew that it was the hope of reuniting such families and of providing some sense of family to prisoners who would never see a swing set again that drove John to cut through bureaucracy, shrinking budgets, verbal abuse from prisoners and guards, and even physical threats.

John had been part of a lockdown five years ago when nine prisoners in the west wing took several guards and other prisoners hostage. The laid-back chaplain served as communications liaison between the outside world and the angry inmates. After a twenty-four-hour standoff, no one was hurt, the prisoners surrendered, but John saw to it that some of their complaints were heard and some conditions met. His ability to keep his cool reminded me of Dan Warren's and was a trait I tried to emulate.

Even John's appearance seemed to instantly put people at ease. Rather short—"Five foot ten is not short to the rest of the world, just you giants," he teased once—and wiry, with a balding crown trimmed by a Saturn's ring of silvery hair peppering black as it slid down his sideburns to form his short beard. He looked rather nondescript until one noticed the light behind his brown eyes and the smile that came naturally and often. Although he dressed casually in basic colors, his banker's eye for details still emerged in his neatly trimmed nails, starched shirts, and polished shoes. He reflected this today with creased khaki pants, a forest chamois shirt, and black boots glaring up shards of fluorescent light. He was one of those people you wouldn't notice on the street, but the more you got to know him, the more handsome, kind, and familiar his features became.

"Uh-huh . . . yes, I will. . . . You too. Bye now. Blessings to you, too," he trailed off as the phone magnetically jumped back to its cradle. "Griffin! As always, good to see you, my friend!" He stood and hugged me, and just the gentle strength in his embrace bolstered my spirit.

"John, am I glad to see you. Thanks for letting me come on short notice," I said.

He motioned for me to take the only other chair in his office, a green vinyl-and-chrome dinosaur donated, I guessed, by some hospital or nursing home who had purchased it in the '60s.

"I will always make time for you. You're family. I'm only sorry we had to play phone tag. I hope it's nothing too serious. . . ." He poured a cup of thick, aromatic black from the Mr. Coffee atop his only filing cabinet and stirred in sugar for me without asking.

"No, no . . . I don't know if you heard it on the news or not, but one of Avenell's faculty was found dead. It was Gentry Truman, the play-wright. I think I mentioned to you last time that he was coming to be a writer-in-residence this year. . . . They—I mean, I—found him . . . in the Martyr's Chapel—"

"Whoa, Grif, slow down. I heard on the radio this morning that Tru-man was found shot, but I didn't hear Avenell mentioned, and I sure didn't know you found the body. Drink some coffee and tell me what happened, from the beginning," John said, soothing me with his focused attention.

For the next thirty minutes I explained the events of the last five days as accurately as possible, making clear distinctions between what was known and what was merely my impression or speculation on the matter. John only interrupted to ask qualifying questions or whistle a low note of incredulity.

During the part where I explained last night's events, about finding the gun and the lit candle in the cathedral and all, I suddenly had an image pop in my head. It wasn't an idea or a deliberate thought so much as a memory, a still photograph. Inside the Martyr's Chapel on Monday morn-ing when I saw Gentry's body and then quickly scanned the sanctuary, one of the half-dozen petitioner's candles was missing or else burned down to the wick. I was sure of it. With so few candles for the small chapel, the white votive wax shone like teeth in a crooked smile on the west side of the room. Suddenly I knew one of the teeth, I believe the second from the end, was missing on Monday morning. Unsure why or if it was important, I made a mental note to ask Dan first thing when I returned.

"Grif? You okay?" John touched my arm.

"Yes, I'm fine. I just remembered something, an odd detail from when I found Gentry's body. I think one of the candles was missing from the petitioner's box beside the altar. I don't think it's important, but I'll men-tion it to the police when I return."

"What an ordeal. And it sounds like it's not over yet," he said. "What say we go out for lunch today instead of eating in the cafeteria? I think you need a little lighter atmosphere than we can provide with our crew here. I know just the place."

I objected, but he just smiled and ignored me, and before I knew it we had been ushered back through the labyrinthine halls of Rockmont and out into the November sunshine. We rode in his ten-year-old Ford Ranger amid two thermoses, half a dozen books and Bible studies, and a plaid wool jacket. It reminded me of riding with my father as a boy and the smell of masculine companionship that was the essence of his pickup: a blend of pipe tobacco, warm leather, cold metal, and Old Spice.

We made small talk as we drove along the state highway to the nearest town of Poplar, Tennessee, population 1,238. John told me that he was pleased with the way area pastors and his assistant were lightening his load. "Harry, my assistant chaplain, really loves the inmates. If I ever have to retire, I'll feel good about leaving this ministry in his hands. He's young and unseasoned, but he's got patience, and he loves the Lord with all his heart." John pulled off into a sandy graveled expanse masquerading as a parking lot beside a small ramshackle diner advertising chicken and dumplings and free coffee for senior citizens. As we walked closer to the structure, it became clear that the heart of the restaurant was a double-wide house trailer with various appendages apparently added during spurts of prosperity. John and I both loved dives full of southern Gothic characters and greasy food, and this one didn't disappoint.

"This is Hube's Place," whispered John as we opened a creaky screen door. "Best barbecue this side of your sister's kitchen."

We settled into a cracked maroon vinyl booth and attracted a few looks from locals until they noticed John, and then several of them smiled and called out greetings. We ordered pork barbecue sandwich platters and sweetened iced tea. Soon our waitress returned with chipped Fiestaware plates covered with a mound of meat, tangy sauce, coleslaw, and crispy fries.

"This has stirred up a lot in you," John observed. "I'm sure it's made you miss Amy."

"Yes, it has," I acknowledged. "But what's surprised me are my feelings about Truman's death, about the kind of man he was, about what would drive him to take his own life. Or what would motivate a person to kill a man inside a church. Yes, I definitely have thought about Amy more than usual—if that's possible—during all this. . . . I'm all over the map today, John."

"It's okay, my friend," he comforted. "It's okay."

"And then I'm thinking about Gentry's service and how to do it well, in a way that honors God as well as Truman's legacy. It feels so difficult, such a balancing act . . . How do you handle funerals where you're unsure of the deceased's salvation and morality? Gentry lived a long, fast life, and I don't want to judge. . . . It's funny, because I've been defending him to others—Sheriff Claiborne, Philip Jackson. I still have to get the bishop's approval since Gentry was not officially a member of our parish."

"To answer your question," John said, "I give as many benefits of the doubt as I can. I concentrate on whatever is known to be good about the person, and if there's nothing there, then I talk about the dying thief on the cross beside Jesus. 'Today you will be with me in Paradise' says our Lord. I don't want to advertise for immoral lives and deathbed confessions, but I don't believe it's my job to be judging a man's life when we're trying to put him in the ground. There's a lot of good things you can say about Gentry Truman. You told me yourself how much you've always admired his work." John took a last bite of coleslaw, and I motioned for him to wipe a dribble of barbecue sauce from his chin.

"Yes, you're right. I'm just troubled by all this, why things like this have to happen, why it hurts so many people. It bothers me that Gentry Truman may have been in the chapel for spiritual reasons. He may have finally found what he spent his whole unhappy life looking for."

I looked up over the counter and the overalled backs of several farmers at the portable TV. CNN led the hour with Gentry's death and reported live from Avenell. I watched familiar places in my hometown and felt a kind of surreal detachment from it all, as if it were just another news story, like unrest in the Middle East or a plane crash—some tragedy that didn't affect me. Only it did.

"You don't think Truman was happy at this stage of his career?" asked John.

Our waitress brought the bill and John snatched it up before I could reach for it. "No," I said, "I'm almost sure he was a most unhappy man. His wife was unfaithful, he couldn't get past writer's block, and I'm not sure he knew how to love his children or brother."

"What's the brother like?" John counted out a ten and two ones and folded the bills neatly inside the ticket at the edge of his plate. We got up and headed out to his truck.

With the door handle between my fingers, I said, "There was no love lost between Gentry and his half brother. My curate thinks Cale Sanders should be suspect number one. Sanders is very snide, very intelligent, and probably was jealous of his brother's career. He delights in undercutting the rest of the family and leaving people speechless. He drinks a bit too much."

John nodded, and we got in and began the drive back to Rockmont.

I wanted to change the subject and enjoy John's company before the long drive back home. "What have you been reading?" I asked.

He smiled and accelerated the old truck onto the highway. "Well, I'm in the Old Testament. It's funny that you were talking about Truman's brother being jealous. Just this morning I was reading Genesis, chapters twenty-five through thirty. Jacob—now there's a wild man for you. Gentry Truman didn't have anything on him. You might take a look at it yourself; maybe it will help you with the memorial service."

I laughed thinking about Gentry Truman donning goatskins as if he were Jacob trying to trick Isaac into thinking he was Esau. But my chuckle subsided as I recalled the enmity between the brothers and Jacob's fear of Esau for most of his life. Maybe I would take a look at that passage. . . .

"Can I pray for you?" John asked, and I nodded, comforted by this older man's words as he kept his eyes on the road but his heart focused on me and my needs. We were silent for a long time until I reciprocated, praying for my friend and mentor, and before I knew it we were back in the penitentiary's parking lot.

————————

The drive home was uneventful. I left with tears in my eyes when

John hugged me good-bye. Miraculously, the miles melted away as fast as they had this morning, and I found myself turning over and over the details of Gentry's death. The missing candle from my mental photograph came back to mind. Marcia Truman's puffy face, waiting inside my house before she even knew of her husband's death. The fragility of Truman's daughter Jenna. I couldn't wait to meet his other daughters. To tell the truth, I simply wanted all this behind me, the service appropriately and elegantly handled, the man's death resolved, everyone's lives back to normal. I selfishly did not want my life disrupted any further.

I stopped for gas at the first Cleveland exit, just north of Chattanooga, and had just opened my root beer while I waited to pay when the woman behind me said, "Aren't you the priest I saw on TV? The one who found Gentry Truman? I'd swear you're the guy on *Prime Edition* last night!" Her country drawl did not match her tailored business suit and sleek sunglasses.

"No, ma'am, sorry," I lied and thrust my credit card to the clerk for my gas and soda. She continued to chatter and had the truck driver behind her convinced that I was a celebrity, maybe even a killer. I shook my head and couldn't wait to get back on the highway.

I listened to NPR the rest of the way home and pulled into Avenell a little before five. The media carnival was full-blown now, and I wouldn't have recognized my town if I didn't know it. I parked in my driveway and noticed a white Cadillac out in front of a news van beside the cathedral. Just what I needed—Joan Dowinger perched and waiting for me. I counted to ten and said a silent prayer for what I was about to walk into.

Taking a deep breath, I slammed my car door and slipped my blazer on. Just then a shrill scream pierced the air from the Cathedral of the Divine. *Oh no,* I thought. *Please, Lord, no more chaos today.* I looked over just in time to see a mane of red hair flash late afternoon sunlight and disappear around the side of the church. Before I could react, Pete Abernathy dashed out behind her and shouted, "Stop that woman!"

Chapter Eight

THE WALLS OF PARADISE

I DROPPED MY SATCHEL and jogged the dozen yards to the front steps of the cathedral. My curate had disappeared around the same corner as the flash of red hair just moments ago. Framing the side of the church, the lawn alley looked like the road not taken, covered with oak leaves from the giant limbs above it. Fingers of kudzu caressed a telephone pole and extended to the edge of the brownstone. I considered joining the pursuit but quickly decided against it; my ankle was still tender from last night's fall. After waiting and shooing off a couple of reporters who caught the same sounds as I had heard, I went inside the cathedral to see if anything was amiss. All appeared as it had last night. Except for the petitioner's box and the inconspicuous absence of three votives next to it, all the details of the church remained as placid as the sheep being carried by the shepherd in the stained glass above my head.

Just as I noticed Peter's book bag on the front pew—black canvas Jansport brimming with paperbacks and newspapers—my curate came huffing down the center aisle.

"Catch her?" I asked and grasped his shoulder.

He shook his head from side to side, his body heaving to catch its breath. We stood there for a good sixty seconds until he could speak without gasping. I handed him my handkerchief, and he wiped the wreath of sweat off his forehead.

"I'm here early for youth group tonight, right? And I'm sitting on the front pew reading, waiting for the kids to show. I hear someone poking around in the back room—you know, the old storage room back behind the choir room? So I head back there, but just as I turn the corner, I literally run into this . . . this woman who's just standing there in the hallway, evidently looking at that big portrait of the campus back at its founding. She screams as we both fall down, and before I can get up or offer to help her up—let alone ask her who she is and what she's doing here—she clocks the hundred meters in about ten seconds." His eyes telegraphed his electric excitement almost as much as his words.

I stood there for a moment, then slumped into the end of a pew a few rows from the front. Peter sat down beside me and held his head in his hands just above his knees. His breaths were almost back to normal now.

"So had you ever seen her before? What did she look like?" I asked.

"No, never. I'd remember someone that striking. You saw the long red hair, I take it. She's . . . well, she's beautiful. Tall, about five nine, slight build, pale freckles, blue eyes—cold, intense blue eyes. She has a little beauty mark right above her jawline on the right—no, left side of her face. . . ."

"That's some description. You must have gotten a good look at her. Could she have been a reporter or someone from law enforcement?" I puzzled over Pete's portrait. He usually wasn't one to be taken in by looks or romantic first impressions.

"I did get a good look. While we were both on the floor, there was a minute there after she screamed that seemed to last forever. It was like neither one of us knew what to do. She hesitated, like she was going to apologize or explain. But then I guess I started to speak, and she was out of here. Funny thing, too. I'm almost positive she wasn't a reporter—I don't know why. Maybe a cop, though, or a federal agent. But seems like she wouldn't have been afraid to introduce herself, then." My curate leaned back, wrapping his outstretched arms over the back of the oaken pew. His cowlick stood straight up like a radar device.

"Yes, I agree. If she were on legitimate business, seems she would have identified herself and asked you the same questions you wanted to ask her."

We both turned as the mammoth castle door at the front entrance swung fading daylight into our line of vision. A large form finally eclipsed the sun, and Dan Warren emerged from the narthex, thudding heavy boots our way.

"More trouble?" he asked, leaning into us. "Got a call from some reporter that a priest was chasing an intruder from the cathedral. What happened?"

I stood to shake his hand, unexpectedly relieved by his kind face and sympathetic eyes. Dan would know what to make of this. "We're not sure, Dan. Good to see you," I replied as he and Pete shook hands and the three of us formed a small triangle at the top of the nave between the first pews on either side. Peter quickly retold his encounter with the mystery woman, and Dan shook his head.

"This case just keeps getting weirder and weirder. Pretty soon nothing's going to surprise me," he said. "I don't know of any local officers who fit that description—I'll check with the state and federal agents for a match. Sounds like it would be hard not to notice someone with those looks, let alone that much red hair."

"Any leads on what we found last night?" I asked, then cut short, wondering if Dan minded my question in front of Pete.

"Pete knows what's going on, Grif. I had to come back this morning and grab two more votives to compare to the one that was lit last night. Pete was here, down in the office, so I filled him in."

"Plus, I talked to Miss Bea," Pete said, smiling. "Her version was definitely much more exciting than yours."

We all exchanged a grin before Dan responded to my question. "Sam told you that all but one of the prints found on the gun belonged to Truman. The votive was clean, and we haven't found the match it was lit with. Even the box lid was clean, which I thought unusual considering how many people use it and drop money in each week. Someone knew what he was doing, all right."

"Or she," interjected Pete, clearly thinking of his lovely adversary.

"Let's take a look round back and see if she left anything," returned Dan, and the three of us headed between the pulpit and the left-side altar, back to the stone passageway connecting a handful of rooms to the sanctuary.

"This hall goes all the way around, correct?" asked Dan.

"Yes. On the other side is the vestry room, which has its own entrance on the east side of the church. Then there's the library, a bride's room, and the deacon's room. Like Peter said, back here is a storage room and another rarely used conference room. The fellowship hall, kitchen, and our offices, along with the bishop's office and canons' rooms, are all in the basement. That's where those stairs lead there." I pointed.

On the other side of the ninety-degree intersection where Pete and our mystery woman collided, Dan stood and absorbed every detail for several moments. My curate and I remained quiet, subject to the large landscape portrait that ruled several square feet of the rear-facing wall. Painted by an unknown artist before the turn of the century, it depicted a pristine, highly detailed view of Eaglehead Mountain and the parcel of land that became Avenell University. It had been donated by the estate of a New York attorney who attended Avenell back in the forties. Really quite lovely, if one paused to look at it, with the shimmering oaks and beeches, numerous deer, rabbits, and squirrels, a bluejay in the far left maple tree, cerulean blue skies, Lake Weston in the distant foreground. If I didn't know better, which I really didn't where art was concerned, I'd guess it was painted by Thomas Cole or another artist from the Hudson River School—more likely an imitator, though, someone taken by the romantic grandeur of the pastoral ideal.

While the artist was unknown, the title was not. Centered on a small brass plate at the base of the flat mahogany frame read *The Walls of Paradise.* Whether graced by the artist himself or some commissioning benefactor back at the university's founding, we would probably never know. The estate had donated it specifically to Avenell Parish, not to the university, which seemed a bit odd but implied tax reasons. Bea had said for some time that we ought to raffle it off at the Fourth of July picnic, but I could never bring myself to do it. There was something grand about it, an awe-inspiring quality that captured some of the magnificent charm of our home in a way that I had not found in other portraits. So in the meantime it languished in the purgatory of the back wall.

"What was she wearing?" Dan broke the silence, completing his mental inventory.

"A black dress, I think," said Peter. "Some kind of dark coat or jacket over it, but definitely dressed in dark colors."

"Perhaps she was only standing here admiring this landscape," I offered the obvious.

"Maybe," said Dan. "But then, why so shy? No crime in looking at a painting. Is the public usually allowed back here?"

"Well, no . . . just parishioners, I guess. But you know as well as I do, Dan, that the Divine is usually wide open. We've got parishioners coming and going, youth group, choir practice, Mrs. Willamet practicing the organ, students doing sketches for art class or examining the architecture, the bishop coming in once a month or so. . . . Everybody has access to this place, as well they should," I defended.

"But everything changes when someone dies," Dan countered. "Especially if he was murdered."

———

We said our good-byes, Dan promising to beef up security around the cathedral once more, Peter greeting the first teenagers arriving for group. I retrieved my satchel abandoned beside my rear fender and remembered that Joan Dowinger was still waiting inside for me—still waiting patiently if she and Bea hadn't tangled in a cat fight yet. The flashing image of fluid copper streaking around the corner of the Divine would not dislodge from my mind as I took a deep breath and turned the knob into my home.

The scene inside contrasted considerably with my expectations and caused me to pause momentarily to take it in. Joan Dowinger was a neat-to-a-fault, heavyset woman, older as denoted by her white hair and wrinkled hands, yet ageless from her regimen of beauty facials and fashionable clothes and accessories. Bea claimed she had to be at least seventy. Joan's great-great-grandfather was one of the founders of Avenell, and her husband, a northern industrialist, had secured her importance to the university by establishing a large endowment just before his death. The combination created a kind of divine right in her bearing and in the execution of idiosyncratic, but often well-intentioned, ideas.

Balancing a saucer on one knee and sipping tea before me now, she looked resplendent in a camel suit and white silk blouse accented by a large golden-framed cameo at her neck. My sister looked well prepared for Joan's visit: her favorite navy print dress, the good china, and a rum pound cake sitting on the coffee table between them. Their voices were low and amicable, like old friends enjoying a leisurely afternoon of prayer and parish news.

"Griffin, we expected you an hour ago," my sister mock-scolded. "Look who's here."

I hurried over to gently clasp Joan Dowinger's small, pawlike hand, which she extended with a kind of expectant grace. "Joan, how nice to see you. Please forgive me for breaking our appointment yesterday. With Gentry Truman's death and all, I've been rather tied up. I hope you understand."

"Of course, dear. A dreadful business, Griffin, just absolutely dreadful. And now they're saying he was likely murdered. Such a distasteful crime to blight our beautiful parish. And I'm told you found the body!" She nibbled a morsel of pound cake.

"Well, yes, I did. However, since it's under investigation and all, I'm really not at liberty to talk about it; I'm sure you understand—"

"Absolutely. Never interfere with the law, I always say," she exclaimed.

I looked at Bea for a reading of the situation, but she returned my gaze stoically. "Now, how can I help you, Joan? Would you like to come into my office?" Before she could answer, the room suddenly seemed to dim and darken, as if we were on a stage and our show about to begin. Outside, the mountain and hills were now casting evening toward us like assorted nets, woven of shadow and intended to capture the last stray particles of light. No sunset was ever the same twice in Avenell, and despite my present state of weariness, the fleeting beauty did not escape me as I illuminated the room with my favorite brass reading lamp. "Perhaps you could even stay for dinner?" I offered, realizing the present rumbling in my stomach was hunger and not anxiety.

"No, no, dear. Lovely of you to offer, but I have to be at the Daughters of the American Revolution by seven. Dreadful meeting tonight—trying to nominate officers for next year's board. No, what I'd like to discuss we can do right here. Now, let that wonderful sister of yours pour you some tea and you have a seat. What I'd like to discuss concerns you both."

Uh-oh, I thought as Joan replaced her cup on its silver-rimmed saucer. I propped myself upright at the edge of the sofa like a soldier at full attention. She not only wanted something from me, she wanted something from Beatrice and the rest of the Ladies' Auxiliary.

My sister poured me a cup of Darjeeling, added one sugar and a splash of cream, and put it on the reading table beside me. "I'd offer you cake, Grif, but it will spoil your supper," she said matter-of-factly.

"Well, I'll get right to the point now that we're all here," began Joan, pursing her lips carefully. She had obviously rehearsed.

"I've been talking to various congregants in our fine parish, and we all feel that it's high time to renovate the Divine. Now, don't get me wrong; it's a beautiful old cathedral. But seeing the way St. Anthony's has turned out with its beautiful new facility . . . well, we don't want to be losing any of our flock to the valley, now do we? I'm all prepared to fund this myself—anonymously, of course—so money is not a consideration. No worrying about those tacky little pledge campaigns or stewardship sermons. Our heavenly Father has blessed me, and I'm prepared to bless others. I would, of course, want to help with selecting the renovation committee, the architects, designers, and all. . . ." She smiled up at me with clear hazel eyes and wiped her mouth with finality on the paper napkin in her palm. My sister choked on her last bite of pound cake and sputtered like an old lawn mower that's just hit a stubborn tree root.

Stunned to say the least, I didn't know where to begin to respond to Joan's suggestion—a plan that, in her mind, had already proceeded beyond conception and was now approaching adolescence. Why, she probably had a list of names of prospective committee members all drawn up in that little leather clutch of hers. Probably right beside a check for the initial costs of beginning the project. I couldn't bear to second-guess how far along this movement was already advanced.

Pictures of the slow, weather-dependent work at St. Anthony's flashed through my mind like thunder clouds: the sanctuary there without a roof for more than two weeks; the skeletal wall of their fellowship hall with its exposed duct work, pipes, and electrical wires; Philip Jackson's office without a door and bookshelves for almost two months. Let alone destroying the beautiful edifice that is one of the only traditional cathedrals in the state.

My mind jumped to before-and-after pictures of the courthouse over in nearby Crescent where its stately, angular-deco marble square was modernized with an annex of mirrored tiles and chrome frames. Then I remembered that Joan had her own home renovated only last year and had allowed her stately tastes and antebellum antiques to be made over in modern silhouettes and monochromes by an L.A. designer. I simply couldn't bear it.

"Joan, I don't know what to say," I stammered.

Beatrice, however, was not at a loss for words. This was far beyond their usual tangle over whether or not the flower committee should use white or red poinsettias in front of the Christmas altar this year.

"Dear Joan, what a lovely notion," my sister began to my surprise, "but it's absolutely out of the question!" Her voice rose on the last few syllables. "There's absolutely nothing wrong with the Divine as it is! It's a historic landmark, for goodness' sake! Griffin, tell her it will never happen."

Joan's lips clenched like a rosebud in reverse bloom. "Griffin. . . ?"

"Now, ladies, calm down," I began. "I have to admit that I'm a bit surprised by your suggestion, Joan. It's certainly one worth considering. But I think I need some time . . . and prayer, and of course I'll have to bring it before the deacons, you know. And then there's the bishop and the university parish committee . . ."

Of course, what was I worried about? The proposal would drown in a sea of bureaucracy. *Thank you, Lord.*

"I've already spoken with the bishop and President Milford," Joan replied with obvious relish. "And they both respect the idea. Franklin even praised me for my initiative and generosity. The bishop's response was favorable, as well. With their support, I'm sure the renovation will sail right through all your little committees."

She had obviously come prepared. This wasn't a whim, like her suggestion to open a parish discotheque for students at a youth ministry meeting a few months ago. She was armed and dangerous.

"Well, I can speak for the Ladies' Parish Auxiliary," snapped Beatrice. "And we will never support tearing down the Divine to build some postmodern tribute to you and your money, Joan Dowinger!"

"As if you even know what postmodern art is, Beatrice Reed!" fired back Joan.

"Bea, Joan . . . please. There's no need to speak that way. As I said, I will prayerfully think through your suggestion, Joan, and then, accordingly, set it in motion before the proper authorities."

The older woman regained her regal bearing. "Beatrice, dear, don't take this so personally. It has nothing to do with me; it's all about what God wants to do through our parish. We must stay up-to-date if we hope to maintain our vital ministry to the university and surrounding area. We must be prepared to embrace the twenty-first century." The short, plump woman stood, smoothed the lines of her pleated skirt, and flattened a silver curl over her right ear, a self-conscious reminder of her hearing aid.

"Well, I'll give you a week to pray on it, Griffin, and then we can meet again. Perhaps you could come to my house for tea next Tuesday—" she looked right at Bea—"and we can discuss how to proceed. Beatrice, thank you for a wonderful tea and conversation this afternoon. I'm sorry to see the prospect of change upset you so. . . ."

"Thank you, Joan," I said, hurrying to help her with a long wool cape trimmed in sable. "Let's plan on tea next Tuesday, then."

"Thank you, Father Grif." She smiled, fastening the clasp of her elegant cape. "I'll see you at Gentry's service. Such an honor for you to be officiating."

"Were you close to Gentry Truman?" I asked, then flipped on the porch light. "Let me walk you to your car."

"Such a gentleman. Well, we knew each other, of course, and traveled in the same social circles." I heard Bea snort as we headed out the door, and Joan twined her hand around the crook of my elbow.

"Such a sad man, so bitter to be so successful," she continued. "I wonder what the university will do about that new play of his that's scheduled to open in a few weeks."

Her comment struck me as rather insensitive as I took the keys from her gloved fingers and opened the Cadillac's door. "I guess they'll have to make a substitution," she continued to think aloud. "It's a shame playwrights don't have understudies." She giggled, and I smiled politely as she situated her hips into the soft tan leather driver's seat. "You think about my proposal now, Father Grif, and we'll talk next week. Good night."

She ignited the engine and raced off toward the interstate. I stood there asking the Lord what I had done to deserve a day like I'd just had.

———

Supper was a warm and comforting little meal of tuna noodle casserole and baked apples. My sister could tell I was worn thin and left me to myself after we had loaded the dishwasher together. I wanted nothing more than to go to bed and read until I fell asleep. Somewhere in the back of my mind, Gentry Truman's memorial service had burdened me all day like an overdue term paper. While I didn't have to deliver the eulogy, nevertheless I was expected to plan and conduct a service that honored one of the most cantankerous literary legends of our time, one that would please all members of his family and capture his legacy for posterity.

I was going a bit overboard in considering the weight of his service, at least the grandiosity of my minor role in it. But I did need to plan something since I was scheduled to visit the entire clan tomorrow night and offer suggestions. After a quick shower, I accompanied a cup of chamomile tea to my study to collect my thoughts and raid the bookshelves for inspiration.

A stack of unreturned phone messages was piled neatly on top of my parish desk calendar. I thumbed through the dozen slips quickly, only pausing at the one I dreaded most. Bishop Thomas Wilder. He would have heard by now, along with the rest of the world, that the Truman service would be held in the Cathedral of the Divine on the Avenell campus this Friday morning. While I did not officially need his approval—the cathedral served double-duty as the seat of his diocese as well as the church of my parish— I still craved it like a father's endorsement of his son's choice. Thomas and I had a solid working relationship, but he was still new enough in the position that we did not always know what to expect of each other.

In the pathways between my head and heart, there was an intersection of conscience I had been avoiding. A caution light, if you will, blinking ominously, prophetically. Since my agreement to conduct the service the previous evening, I wrestled with the kind of service to give this man. Even though Gentry Truman had been baptized as an infant into the Episcopal Church and had every right to a full Christian burial, I had reservations about conducting a high service complete with the Eucharist. Mrs. Truman seemed to be relying on my judgment regarding the order of service. Thomas would likely leave it up to me, as well, although I suspected there would be an undertone of disapproval whatever I chose. Honestly, I knew that a lighter service would be more appropriate for almost everyone concerned. I did not presume to fully know the Lord's point of view, but I had always believed that the service should fit the personality of the deceased as much as possible.

The clock was going on half past nine by the time I picked up the phone and called the bishop. We exchanged pleasantries, and he expressed his genuine concern for me regarding this entire affair. I brought up the matter of the service.

"If it weren't for the tragic circumstances, Grif, you and I both know that Truman's widow wouldn't even have considered having the service here. I received a call from Franklin Milford this morning requesting my endorsement and attendance. He says we must show complete university support, a unified body. I told him I would be there, but that I still wanted to talk to you before I approved the media circus on Friday." His baritone voice crackled across the wire from Nashville, where his home parish and permanent office were located.

"Thomas," I began, "neither you nor I have any idea what transpired between Gentry Truman and the Lord in the Martyr's Chapel before his death. Why, he may have come there on his own accord. He may have been praying when his murderer caught him by surprise." My voice faltered at the end and betrayed my weariness of spirit.

"You're right, Griffin. We have no room to judge. And, on the other hand, perhaps carrying out a dignified service for this man can eliminate some of the ridiculous publicity circulating about Avenell. How is the order of service coming?"

I quickly described last night's visit to the Truman home and my return visit scheduled for Wednesday.

"Will it be a high service, Grif?" he asked, lowering his voice into a whisper that reminded me of the call I received from Gentry Truman less than a week before. It seemed like years had passed since that plea.

"No, I think the second order of service, modified a bit, is more what the family is looking for," I explained.

"I agree. Perhaps we could discuss the order of service on Thursday morning, after you've finalized plans with the family."

"Thank you, Thomas. I always respect your counsel," I said.

"You know God as well as any man I've ever met, Grif. And you know people almost as well. I trust your judgment implicitly. Good night, my friend."

Before I could respond he hung up, and I stood there with the phone in hand, incandescent in his encouragement of me. He continued to surprise me, as did the Lord.

Nonetheless, as I replaced the phone and sipped my tea, my own reservations of heart were not totally diffused. I recalled my few exchanges with Gentry Truman and his contempt for the church.

"The problem with you people," he once drawled at a dinner party, *"is your insistence on superstition. If God does exist, why, he ought to at least take a curtain call for some of the spectacles he stages in this old adult theater of his. . . ."*

He had laughed ebulliently at his arrogance before I could even attempt any rebuttal. My dinner companions all laughed politely, and I smiled out of deference. I regretted my silence, and Christ's words in the tenth chapter of Matthew haunted me for a week: "So every one who acknowledges me before men, I also will acknowledge before my Father who is in heaven; but whoever denies me before men, I also will deny before my Father who is in heaven."

In honesty, my star-dazed infatuation aside, I really had not cared for the man himself. His genius with language and drama, yes. His relational style and personal philosophy, no. I wanted to emerge from the Divine Cathedral on Friday with my own integrity intact, not compromised as if I were some sophomoric sycophant.

I had agreed to do the service without even considering my own heart's stake in the matter. So typical of me. The grief counselor I saw after Amy's death spent many months on my pastor's complex, as she called it.

"You forget," she told me often, *"the Lord's command to love your neighbor as yourself. You love the world around you, Grif, more than you're willing to love the world inside you."*

Her simple wisdom had revived my ministry in many ways, but I still struggled with an awareness of my own integrity.

And this was not a time I felt the Lord would have me decline; I felt called and uniquely qualified to deliver this service. Scanning the small bookshelf closest to my desk, I pulled my weathered *Book of Common Prayer* and thumbed slowly through its wisdom. Then it seemed very clear, an obvious inspiration leaving an immediate residual of peace. I would not use either of the two burial rites provided in the prayer book. Instead, I would use the suggested order reserved for "pastoral consid erations," a euphemism for similar services for nonbelievers, terrible backsliders, or uncertain deathbed conversions. I would include enough of the regular order, excepting communion, that it would still be a holy affair, as well as an honorable time for the deceased.

The oldest son of the Janzen family, Tyler, came to mind. Yes, that service would make an excellent model for Gentry Truman's memorial. I pulled a manila folder from the iron gray file cabinet that guarded my door like the officer now posted outside the church. Tyler Janzen was nineteen years old and a freshman at Vanderbilt when he crashed into the oldest sugar maple on the Murfreesboro Highway. Dan Warren had told me that his blood alcohol was .35, over three times the legal limit. A wild one, always had been. Parents some of the most caring, godly people in the parish. Even though he had been baptized as an infant, he hadn't stepped foot in the church since grade school. A tragic loss— turned out in the end to be a suicide. Oh, it was never publicly disclosed, but the family discovered his journal in his dorm room. Seems he felt like such a failure for not shaking his addictions. The mother had grieved for years, blaming herself, before releasing her grief before God. Yes, his ser vice, which did include communion, would make an excellent model.

Since Truman was to be cremated, I assumed there would not be re mains present. We would begin with music, some classical hymns, Men delssohn or Beethoven perhaps. I made a note to call Mrs. Willamet, our organist, for other suggestions. Psalms 90 and 121 would work just fine. Then perhaps several passages from John, chapters five and six and part of ten and eleven. I had to leave room for Cale Sanders' eulogy and my own short homily that would include Truman's best legacy: poetic dia logue from his plays.

What a gift from the Lord—it all seemed very clear and cogent in my mind. I scribbled notes and marked passages to read through in the morn ing. With my rough order of service sketched out, I began to consider what exactly I would say about the man and his work. I sorted through the stack of unauthorized biographies, playbills, my own old class notes, and newspaper clippings about Gentry Truman collected on my desk. Only one thing was missing. I scanned my bookshelves that housed the usual reference texts and Greek concordances, Anglican journals, and how-tos on contemporary Christian living. But my favorite section, of course, was the unit of five shelves in the window corner where Wordsworth waxed poetic and Shakespeare revealed every facet of human capacity.

Mostly classics and eclectic personal favorites comprised the collection, and it was here that I found Gentry Truman's *Collected Works*. It contained all the major plays, a few early one-acts, and sketches. Only the terribly received play from about ten years ago—I couldn't recall its name just then—was not included. What a blow it had been to see Truman raked and punctured by every critic from L.A. to New York. Yes, I had clipped a few reviews. *"Lacks the poetic depth of his previous works. Truman settles for recycled characters and leftover plots, hoping we won't notice because he's contemporized the historical references. Our greatest living playwright needs to bask in the afterglow of his prime rather than pretending to sustain a zenith that has long since passed. . . ."* It had to have been simply excruciating for Gentry to read review after review reminding him that his talent had evaporated, that his career was finished.

I had never seen the work staged, but I had to confess that I, too, found it sorely lacking. It was basically a diatribe against organized religion and the apparent cruelty of God. A traveling Baptist revivalist seduces an aging spinster, promising to make her his wife. When he reneges on his promise, she kills herself and he continues preaching the Gospel without a shred of conscience. Very Flannery O'Connor-esque, but it lacked any of her vigor with language. What was its name? I shuffled through more paperbacks and newspaper clippings.

Here it was. *The Walls of Paradise.*

Chapter Nine

FIRST CONFESSION

I DROPPED THE BOOK, knocking over the dregs of my tea. Truman's failed play bore the same name as the painting our red-haired mystery woman had perused in the cathedral today. This seemed much more than a co-incidence, but I wasn't sure what to make of it. I only knew that it left a cold streak like dominoes toppling down my spine.

Although I rarely called Dan Warren this late—it was after ten now— I wanted to tell him about this. Chiding myself for not remembering to tell him about the missing candle at the crime scene when I saw him this afternoon, I got his machine and left a message asking him to call me the following morning. Since I wasn't sure of the significance of either piece of information, I couldn't justify paging him down at the sheriff's office.

I mopped up the small puddle of tea and wiped off the cover of Gen-try Truman's worst play. My original purpose came to mind—to gather some ideas about which of Truman's works might be appropriate for his memorial—and I collected the stack and headed to bed. Classical music, Mozart perhaps, wafted from beneath my sister's door, along with an oc-casional flick of paper as she turned a page.

After brushing my teeth and reading Psalms 4 and 5 ("For Thou art not a God who delights in wickedness; evil may not sojourn with thee"),

I settled under the down comforter and Amish wedding quilt that old Mrs. Lapp, from the community down near Tremont, had given Amy and me as a wedding present. It was pieced in the bold, solid colors the Amish are known for: navy blue, dark green, burgundy rose, and violet. As a result of its origin, I never went to sleep without thinking of Amy, of what our lives would be like if she were still with me. An odd kind of comfort.

I wondered what Amy would have thought of Gentry Truman. Like me, she loved and respected his work, but how would she have perceived him? She had a gentle yet shrewd intuition about people, the way a good kindergarten teacher should, gauging her pupils' kindnesses and weaknesses the first day, yet leaving room to be surprised.

Arranging my texts in a barricade alongside me, I began skimming the stories about this man's life, this man whom I did not even know well but whose service I had agreed to render. I decided to play a little game then, reading these like Amy would and forming an impression based on her sensibilities.

Most biographies of Truman recounted his dirt-poor upbringing by his grandmother just fifteen miles away down in a little community called Harpertown. In fact, his parents proved to be the impetus behind most of his best dramatic creations. His rakish, bootlegging father, Spencer, came from an old-money family in Savannah. When he fell in love with Truman's mother, Ellen, she was a single mother working as a waitress in a roadside diner off Highway 64 over near LaFayette. The son she was raising from a previous affair was Cale. It was hard for me to believe he was actually two years older than Gentry. I guess Gentry's fast lifestyle and alcoholism took those two years and more off him.

The dashing Spencer Dunlap Truman and poor, pretty Ellen Hope Sanders were a typical southern Romeo and Juliet. Socioeconomically star-crossed, they were never allowed to marry by his family, who forbade it even when she discovered she was pregnant with his child. Their relationship continued on-again, off-again until Gentry—one biographer commented on Ellen's appreciation of irony in selecting her son's name—

was about eighteen months. Except for one summer spent in Savannah when he was eight years old, Gentry Truman never saw his father his entire life. In pursuit of her faded dream of being a successful country singer, a Patsy Cline–like persona she perceived the Trumans as accepting (which I doubted), Ellen proved an alcoholic, unstable parent, as well. Consequently, Cale and Gentry grew up together in Harpertown with their mother's mother, Lucy Gail Sanders, the delightful "Nanna" character of Truman's one-act play *Country Store*.

Ellen died in a honky-tonk fire in Marietta, Georgia, when Gentry was only fourteen. Shortly thereafter, he left Nanna and Cale behind and hitchhiked to Atlanta and eventually to New York. From there, the boy's innate talent for poetry and drama could not be suppressed. He worked as an usher for the Clairmont Theater on Broadway until he got to know the actors, writers, and directors well enough to show them the scenes he'd written. He married at age nineteen to a showgirl, someone, most critics think, much like his mother.

That relationship lasted two years and produced one daughter. By then, though, Gentry Truman had been discovered, a wunderkind. He quickly became the darling of Broadway, toasted and feted by every producer on the Great White Way. His next marriage at age twenty-eight was to film actress Charise Chandler, a union lasting five years and producing daughter number two. At age thirty he was awarded his second Pulitzer prize for drama for *The Color of Night*. Warner Brothers snapped up the film rights and cast Charise to star. In the middle of their messy divorce, Truman balked at her casting and won out. Much of his spite for his ex-wife did not come out in the press at that time, but he quickly gained a mercurial reputation for disparate extremes of kindness and cruelty.

A recovering Vivian Leigh was cast instead with newcomer Marlon Brando, and the rest, of course, is film history. The front-porch scene alone won Brando an Oscar and Leigh a nomination with his raw, brutal vitality and her frail, fading sensuality. Despite the unhappy ending where Leigh's character is institutionalized, the film was one of mine and Amy's favorites. "*What color's the heart, Mr. Primrose? Why it's the color of night, as black and dark and scarred as the sky above us. . . .*" the lovely actress's exaggerated southern drawl echoed in my mind.

After that success Gentry Truman was more persona than man, I believe. He succumbed to the cycle of alcohol and drugs in the New York party scene. Refused to marry during the '70s and '80s, yet he did produce another daughter to a young woman whom he met in a writing class he taught at Columbia. I couldn't find her name anywhere, but she must be the mother of Jenna—the daughter I'd met the previous night.

He was also in a terrible plagiarism lawsuit as a result of his stint at Columbia. A graduate student claimed that Gentry had stolen scenes from her graduate thesis project and inserted them almost verbatim into his work in progress, which turned out to be *The Walls of Paradise*. After his play was so poorly received, Gentry quickly settled out of court for a small amount, never acknowledging anything but that the poor woman was deluded. He claimed only to have settled to avoid further litigation costs. He cruelly joked in one interview that he wished he had plagiarized so as to explain why the critics "chewed it up sideways like a coon dog on a rabbit's carcass."

I wondered if this former student could still be harboring a grudge for over a decade. Of course, I knew people harbored grudges for lifetimes, let alone decades. But if this woman, named Carol Tyson-Burks, hated Truman enough to kill him, why wait over a decade?

I was sure the police had already thought of this and interviewed her, but I added her name to my mental inquiry list for Dan in the morning. My eyes felt the weight of the day, and I began transferring my wall of books to my nightstand. The room was beginning to seem dimmer, cold air pressing against my window that faced the side of the Divine. I could tell fog was rolling in from the dusky glow of the muffled streetlight, and I took this as my cue to embrace rest.

I slept in shifts, waking every couple of hours, and except for the absence of those hard waiting room chairs, my fitful state reminded me of so many nights in the hospital with Amy, so many nights where the most I hoped for was four or five hours. I deliberately stayed in bed, refusing to read or make a cup of tea. Dreams rolled in like trailers for foreign art films, incoherent, disturbingly violent, in a language beyond my comprehension.

I welcomed dawn's entrance into the cotton-packed world of fog with impatience. I did not feel rested, but I had regained enough energy that I did not wish to remain in the terrible purgatory of my bed any longer than I had to. A morning run, perhaps? Would I ever be able to enjoy one of my favorite pursuits again without remembering the grisly sight at the end of my last trek?

I figured the only way to reclaim it would be to get back on the horse that had thrown me as soon as possible. If ever I needed the solitude and stress relief that my morning jogs provided, it was now.

Outside, the day was much like it had been just two before. Only now, dark figures with walkie-talkies and cell phones dotted my course like statues. I made up names for each tableau, as if they were modern works of art, the kind I'd see on campus over by the art building occasionally, or the kind I remembered from Central Park when I attended Union. *The Waiting Reporter* knelt in her trench coat with a phone to her ear . . . or was that a microrecorder? A block over stood *Police on Patrol*, a cluster of three officers of various heights who looked oddly comical, like overgrown penguins sifting through the fog for the rest of their clan.

As I turned off State Street, the President's Manse loomed silent and dark behind its white brick walls and shuttered windows. For a second I thought I saw Franklin Milford standing out on the widow's walk on the far right of the second story, but the image disappeared in a breath of fog, and I didn't look back. After I'd seen the way he comforted Marcia Truman the other night, he seemed the obvious candidate to be her mystery man rekindling a romance from their past.

He was a distinguished man, neat to the point of fastidious, and his bachelorhood seemed to reinforce his desire for singular focus and devotion to the university and his career. Yet every man has his weakness, and Mrs. Truman is a striking woman, a powerful woman, an actress of considerable talents and wealth. Perhaps I was letting my imagination run away. Franklin Milford had an impeccable character, and I hated to tarnish it with speculative projections from my own attraction to Marcia Klein Truman.

More human statues were along Southern Avenue, increasing in number and similarity as I neared the Grove Park enclave of faculty homes where Gentry Truman once lived. Just as I entered the mouth of Pine Woods, I heard the sound of another runner, the labored rhythm of breathing as familiar as my own. It grew closer, the runner's approach punctuated by snapping twigs and footfalls. My mystery chaser from the other night jogged through my mind, starting the treadmill of adrenaline that was beginning to seem regular in my body this week.

Maybe it was the morning light—regardless of its shroud of fog—or perhaps it was my agitation from a poor night's sleep, but I quickly decided to face my coming fear. Probably a student or Coach Granger or one of the other dozen people I often saw on any typical morning jog. It was foolish to be afraid. I stopped on the footbridge binding the skinny leg of the Jackson River and planted my right foot on the cement brace and retied my laces. The runner continued his approach, nicely paced, and soon appeared through the trees on the bank opposite me.

A sleek blue form bounded across the rough-hewn planks of the bridge. Pink cheeked and pale complected, the runner stopped a few feet before me as I completed the double knot on my left Nike.

"Father Reed? Is that you? It's Caroline Barr." She jogged in place, her auburn hair pulled straight back in a tight ponytail, her eyes alive with sapphiric color.

"Dr. Barr—Caroline—how good to see you. I didn't know you ran." I stood and offered my hand, which she took.

"Nor I, you," she puffed.

"Thanks again for your help the other morning. Sorry we couldn't have visited under less tragic circumstances," I replied.

Her breathing was slowing down. "I'm just sorry you had to find what you found. A terrible loss. Are you running? Which way?" Her feet continued to shuffle as if she were practicing tap.

"I'm heading toward your house, over by the chapel," I said.

"Mind if I join you? I usually turn back here at the bridge."

"Please, I'd love the company. You're probably faster than me, though. Don't let me slow you down."

"No problem. I . . . I'd like to talk to you anyway." She blew on her hands for warmth in the cold morning air and began lifting her knees higher again.

"Great, let's go," I said and continued my route that Caroline Barr would now retrace for herself.

We ran in silence for several hundred yards, with me following her lead when the path narrowed to one lane. Side by side for most of the way, we found our pace was well matched, although I could tell she was holding back a tad, confining the energy that coursed through her neck and lovely cheekbones. I kept waiting for her to speak her mind about whatever she wanted to tell me, but my attempts met with small talk about the loveliness of campus and the exceptional colors this fall. As we approached the Martyr's Chapel, I stopped to survey the scene.

Yellow police crime-scene tape decorated the perimeter of the chapel like tattered crepe paper after a parish picnic. The area appeared forlorn, the hung-over expression of a place trampled and abandoned, a place aware that it has been violated beyond repair. Only the stone spire and cross atop it seemed to offer hope, piercing the fog like a kind of periscope, peering up to test the water after the tumultuous undercurrents of Gentry Truman's death. A county sheriff's Blazer blocked the rudimentary tire trail formed by the influx of traffic over the past two days. Two officers waved us off, suspecting more reporters, and we continued on our way.

I hadn't planned on accompanying Caroline Barr home, but that was the direction we pursued. The distance passed by quickly, only the sound of our breathing communicating between us. Approaching the drive of the trim cottage she called home, we gradually slowed our pace to a fast walk.

"Would you like some water? Maybe some juice or coffee?" she asked, stretching her lean form unselfconsciously.

"Water would be wonderful," I said.

Inside the kitchen with the black-and-white parquet floor and the painted cabinets with ceramic pulls shaped like different fruits, I downed two glasses of water from the large dispenser beside her refrigerator. She excused herself momentarily and returned in baggy sweats. Her face remained flushed with color that matched her hair, now released to frame her beauty. I momentarily remembered our red-haired mystery lady and wondered if she could have been the one. She certainly had the speed, but the hair color and length were all wrong. The mystery woman's hair nearly went to her waist and was bright copper, which could be taken care of by a wig, I supposed. Yet I was certain the mystery woman was taller, as well.

"I . . . I'm not sure where to begin," she said softly. "Do you have time to sit for a cup of coffee?"

"That would be nice," I said. "I know we don't really know each other, so take your time if you have something you want to say. Remember, too, that I'll keep it absolutely confidential." She smiled and turned her eyes away to the window.

Caroline appeared lost in thought for a moment, or lost in the white spun-sugar vista out her window: Eaglehead Mountain's eastern slope draped with fog and frost. She found herself then and poured two cups of coffee from an old-fashioned silver percolator that had been brewing on top of her stove.

I scanned the room and found her sense of style and appreciation of the simple carried over to the cherry dining table and matching hutch. I liked her home, its charm and comfort. She brought out cream and sugar, and we sat down at the table as she released a deep sigh.

"I'm not even sure why I want to tell you," she began. "Maybe because you've been kind to me ever since I came here last year. You were so friendly at that new faculty reception, and your sister was so sweet to bring me banana bread and that little African violet"—she pointed to the windowsill above the white enamel sink—"over there. I guess I need someone I can trust right now."

I nodded, and she sipped her coffee. "I spent most of yesterday afternoon talking to the police." She looked intently at my reaction. "About Gentry Truman's death," she added dramatically.

My gaze remained fixed on hers and the pain behind it. It didn't surprise me that the police would question her. If nothing else, she was the closest in the vicinity. But I sensed their inquiries were more than routine.

"Father," she continued, "I need to tell you a story. It takes place many years ago with a young woman in college, my best friend. She was terribly insecure but was very smart. Her parents wanted her to be a doctor, but she herself wanted to write. She loved the movies, loved plays, would lose herself for hours watching old classics, musicals, everything. My friend decided not to be a doctor and her parents were bitterly disappointed." She paused and motioned me over to the small sofa.

"I'm very sorry," I said. "What happened to your friend?"

"Well, things got worse before they got better. You see, instead of medical school, my friend entered graduate school to become a better writer. She was fortunate enough to get into a program facultied by some of the greatest living writers at the time." Her voice became more forceful and controlled, as if she were reviewing the scene in some mental film clip. It's a tone that I imagined her students would recognize from class lectures. She continued. "Then one day, while she was waiting for her faculty mentor in his office, she noticed his new work sitting on his desk. She knew she shouldn't, but she began to skim through it, thrilled at the prospect of seeing the next great drama from this master playwright before the rest of the world.

"She was shocked, however, to discover some of her own scenes in her mentor's work. Even though he changed the names, several runs of dialogue were exactly the same as her thesis project—something only her mentor and a handful of classmates had seen. She ran out of that office terribly disillusioned. She sued her teacher for plagiarism, and he tried to discredit her as crazy. The process became very messy and very expensive. Eventually, he settled out of court, but the settlement barely covered my friend's legal fees. . . ."

Our coffee was cold by now, but Caroline gulped the rest of hers down and hurried over to place the mug in the sink. She stood at the window and seemed to lose herself in the lifting fog steaming off the dew-kissed mountainside.

I walked over to her, placed my own mug in the sink, and gently placed one hand on her shoulder. "Caroline," I whispered, "I understand that you were that young woman. And I know that Gentry Truman was the mentor who let you down so terribly. You are Carol Tyson-Burks, aren't you?"

She spun fiercely, tossing my hand back to my side. "Was," she said. "I used to be Carol Tyson-Burks. But she died when she discovered what a wretched, unfair place the world can be. . . . She died just as sure as if Gentry Truman pulled the trigger. I'm sorry, Father, I—" she stopped, as if thinking better of her next words.

"So what happened after the lawsuit was settled?" I asked.

"Well, I remained depressed for many months but slowly began to put my life back together again. I quit the creative writing program and entered the literary studies track, got my Ph.D. . . . taught part time here and there until I got this job last year." Her defensive edge receded back into the vulnerable ocean inside.

"And Caroline Barr was born," I said. "Didn't Truman recognize you when he came here this fall?"

She smiled out of one side of her mouth, oddly amused. I didn't like the look in her eyes, one of possession. Or obsession, perhaps.

"No, not at first. I . . . well, I used to be very different. I was very shy and quiet, with thick glasses and a curly perm and about forty pounds heavier. Carol Tyson-Burks was not someone I liked very much." She shifted uncomfortably and folded her arms across her chest. I couldn't

imagine her with these features—she looked so . . . well, natural and unselfconsciously attractive now.

"So gradually, about halfway through my graduate program, I began
to change—I exercised and the weight came off. I began letting the things
I didn't like about myself melt away. I decided a new name was in order,
as well. I occasionally still got recognized as the girl who took on Gentry
Truman. Caroline was my full given name and Barr is from—"

"Barr is from the Afra Behn manuscript you discovered, *The Bartered
Bride*," I finished.

"I'm impressed, Father. You've read my dissertation?" she asked,
clearly animated.

"Yes, I saw it listed under new faculty publications in the *Avenell
Eagle*—an easy find in the library. From your research, it sounds like the
character of Victoria Barr is certainly a good role model." I smiled, thinking of the title character who disguises herself to avoid going through with
a prearranged marriage.

"She's been good for me, for who I am now. No, Truman didn't recognize me at first. I kept my distance, and the only time we officially met
was at the president's dinner party. Truman was too sloshed to notice me,
though, and like I said, I've changed quite a bit since my days at Columbia."

"So that's why the police were here yesterday? They traced you to
Avenell and thought it too much of a coincidence that one of the people
who had a great reason to kill Gentry Truman, publicly at least, was so
near the scene of the crime. . . ."

"Yes. And you have to admit, what are the chances? I was stunned
when I heard Truman had accepted an invitation to come here. I almost
left. But I like it here—the students, the department, the beautiful setting. I wasn't going to let Truman ruin my life again. Besides, I figured
he'd be gone by the end of spring semester having never known I'm here
. . . and now this."

I glanced at a large clock shaped like a cat's face and realized that over
an hour had passed since we completed our run. My sister would be riding

in a police cruiser by now, combing the ditches for my remains.

"Caroline, may I use your phone? I'm usually back by now, and I don't want my sister to be alarmed."

"Of course," she replied and pointed me to it for the second time that week. She returned to the sofa casually, trying to give me some privacy. Bea was livid but relieved nonetheless. She had just paged Dan Warren. "I'll be home soon," I promised and hung up.

"Father Reed," said Caroline, "I have one more thing I want to tell you. Perhaps the main reason I'm telling you any of this. There's something I didn't tell the police yesterday."

I had planned to leave but resumed my seat next to her. "Yes?" I encouraged.

"This must remain confidential for now. At least until I figure out if it even matters," she said, and I nodded. "You asked if Gentry Truman recognized me, and no . . . not at first, just like I said. But then last week I was in the faculty lounge up on the fifth floor of Hammond Hall. Truman came in, and I discreetly prepared to leave when he struck up a conversation. Then, out of nowhere, he says, 'So, little Carol thinks she's been able to fool Uncle Gentry.' I could have died on the spot—his tone of voice was so . . . so spiteful. I was frightened and grabbed my briefcase and lunged for the door. But not before he jumped in front of it." She closed her eyes. "He said, 'Oh, you fooled me at first. But then I read your vita in one of the university brochures. It listed works you've published, and so I had my teaching assistant fetch me a copy of your endearing little feminist treatise on Shakespeare's comedies. I remembered a similar topic from one of my most promising students back at Columbia. The writing style was the same . . . the same pathetic, no-talent little writing style that made you give up drama in the first place. I guess it's true—those who can't write, teach.' He sneered at me, literally sneered at me like a cartoon villain. I . . . I slapped him. I told him to get out of my way."

She subtly shifted toward me but said no more.

"What did he say? Did he let you go?" I asked, riveted by the animosity in her voice.

She leaned closer. "He said that if I wanted to keep my job, then I better be a lot kinder to him." She took a deep, diaphragm-centered breath.

"And what did you do?"

Caroline Barr enunciated very carefully. "I told him that I would kill him before I'd let him ruin my life again."

Chapter Ten

THE CORNER HOUSE

———

I COULD IMAGINE IT. If this young, vibrant woman, as intelligent as she was, felt that the man who changed the direction of her life forever was threatening to do it all over again, I could imagine that she would kill him.

"Forgive me, but *did* you kill Gentry Truman?" I asked calmly.

She looked hurt. "No, Father. No, a thousand times no. I hated his guts, and even though I said that, I would never follow through. But I know how this all must sound, and that's why I want to know if you think I should go to the police or not. I can't see how this would help them. The only thing it could do is cast more suspicion on me."

"Could anyone have overheard you? Another faculty member or student perhaps?"

"No, I don't think so. It was late in the afternoon last Wednesday, a week ago today. The last class period had ended, and most faculty were gone for the day," she said.

"What did Truman do after you threatened him?" I continued the interrogation.

"Nothing. My bluff worked, I think. He just sneered and stepped aside. I slammed the door in his face and ran out of there as fast as I could. I was sick at heart all weekend, just waiting for my department chair, Dr. Stanley, to call me in and fire me. But nothing . . . until Truman turns up dead, and not far from my house at that." Caroline Barr wrapped a strand of ginger hair behind her ear and rested her hand at the base of her angular jawline. I wasn't sure why yet, but I believed she was telling the truth. I had no doubts about the limits of Truman's words or actions.

"I think you should tell the police, Caroline. I know I'm in the truth business, but I think it's what's best for you. If someone did overhear you, then you've beat them to the punch and shown you have nothing to hide. If not, then you've released your conscience and shown your integrity to the police. Would the murderer recount an incriminating incident un-solicited to the police? I'll go with you if you want," I pushed.

"I . . . I don't know what to do. What you're saying sounds good, but I'm scared. Even in death, Gentry Truman has my life coming apart at the seams. . . ." She began to release the torrent of emotions swirling in-side, and I let her cry it out, her face in her hands as she shrank into the corner of the couch. I scooted closer to comfort her, aware of the ap-pearance of impropriety if someone happened to walk by the dining room window. But to withhold comfort would have been cowardly and would violate the courage required to carry out the counsel I had just given. She nestled her head against my shoulder and slowly the tears stopped.

"Thank you for believing me, Father," she whispered and patted my hand.

"You're welcome, Caroline." I paused awkwardly. "I know this sounds trite, but may I pray for you? Right now?"

She smiled through the moist veil of her eyes and nodded. "That would be very nice."

"Abba Father, thank you for Caroline and her willingness to risk trust-ing her secret with me. I pray that you would give her peace and protect her from the enemy, from those who would harm us. We ask that you would guide and direct her steps to help her know when or even if to share this information. I ask for your blessing on her and her step of faith today. In the holy name of Jesus. Amen."

We sat in silence for several moments, long enough for her cat to enter the room and leap into my lap. Caroline began to shoo her away, but I smiled and began to stroke the gray tabby.

Finally she said, "I can't thank you enough. I feel much better. I don't know what I'm going to do, but I'm grateful to have someone believe I'm telling the truth." Her composure returned, and I smiled, trying to dismiss the intimacy that confession and prayer often bring.

"I'm not much of a pray-er," she said as I rose. "But your words for me just now . . . I don't know. I like your faith, Father."

I nodded, and we hugged briefly before she escorted me to the door. "If you need me to go with you, or if you only want to talk some more, please call me. I'll do whatever I can."

"I will," she promised.

I strolled down the drive and marveled at the sun's brightness now engulfing the woods. Under a canopy of branches, the light seemed trapped, like neon under water. In my mind I wondered if she could have murdered Gentry Truman, while in my heart I knew she did not. I was learning to trust my spiritual intuition, as Bea called it, more and more. But I still didn't like the fact that I couldn't explain it.

———

Back at home Bea scolded me for not calling sooner. Once again, she had stopped answering our phone because so many reporters continued to harass us for details about Gentry's death. I hoped that once more information was released, they would leave us alone. Two press conferences were scheduled for the day; one by the district attorney's office to announce that the case was being treated as a homicide, and the second by Marcia Truman's personal assistant, Claire O'Brien, announcing the memorial service on Friday and asking the public to contribute to an Avenell scholarship fund that had been established in Gentry's name in lieu of flowers.

When the phone rang at ten-thirty, I had just stepped out of the shower. Bea had left a note saying she had to run to Mr. Spradley's market for cinnamon—she had run out while baking snickerdoodles for me to take to the Trumans that night. Still in my no-nonsense mood, I grabbed the phone and snapped, "Yes?"—expecting to take some reporter from the *National Examiner* by surprise.

"Grif? It's Dan Warren. Are you all right?" came the sturdy voice.

"Dan, sorry. I expected you to be one of the parasitic press who keep calling here. How are you?" I asked, unburdening my tone.

"Fine, under the circumstances. Your message said you had some information to share?" Dan's stress pressed through the seams in his voice.

"Nothing significant . . . or at least I don't think. Can you sneak away for lunch? My treat."

"Every place in town is packed out, Grif. I'd love to, but I'm not sure now is the time. . . ." I could hear the whirl and clang of other phones, faxes, voices, and keyboards in the background.

"How about the Corner House in Harpertown? I doubt many of the reporters have discovered Miss Georgia's place yet."

"Well, all right. I'm sick of eating out of the vending machine. I'll meet you there in two hours, Father," said my friend.

"The food will do you good, Dan. Hey, I may bring Pete with me—do you mind?"

"No, not at all. I'll see you shortly."

I called Miss Georgia Epps while the phone was still in my hand and reserved the back porch table. She said she'd save the space as well as a piece of derby pie for each of us. Pete was a little harder to track down, but by noon I found him coming out of the library, and he was glad for the company.

"I've checked all over campus," he began, "and no one knows anyone who matches the red-haired woman's description. I thought I was close a couple of times, but they only turned out to be students with similarities—one with bright red short hair, the other with long strawberry blond. I'm beginning to think she doesn't exist."

Our narrow road leading out of campus was congested with more news vans and portable satellite hook-ups. There was even a limousine stretching itself like a drowsy cat in front of the Pepper Tree Grill, a student favorite. As I guided my big sedan through the intersection and onto Highway 64, the traffic thinned to the usual semis, pickups, and student Hondas. I debated whether to share my discovery about the name of the painting being shared by Gentry Truman's worst play. Did the mystery woman know of this apparent coincidence? Her face refused to come into further focus in my mind.

"Do you think the hair could have been a wig?" I asked instead, choosing to wait until Dan was with us to share about *The Walls of Paradise*.

"I wondered that, too," Pete replied. "I suppose it could, but I don't think so. During the moment when we fell and our eyes met, she looked too natural, too beautiful for it to be a wig. Besides, I think it would have fallen off as fast as she was running!"

The comical image made us both laugh. I found myself still smiling as we made our way down the mountain, enjoying the autumn palette once more but feeling an edge of melancholy rustling through the last leaves. The hairpin curves doubled back again and again, winding us slowly, gradually down Eaglehead's steep leaf-strewn descent, reminding me of a snake coiling and uncoiling to shed its skin. While one of the tallest peaks in the state, Eaglehead was still nothing to worry about on paper at only 2,000 feet above sea level. However, its incline-to-base ratio rivaled those of many grander peaks. When the fog set in, or the occasional snowstorm, traversing these curves had proved deadly to more motorists than anyone cared to remember. New Avenell students were especially susceptible, dismissing local warnings as unfounded.

As if reading my thoughts, Pete murmured, "Whoa . . . I left my stomach at that last curve, Grif. I don't care how many times I drive this mountain, I'm always a little nauseous by the time I reach the base."

"Let me know if you need to stop," I said, gently braking into the next turn. "Only three more curves until we're down."

"You know how many curves this highway has?" he asked incredulously.

"Pete, I grew up here. Of course I do. When Amy was sick and we'd drive back and forth to County General for chemo, she'd be too weak to talk coming back. So I'd pray or count trees or curves in the road. It's funny what we find to occupy ourselves with . . . when we're in pain."

My curate nodded and clutched the armrest as we turned the last 180-degree curve. "Oh yeah! Speaking of distractions—I talked to Dylan Klein yesterday. I'd almost forgotten with all the excitement over Lady Red. He seemed pretty shook up, more worried about his mother and how his stepfather's death will affect their finances than about missing Gentry himself."

"Did he say that?" I asked.

"Pretty much. Said he hoped he'd be able to stay on at Avenell without Truman footing the bill. Said he's worried about his mother's fragile state. Kind of a weird guy," explained Peter.

"But obviously there will be a sizable estate—I'll bet publishing and film royalties alone bring in a million dollars a year. I can't imagine that there's anything to worry about there—unless he knows something the rest of us don't." My curate's assessment finally caught up to my thoughts. "Why weird, Pete? In what way? Scared, blasé, angry?"

"No. More detached, stoic. A bit . . . effeminate, you know." He fumbled for words.

"Hmm, maybe he's simply in shock. And let's not jump to any conclusions based on his mannerisms—he hasn't had many male role models in his life. Maybe you could invite him to Next Generation services?"

"I did. He said he might come some time, if his schoolwork and drama production schedule didn't get in the way."

"Good," I said, and each of us returned to our own thoughts as the highway transformed into a nice linear plane. Miss Georgia's was only another ten minutes away, and we both lost ourselves in the Irish-green meadows and stalk-littered cornfields. I wondered if Dylan knew something about Gentry's finances or will that would have precipitated his fear of leaving Avenell. I wondered how Marcia and Cale would react if they knew Dylan had expressed this fear.

More loose ends. I was pleased to find a Carroll County Sheriff's cruiser backed into the last spot in the tiny parking lot behind the Corner House, a quaint lavender two-story with violet shutters that guarded the corner lot across from the Andrew Johnson Elementary School in downtown Harpertown. I remembered then that this was the area where Gentry Truman had grown up with his grandmother and half brother. Maybe I could talk to some of the folk who knew him as a boy, gather some more impressions for the memorial service.

Miss Georgia Epps welcomed us herself, her ebullient smile lighting up the small restaurant. Like her white counterpart, Miss Percy at the Scenic in Mumford, Miss Georgia was a local institution, synonymous with Cajun cooking and southern-fried vegetables. Her clientele ran the gamut from bricklayers to lawyers who wanted privacy with their clients and thus avoided the restaurants on the square in Mumford.

This day Miss Georgia was dressed in a long flowing floral dress comprised of sections, each with a different, although kindred, print of burgundy, cobalt, emerald, topaz, and scarlet pansies. A starched white apron embraced her wide hips and heavy bosom, highlighting the sienna glow of her flawless complexion and large brown eyes. The woman was ageless.

"Father Griffin, so good to see you, my dear! Father Peter, if only I were a few years younger!" boomed the sweet, husky voice. "I have your special table all set, and your very good-looking friend is there waiting for you already!"

She led us discreetly through three adjoining rooms of cozy round tables and ladderback chairs, each room with a different flower motif: the first, daisies; the second, roses; the third, pansies. Behind the pansy room was the back porch, decorated year round with ivy, ferns, and philodendron. The back porch was partitioned off from the other areas by glass French doors and often hosted birthday parties, receptions, and more than a few marriage proposals. Today the intimate locale looked rather forlorn, with only Dan Warren anchoring the large white pedestal table in the center. We men shook hands and took our seats.

"You want my special today, gentlemen? It's my secret gumbo—

mighty fine. Or would you like the menu?" our hostess asked.

"Sounds good, Miss Georgia," said Dan. "Just make sure you have a pitcher of tea handy."

Her hearty laugh bounced through the small room, shaking a glass shelf of African violets behind her. "I put extra hot sauce in it today just for you!"

"I'll have the usual, Miss Georgia," I said. "Fried tomato sandwich on honey wheat bread, Cajun mustard, and Swiss cheese."

Pete bridged our two orders by requesting a cup of gumbo with half a sandwich.

As the large woman swished skirt and apron through the French doors, Dan smiled. "Good idea, Father Grif. Nothin' like Miss G's gumbo to take my mind off a case. 'Course, depending on your information, my mind won't be off of it for long. What's up?"

"Two things, Dan. I went up to see my friend John Greenwood at Rockmont yesterday and remembered something inside the Martyr's Chapel when I found the body. For some reason, I'm almost positive that a candle was missing from the votive stand. Either it was missing or else the candle had burned down to the wick. Is this accurate, Dan, or did I just dream it up after what happened in the cathedral the other night?"

Dan thought a moment. "Yes. One of the candles in the votive stand had been lit, presumably around the time of death, and had burned down to nothing but wick."

"So that means either Truman or the murderer lit it?" Pete interjected.

"Apparently," said Dan. "Unless someone else visited the chapel in between Truman's death and Grif's discovery of the body."

"Is that likely?" I asked, recalling my conversation with Sam Claiborne.

"It's a possibility," he continued. "There were no unidentifiable prints on any of the candles in the Martyr's Chapel, but we still haven't identified the mystery prints from the chapel that match the one found on the gun. So we're widening our net, taking more prints today of the rest of the family, acquaintances, students in Truman's classes, and faculty who knew him."

I immediately thought of Caroline Barr's dilemma. Could it be her print? Was she telling me her story ahead of time to win my sympathies in case she was charged with murder? I tried to imagine her arranging to meet Gentry Truman in the Martyr's Chapel late on a Friday night. It was close to her house, giving her an easy jog back to her cozy cottage in no time. But if she planned to murder her former mentor, would she choose a site so obviously close to her home?

And if she did arrange the meeting, how did she manage to overcome him? Truman certainly wasn't a docile lamb being led to the slaughter. Did she drug him first? Or take him by surprise with a blow to the head? Was this lovely woman—with whom I ran, drank coffee, and prayed this morning—capable of murder?

Somewhere in the spectrum of my theology, my view of human nature's sinful capabilities had always leaned toward the liberal. Cynicism aside, I understood that any one of us was capable of any transgression imaginable—including murder—given the right circumstances. I wasn't arrogant enough to believe that one could never rise above the selfish inclination—no, that was why Christ came, as St. Paul explains so well in Romans seven and eight. But I had also learned never to trust too much in the appearance of goodness, regardless of a person's sincerity or my desire to trust him. Or her.

"Grif? Are you praying without us or what?" Dan chuckled and brought me back to the table. Our food had arrived and the gumbo's delicious aroma permeated the enclosed air—onion, pepper, garlic, oregano, tomato.

"Sorry. Pete, why don't you pray for us," I said.

We enjoyed our first few bites in silence, my fried tomato sandwich grilled to golden crisp perfection.

"So what were you thinking just then?" Pete asked. "How's your morning been?"

"I was just thinking about someone I ran into today, that's all. I had a very pleasant morning. Went running—decided I don't want to let all the hoopla keep me from my routine, from what's good for me."

"Were you the one running by the Martyr's Chapel this morning?" asked Dan. "Keith Lockwood reported seeing a couple of runners—he figured they were more press trying to get pictures of the crime scene."

"Yep, that was me," I said, thinking quickly how to change the subject.

But not quick enough. "So who were you with?" Pete tried to sound casual. I could tell by Dan's raised brows that he, too, was curious.

"Oh, just a new friend," I said. "One of my parishioners needed to talk, and so we decided to run together."

Dan and Peter exchanged glances and I bit into the second half of my sandwich. They took the hint and let it go, and I was grateful that I didn't have to come right out and tell them it was confidential.

"You mentioned two things, Grif. What was the second?" Dan inquired.

"It has to do with a rather unique coincidence I discovered last night while I was researching Gentry's life for the service on Friday. Let me back up. When we were in the cathedral yesterday looking for clues, after Peter's mystery woman ran out, I spent a long time gazing at the large landscape of Eaglehead Mountain that hangs there at the corner where she and Pete collided. While the artist is evidently unknown, the work is titled *The Walls of Paradise*. Well, last night as I was reading through the canon of Truman's work, I found that the last play he had produced over a decade ago—was called *The Walls of Paradise*." My voice could not contain my excitement.

"What do you know about either of them?" quizzed Dan.

My words flowed rapidly, providing details about the painting's prior owner and benefactor and about the dismal quality of Gentry's last attempt at greatness.

"So there's no apparent connection?" Pete half asked and half observed. "But you're right, this does seem like a very odd coincidence."

"Could Truman have been that benefactor who donated the painting?

Or could he have known this person and seen it in his possession first? Since the artist is unknown, could the painting be an undiscovered Rembrandt or Picasso—worth millions?" Dan bombarded.

"I doubt it. And Gentry was not the one who donated the piece." I wiped a trace of the last homegrown tomato I'd likely have this season from my mouth's corner.

"I'll get on it right away—I'm sure the federal boys have an art expert they can spare to evaluate the painting and trace its origin. Good work, Father Grif," my deputy friend praised. I tried not to beam too proudly— it could still be what it appeared to be now, a coincidence. Our bill had mysteriously appeared by then along with three slices of derby pie, although I didn't recall Miss Georgia or anyone else delivering them. The rich confection of pecans layered with chocolate filling, graced with a dollop of real whipped cream, sent us beyond the comfort of full, but didn't keep me from risking the sin of gluttony. Dan and I both reached for the check at the same time. I won.

"What kind of man lets his priest pay for his lunch?" Dan kidded.

"A smart one," chimed in Pete.

"Glad to do it," I said and meant it.

"Well, I've got to get back. The DA's press conference is at two, and then it's back to the office. I'll see you both on Friday." The dark giant rose, brushed crumbs of pie crust off his uniform, then squared his shoulders for departure. He turned before exiting through the French doors and said, "You both be careful. I appreciate what you've found out, but don't put yourselves in any danger. Understand?"

His caution wasn't condescending, only fraternally concerned. We both nodded, and Sergeant Dan Warren made his way back to a world of scanners, forensic details, and circumstantial conjecture.

———

Back in the car I asked Pete, "Do you have time for a little side excursion?"

"Of course. Where to?" he asked, like a retriever invited hunting.

"Well, Gentry Truman grew up here in Harpertown. I thought we might mosey over to the library and see what we can turn up. Maybe see if the house he grew up in is still there." I felt a twinge of guilt, knowing I ought to get back home, lock myself in the office, and work on my homily for the dead man's memorial. Bea's voice, so much like my mother's when she'd scold me as a boy for playing football instead of doing homework, rang in my ears: *"Now who thinks he's playing TV detective, dear brother?"*

I turned her voice's volume down to a level I could ignore and tooled the LeSabre down Main Street toward the Harpertown branch of the Carroll County Library. I wasn't playing detective, for heaven's sake. I was only trying to find out more about a man I was expected to honor in two more days, a man I knew a lot about but still hardly knew. I was only doing my job; I had no desire to do Dan Warren's for him.

The parking lot was empty, and the afternoon sky had dimmed to a sultry gray. Getting out of the car, I smelled the moist wind and saw the backs of oak leaves flapping in the row of big trees behind the Romanesque building. We'd have rain by suppertime.

The interior was shabby but clean—faded orange carpet, stacks from veneered shelf kits circa 1965, and squared-off chairs and worktables. The place was deserted except for a lovely young African-American woman sorting paperbacks behind the reference desk.

"May I help you?" she asked as we approached.

"Yes," I began, choosing a direct approach. "I'm Father Griffin Reed and this is my curate, Father Peter Abernathy. We're down from Avenell looking for some information on Gentry Truman—"

"The writer who got shot up there in a church? Yeah, we've got some information." Her pleasant expression wilted as she turned and led us to a small reference room partitioned by a glass wall.

"I'm scheduled to lead his memorial service this Friday, and I read that he grew up around here. I just thought I might get a better idea of what his ties to the community were if I saw where he grew up," I finished explaining.

"Of course," she said, holding the door for us. "You don't need to explain to me, Father. This place has been like a bus station the past two days. Everybody wantin' to know 'bout Gentry Truman."

"Really?" I asked, following Peter into a room no bigger than a walk-in closet.

"Uh-huh," she said. "Somebody in here right before you, wantin' the same thing. Mrs. Potts said yesterday she had at least three visitors with the same request."

How foolish I'd been to think that no one else had thought of this place. Peter sensed my embarrassment and leaned toward me as if in support.

Our guide continued. "Harpertown's most famous resident has his own little shelf and glass display case. Seems he had an aunt who used to work here—she done made him a scrapbook and everything. Baby pictures, old programs, scripts, newspaper clippings, the works. It's all right over here."

She took three steps and waved her hand like Vanna White in front of an eye-level shelf crowded with hardbound versions of Gentry's plays, an early book of poems that I had seen referenced but never read, two biographies—only the favorable ones, I noticed—and the autobiography he had penned five years ago. Beneath the shelf a small glass display case, looking like a flattened aquarium, held some handwritten pages from *The Color of Night* script, a premiere program autographed by Vivian Leigh and Brando, and several photographs of Gentry with various stars and literary celebrities.

A darker square of the plush blue fabric lining the case spotlighted a conspicuous absence.

Chapter Eleven

SECOND CONFESSION

"WHERE'S THE SCRAPBOOK you mentioned?" I asked, already afraid of the answer.

"It should be right here!" she burst out. "It's gone!"

"When did you last see it?" I asked calmly. Pete's mouth hung open, as if the book had been snatched before our eyes.

"It was here yesterday when I worked my shift, I know," she proclaimed. "An old blond lady came and spent over an hour in here, then there was that cute young reporter, and the last person I saw in here yesterday was an old man. He was still thumbing through the scrapbook when I left."

"And this morning?" I continued.

"Hey, I just came on at noon. Mrs. Potts opened up this morning. She's at lunch now—should be back any time. She'll know if anyone was in to look today."

"Okay if we look at what is here?" asked Peter, finding his voice.

"Sure, honey, help yourself," said the young woman. "When Mrs. Potts gets back, I'll send her your way." She marched back through the door and behind the circulation desk and began reassembling newspapers.

"So . . . you think someone stole the scrapbook Gentry's aunt put together about his life? Maybe a reporter?" Pete ventured.

"Maybe. Or perhaps the federal investigators wanted it. Something charting a man's life could prove very helpful in determining who would want to end it. I wonder if the aunt is still alive."

"We can try Miss Helpful again." He smiled.

"Let's just wait on Mrs. Potts," I returned, picking up a copy of *Country Store* inscribed *To dear Marie, Thanks for everything—including the saltines!* XXX *Gent.* We took seats at a reading desk about the size of a card table; it may have even been a card table. Peter whistled softly and began sorting through a stack of first editions, signed copies, and playbills.

"Wow—check this out," he said momentarily. "A playbill from *Breakfast in Birmingham* signed by the original cast, including Jaspar Owens, Peggy Ashcroft, and Helen Hayes. This must be worth a fortune—it's a wonder someone didn't steal this!"

"You're right; this place could probably use some security until after all the commotion simmers down," I said. "I'll mention it to Dan next chance I get."

Since we were facing the entrance to the library and had been surreptitiously keeping Miss Librarian in our vision (especially Pete), we knew at once that the lady entering just then had to be the venerable Mrs. Potts. A tall, slender black woman with curly white hair, she wore a trim, navy colored skirt and jacket with a blouse that tied a draping bow from the neck down to her chest. A pair of bifocals hung from a silver chain over the bow, with accentuated black rims beneath the lenses that looked like they would give the wearer black eyes. She spoke curtly with her younger counterpart before striding confidently our direction. I looked up as if I hadn't noticed her yet and smiled at her entrance.

"Fathers? I'm Abigail Potts, the main librarian here. Charlotte said that the three of you had discovered the Truman scrapbook missing. No need to be alarmed. I had it locked up in my office—sorry you had to wait," she explained apologetically. Up close her face contained fine-woven amber lines around the eyes and mouth, like molasses poured out of a jar and recursively over itself. It was a face that exuded kindness.

"Well, that's a relief," Pete sighed.

"Yes, Mrs. Potts, thank you. I'm Griffin Reed, rector of Avenell Parish up on the mountain, and this is my curate, Peter Abernathy. Pleased to meet you," I returned. She extended a thin, rubbery hand and gingerly shook with each of us.

"Would you like to see it, gentlemen?" she asked.

"Yes, please. I'm in charge of the memorial service for Gentry Truman this Friday, Mrs. Potts. I was hoping to learn a little more about him here. I know his work, and I talked to him a few times casually, but I didn't really know what kind of a man he was."

She smiled knowingly. " 'Follow me, and leave the dead to bury their own dead.' "

"Matthew 8:22, if I recall," I replied. "What are you telling us, Mrs. Potts?"

Her smile faded but did not leave her lips as she motioned for us to follow her. She led us behind the reference desk—her co-worker tried not to look surprised—to a smallish office with *Abigail Potts, County Librarian* on a brass placard screwed to the door. She shut it behind us and motioned for us to be seated. The room was lined with books competing for space—some vertical, some stacked horizontally, some towering in top-heavy piles from the floor. A ream of old *Life* magazines were in the midst of being catalogued on a small worktable behind her. The sky through the window over her shoulder shone as dully as unpolished silver against the fluorescent lighting overhead. She handed us a dark, faded crimson leather album. Peter and I pulled our chairs close together and opened it across our knees.

" 'The dead do not praise the LORD, nor do any who go down into silence. But we will bless the LORD from this time forth and for evermore. Praise the LORD!' " she exclaimed. Her voice conveyed a passionate appreciation for poetry and worship.

"Umm, Psalm 116?" guessed Pete.

"No, sugar, the one before it." She smiled again, this time revealing teeth and gums.

While I love Scripture as much as any person, I found myself a little annoyed—was she coyly inferring her view of Gentry's character or trying to impress us with a concordance-like memory of verses? In either case, I was distracted by the fascinating collage of memorabilia surrounding one man's life. Baby pictures, crayon drawings from when he was a boy, a spelling test, third grade report card . . . a leap to adolescence in assorted snapshots. A blank square, darker than the rest, bore the caption, *Gent and Cale—Sweet Sixteen.* Next came newspaper clippings and magazine articles once he achieved fame and fortune. Glossy photographs with movie stars and ex-wives.

"Do you know what happened to this photo here?" I pointed to the vacant rectangle.

"Oh my. No, I don't Father. I'm sorry. One of our recent visitors must have swiped it as a souvenir. Probably that reporter I talked to this morning. I could've sworn that picture was there last night."

"Did you know Gentry Truman at all, Mrs. Potts?" I asked.

She fished her bifocals from their silver chain and looked down at me, as if I had asked her to describe my features. "I knowed his mama and grandmama, Father. His grandmàma was such a fine woman. Miss Lucy Gail was hard workin', decent, never made no difference between white and black. His mama . . . well, let's just say poor Ellie had too many troubles to ever be a fit mama for Gentry and Cale. He was a sweet young'un growing up. Why, he'd come in my pappy's store and buy a penny's worth of snuff for Miss Lucy and a penny's worth of spearmint gum for himself. But when he got all high-and-mighty famous, Gentry Truman wasn't worth shootin'. No, you just stick to helpin' the livin' in your funeral service for Mr. Gentry Truman. That man been walkin' round dead for years." Her voice trailed into anger at the end, refined sugar becoming ground glass.

Pete shifted his foot at the irony of "Gentry Truman wasn't worth shootin'." But the image she sketched with those words intrigued me, took me back to a hard-times little boy who wanted nothing more than a stick of gum and to be loved by his mother and father. But Gentry Truman had neither.

"You're welcome to take the scrapbook back to the conference room," she added.

Her voice remained caustic—could she have some personal reason of her own for disliking Truman or his family? I nodded, undeterred by her sudden shift in demeanor.

"Do you know where he grew up, Mrs. Potts? Is the house still there?" asked Pete.

"Land's sakes, son, that house burned down, I guess, twenty-odd years ago. Wasn't much to look at to start with, just a little clapboard with four rooms and a sweet gum tree beside it. It's out off the gravel road by the old Sand Plant, near where the county dump is now. If you get to Siler's Bridge, you've gone too far."

Pete scribbled this down on the back of a yellow Post-it note he dug from his pocket. I kidded him about being an Eagle Scout, but he really was one.

"Does Gentry have any blood relatives left, besides Cale Sanders?" I inquired.

"The scrapbook maker herself—his Aunt Olive Merriweather—is still alive. In her nineties, honey, but sharp as a tack. She's at the Eagle's Nest Retirement Home over in Mumford—you know the one? I try to make it over there when I can, but it's been—why, I guess it was last Easter since I been to the home to visit her."

I nodded, recalling the place where several parishioners had spent their last few years. My only member there now was Dr. Cantrell, our family dentist when I was a child. While the place was clean and staffed by caring attendants and health care professionals, I had to make myself visit regularly. The dim lighting, ammonia and body-waste smells, and crying voices always took their toll on my heart. I either had to take all those folks home with me or trust God's goodness for them there at Eagle's Nest.

"You've been very helpful, Mrs. Potts," I said, rising to return the scrapbook to her.

"I'm glad to be of service. Now, you call me Abby, and if I can do anything else for you, just give me a call." She handed over a neatly embossed black-on-cream business card with her number, address, and the library's email address. Her voice had returned to her initial lilting cadence.

We showed ourselves out and decided there was nothing in the special collection worth more time. Like the visitors before us, we concluded that the scrapbook was the only treasure the place had to offer.

"She was helpful," Pete said as we slid into the car. "What do you make of her?"

"Yes, very kind," I replied. "Shrewd too. I can't help but think she was telling us more than we know." The look in her eyes when she said, *'Let the dead bury their own dead'* expanded in my mind to billboard proportions. Only I didn't know what she—or the Lord through her—was advertising. Not yet, at least.

———————

It was after three by the time I deposited Peter at Otey Hall for his Wednesday afternoon Bible study with several members of the Avenell Tiger football team—"Jesus' Jocks" they half-jokingly called themselves. I invited him to accompany me to the Truman's pink monolith that night to plan the service, but he reminded me that his usual Wednesday night commitment, the Next Generation service, was that night in the conference room of the Divine. My week, usually so predictably ordained, was totally off-kilter.

I was especially proud of what my curate had done with this midweek young adult service. Attendance was up to more than fifty students and locals now; word of Peter's passionate faith and engaging handling of Scripture had quickly spread. Bea and I attended when we could, captured by the youthful buoyancy of so many lives and faith journeys just beginning. I enjoyed it—though sometimes Bea was a little alarmed by pierced noses and lips, tattoos, and the hip mix of retro '60s and '70s clothing with J. Crew. But her love of others ultimately transcended her first impressions.

It was yet another trait I loved in my sister, and one I was counting on in her suspicious regard of Truman's survivors. These were my thoughts as the clouds gathered like luminous black pearls, expanding, inflating with their burdens of cold, wet air from the east. I was glad to make it back home before the rain set in and doubly blessed to find Bea lighting a small fire in the shadowy living room. Amid all the thoughts of murder, suspicions of motives, and speculations about the deceased, it was wonderful to come home to such a domestic scene as my sister streaked with flour, hair dangling at her temples, the smell of cinnamon and sugar wafting from the kitchen.

"Still baking?" I asked. "Smells wonderful, sis." My jacket hung itself in its usual spot on the hall tree magnetically. "Have any cookies to spare? It's perfect weather for a hot cup of tea and a few of Miss Beatrice Reed's famous homemade snickerdoodles."

"Flattery will get you everywhere." She looked up at me, brushing a wisp of feather-gray hair behind her ear. "I thought you ate at Miss Georgia's today—you're usually stuffed when you get back. Why, last time you lunched there I don't think you ate supper."

I followed her into the cheery kitchen with its Delft tiles and accompanying blue-and-white motif and related most of the afternoon's findings. She was as intrigued as I was about Truman's boyhood.

The kettle, a cobalt enameled Chantal given to Bea last June on her birthday by the Ladies' Auxiliary (she almost did not accept it because she knew Joan Dowinger probably paid for it), whistled its clear harmonic train notes. Good heavens! I'd managed to put that woman's plan for renovating the Divine out of my mind for nearly twenty-four hours, but the sight and sound of the kettle set off my apprehensions like a fire alarm. I should have mentioned it last night to Bishop Wilder.

"Grif! The kettle!" shrieked Bea above a cloud of steam.

I removed the angry pot from the ember-glowing stove eye and poured water into china cups into which my sister had placed apple zinger tea and cinnamon sticks. A plate mounded with fresh cookies waited, as well. I noticed these were segregated from a large plastic container filled with the same, obviously intended for delivery that evening to the Trumans.

"Joan Dowinger called for you twice today," Bea said, removing her apron.

I sat at the breakfast table and watched the first plops of silver rain out the window—heaven tethering itself to earth. Some poor officer was getting soaked even as he backed under the inlet of the front door and overhanging arch of the Divine. The downpour's sound was one I loved . . . comforting, rhythmic. If only I didn't have to go out in it tonight, it would be a perfect night for reading by the fire, sipping hot chocolate, or maybe a game of backgammon or whist.

"More renovation plans?" I asked, forcing my attention back to the unpleasantness at hand.

"I suppose; she didn't say. Only that she wants to talk to you tomorrow—it can't wait until next Tuesday," said Bea.

"Please remind me to call her. It was rather nice today. For several hours at a time I did not think of her at all," I replied, munching my third cookie. "Probably denial."

My sister placed her hand on my wrist. "Don't be afraid to put your foot down, Grif. You want people to like you, I understand that. You want to be all things to all people as you live out the Gospel. But there are times when we're more afraid of what's *inside* ourselves than we are of the conflict that's outside. Why, even our Lord ran the money changers out of the temple!" Her voice rose in an animated appeal.

Startled at her sudden directive, I leaned toward her and whispered, "Indeed," then stood up from the table. "Thanks for the cookies."

"I'm only trying to help, Grif. You know that," she added.

I nodded and leaned to kiss her forehead. "Yes, I do."

I had not been in my office for more than an hour, sifting through a handful of books on grief counseling, when Bea's sharp rap on the door snapped my concentration. Glancing at the clock, I found it too early for dinnertime.

"Come in," I replied wearily, half expecting to see Joan Dowinger's fur-trimmed shoulders fill the doorframe.

My sister poked her head in instead. "Sorry to interrupt, but you have a visitor I think you'll want to see. Ms. Florence Lipton, assistant to Mr. Gentry Truman." Bea gave me this knowing look as if to communicate that I'd better be interested.

"Send her in," I sighed. My eyes burned, and I removed my wire-rimmed reading glasses and massaged the bridge of my nose.

Short, brisk steps on the hardwood hall floor. Bea held the door, and a trim woman entered tentatively.

"Father Reed, I'm Florence Lipton. I know we've never officially met, but I've attended many of your services since I came here this fall with Mr. Truman. I always like what you have to say . . . and I'm not really a very religious woman. . . . I need to talk to someone, Father. And . . . well, you seem like someone I can trust." She had obviously left a raincoat at the door, for her appearance was dry—crisp, even—and casually profes-sional.

"Please sit down, Ms. Lipton. I'll be glad to help however I can."

I offered her the bold tartan wingback that faced the Cumberland Plateau and its exquisite palette of colors, now a watercolored blur of henna and gold, milk-washed in the gray twilight rain.

"Can I get you some coffee or tea? My sister will be glad to make us some."

"No . . . no, thank you, Father. I want to get right to telling you what's on my mind before I back out." Even though her dark silvery hair be-trayed her as my peer in age, she displayed a youthful poise. In her casual knit skirt, turtleneck, and green cardigan she was . . . well, quite attrac-tive. I glanced at her left hand and then forgave myself just as quickly when I saw the safety of a thick gold band on her ring finger. I had not been out with another woman since Amy's death, and I wasn't about to start with someone in the confessional. Women with burdened consciences seemed to be the only ones I was attracting today.

Obviously uncomfortable, she glanced over at my bookshelves, then out the window. Her eyes shone wistful and clear, a beautiful steel gray that matched our present skies. "Oh, Father, it's so horrible . . . I don't know what's going to happen. . . . I mean . . . oh . . ." her voice trailed off as tears formed. She pulled a tissue from her skirt pocket.

"Yes, it's a terrible tragedy. I'm sure the blow must be devastating for you, working so closely with Mr. Truman and all." I wasn't sure how to draw her out without seeming to pry. In matters of confession, I had discovered that a patient nod goes much further than a direct question.

"It's such a mess. I don't know where to begin. . . ." She paused and gazed out the window again. Beads of rainwater inscribed rivulets outside the panes while moisture, condensing as the temperature dropped, formed on the inside.

"Thanks for your patience, Father. I'm usually a very direct person, very efficient about my own time and the time of others." She clutched the tissue like a security blanket even though she had regained her composure.

"A very necessary trait, I would imagine, for anyone working for Gentry Truman. I've heard he was not the most patient person."

"Yes, what you've heard is true. Mr. Truman was very much a perfectionist, not one to suffer fools. I'm good at what I do. I've been with him for some time. It would have been coming up on ten years now. Let's see . . . yes, right after *The Walls of Paradise* premiered."

"Baptism by fire, then. I imagine you transcribed some scathing letters to quite a few editors and critics first thing." I smiled, and Florence Lipton returned it.

"So you know his work? Yes, indeed, Father. I admit, I secretly admired Mr. Truman's talent for writing blistering letters. He once had me address Pauline Kael at *The New Yorker* as 'you old blind, cud-chewing, ego-milking cow.' It was right after the film version of *The Ghettos of*

Heaven came out, the remake with Sharon Stone."

"Ah yes," I chuckled.

"But Gentry could be incredibly kind, as well, Father. In fact, that's why I'm here." Another doleful glance out the window. "You see, I stole some money from him, and he didn't call the police. . . ." She continued focusing outside the window, although it was practically opaque by now. The rain continued to press against the glass, and perhaps she found the rhythm as soothing as I did. "As far as I know, he didn't tell anyone."

She continued in monotone. "When Mr. Truman accepted this writer-in-residence position here at Avenell, one of the perks was a university expense account in addition to his salary. Gentry had money enough, of course, that he rarely used the account—he paid his own travel expenses, bought his own books, that sort of thing. For the last few months I've been turning in various fabricated expense vouchers to the university accounting office. They write a check either reimbursing Gentry or prepaying an approved expense. Both are drawn on his university expense account."

She cleared her throat, her eyes searching mine as if for some sign of judgment.

"I then forged those checks with Gentry's signature—a talent all good secretaries develop as a practicality. It really wasn't that hard at all."

Good heavens, I thought, *she almost sounds pleased with herself.*

As if reading my mind, she said, "I'm not a bad person, Father, and Gentry knew that. He discovered my crime this past Thursday and replaced the money I'd stolen right out of his own pocket. Sat down and wrote a check and had one of his teaching assistants deliver it to accounting right then. He scribbled some note about a mix-up in his personal and professional accounts. I couldn't believe it." Tension lines visibly lifted from her forehead.

"Then he didn't fire you?" I asked.

"No, he said he couldn't afford to lose me—not now. That with everything that was going on, money was the least of his problems. I suppose he was referring to his problems at home and his writer's block. He did tell me that he was disappointed that I didn't come to him and ask to borrow the money. Funny thing—and I didn't mention it at the time—but I had asked him for money before. Last year after my husband died, Gentry turned me down, told me I was paid well enough as it was. He was so funny about money sometimes."

"I'm sorry to hear about your husband—I know how difficult it can be to lose a spouse." I glanced at a wedding photo of Amy and me in a silver frame on the shelf just above Florence Lipton's left shoulder. Something in me warned, *Don't go there*, as I diverted from my own private loss. "So the writer's block rumors were true? How unfortunate."

"Yes, he's been writing like a madman trying to finish this new play that was supposed to premiere here in a couple of weeks. He's really struggled with this one. He knew everyone was waiting to see if he still had the magic or if—as they claimed last time—he was washed up. His brother, who's directing, had been pressuring him and undermining his confidence at every turn. On top of that, there's the business with Marcia—Mrs. Truman."

I shook my head. "What business, if I may ask?"

"Well, I just imagined you'd heard by now. It's all over campus, it's even been in the tabloids about the affair she's having. I knew it would never last when he brought her here. Avenell is too small, too quiet for her larger-than-life style."

Was that jealousy or just resentment I sensed? Was her relationship with Truman more than professional?

"Mrs. Truman has been seeing someone here?" I felt like a gossip, like Bea at one of her Auxiliary meetings, feigning ignorance only to gather fresh data.

"I'd rather not say, Father. If you haven't heard already, it would be better for both of us if I didn't say." She folded her arms and examined the remnant of shredded tissue still in her hand. Was the knowledge potentially dangerous, or was she merely being coy? Perhaps she was hoping to find an administrative job in the university and did not want to upset Franklin Milford—if indeed he was the mystery lover.

I nodded and decided to change tactics. "Why did you take the money? May I ask where it went, Ms. Lipton?" I tried to sound sympathetic, not accusatory.

She expected such a question and had fully rehearsed her response. "My daughter, Father Grif . . . she's a freshman at Yale, and everything's so expensive. I simply wanted her to have the best. I got tired of telling her I couldn't afford things. I got tired of doing it all alone. It's been hard for me since my husband died, and I've had to rely on one income—most of the insurance money went to pay off numerous debts. I resented seeing how Gentry Truman spent money like pouring water. Besides, this school is not exactly cash poor itself. I figured what I took was a drop in the bucket."

Her tone of justification returned, and I raised my eyebrows inquisitively. "How much are we talking about?"

"A little over twenty thousand dollars. I hope you can understand . . . I'm really not a bad person."

"I'm sure you're not. But why are you telling me this? I'm more than happy to assist you in seeking our Lord's forgiveness, but is there anything else I can do? Would you like me to pray for you?"

"I figure I'm a suspect now." She looked at me intently and adjusted her skirt, returning to her businesslike approach. "A suspect with a good motive. It's only my word that Gentry didn't fire me or threaten to have me arrested."

"There is the money he replaced in his expense account to back up your story," I said.

"Yes, true. But who's going to take my word that I hadn't stolen more money than what he discovered? There will be audits of all his accounts. The media vultures will have a field day. His family already dislikes me. My daughter will be so embarrassed. I won't be able to find another job. It will only get worse." Her eyes revealed genuine fear. "I do feel better for having told you, Father," she continued, "but I wonder if you think I should tell the police, or if I should just wait and see what happens."

The moment transcended déjà vu. How many people were going to confide in me and ask advice? How many secrets, infidelities, and harbored grudges could one dead man produce?

"There is no terror in threats when we are armed with honesty, to paraphrase Shakespeare," I offered, hoping she would prefer his authority to Scripture's. "I'd go to the police right away. What you tell them might actually clear any suspicion on you and help them find the real murderer."

She nodded obediently. "I knew you'd say that. I just needed to hear it out loud. What's the saying? 'Advice is what you know already but don't want to do.'"

"Sergeant Dan Warren with the county sheriff's department is an active member of my parish here. He's a very understanding man and a personal friend of mine. Would you like me to call him for you? I could accompany you to the station."

"No, Father. I appreciate your suggestion, but I'm not sure I'm ready to talk to the police tonight. Maybe tomorrow, or maybe after the service on Friday. I need to sleep on it, decide what the next step is for me, what's best for my daughter."

"I understand. But I encourage you to talk to the police as soon as possible. You'll feel better once you're cleared."

A sudden combustion flared in her eyes, making her look catlike, predatory. "Father, how can you be so sure that I didn't kill Gentry Truman?"

Her question surprised me, and I cocked my head. "I can't," I said. "I'm simply taking your word until I have reason to believe otherwise." She smiled the way I had seen Amy smile at my prayers for her healing.

As I walked her to her car, a new two-door compact, I wondered if Florence Lipton was glad she had unburdened herself to me. Just as I was about to shut her door, she caught my eyes. "Father," she asked, "what Shakespeare play is that quote about honesty from? I don't recall it."

"*Julius Caesar*," I answered, "Act IV, scene iii, I believe."

She smiled feebly and turned the ignition. "And we all know what happened to him in the end."

Chapter Twelve

FAMILY SECRETS

BEA PESTERED ME throughout supper for the smallest detail of Ms. Lipton's visit and became irritable when I refused. "You know I can't tell you people's private business even if I wanted to," I stressed.

"It has to do with Gentry Truman's death, though, doesn't it?" she asked. "You're in danger now from every direction because of what you know and won't tell anybody. If it's not the black widow spider wrapping you in her web, it's the attractive personal assistant."

"You think Florence Lipton is attractive?" My question surprised me, but at least it would divert my sister. Bea had been on me for some time to begin dating and was forever listing prospective parishioners who had all the qualities for a pastor's wife. Her job description rarely considered my personal preferences in the equation.

"Yes, in a rather L.L. Bean, catalog-model kind of way. Why, do *you*?" She raised her eyebrows, excited at the prospect, and began to clear the table.

"Yes," I smiled, "I suppose I do."

"Well, it's about time you started noticing women again. You know that nice Cecilia Winningham down at the post office certainly is attractive. She's been coming to our Ladies' Auxiliary for over a year now."

"I thought we were discussing Florence Lipton," I said.

"Once it's clear she didn't have anything to do with shooting her boss in our chapel, then you can ask her to Sunday dinner. In the meantime, you might ask Cecilia if she would like an escort to the parish Homecoming potluck next week."

"Well, maybe I just will," I said and drained the last of my iced tea.

Since the rain had stopped, I debated on walking to the Trumans but thought it unwise considering my last experience. Fog was rolling in over the soggy mountain and would likely obscure even the streetlights by the time I came home. No, I'd drive and play it smart, even if I felt like my sister's paranoia was wearing off on me.

Outside I inhaled deeply before starting the car, taking in the smell of moist earth mingled with the lingering smoke of burning leaves, that timeless scent of autumn. Driving through campus, I found most of my ghostly statues anchored to their former positions, milky apparitions guarding, searching, reporting.

A silhouetted couple, probably students, kissed a farewell in front of the Eastman Library. I chuckled to myself, knowing I had no intention of asking out Cecilia Winningham. Amy had been such an extraordinary woman, from her stunningly beautiful eyes down to her warm, compassionate heart. I was so sure of never encountering another woman like her that the prospect of even considering another woman attractive seemed futile. Florence Lipton was attractive, but was she my type? If I had to ask someone to the Homecoming potluck, who would I ask?

Caroline Barr's lovely visage surfaced immediately, like a sharp photograph emerging in the developer's dark room. Yes, she was attractive . . . and seemed kind, intelligent. I wasn't sure about the depth of her faith, but at least she did seem to have one. And to be honest, her vulnerability reminded me of my late wife's.

However, my theory had always been that if I were to start dating or even considering the possibility, it would have to be with a woman who was so different from Amy as to be her opposite. I'm surprised I hadn't recognized it sooner: Caroline Barr did remind me of Amy. In a younger sister, family-photo sort of way, Caroline even resembled Amy. That troubled me.

Florence Lipton might certainly fit my opposite category. But could I go out with a woman who had embezzled? I recalled how she described the accomplishment of her crime. A kind of self-satisfaction. That air of justification and the emphasis on the material. Yes, in that respect she was the antithesis of my dear humble wife, a woman who never knew how much money we had in the bank or cared.

A sudden shiver engraved my back. How self-righteous I sounded to myself, so judgmental. I realized then that I was guarding Amy's memory, protecting my love for her. Somehow it still seemed, after four years, that if I noticed other women I was betraying her, selling myself, and erasing the life the two of us shared. In this defensive mind-set it was easier to adopt self-righteousness than to face the multifacets of guilt and loss.

It was time to change, to move on. It's what Amy so wanted—for me to be happy, to love again. Should I give Ms. Lipton a call tomorrow? Just to be friendly, to let her know that I took her confession seriously and that I'm praying for her? It's what I'd normally do, if I weren't so busy worrying about attractions and betrayals. But then if I called her, I ought to call Caroline Barr, as well, and offer the same kindness.

I was relieved to take my mind off such analysis when I rounded the corner of Evergreen and Poplar and focused on the gingerbread mansion Gentry Truman had called home. Florence Lipton's embezzlement made me question just how much money Truman was worth and who in the house I was about to enter would benefit most. Marcia Klein Truman, of course, seemed the most likely beneficiary. However, if she had indeed been having an affair, he might have cut her out. The three daughters, naturally. Cale Sanders, perhaps. I imagined President Milford was counting on a rather substantial endowment to the university, as well. He had been wanting to build a new theater on campus for some time and knew that Gentry loved donating money for buildings that would bear his name. I wondered if other beneficiaries would produce new suspects. Perhaps old lovers, unknown children. Maybe Florence Lipton herself would even be named in the will.

As I identified myself once more to the security guard monitoring the wrought-iron gate in front of the house, an unnerving shriek, like that of an animal, pierced through the misty November night. The cop immediately dashed to the porch and bounded through the door.

With a deep breath and a shallow prayer, I followed the guard's dramatic entrance and nearly tripped over Scotch, the little terrier, who darted through my legs and out the door as quickly as we had darted in. A maid, younger than the one who had served coffee the night before, pointed upstairs and yelled, "Up there!"

What followed, as I would later discover when I tried to describe it to Dan Warren and Peter, might best be described as a dress rehearsal for a Fellini film. The tasteful entryway looked like a florist's greenhouse, overflowing with potted ferns and chrysanthemums, baskets of cut gladiolus in rainbow hues. The young guard and I waded through the expressions of sympathy and thudded up the wide staircase just as Marcia Truman and a striking brunette began to descend. We collided and all began talking at the same time, asking questions, barking orders, and clamoring for answers.

Marcia's son, Dylan, came back inside with Scotch, who began yapping furiously at the widow's feet. Jenna Truman emerged from a bedroom door looking visibly shaken and drained of all color. Finally, Cale Sanders appeared at the end of the long hallway above us and began laughing so hard I thought he would burst. Like his brother at the dinner party that time, he seemed to delight in the absurdity of the situation, as if he had just accomplished a great practical joke. Our commotion of different voices at different volumes, the dog's barking, and Sanders' laughter made the Tower of Babel seem like parliamentary procedure.

"Silence!" I boomed, louder and deeper than my usual baritone. To my surprise and theirs, everyone immediately froze.

"Well, well, if it isn't Father Brown and the keystone cops," chuckled Sanders.

"Thank you, Father. Let's all go downstairs, please," ordered Mrs. Truman, seizing the moment's stillness. Everyone began to file down like children in a fire drill.

"Shouldn't Jenna be lying down?" Sanders sniffed. "Do you really think we need to go into all this with strangers?" His eyes glanced a blow my way.

"I'm not sure we have a choice now, Cale," Marcia replied, regaining her usual composure. "Jenna dear, come and sit down in front of the fire. Jeanette will get you a brandy and all of us some nice hot tea. Officer Arnold, you may resume your post. Dylan, take Scotch to his room. Now, let's all be seated so we can discuss the service with Father Reed. Please, have a seat, Father."

Marcia Klein Truman was a resourceful woman used to taking charge of situations. It was easy to see how she produced a cosmos from the flat chaos of a dramatic character on the page. She smoothed her hair and adjusted the multicarat diamond pendant hanging above her pale neckline. A pink silk blouse and taupe skirt gave her a softer look tonight.

Cale Sanders stood by the mantel with a devious smile playing his thin lips, a sympathetic Mephistopheles with the flickering shadows from the hearth dancing beneath him. He looked relaxed, even elegant in his black trousers and baggy turtleneck beneath a gray herringbone blazer. How quickly he had assumed the air of Lord of the Manor, the demeanor of entitlement. Difficult for me to believe for a little boy from Harperstown, yet he definitely seemed pleased with himself. He helped himself to a whiskey from the bar in the corner as we were all being seated.

"Is everyone all right?" I asked. "I heard a scream as I came in and naturally thought someone was in danger. . . ."

"That was Jenna. She thought . . . well, she thought someone had broken into Father's room," said the brunette stranger. "We haven't met. I'm Lucy Truman."

I rose to take her cool hand. She had a creamy complexion sprinkled with freckles like pale strawberry stars. Her blue eyes were her father's—penetrating, deep-set, and fierce, with subtle crow's feet nearly undetectable in the lamplit room. Looking at least ten years younger, she was likely older than me or at least my age—the first offspring of Gentry's overnight sensation on Broadway. I could not read her greeting and wondered how she related with the rest of the family.

"And I'm Lisa Chandler," said another woman entering the room. "How do you do, Father."

Taller and thinner than her sisters, Lisa resembled Cale Sanders more than the other women. Darker in complexion, with deerlike brown eyes and blond hair, she was the exotic product of Truman's marriage to Charise Chandler, Oscar-winning actress of the 1962 film *Angel Falls*.

I felt a bit star-struck and took her hand just as Jeanette returned with a silver tea cart and began serving. Jenna had not moved since being positioned in the club chair next to the fire. She stared hypnotically at the tangle of dueling flames.

"It's my pleasure to meet you both," I said. We all reseated ourselves, tea in hand, and sipped quietly. "So was there an intruder in the house tonight?" I asked.

"No, Father Reed." Marcia sighed, perhaps a bit exasperated at my tenacity. "Jenna had a bad dream is all. She was sleeping and must have wandered into Gentry's room—just across from hers—before she awoke," she explained.

"Either that, or she forgot to take her meds today," added Cale. Our eyes met, and he winked at me before continuing. "She's bipolar, you know. A day off the drugs can do nasty things to one's mind."

Jenna glared at him, and I thought she might spontaneously combust and be absorbed up the chimney in a cloud of angry smoke, taking all of her family with her. I shared her contempt for her uncle's disclosure.

"I know what I saw," the young woman said resolutely.

"An intruder in your father's room?" I encouraged her.

"Yes . . . I was coming out of my room, and yes, I had just awakened from a nap. I heard something fall in Daddy's room. I opened the door and saw *him*. . . ." Her words trailed off and the only sound was the crackling from the hearth.

"Saw who, Jenna?" Lisa Chandler asked.

"Daddy," she replied. "My eyes didn't have time to adjust to the dark, but I know his profile, his silhouette. He was standing by the window, in front of that monstrous desk of his, with a page in hand. It's a pose I've seen him strike hundreds of times. I saw my father tonight, and that's why I screamed. And yes, Father Reed, in case you're wondering, I do take medication for manic depression."

I recalled what her stepmother had confided at my last visit, her estrangement from her father, his hopes that bringing her here would strengthen their relationship and help her become an adult. Marcia also mentioned something about money troubles, which struck me odd just then because Jenna did not seem like the kind of person concerned with wealth, status, or appearances. Perhaps that's what distinguished her from the rest of her family.

"Jenna, couldn't it have been a bad dream?" soothed Lucy.

"Or maybe it was one of the staff," offered Lisa.

"No, the room is supposed to be locked," said Marcia. "Unless you were in there, Cale." Her tone carried more accusation than inquiry. She, at least, implied that Cale knew where the key was kept.

"Why in the world would I be in there? There was nothing to find in there when Gent was alive, let alone now that he's dead. Unless he's come back as a ghost to finish *Chameleon, a Tragedy in Two Acts* his so called masterpiece—the one we've all been waiting on for months, the one that's been in rehearsal without a complete script for the past six weeks. No, I wasn't in the old fool's room." Cale marched to the bar and refilled his glass.

Jenna clenched her teeth. "I know what I saw."

"I wouldn't put it past Gent to come back and haunt us all if he could," said Cale, sipping his whiskey neat.

"And why's that, Uncle?" asked Lisa naïvely.

"I'm sure what Cale means . . . is that we all wish we'd had more resolution with Gentry before this . . . accident occurred," Marcia replied, carefully navigating her words. She seemed quick on the draw, and I would have preferred to hear Sanders' response. I silently prayed for such an opportunity before I left; I wanted to delve beneath the curmudgeon's facade and discover if he hated his brother as much as he tried to appear to.

"I thought we were here to plan Gentry's service," said Lucy.

"Yes, let's get on with it," echoed Lisa.

"Are we expecting anyone else who needs to be included in our discussion?" I asked. Just as Dylan Klein came to mind, he returned minus the little terrier in his arms. He seated himself at his mother's feet on the Kiristani rug that depicted in muted jewel tones the tree of life pattern. From our last gathering, only Gentry's agent Casey Atwood and President Milford were absent tonight.

"No, Father," said Marcia, "we're all here now. Let's begin." She might very well be calling a board meeting to order.

For the next ten minutes I held the floor, explaining the order of service and offering my tentative selections for Scripture readings and committal. No one interrupted and everyone, even Cale Sanders, seemed pleased with my plans. I concluded by reading them selected verses from the third chapter of Lamentations in the thick rose-cloth bound Revised Standard Version Bible I had brought with me: " 'Remember my affliction and my bitterness, the wormwood and the gall! My soul continually thinks of it and is bowed down within me. But this I call to mind, and therefore I have hope: The steadfast love of the LORD never ceases, his mercies never come to an end; they are new every morning; great is thy faithfulness.' " The words lingered. No one moved, no sounds intruded, and each person seemed lost in his own thoughts of the deceased, of life without Gentry Truman, of why and how this had all happened. And perhaps, most of all, they were considering God's faithfulness. . . . I confess I chose the passage for my congregation tonight as much as for the one at the memorial service. I didn't think they would be comfortable if I prayed aloud for them, so my reading was the prayer I offered for us all.

"Very nice, Father Reed," the widow whispered. "You have assembled a thoughtful, tasteful service. Gentry would have been very pleased, and so am I."

"Am I leaving out anything?" I asked.

"Well, my only addition would be to allow Gentry's daughters to read a selection—"

"I'd rather not," Jenna countered.

"Well, I would like to very much," said Lucy, rising to stretch.

"Yes, I don't want to do it, but I think it would help us all to begin the grief process." Lisa exchanged a nod with her older sister. So far tonight they seemed to agree on most everything, surprising since they had different mothers and had apparently been raised apart from each other. I had gleaned from the morning's *Tennessean* that Lucy Truman grew up in Swiss boarding schools while her mother left acting behind and climbed the corporate ladder in a cosmetics firm—a career change precipitated when Truman divorced her. His oldest daughter then inherited her mother's large estate several years ago and started her own film company, producing several independent pictures and a series for public television.

Lisa Chandler, similarly, had grown up in affluence as a Hollywood brat—going through several stepfathers with her famous mother's numerous divorces. She attended private schools with peers like Carrie Fisher and Scott Redford and had made a successful career for herself as a costume and fashion designer for films.

Young Jenna, on the other hand, grew up with a single mother who refused to grant interviews about her liaison with legendary playwright Gentry Truman at Columbia—which reminded me to ask Caroline Barr if she knew Jenna's mother there. When the affair cooled and Jenna was born, the woman accepted generous child support but kept on teaching at the university level. An only child, Jenna reflected the quiet demeanor of someone more mature than her peers, always aware of her aloneness.

I suddenly thought of *King Lear* and the similar dynamics within that monarch's household. My first impression, however, of Lisa and Lucy found them much too kind to hide the heart of a Goneril or Regan.

"It will only be meaningful if we all three do it, Jen," continued Lisa. "It's one of those hard things that you'll regret if you don't do." She rose and stood behind her sister's chair. Perhaps the sisters were closer than I perceived.

"Oh, all right," replied the youngest Truman daughter, "as long as it's short, Father Reed." She offered up a wan smile to the blond goddess above her.

I nodded. "Of course."

"Very good," said Marcia. "Have we left out anything, Father? Oh, I jotted down a few pieces of music that I know Gentry would want played. The Beethoven for the processional is fine, but we have several musician friends who will want to perform."

I scanned the list on the monogrammed note she passed me. It included a famous bagpiper from the Glasgow Orchestra; "Amazing Grace" sung by Annetta Fielding, the aging black diva of the New York Metropolitan Opera; and a popular Los Angeles string quartet's interpretation of highlights from Mozart's *Requiem*. This service was going to be a spectacle indeed.

"This is acceptable, Father Reed?" she asked.

"Of course, Mrs. Truman, certainly," I said. "Forgive me for pausing—I'm so impressed by these performers. Annetta Fielding is one of the greatest operatic voices of this century. I'm delighted that all of these friends of the family wish to contribute."

Lisa now joined her older sister in front of the fireplace, curious twins in the soft light from the Tiffany shade on the end table. Side by side they looked remarkably alike—only the slight differences in hair color and height betrayed their maternal variance. Jenna approached, and the resemblance remained intact. Anyone viewing them would instantly know they were sisters, even their father's daughters if one knew Gentry's features.

Dylan stood and refilled his mother's teacup. This young man, on the other hand, reflected his mother's beauty but was clearly not a Truman. With short, curly brown hair, a pale face, and his mother's aquiline nose and full lips, he looked young for his age, and his blue sweater vest over a white T-shirt and jeans made him look even more boyish. His father had been the aging film director Louis Valjean, who died shortly after Dylan's birth. Consequently, he grew up devoted to his mother amid the turbulent throes of her career and love life. Pensive, with narrow eyes and rimless glasses, Dylan looked scholarly tonight. He seemed pleased with the results of our meeting only because his mother was pleased.

Cale prepared his third—or was it fourth—Jack Daniels. The crowd was getting restless.

"Franklin was kind enough to cancel classes and most university operations for Friday," said Marcia, stirring a silver spoon into the bone china teacup. "And the service is set for noon, not eleven as I suggested the other night. So many friends are coming in from the coast, and they'll have to drive over from Nashville or Atlanta."

Recording this change, I checked my own short list inside the cover of my Bible. "Oh, I'm terribly sorry to have to ask this," I prefaced, "but will Mr. Truman's remains be present at the service?" I tried not to look away but didn't wish to look her in the eyes.

"No, they won't. Don't be embarrassed, Father. I know I speak for all of us in extending our warmest thanks for your tact and consideration here. We realize not everyone would agree to hold the service for us." Her voice sounded soothing, apologetic, conciliatory. "As I mentioned the other night," Marcia continued, "Gentry requested to be cremated, so that will take place tomorrow, granted the police release the body from the coroner's. We will have a private family time on Friday morning to disperse the ashes in one of Gentry's favorite spots, the grove of maples over by the Natural Bridge."

"Ah yes," I said, "a lovely spot. Very tranquil." I rose and placed my teacup carefully on the rosewood coffee table. "Well, I guess that covers everything. I'll be going and leave you all to get some rest. If I can do anything at all, please give me a call."

"Good night, Father." It was Jenna. "Thank you for coming. I'm sorry if I frightened you when you arrived." She took my hand, and her half siblings assembled behind her in an informal receiving line.

"If you have time, Father, I would like to speak to you alone before you go," Marcia whispered just as Jenna, Lucy, and Lisa ascended the stairs.

"Certainly." I nodded, recalling her tone on Monday morning in my office. Her perfume overwhelmed me, a sharp floral scent, simultaneously fragile and pungent.

"Good night, Father Reed," offered Dylan cordially, sounding much older than his demeanor. "Mom, if I can speak to you before I go back to the dorm?"

"Of course, dear," replied Marcia. "Excuse us for a moment, Father." They retreated to the foyer and whispered in low, familiar tones with their backs to me. Only Cale remained, pacing like a caged panther back and forth before the hearth. He took a cigarette out of a silver case from inside his jacket and fired it from a matching silver lighter.

"Care for one, Father?" asked the dead man's half brother.

"No, thank you," I said. I tried to imagine what it must be like to be related to one of the greatest literary talents of the last four decades. Surely he was jealous of his brother's success, the accolades and fame. Although I'd heard about Truman's brother, it wasn't until he came to Avenell this fall to direct the new play that I learned anything of substance. If I recalled the campus newspaper correctly, he had been directing a network sitcom that was just canceled before coming here. I would have to look up that article again.

Jeanette came in and began clearing away the cups and saucers. I heard Scotch growling playfully somewhere from the area of the kitchen. Marcia called out, "Be careful, darling," from the front porch as her only child departed.

"Smoking is such a nasty habit, eh?" Cale chuckled in that devilish way of his. "Sure I can't persuade you?"

"No, thank you." I smiled.

"Give me one, then," said Marcia, reentering the room, "on your way out. I wish to speak to Father Reed alone."

"I'm sure you do, my dear," replied Sanders, offering her the silver case. "You've got to confess all those naughty-girl sins of yours before you play all sweet and innocent at dear old hubby's funeral."

"That's unkind," I protested.

"The gallant knight protecting the sacred widow. I knew I could count on you, Father Reed." Cale lit his sister-in-law's English cigarette and she accepted stoically.

"No," he continued, "it's not unkind. In fact, it may be the truest thing you've heard all night—what's that line of Shakespeare's? 'More truth in jest than the world shall ever know'? Good night. See you at the circus Friday." He strode across the room, and I was struck once more by his nervous animosity.

"I'm really sorry to put you through this, Father," comforted Marcia Klein Truman. Would she change her name back, I wondered, or maintain the recognition that would come with her husband's reputation—now forever secured.

"No need to apologize, Mrs. Truman. Different families grieve in different ways. I apologize if I was out of line with your brother-in-law just now. It's just . . . I don't like seeing someone punished for their past mistakes. I don't think we can judge one another. That's our heavenly Father's job alone. Now, how can I help you?"

She strode to the heavy paneled doors and closed the study from the entryway. Reseating herself in the spot where her eldest stepdaughter had sat moments ago, Marcia smoked quickly, deliberately, exhaling thin tendrils of white vapor toward the fireplace.

"I'm most appreciative of your discretion, Father," she began. "Thank you for the kind defense. It's been such a grueling week. . . ."

"Indeed it has. Not only have you lost your husband, but you've been questioned innumerable times by the police, had your privacy assaulted by hordes of reporters, cameramen, and helicopters. You've had to make arrangements for the memorial service, for the logistics of getting friends and family to Avenell—it's grace that you're even able to stand up."

"As you can see, I'm not," she laughed.

We smiled together, and I seated myself opposite her in the club chair still warm from Jenna's presence. I longed to prop my weary feet on the ottoman but refrained. I made a mental note to polish my wing tips for Friday's service.

"You're very kind. I just needed someone to talk with, and you were so kind on Monday as I explained the situation. . . ." She paused to exhale another breath. "As I told you before, Gentry and I quarreled terribly the night before his death. We both said a lot of cruel things neither of us meant."

I nodded encouragement and braced for my third confession from one of the many women in Gentry Truman's complicated life. The little Scottie dog now nestled at my feet. He liked me.

She started to continue, then stopped herself, lips parallel, rose lipstick perfectly accentuating a pained smile. "Father, I don't want you to feel as if you're being pulled into something that you'd rather not be part of. . . ."

Too late for that, I thought but said, "No, not at all. That's my job."

She hesitated and then launched in. "Very well. I want to tell you the other half of what I started on Monday morning. It's just that, well, there's another reason for my feelings of guilt. Not only did Gentry and I quarrel, but I told him that I planned to divorce him." She paused dramatically. "I had planned to wait until after his new play opened, until after Christmas, perhaps. But in the heat of the argument, I just blurted it out."

"Did Gentry believe you? I mean, forgive me for asking, but had you threatened to divorce him before?" I asked.

"Yes, on both accounts," she replied, stubbing the last of her filtered cigarette into a crystal ashtray. "I had threatened before, but always in vague terms. This time . . . well, I meant it, and I think he realized it. I told him that I planned to marry Franklin and that I would be seeking a divorce immediately." Her eyes darted across mine to gauge the weight of her lover's identity.

"I understand. And you're afraid that somehow this drove Gentry to . . . take his own life," I responded.

"I suppose. I don't really know how or even if it's related to his death. It just seems like such an odd coincidence. Franklin was furious with me for letting the cat out of the bag. I've never seen him so enraged. . . ."

Was she trying to cast suspicion on the man she threatened to leave her husband for? For the briefest second I tried to imagine our distinguished university president killing the husband of his lover, the woman he planned to marry. I wasn't surprised at this confirmation of my suspicions and the many rumors I'd heard, but I was still disappointed, dismayed at Franklin Milford's moral failure. Although a lifelong bachelor—thank goodness he was not married—he was involved outside of marriage with a woman married to someone else. And once the press got hold of this—and I knew it would only be a matter of time—how would it reflect on the university? On our community, parish, and church? Or worse yet, what if Milford did have something to do with Gentry's death? My mind swarmed with possibilities.

Chapter Thirteen

DAY OF REST

———

WHILE I MUSED ON the repercussions of Avenell University President Dr. Franklin P. Milford becoming an adulterous murder suspect, I realized Marcia had continued talking.

" . . . Not that he didn't have every reason to be upset."

He, Gentry or he, Franklin? I realized I had better pay closer attention.

"Life is so funny with its twists and quirks. . . ." Her voice became thin and trailed off toward the fireplace like smoke before resuming. " 'How could a girl like me ever think that love in this life would amount to any more than a star in the sky, a child's wish for some fairy tale shot at love and happy endings? Well, I won't give up yet! What I hope for is no more than a blanket of stars, a field of tiny sparks to illuminate the color of night itself. . . . ' "

"Rachel's monologue, outside the bar in *The Color of Night*," I whispered. I was shocked. To suddenly see a character, an icon of contemporary drama, a character as well known as Willy Loman or Blanche DuBois, come to life was like watching a statue suddenly breathe with a passion inherently human. Marcia Truman averted her eyes as if embarrassed by her talent, as if shamed by her ability to so easily shift into character.

"Yes, that's always been my favorite. That's how Gentry and I met," she said.

"Yes, that's my favorite, too. Perhaps I'll include that passage in the service Friday." Was she performing for my benefit? To win me over?

"Gentry told me what a fan you were. All the selections you shared tonight were exquisite." She instantly regained her widow's role; Rachel Harper vanished back into the scripted imagination of her audience. What a fine actress Marcia Truman was. How much of her true self did she reveal to those around her? Her dead husband may have been the only one to know the answer.

I still wasn't clear on why she had told me about her threat to divorce Gentry, yet I was at a loss for how to exit. "Is there anything else I can do?"

"No, Father, you've been more than kind. Thanks for listening. I'm not a religious woman myself, but please keep all of us in your prayers. My poor Gent is dead, and it's creating all kinds of ugly suspicions and doubts. Of course, our marriage had its ups and downs, as anybody's does, but I would never . . . I don't know anyone who hated Gent that much. . . ." Her eyes filled with tears, and she fidgeted with her diamond pendant.

I stood awkwardly, wondering how to comfort her when she continued. "Actually, there is something you could do. That young curate of yours—Father Abernathy, I think—if you could have him talk with Dylan . . ." Her tears pooled and cascaded down the lovely face and darkened the silk of her blouse.

"Of course. In fact, I think Peter offered his condolences to your son yesterday." Had he mentioned the visit to her? "How is Dylan taking all this, if I may ask? Was he very close to Gentry?" I inquired.

She looked a bit defensive, the proud mother hen guarding her chick. "Honestly, it's hard for me to tell. He's a very mature young man. He and Gentry did not get along too well. I'm afraid he may be dealing with his own guilt, and—no offense—I thought he might be able to relate to your young curate and would benefit from . . . talking."

I lifted my brows to encourage further explanation.

"My son's quiet manner and European sensibilities—his father was French, so he grew up in Paris, when he wasn't with me of course—did not suit Gentry. But Dylan's a fine young man, Father Reed."

"I'm sure he is. He seems very devoted to you."

"He's never given me a moment's trouble. Always been so independent, a 'little man' even as a baby. It's just . . . he's never had a father figure . . . and I think he hoped for more with Gentry, but Gent was simply not cut out for parenting. Ask any of his daughters, and they'll tell you the same thing." She slid her diamond pendant back and forth on its golden chain.

"Do you have children, Griffin?" It was the first time she had used my Christian name.

"No, I'm sorry I don't. My wife and I had hoped to before she died."

"Forgive me, I didn't know. You would make a good father, Father."

We both smiled at her little joke and knew it was time for me to go.

"I've kept you long enough," she said, wiping the corners of her eyes with her index fingers. "I can't thank you enough. For everything. I feel much better now. I know the next few days will be difficult, but it will be easier if we all concentrate on Gentry's best qualities."

"As well as our own," I added, collecting my jacket and wool cap. "Good night," I said, admiring several bouquets and foil-wrapped peace lilies on my way out.

"Good night, Father Reed," she returned, walking me through the foyer and to the door. Back to formalities, I noticed.

I stood for a moment on the porch and adjusted the bill of my cap. The night air provided welcome ventilation from the stuffy warmth of the old house. Although the fog lingered in shreds along the treetops, above them the sky shone remarkably clear. Stars glistened like the moist tears in firelight I had just witnessed, or like sparks of hope piercing the color of night, as Gentry Truman had put it so well over thirty years ago.

A hundred yards from me, the light from the end of Officer Arnold's cigarette flickered like a firefly in the mist as he made his way toward the end of the block. I drove the five-minute route home on automatic pilot, bone weary and soul tired, so exhausted that I could no longer think, or perhaps even care, about the strange secrets and hidden motives within the Truman household.

————————

Thursday morning seemed almost normal. My calendar told me it was my day to fast, a spiritual discipline I enjoyed and practiced at least once a month. Since circumstances seldom seemed conducive to fasting—in other words, I often found excuses not to—at the beginning of the year I went through my desk calendar and randomly chose a day to fast for each month. My fasts had lasted several days in some months, especially spring and summer. Sometimes I relinquished food for just twenty-four hours, easily skipping three meals in order to devote time to prayer and listening to God.

I never liked explaining my fasts to others, so I usually canceled any lunch appointments scheduled for that day. Bea had understood immediately when I explained it to her last January, so she kept a list of my fasting dates and cooked only for herself accordingly.

At first the timing of today's fast did not seem particularly fortuitous, but after a sound night's sleep, I decided a day of rest would be most appropriate before the busy, busy day of the Truman memorial service. In addition, Marcia Truman had called this morning to invite Beatrice and me to the "small reception at the house" immediately following to-morrow's ceremony. Bea was ecstatic over the invitation, and I decided that the rich buffet would be much more enjoyable coming off my fast.

So I spent the morning reading St. Teresa of Avila and Eugene Peterson on the Psalms, praying for my parish, for individual needs.

Outside my office window, this autumn was clearly announcing the passing of its peak. In the flashbulb-bright morning sunshine, with the mountain sky a cloudless blue like a photograph of heaven's gate, even the officers in front of the Divine seemed a normal part of the landscape. Similarly, the parade of cleaners, florists, and groundskeepers taking orders from my sexton, Joe Brewer, carried out tasks as if this was their typical Thursday morning routine.

Far from it, however. A dark burgundy awning was being assembled over the front entrance to the church in case of rain. Wreaths and swags of laurel and evergreen hung on the doors and above the stone arches. Florists' delivery trucks, from as far away as Nashville, were being turned away because the cathedral was to be decorated only with the plants and flowers that Marcia approved. So they drove to the house first and, if their wares passed muster, returned to discharge dozens of tastefully arranged roses, foil-wrapped miniature fig trees, and baskets of magnolias (flown in from South Carolina, Bea told me later). It was going to be some show.

And as I reflected and prayed about my ringmaster duties, I heard a crisp knock on the door. Joan Dowinger burst into the room with Bea saying from behind her, "I *told* her you were—"

"Beatrice told me you were preparing for Gentry's service tomorrow, but this simply can't wait, Griffin. I knew you wouldn't mind." She removed a blue leather midlength jacket and positioned herself upright in the club chair before my desk. She wore all blue beneath, as well, with varying degrees of success in matching the shades. A navy skirt, periwinkle blouse, teal jacket, and sapphire earrings. So typical of Joan, so deliberate in her tastefully subtle attempt to attract attention, like a debutante wearing pink.

Bea huffed out, then turned at the door. "As long as you're being interrupted, Dan called. I told him you'd call him back at lunch." She closed the door as forcefully as a windstorm, but not as indeliberately.

"Yes, Joan, I trust your judgment. If this can't wait, then it can't wait," I replied, hiding my frustration within the pages of the book on my lap as I pinched the cuticle of each thumb with my index finger. "However, if this is about the renovation—"

"Of course it is. What else could be as urgent? Now listen, I just found out yesterday that Peyton Fentriss will be attending the service tomorrow." Her voice became clipped with excitement, and her eyes indicated that I should immediately recognize his name and be just as elated.

"And who is Mr. Fentriss?" I asked.

"Oh, Griffin, please . . . you disappoint me. Why, Peyton Fentriss is only the best renovation architect in the South, maybe in the whole country. He lives in Savannah but has offices in Atlanta and New York. I met him several years ago at a party for Blanton Stewart IV, who was running for governor at the time—it was at Naomi Judd's home in Franklin. Well, anyway, Peyton renovated the Trumans' penthouse in New York and became great friends with Gentry. So he'll be at the service tomorrow." She was out of breath and clutched a diamond-ringed hand to her bosom as if to slow herself down.

"So you want to ask Peyton Fentriss if he'll consider renovating the Cathedral of the Divine tomorrow?" I asked, incredulous for many reasons.

"Well, of course. It's the perfect opportunity. He'll get to see for himself what terrible shape it's in. I was hoping you could meet with him at my house tomorrow after the service." Joan fumbled through her small navy clutch and produced a roll of LifeSavers.

"Mint?" she asked in a maddening way, as if we were at a tea party she were hosting instead of in my office discussing a matter upon which we might never agree.

"Joan—no, thank you—you don't understand." I could literally feel the physical sensation of my blood rushing through my veins. "I am not convinced that the Divine needs renovation, that the parish budget can afford it, that such a renovation—if needed—is a worthy endeavor of stewardship. And furthermore, even if I am convinced of all the above, it has to go through the deacons, the elders, the bishop, perhaps the board of canons, and the university! We are not in any position to be discussing renovation plans with any architect, even if he is the most famous one in the country!" The volcano inside could not be contained any longer.

Joan Dowinger sat there in her multihued ensemble, likely some designer's latest creation, and did not blink. After the echoes of my outburst had washed over her for a few moments, she said, "I see." Then added, "You proceed with your various committees and approvals, Father Reed, and I will meet with Mr. Fentriss tomorrow about the *possibility* that we may acquire his services in the future."

She arose and collected herself and said coolly, "Good day, Griffin. I will see myself out."

After the woman closed the door, I had to stop myself right then, get on my knees, and ask forgiveness. Oh, the things I thought to myself about that woman. What nerve! I wanted to blame it on the audacity of wealth, but I had plenty of successful parishioners and knew plenty more wealthy people who never presumed or demanded the way Joan did. I stayed on my knees until my heart rate subsided and my blood pressure descended back to its normal range.

My reverie seemed shot for the day, so I put in a call to Dan Warren, hoping to catch him.

"Can you call Pete and the two of you meet me in the library, second floor, periodical archives? Say . . . one o'clock?" Dan ordered more than asked after initial greetings were exchanged. "There's someone I may want you to help me interrogate." He abruptly hung up, and I stood bewildered—it wasn't like Dan to be so curt or mysterious. The case was taking its toll.

Peter answered on the first ring and seemed excited about the prospect of once more putting our heads together with Dan's to sort through the mess of loose threads surrounding Gentry Truman's death. I related my morning's encounter with the indomitable Mrs. Dowinger, and Pete responded: "Boy, you're getting it from all sides—but it sounds like you handled her perfectly. I would have lost my temper and told Joan Dowinger where to put her renovation plans!"

My curate decided that I needed some stress relief, especially before tomorrow's "big game," as he called it. Sometimes his exuberant sarcasm made me feel like an old prude. So I accepted his challenge to a game of racquetball in the Alumni Gym and promised to remember my gear.

I drank my fifth glass of water for lunch, packed my gym bag with fresh sport clothes, and went over the order of the memorial service for the tenth time.

Inside the cathedral I conferred with Joe Brewer about how the cleaning and decorating was coming.

"Everythin's gonna be just fine here, Father Grif," assured our parish sexton, a short mahogany-colored man from Louisiana. He was capable in the most relaxed manner I'd ever witnessed in an individual—seemingly diffident, but always in control. He smiled a wide-toothed smile and patted my back. "Don't worry none. It's gonna be a lovely service. The Lord bless you and give you peace."

I had to smile back at him as I turned to keep my appointment with Dan and Peter.

The temperature had climbed to the high sixties, a throwback to the kind of Indian summer days we had for most of October this year, and the air smelled moist like spring. So I decided to work off my nervous anxiety and walk the five blocks to the George Eastman Undergraduate Library, the one everyone on campus meant when they said "the library"—not the music library over off Ivy Circle beside the theater or the seminary's Leonidas Polk Theological Library. Now, *there* was a legendary Episcopalian! A bishop of Louisiana who left his diocese to become a Confederate general—he allegedly strapped his sword on over his vestment gown.

But our main library's story was nearly as colorful. Originally located in the basement of Otey Hall, as the school grew the library became divided among four different class buildings and even the women's dormitory. Right before World War I, ground was broken between Otey Hall and the old Sigma Chi fraternity house for a new brownstone edifice that would house all university volumes. It was to have been named the Ryan A. Northrop Library after the university president at the time. However, like the suspension of campus construction during the War Between the States, WWI caused major delays as building supplies were rationed, not to mention the lack of laborers.

During that interim, George Eastman, the inventor of the dry-plate process for developing photographic film, wished to make a large gift to the university. It seems that during the time he was trying to develop his new color film, he visited his mother over in Lewiston. One Sunday afternoon they drove up to Avenell to see the campus and have a picnic at the Natural Bridge. There Eastman found the mountain wild flowers so brilliant that he began thinking again about how to take color photographs. The story goes that he had an idea—a way to correct the problem that had blocked him so far—and became so excited that he leapt up from the picnic grounds and ran more than a mile back to the campus library. Inside the scruffy basement crammed full of books, the librarian helped Eastman find the chemical formula he was looking for.

Needless to say, this led to his discovery of color film, and the rest, as they say, is history. Eastman felt so kindly disposed toward the university that he wanted to fund the building of the new library. Poor President Northrop got his feelings hurt and resigned because the board of trustees insisted on naming the new book depository after Eastman.

An imposing, multistoried building with Romanesque features and rows of mullioned windows, the ivy-wrapped Eastman Library exuded tradition, scholarship, and was often featured in Avenell view books and postcards. Tony, the Avenell Tiger—an oversized, exquisitely detailed bronze sculpture of a male Siberian—guarded the courtyard. Today it seemed a busy hub of activity, and I noticed Dan had parked in the fire lane in the semicircular drive fronting the structure.

No matter how many times I walked through the bold, oversized doors, I still felt a twinge of pride, a hunger for wisdom, a love of the thousands upon thousands of volumes housed here. Inside, students browsed in the lounge area beside the bar-shaped reference booth and U-shaped circulation desk. Dozens of computer terminals lined the walls, complete with online card catalogs, CD-ROM databases, and Internet access—research was certainly not what it used to be in my day. However, the old walnut and oak card catalog drawers from my golden era were such beautiful pieces of furniture—most of them handmade exclusively for the Eastman Library by craftsmen in Hickory, North Carolina—that they were lovingly retained as decorator pieces.

I loved them so much that one, an odd cherry piece with twenty-four card drawers, anchored my office at home. Amy bought it for me as a birthday gift the year before she died—had Bea explain how much I loved the piece to Norma Slater, the university librarian. She charged Amy one dollar and had it delivered to my office.

"Grif! Over here!" Peter's voice sliced through the "quiet" din of loud whispers, laughter, student questions, and librarian responses. He looked sporty in khaki pants and a denim shirt. My white button-down and corduroy trousers made me feel old by comparison.

"Have you seen Dan yet?" I asked.

"No, I was waiting on you. Let's go on up to periodicals and see if he's there," he replied.

"I thought I saw his car outside," I mentioned as we climbed the gleaming oak staircase to the second floor. Inside the glass-fronted periodical room, rows of microfiche cabinets, copiers, and stacks of current magazines and newspapers from around the world were aligned like dominoes.

"Hey, you two—back here," came a familiar bass voice from the SC–ST stack at the back of the Berber-carpeted room. Dan beamed as we turned the corner, his developed arms towering with a couple dozen glossy issues.

"A little light reading to take your mind off the case?" I asked as we followed him to a large study carrel that he had obviously procured before our arrival.

"You might say that," he shot back, smiling. Inside were his briefcase and a legal pad adorned with neat, tilted block letters. "I checked already—this place is soundproof. Perfect for what we need to discuss."

"Which looks like recipes for strawberry shortcake and the best rates at Disney World," said Pete, leafing through the pile of *Southern Living*, *Country*, and *Volunteer*, a state homemaking magazine out of Memphis. "Feeling domestic, Dan?" he kidded.

"You just wait and see, buddy boy," replied Dan. "I've got so many new irons in the fire to tell you both about, I don't know where to start." He scratched his head absentmindedly before continuing. "Since you're already into 'New Light Suppers with Squash,' I'll begin with you, Father Abernathy. You remember your mystery woman?"

"I'm still praying that she's single and not a murderer, art thief, or agnostic," he said. "Of course I remember—she was beautiful."

"Well, I'm talking with my wife, Diane, at supper last night about the case. I know I'm not supposed to, but she's my best friend. And as corny as it sounds, I trust her judgment better than anyone's."

I nodded my understanding. I had exchanged more than a few parish confidentialities with Amy.

"So I'm telling her all about your lovely, long-haired redhead, and while Diane thinks the description sounds familiar, she can't recall anyone in the county who fits. Then we started loading the dishwasher and all of a sudden she screams, 'That's it! That's where I've seen her! The Tremont Quilt Show!'"

"Tremont? The Amish Community?" Pete asked.

"Why, the quilt on my bed was made there—a wedding present from a friend of my wife's," I exclaimed.

Dan relished his wife's discovery. "Diane swore that she saw a young, striking redhead—one of the Amish—behind a booth at their annual quilt show this past July. It was especially windy and the woman's bonnet blew off, and out fell this long gorgeous braid of scarlet hair! The woman was so embarrassed, but Diane only complimented her beautiful hair."

"So we're looking for articles on quilts?" Pete asked.

"No, no. Diane recalled an article in a magazine last year about Tremont and the Quilt Show, but she couldn't remember which one. She narrowed it down to these three."

"But the Amish do not allow themselves to be photographed," I stated.

"Exactly, and that's what's so unusual about this article, according to my wife. Most of the pictures show quilt patterns, hands pulling stitches, and farmhouses. But in one of the photos—Diane's sure it must've been shot with a telephoto, unbeknownst to the subject—a lovely young woman with straight red hair blowing in the breeze hangs a quilt on a clothesline."

We quickly divided the stack and began flipping through tables of contents and slick color pages. It didn't take long.

"Oh my—that's her!" shouted Peter. We circled around, peering over his broad shoulders as he held up the very picture Dan had just described: a lovely photograph with excellent lighting catching the early morning summer sunshine, the deep emerald green hills, a plain four-square farmhouse in the far right background. A radiant woman in a black dress and white apron, definitely unaware of the eyes fixed on her then or now, reached to fasten a wooden peg clothespin to the corner of a lovely white-and-blue log-cabin patterned quilt. It could have been an art poster or a travelogue's cover.

"Are you sure it's her? You can only see a profile here," Dan said.

"I'm positive," my curate proclaimed. "How far is Tremont anyway?"

"It's only about forty miles from here, but the roads are unpaved the last ten, so you can count on it taking close to an hour," I explained.

"Can you go with me this afternoon to identify her in person?" asked Dan authoritatively.

"Of course," Pete and I said in unison, like eager children.

Dan frowned. "Good. Pete, you can ride with me down to Tremont to see about our redhead. Father Grif, I have a rather large favor to ask of you. It involves another lead we have."

I tried not to show my disappointment. "Anything. I'm free all afternoon."

"We traced that partial print from that .45 dropped in the Divine," Dan explained. "Found a match in the FBI's veterans databank, and—you're not going to like this—it belongs to Charles John Baxter, Jr."

"Charlie Baxter?" I asked. "That's impossible."

"The town drunk? Old Stinky?" echoed Pete.

"Peter, please." I found the students' nickname for Charlie—based on his infrequent bathing habits—accurate but unkind nonetheless.

Dan continued. "That's right. Old Charlie's a former Vietnam recon pilot. We picked him up this morning, about half-sauced of course, and questioned him. At first he denied knowing what we were talking about. Then he started rambling about being behind enemy lines and the Gemini project—we got nowhere. Grif, I was hoping you'd maybe talk to him this afternoon—he's still at the office in the holding cell—and see what he knows. He likes you, our church has been good to him . . . maybe he'll feel more comfortable."

"I'll go, but only if I can make it clear to Charlie that I'm helping you, that anything he tells me about Gentry Truman's death or how he came to have touched Truman's pistol will be passed on to you. I don't want to exploit my role as his pastor."

"Good enough, then," Dan replied. "Let's get going."

Chapter Fourteen

RED HERRINGS

PETE AND I AGREED to postpone our racquetball game until after dinner, which suited me fine. As I walked back down Southern Avenue, I was disappointed that I wasn't accompanying him and Dan to Tremont to find the mysterious Amish woman. Nonetheless, I was glad to help out however I could.

My sister was at an Avenell University faculty tea, so it was nice to leave the house without fabricating a reason; Dan had cautioned me not to mention Charlie Baxter's fingerprint to anyone, including Beatrice. The mile down to the sheriff's office was tedious but faster than I'd expected. It seemed as if media coverage had reached saturation level and would conclude with the memorial service tomorrow. The mobile homes, vans, cables, and satellites lining our main thoroughfares made Avenell look more like a Florida trailer park than the dignified university town it prided itself as.

The Carroll County Sheriff's Office had become the mini–command center for the State Bureau of Investigation, as well as the FBI and campus security. Avenell did not have a police force of its own, although Gentry's death would certainly add fuel to the argument for one. Harold Littlefield, head of campus security, had been asserting the need for a "real" campus police department for the past five years. Usually, however, Avenell barely needed any kind of security whatsoever. Sure, there were the overzealous fraternity parties and pranks, the occasional fistfight or panty raid, but rarely did an actual crime—theft, rape, or murder—occur in our little community.

The CCSO overflowed with assorted uniforms: blue police-types for campus, khaki and hunter green for the sheriff's team, and so many black and navy suits it looked like a funeral home. Men in sunglasses and women with sleek, tight hair scurried from cars over to the garage and back. Inside the tiny lobby, Maria Alvarez tried to maintain some kind of order. "Can you believe this?" she asked me. "It's like *NYPD Blue* comes to Mayberry." She pointed me down the hall, frowned, and went back to typing a report while answering the phone.

Sam Claiborne himself strode out of the same office where Bea and I had been questioned only days before and greeted me warmly. "I really appreciate your help on this one, Father Grif," he said. "Our people are getting nowhere fast. And because Stink—I mean Charlie—was in the military, he thinks everything's a secret operation or some kind of conspiracy. I'm hoping maybe he'll trust you."

I nodded and repeated the same caveat I'd discussed with Dan.

"I understand your position, Father," assured the sheriff.

I followed him to the end of the hall and down to the holding cell in the basement. Since the federal agents had taken over the conference room, usually reserved for interrogations, I entered the cell and had it locked behind me. The small room smelled hospital-clean—only found in a small town jail, I thought to myself—and looked remarkably fresh with new white paint, fluorescent lighting, a starched sheet on the iron cot, and bright porcelain fixtures gleaming in the far back corner.

Only Charlie Baxter looked out of place. He sat quietly, almost dejectedly, on the cot with bowed head and dirty hands in his lap. A torn, red tartan flannel shirt was layered over an Avenell Tigers sweat shirt that was at least ten years old, before the new mascot. Faded, dirty jeans led down to the biggest surprise, a pair of new-looking penny loafers. He smelled of gasoline, beer, and fermented perspiration.

"Charlie?" I said calmly. "It's Father Grif, from the church at school."

No response. His bushy, gray-haired head dipped slightly as if he were sleeping.

"I just want to talk to you, to help you. I want to try to get you out of here if I can."

He looked up briskly. "Who are you? Password?" Unshaven cheeks and neck, long, thick porkchop sideburns. Wild blue bloodshot eyes, forehead wrinkled like a worn, unfolded map. Wide nose and loose jowls, a tired bloodhound. He probably wasn't much older than me, but most would think him my father. We were certainly different men, but I knew inside we were much the same.

I combed my mind for a logical password but none came, so I played it as if we were boys. "The password is 'Go Tigers.' Charlie, I'm working with the sheriff to help him find out what happened to a man who's dead now, a man found shot in the Martyr's Chapel. I'd like to tell him whatever you know about the gun that had your fingerprint on it."

He nodded and smiled. "What took you so long? You know how many months I've been here?" His eyes flashed like foil in the purplish glow of clean, fluorescent light.

"Charlie, it's me, Father Grif," I repeated. "How are you? I want to talk about the gun you left in the church."

"Oh, they thought they were so smart catching me the way they did," he said slyly. "Well, they don't have a thing on me. I cleaned the last job smooth as a whistle." He puckered his lips and bird-called a few notes.

"What last job was that? Did it have to do with a pistol you found— maybe out at the Martyr's Chapel?" I didn't want to lead him too much.

"*Boom!* And I ran back to my plane. Then there was another *boom* and I had to take cover under a sycamore tree. The Gemini had landed! Pilot and copilot! Friendly fire! I barely escaped alive!" His voice was animated like a child's, his sad eyes replaying a scene from the war still raging inside him.

Or maybe not. "Charlie, were you out at the Martyr's Chapel last

Friday night? Did you see something? See a man shoot himself?"

He grabbed my shoulders and pulled me in excitedly. "You were there? I ain't a prayin' man, Padre, but I got it all squared away with the Big General in the sky. I was so hungry, and God's so good to feed me. Manna, it's called. Bread and cheese and meat and soda pop from the sky!"

"You were eating in the chapel? Friday night?"

He nodded, eyes like glass saucers. "They meant to take me by surprise, but I hid outside. Gemini, this is Air-Boy 12, come in? Roger!"

It was like talking to a parrot—random thoughts, old memories . . . like forgotten photographs shuffled into a new deck of playing cards. Only I sensed that he was telling me something, that he had been at the Martyr's Chapel and seen someone else there Friday night.

"Charlie, who did you see? What did he look like?" I asked patiently.

"Only I grabbed his weapon—Man down!—but it was too late then. The mission was over. Man down, nothin' left." His voice dipped, sounded despondent, melancholy.

"Did you see a man down in the chapel? Did you take the gun from his hand?"

His head bobbed mechanically. Then Charlie's eyes glazed with water as tears brimmed forward. It was heart wrenching, and I took his hand in mine and whispered a prayer. "Lord, in your bountiful goodness have mercy on this man, on his mind and heart. Give him peace, your peace that passes beyond understanding. Let him know he is loved and that he can trust you. Amen."

He whined, "I didn't know what else to do with it, Father. I lit a flare so our boys would spot it. I didn't want God to quit sending the food. I didn't want her to think I hurt nobody. I can't hurt anybody ever again, I just can't. Can you understand that, sir?" His voice rose at the end.

"Yes, soldier, I can. And I'm going to do everything I can to get you an honorable discharge."

"I'd be much obliged, Chaplain." His eyes looked vacant and spent, heavy-lidded.

"You rest here, Charlie, for now. I'll be back, I promise." I helped him recline on the small cot and went over to the cell door. With a motion from my hand, a guard came and unlocked the door. If only I could release Charlie Baxter's spirit as easily.

The guard led me back upstairs to the sheriff's office. Sheriff Claiborne was cradling the phone on his neck while he juggled a cup of coffee and a file with his hands. "Got it . . . okay, yeah, thanks," he spoke into the phone before replacing it.

"Any luck?" he asked intently. "Have a seat. Cup of coffee? Coke?"

"Maybe some water," I said as my stomach grumbled. "I may have something; I'm not sure." I sat in front of his desk in an uncomfortable, straight-back vinyl chair.

"What do you mean?" he asked, handing me a bottle of Evian from the portable fridge beside his desk.

"Well, I do think Charlie was out at the Martyr's Chapel last Friday night. I think someone drops food off there for him. So he's out there eating, and Gentry Truman shows up, maybe alone or maybe with someone else—it's impossible to tell from what Charlie said. He keeps drifting in and out of the distant past and the present."

"So he sees Truman go into the Martyr's Chapel late Friday night," Sam repeated, picking up my thread. "Charlie hears a gunshot and goes in. He sees Truman dead up front, checks the body, picks up the gun, then panics. He realizes that he could be implicated—or maybe his paranoia kicks in. He leaves the scene. Later, he's afraid to keep the .45, so he drops it off in a safe place—the church donation box."

"Maybe he was the man running after me Monday night. He wanted to tell somebody what he'd seen but was too scared. So he dropped the gun off later that night and even lit a candle so it would be found sooner rather than later. It sounds plausible enough."

Sam seated himself behind his desk and began digging around in his top left drawer. "Bagel?" he offered.

"No, thanks," I said. "Charlie kept talking about Gemini, and pilots and copilots, and man down. Somehow what he saw seems to have reminded him of something from the past. Is Gemini a military term for a weapon or project? An aircraft carrier maybe?"

"Not that I know of," the sheriff replied through a mouthful. "It's a sign of the zodiac. Corresponds to the month of June, I think. Could've been a code word for virtually anything. Or maybe nothing. You know Charlie, Father Grif. He's harmless, but he's never made much sense . . . even on a good day when he's sober and rested."

"So you don't think he had anything to do with Gentry's death?"

"I didn't say that." He chewed ravenously before continuing. "What if Truman was the one bringing Charlie food—"

I laughed and then tried to stop myself. "Sorry, it's just—"

"I know, Truman didn't exactly strike me as the Mother Teresa type, either."

"It's funny because Charlie said that God provided his food, that it was manna from heaven, but then he referred to God as 'her.'"

"Hmmm," growled Sam Claiborne, wiping a sesame bagel crumb from his mouth's corner. "Anyway, let's say that Gentry was the one bringing Charlie food—or maybe Charlie mistakenly thought Truman was his guardian angel. It spooks Truman, the two of them wrestle over the gun, it goes off and kills Truman. Now Charlie's the one who's spooked—"

"So he elaborately stages the scene to look like Gentry shot himself in the head and then takes the .45 with him? That doesn't sound likely."

"You're right. We're still missing too many pieces."

"Did you run any tests on Charlie to see if he'd fired the gun that was found?" I asked.

"Confidentially, yes—a powder residue test, and it was negative. But keep in mind it's been almost a week since Truman was shot. Charlie could've washed his hands hundreds of times by now."

"But I doubt he has," I replied matter-of-factly, and we both laughed.

The sheriff wiped the last bread crumbs from his hands. "I've got to run—meeting with the feds and Doc Graham. Thank you, Father Grif. This helps a great deal."

We shook hands and filed out of the room. "Will Charlie be released today? He seems comfortable enough, but he equates a cell like that with imprisonment and wrongdoing."

"We'll hold him until tomorrow, then release him if nothing else turns up. We will require him to stay in Carroll County, though. Maybe at the Y down in Mumford."

"I'll check on him, Sheriff. I promised him he'd be okay."

"He will, Father Grif. We'll take care of him. Thanks again for your help." The short, thick-muscled bulldog of a man bounded off toward the door with me several paces behind. I felt reluctant to leave Charlie here without saying good-bye, so I stood in the cramped lobby and wrote out Psalm 27 on a note pad provided by the dispatcher. I added, *You are safe here. I'll see you soon. Go Tigers! Blessings, Father Grif* and folded it in thirds. Maria promised that she'd have a guard give it to Charlie right away.

Just as I was heading out the door, realizing almost two hours had passed since my arrival, I bumped into a familiar face.

"Father Grif? How good to see you!" exclaimed Dr. Caroline Barr, out of breath.

She looked youthful and vibrant in jeans, a red Shaker sweater, and an Avenell baseball cap. If I didn't know her, I'd think she was a student or novice reporter.

"Caroline! It's good to see you. How are you?" I asked.

We were blocking traffic through the busy door, so we stepped outside to the edge of the asphalt parking lot. She stood very neatly on a yellow parking line, a gymnast on a beam.

"I—I came to tell the police what I told you the other day. About my threatening Truman and all. I don't want it hanging over me. I don't want Truman to have any more power in my life. Telling the truth is the only way to face my fears." She lowered her eyes beneath the navy brim of her cap. Her lovely auburn hair glinted in the late afternoon sun as a breeze blew it off her neck.

"You're doing the right thing, Caroline. I promise. I'm proud of you, and I trust God to honor your choice." I wanted to reach out and touch her hand, to encourage her in some way for the battle ahead, but some unnamed fear of my own held me back.

"Thank you, Father Grif. I wouldn't be here if it weren't for your words the other day. Thank you." She took a deep breath and looked me in the eye. I wondered what was on the other side of those blue portals flecked with green.

"It's nothing at all. I'll be praying for you as you talk to the police." I didn't want to leave her there alone, but I was running out of things to say. "Would you like me to go with you?"

"No . . . no, thank you. This is something I need to do alone. May I ask why you were here?—I'm sorry, it's probably none of my business." She turned as if to leave.

"No, wait. I . . . came to visit someone. I'm friends with the sheriff, and so we chatted a bit. You can imagine the toll a case like this one is taking." Which was mostly true.

"Of course. You may be visiting me here, as well, before it's all over." She smiled. Deep sigh. "Well, I need to get it over with. Thanks again."

"Perhaps we can have lunch sometime soon? Next week?"

"That would be nice. I hope I can make it." She turned and nearly walked into an officer coming out the front door. I waved and headed to my car.

Driving back home, I said more prayers for her and for Charlie Baxter, for Marcia and Jenna, Lisa, and Lucy. Even for cantankerous old Cale. For all the lives touched by the loss of this talented man and the hard things ahead. I concluded by praying for Caroline Barr again. Silly I know, as if God didn't hear me the first time.

———

While I spent the rest of the afternoon talking on the phone to John Greenwood and reading Thomas Merton's *Seeds of Contemplation*, my curate and Sergeant Dan Warren were conducting their own interrogations in the Amish community of Tremont. As I sat in the club chair dragged close to the window, drowsing like a cat in the warm, extended fingers of autumn sunshine, I could imagine the lovely hour's drive.

Enough color on the trees to keep us lingering on our own losses, checkerboard fields of upturned earth, winter wheat and soybeans, dry-parchment husks of harvested cornfields, flagging scarecrows, houses fewer and farther between. The gravel road off the state highway rising up in a cloud of chalklike dust from the last buggy heading back to the small farming community. The Cumberland Mountains rising and falling like the curves of a giant sleeping on his side. The air crisp with the smell of ripe apples and hickory-wood smoke.

"It wasn't quite that idyllic," Pete told me a few hours later as we prepared for our racquetball match. "I'm sure it was a nice drive, but I was so nervous I didn't notice. Dan and I discussed our approach on the way down and decided to let me do most of the talking. We figured maybe the Amish folk would open up to a man of the cloth."

I nodded and folded my sweats into the top locker space. The air felt brisk on my knees below my gym shorts. "Go on," I encouraged.

"Well, I had changed into more conservative clothes and collar before we left, but it still ended up being Dan's badge that got results. We stopped in the little village square at Tremont. Very quaint with its folk art and Pennsylvania Dutch signs everywhere. We went from place to place asking about our mystery woman, showed the magazine photo to whoever would look. Most just shook their heads and pursed their lips like we'd asked them to denounce their faith. I was getting frustrated when we stopped in the bakery."

He pulled on clean white socks and laced his court shoes. I smiled thinking about the tenacious resistance of most Amish to outsiders.

"The bakery smelled wonderful," Peter emphasized. "Cinnamon rolls and carrot cake, banana bread, German chocolate cake—it was fabulous. A very different smell than the one in here." My curate smiled and motioned around Alumni Gym's sweaty locker room. "We bought some date cookies and asked the Amish woman there about our redhead. She looked sternly at the photo and just shook her head. She said, 'Such stubborn, prying people, the English, taking photographs uninvited.' That's when

Dan intervened and told her that the woman might be in danger. That did the trick."

"Yes, that works for most of us," I replied, fully engaged with his tale.

"So it turns out our mystery woman is named Leah Schroeder. Our Amish baker reluctantly gave us directions to her family's farm a few miles down the road. We found the place without any trouble, a solid clapboard farmhouse with a fieldstone chimney and two Dutch barns. Two boys were playing on the front porch as we pulled up."

I began to feel anxious and took a hard rubber racquetball out of its can. It bounced effortlessly against the adjacent cinder block wall and back to my palm.

"The boys hurried in to fetch their mother for us. She was tall and matronly, with a neat bun of fading red hair tucked under her cap. She was polite but obviously frightened. When Dan explained that her daughter might have something to do with Truman's death, she got upset. She insisted that her daughter never left the farm unless it was to go into town or to church. She said that we couldn't talk to Leah until Mr. Schroeder returned at supper time."

"Good grief," I said, still bouncing the burnt-red racquetball.

"Yep. So we waited on the porch for almost an hour. Mrs. Schroeder didn't warm up to us, but she did give us a glass of cider." Pete grinned boyishly. "I was sitting there scratching an old orange tabby behind the ears when our mystery woman bounded around the corner of the house. It was all I could do not to jump up and tackle her."

I leaned in closer to hear him as a group of students returned from the showers.

"She was so rattled that she dropped her cloth bag and this big canvas she carried under her arm. I helped her pick up a mess of brushes, paint tubes, and sketches. Then the canvas—Grif, it was breathtaking! A beautiful landscape, impressionistic, of the large Dutch barn behind the house, a length of creek and a row of cottonwoods running alongside it.

She had nailed the lonely beauty of the area. I was very impressed."

"I can tell," I said.

"But that's not the best part. After we'd introduced ourselves and Dan had recounted the situation again, Leah Schroeder confessed."

Chapter Fifteen

THE NIGHT IN QUESTION

As I sat in the locker room listening to my curate's tale, I forgot all about our racquetball match. Between his words and my imagination, it was better than being there. It seems that just as they had all sat down on the porch—Leah, Mrs. Schroeder, Dan, and Peter—up drove Mr. Benjamin Schroeder and his eldest son, Jacob, in a horse-drawn buggy. So introductions and explanations were made all over again. The father's initial hostility transformed into a curt respect for the law and a desire to get to the bottom of whatever crime his daughter had committed. Leah's tall, thick-shouldered brother, who shared her good looks, seemed quietly protective as he grimaced at the interlopers.

Leah herself became more composed, almost serene, as she began explaining her presence in the Divine Cathedral. Pete quickly realized that she was confessing to her parents, not to her visitors. Like a seasoned raconteur, he related the conversation which followed.

"I was not at Ruth's on Tuesday to help her can squash," Leah explained. "I lied to you, Mother. Please forgive me."

"Then where were you, daughter?" asked her father.

"I . . . I was—"

"She was with me," interrupted her brother Jacob, speaking for the first time. "I allowed her to ride with me to deliver the preserves and winesaps up the mountain. I must ask your forgiveness also, Mother, Father. Please forgive me." He remained impassive.

The parents exchanged curious looks. Peter and Dan were equally confused.

"That's quite a day's journey if you traveled the entire route by buggy," observed Dan. His tone was not accusatory, but nonetheless pressed the reliability of Jacob's claim.

"We drive the Yoders' van when we deliver to the mountain," the young man explained. "It is a Ford Windstar," he said proudly. Peter couldn't help but smile at this.

"You are forgiven, my children," declared the Father. "Leah Rebekah, why did you wish to accompany your brother? Were you the woman these gentlemen saw in their church on Tuesday afternoon?"

"Yes," she began. "Do not blame Jacob. It is my fault. I begged him to take me with him. I wished to view the paintings in the gallery and in the cathedral at the university. I intended no harm."

The Avenell Gallery was widely known for its diverse collection of folk art, watercolor landscapes, and a handful of Georgia O'Keeffe's works. It sold a piece from time to time, especially to wealthy alumni, but its owner, Monica VanDegraff, was a wealthy woman herself and enjoyed discussing the works with students more than turning a profit. Peter immediately empathized with the young woman's appreciation of beauty.

And she must have found out about *The Walls of Paradise* from Monica, as well. Or perhaps she was simply enjoying the flying buttresses and stained glass and chanced upon it.

"Leah, I have warned you about the vanity of art, have I not?" said her mother sternly. "Do you know anything that would be helpful for these men?"

"I know nothing about a dead man in the church or a weapon left behind," she proclaimed. "I simply had to see the paintings. That one in the back corner is truly remarkable—the lighting is so exquisite. I am certain that it is a work by Albert Bierstadt. I have studied his work for some time now. Although the painting is unsigned, it is likely worth a great deal of money to a collector. You really should not leave it unguarded like that. Anyone could walk off with it."

Dan burst out laughing. Pete joined in and the contagion spread as all four Schroeders found themselves guffawing as well.

"That's the moment I knew she was telling the truth," Peter told me that night. "Her passion for art is so intense, so innocent and genuine. Her laughter was like music, like wind chimes in the breeze. Her pale, freckled face looked so beautiful in the late afternoon sun. Her smile . . ."

My curate, so casually unaware of the opposite sex in his ministry to students, was clearly smitten with Leah Schroeder, and I wasn't sure how to respond. Perhaps she was attracted to him, as well. My fear was that their worlds revolved too far apart.

"So that was that," Peter concluded wistfully. "Dan took her official statement, asked her not to leave the state for thirty days without notifying him first, and we headed home."

I avoided the subject of romance for now. "Do you think *The Walls of Paradise* could really be an authentic Bierstadt? Leah's no art critic, but it sounds like she may be onto something. Remind me to ask Dan if they had a professional assess it yet."

"She sounded very sure of herself," replied Peter. "I honestly don't think she had anything to do with Gentry Truman or with the gun you found in the Divine."

"I believe you. Guess it's just one of those wild goose chases that comes up in a case like this." I retied my tennis shoes for the third time. A handful of male students changed behind us and headed off to the weight room.

"Maybe so." He laughed. "Or maybe it's my own personal red herring from God. I sure wish I could see her again."

"That's not very likely, is it? It doesn't sound like her parents approve of her interest in art," I cautioned.

"No, they don't. I talked to her alone for a while before we left. She's very frustrated. She can't hide her passion for painting—nor her talent—but art is not regarded seriously by her community. But as she told me, she's twenty-one years old, a legal adult. She implied that her parents can't keep her from using her gift forever."

"Peter, I know very little about this situation. But I would caution you not to get involved in a family matter in a very different culture than our own," I said firmly. "Should we finally get to our game?"

"I'm surprised, Grif. I thought you'd be excited for me—aren't you relieved that Leah had nothing to do with Gentry's death?" He could not hide the hurt in his voice.

"Of course I am. And I'm glad you find Leah so interesting. But I care about you, Peter, and I don't want to see you get hurt."

"Fair enough," he said, turning away. "Let's play if we're going to. But I still want to hear about your conversation with Charlie Baxter."

I was relieved that he was willing to change the subject and move on. As our shoes squeaked on the gleaming hardwood floor, I quickly summarized my afternoon at the sheriff's office. My curate nodded and concurred with my interpretation of Charlie's responses.

We entered the tall, narrow racquetball court, like a giant shoebox set on its end, and lost our voices in the cavernous echoes. Goggles in place, we warmed up with several extended volleys. We were well matched. Although Pete was younger and more agile, I had been playing the game since I was a teenager, and my experience usually gave me the edge. However, we each played beyond our ability that night as we unleashed the torrent of frustration, stress, and anger lurking within us.

While I imagined that Peter saw my face, and perhaps Leah's father's, on the small rubber ball, I confess that on many returns Joan Dowinger's face popped into my mind. We each took a game, but drenched and determined, I broke the stalemate for the match with a fury that surprised even my curate. Looking back, my determination had nothing to do with Peter and everything to do with my desire for justice, my angry conviction that Gentry Truman's murderer, if indeed he was murdered, would be caught and appropriately punished. This side of me—what she used to call my Old-Testament-God side—had always frightened Amy.

Dan Warren was waiting for me when I returned home a little before nine. He and Bea were just starting their second cups of decaf when I walked in the back door, still flushed with color and out of breath from my victory. My home felt light and warm and safe, and I was grateful for its comfort.

"We were about to send a search party out for you," Dan said, patting my shoulder. "You okay? Or did Pete beat you too badly?"

"I defeated the youngster soundly," I said. "But not without considerable effort. He told me about your . . . trip today." I almost revealed too much and looked warily at my sister.

"You be careful exerting yourself like that. You're not as young as you think you are," Bea warned.

I poured myself a glass of water and realized I hadn't eaten the entire day. Playing racquetball tonight was probably not the smartest move, but I downed a second glass and promised myself a big breakfast. "Grab your coffee and let's chat in my office, Dan."

"Well, I know when I'm not wanted," grumbled my sister half-jokingly. She topped her cup and headed for the living room's TV set.

I shut the heavy oak door behind us and peeled off my sweat shirt. Dan sipped his coffee, scanning my shelves' popular section for new mystery novels. He waited on me to begin, and I appreciated it.

"Anything new? Any more luck with Charlie?" I asked, as we both took seats.

"No. Although he has asked for you. He will be released tomorrow—I'll have Andy McDermott drive him down to the Mumford YMCA. Thanks again for talking with him. I'm not sure of the details, but I agree that he saw something the night of Truman's death."

"What else do we know about that night?" I asked. "I assume most of the family have alibis for late Friday, early Saturday? Didn't Sam say that Truman's watch stopped at 2:17 A.M.?"

Dan stood again, restless with the frustrating dead-ends so far. "Yep on both accounts. The wife and her son were at the ballet in Nashville and then back home by midnight. Cale Sanders ate alone in the Tiger

Bay Pub, caught the late showing of *Citizen Kane* in the student center theater, returned to the pub for a nightcap, and headed home. The servants verified seeing him come in around midnight. Jenna—"

"Any witness see him at the movie?"

"Yes, the student selling tickets recalled him as did a couple of drama majors."

"How much time passed between when Cale left the pub the second time and midnight when the servants saw him?" I asked.

"Roughly an hour. He says he went for a walk around the block to smoke before going in the house."

"Enough time for him to shoot his brother and return as if nothing happened?" I wondered.

"That would give him enough time to drive out there and back, but not much time for anything else. In other words, he would have had to orchestrate it ahead of time, to have known that's where Gentry would be waiting."

"He strikes me as too much of a loose cannon to be that premeditated," I said.

"He tore up a speeding ticket in Andy McDermott's face last month," explained Dan. "Refused to pay it until Andy could prove that Sanders was speeding. He scared the kid to death."

I chuckled. "What about the daughters?"

"Jenna Truman ate in Chattanooga with a friend and then went shopping. She drove herself back and thinks it was around two when she returned to Avenell. The maid, Jeanette, thinks she heard her come in but can't be sure—she didn't get up to check."

"So she had plenty of time to meet her father, shoot him, clean herself up, and drive back to the house," I conjectured.

"Yes. She also has a history of mental health problems."

"I know. She gave us all a scare when I first arrived at the house last night." I recounted Jenna's scream and ghostly apparition, the ensuing confusion and her family's eagerness to dismiss it as a dream or resulting from medication.

"Just nerves, you think? Or did the girl really see someone?" asked Dan.

"I believe she saw someone. Obviously it wasn't her father, but I think Jenna Truman may be the sanest one of the bunch. Just intuition," I said.

"Now, again, it's all off the record, but six weeks ago, Jenna L. Truman, age twenty-two, dialed 9–1–1 after trying to take her own life with an overdose of Lithium, Prozac, Valium, and whatever other candies were lying around the house. Carroll County General pumped her stomach. Mrs. Marcia Truman refused to discharge her stepdaughter until her husband returned from New York. Proof of psychiatric treatment was provided by Gentry Truman two days later, and she was entrusted to his care."

"Does that negate my claim that she's the sanest Truman I've met yet?"

"Nope, it may even support it. Maybe she couldn't take the craziness any longer and decided to check out of the hotel."

"I'll see if she wants to discuss her home life with me or, more likely, with Peter."

"Truman's other daughters were verifiably out-of-state—Lucy Truman was shooting a documentary in Prague, and Lisa Chandler was at a wrap party for a new film in L.A."

"What about Truman's agent, Casey Atwood?" I asked.

"He was supposedly at his health club right outside of Nashville, the Green Hills Racquet Club, but we haven't found any witnesses yet. His membership card was recorded, but the clerk doesn't recall what he looked like or him being there."

"Hmmm," I said. "And Franklin Milford?"

Our eyes met in an acknowledgment of our university president's role in the sordid drama.

"Fund-raiser in Nashville until ten, then he drove back alone. His housekeeper, Emma Prescott, had the night off, so no one can verify his whereabouts after ten-thirty, when he stopped to fill up in Lewiston."

"So Marcia, Milford, and Atwood were all in Nashville that night,"

I thought aloud. "Interesting coincidence. I wonder if Marcia and Milford arranged a rendezvous?"

Dan agreed that Marcia Truman's affair with President Milford would likely cause a scandal if revealed. "It's likely to come out in the tabloids eventually with this many people working the case," said Dan. "But Sam said to make sure that it doesn't leak from one of us."

I nodded. "It could devastate Franklin's career. And the university's reputation."

"What does your gut tell you about all this, Father Grif?" asked Dan suddenly.

He looked at me intently, as if I held the secret of Gentry Truman's death deep in my subconscious.

"Nobody's a better judge of character than you are." He smiled. "Even Miss Bea admitted that tonight before you got home."

"My sister said that?" I asked. "Well, I'll be . . . I'm flattered that you value my judgment so highly, Dan. I guess my gut is still processing all this. . . . Right now, I think there's a strange dynamic between Marcia Truman and Cale Sanders."

"Based on?"

"Oh, just little things. The way he's so caustic and sarcastic and yet she defends him. I know that they were involved once years ago."

"Yes, that's what they both said. But evidently there are no sparks there to rekindle."

"I don't believe they're involved romantically. But I do believe they share a secret."

Just then the phone rang, followed by my sister's voice. "Grif, it's for you." She stuck her head in the door and silently mouthed, "Marcia Truman."

While I took the call at my desk, Dan scratched his head and stood to stretch for the third time. He thumbed through my collection of Gentry Truman memorabilia and selected the anthology of his greatest works.

"Hello? . . . Yes, how are you, Marcia? . . . No bother at all. . . . Yes, I see. So you'll be delivering the eulogy, then? . . . Right. No problem. . . .

Of course. . . . Yes, right. Tell your brother-in-law that I hope he's feeling better. I'll say a prayer for him tonight."

I shifted uncomfortably. "No, I don't think so. I'll be happy to ask, but I'm afraid the sheriff is a man of his word. . . . Yes, good night."

"Problem?" asked Dan as I hung up.

"Sanders isn't feeling well and doesn't think he's up to delivering the eulogy tomorrow like we'd planned. So Marcia will speak instead. Then she said that Sam refused to release the body for cremation—he told her that Gentry's death is still being treated as a homicide."

"How did she sound?"

I thought a moment. "Like a cheerful mother calling her child's teacher to tell him that little Cale is sick today but it's nothing serious. And would the teacher please ask the principal for a favor."

Dan laughed and I smiled.

He picked up the Truman anthology again and opened to a page he had marked with the jacket cover. He began reading in character with a more pronounced southern drawl and a deliberate dramatic air.

" 'I'll tell you what it's really like, Mary. It's all a big conspiracy set up by the Klan? You think you know everything? They take boys like Johnny Ray and me and make us feel like men. More 'n you ever did. We got a cause, see. Go 'head and say it's a wrong cause, a selfish cause, but it beats no cause at all. Nobody's gonna fight for my interest except me and others like me.' " Dan thoroughly captured the passion and cadence of Truman's dialogue.

"Marvin's speech to Mary outside the church, Act II, scene ii, *Breakfast in Birmingham*."

"Very good, Padre. You win Final Jeopardy. Is all his stuff like this? Racial and southern and as melodramatic as kudzu choking us on the front porch swing?"

"Well, not all of it is quite so charged as that scene," I explained. "But yes, he does tend to address human themes in the context of the South, and you and I know what a strange place this can be. . . ."

I continued. "Actually, that play in its entirety is clearly anti-segregation, anti-racism. Go ahead and borrow it—that was Amy's copy. I have mine for the service tomorrow. Maybe it will give you insight on the case."

"The Lord knows I need it. All right, thanks. Speaking of the service tomorrow, are you ready? I'll be there on security detail, plain clothes, probably sticking out like Monopoly money in the offering plate."

"The family agreed on the service plans. I've got an outline but still feel a little uncertain about how everything will go. I'm having second thoughts about my selections for some parts of the service; I'm trusting God to speak to me between now and then."

"I know He will. Even if it's a whisper." He patted my shoulder and we said good-night.

———

Friday morning proved brisk, cold, and clear. A heavy frost was on more than just the pumpkin. A damask layer of ice encased the multitude of fallen leaves like giant snowflakes, tree limbs rose like stalagmites from some arctic underground, and the grass shimmered like a glass-spindled carpet of snow. The sky, however, was cloudless, bringing a perfect autumn azure color to life before my eyes; it was like hearing the volume raised gradually on a beautiful Mozart sonata.

Nervous energy collided with sharp hunger pains as I came off my fast. Nothing too heavy, though. I'd learned not to overeat when coming off a fast. A little wheat cereal and some cantaloupe were just the thing, a cup of hazelnut coffee for dessert. Bea was up humming and ironing, torn between her black linen suit—"I'm afraid it's too summery"—and her navy silk dress—"It's a little snug in the bosom." I went straight into her perfectly arranged, Victorian-rose bedroom, over to the closet, and pulled out a charcoal wool suit and white blouse.

"How about this?" I offered.

"Oh no, Grif, that's too wintry. It makes me look heavy."

I sighed, wondering why I had even bothered. I pushed the suit back in. "What about this one?" A deep green, almost black dress with simple lines, a square neckline, and onyx buttons up the front.

A sharp little cry erupted from my sister, like an ice pick breaking a frozen surface. "Oh my goodness!" Bea exclaimed. "I'd forgotten all about that. It's perfect!"

"Is it new? I've never seen you in it before."

"Thelma Osgood gave it to me when she lost all her weight last spring. Said she bought it after Christmas at Macy's in Atlanta. Oh, Grif, it's perfect! Thank you." She kissed my cheek as if I were the gift giver.

"You and Thelma Osgood don't look anything alike. I can't believe you wear the same size."

"Used to. She's lost over fifty pounds now and is down to a size ten. But, yes, we *were* the same size."

"But you're at least a foot taller than she is."

"Yes, but unless she wears a petite—which she doesn't—we still wear the same size and simply adjust it to our proportions. A roll-up here, a loosened hem there." My sister inspected the dress and found it still bearing a price tag.

"I see."

"Every good actress knows how to make the most of her costumes. Just ask Marcia Klein Truman."

"Don't start," I warned. "She did invite you to the reception, after all."

I left my sister on a giddy search for appropriate earrings, purse, and shoes, but turned over what she said about costumes. Outside the cold, crisp air was like the snap of a wet towel. I inhaled and relished the sharp tickle in my lungs. Already the streets were lined with reporters, camera crews setting up stationary positions outside the cathedral, and curious onlookers dressed as if waiting for a parade.

I drove to the downtown strip in Avenell to keep my seven A.M. appointment at Walter Frasier's Campus Barbershop. Walt had kindly agreed to work me in first this morning, Friday being the one day that he took appointments. I usually visited him on the last Friday afternoon of each month, but I'd had to cancel last week because of a Mumford Rotary Club luncheon where I gave the devotion.

Despite the fact that I sometimes felt older and slower, my hair had not quit growing and was now needing a serious cut. Patches of gray continued multiplying in my temples, and the front cowlick on the left side was now giving my dirty blond hair a shaggy, unkempt look. Walt sensed the urgency in my voice when I had called him yesterday afternoon after Bea had offered to give me a trim. He knew that a couple of years ago, right before I was to officiate a wedding, a similar oversight on my part occurred. I had forgotten to get a haircut but wanted to look my best for the wedding, so my sister gave me a trim that harkened back to my boyhood days of buzz cuts and whitewalls around the ears. Although not my custom, I wore an oversized biretta for that service. I still feel guilty because that was the only ceremony where I did not purchase a photo of the wedding party.

So in Walt's capable hands, I inhaled the deep, rich scent of pine cleaner, floor wax, lemon shave cream, and bay rum. He had locked the door behind me, knowing that reporters, whom he'd gladly cut all week, might look in and corner me like a wild animal. Besides, his first appointment wasn't until eight, so we had plenty of time to visit.

"It's a shame about that writer fellow," Walt said matter-of-factly. "Did you know him very well?" The hum of his electric barber's shears lulled me into a drowsiness I had overcome only an hour ago.

"I knew him a little," I said. "Yes, it is a shame."

Walt, an affable man in his mid-forties with nimble fingers, a keen eye for symmetry, and an inarticulate knowledge of the male ego, had inherited this shop from his uncle. He sensed my reluctance to discuss the case and remained comfortably quiet, letting the *snip-snip* of his scissors do the talking. Tufts of blunt-cut hair fell into the canvas smock draping my lap. I was used to the mingled gold, wheat, russet, and pale blond hairs, but the new silver ones still startled me. I was fifty years old.

"Walt," I asked, as he daubed warm shaving cream around the backs of my ears and neck, "do many men color their hair?"

"Thinking of getting rid of the gray, Father Grif?" he chuckled.

"Oh, I don't know. I'm as vain as the next man, but I guess I'll keep it. I'm just curious if many men actually cover up their gray—or even change to a color they like better, for that matter."

Walt raked the sharp razor over the cream in deft strokes. "More than used to," he said, standing back to assess the clean lines left behind his blade. "Some students experiment with every color of the rainbow." He paused. "Certain university administrators have been known to use a little Grecian Formula." He crossed in front of me and smiled. Our president came to mind. Yes, Franklin Milford always looked crisp and cleanly defined, like a fresh-starched, buttoned-down oxford cloth dress shirt. He would be mortified to know Walt had just obliquely revealed one of his secrets.

"Did Gentry Truman ever get his hair cut here?" I asked, bracing for the warm towel on the back of my neck. The moist eucalyptus steam was my favorite part and it enveloped me like a cloud.

"Are you kidding, Grif? Gentry Truman wouldn't set foot in here. He came in to pick up that stepson of his one afternoon, and you'd think he was having to wade through the manure pile in the barn."

I smiled. "So Dylan Klein gets his hair cut here?"

"Yep. Most guys on campus do. Good kid. Quiet, very studious, but I like him."

Walt peeled the white towel off my neck.

"What about Truman's brother, Cale Sanders?" I continued.

"Hmm, he came in only once, back when he first arrived in September. Now, there's a well-groomed man. He probably felt like this shop was beneath him, just like his brother, but he needed a cut before an interview and photo shoot with the campus arts magazine. He was a good sport. Talked about growing up down in Harpertown, about things that had changed in the county since he was here last."

"You like him, then?"

Walt was dusting his bristle-brush with talc. "Yes. And if you promise not to breathe a word, I'll tell you something about Mr. Cale Sanders." He shuffled in front of me and began brushing stray hairs off my forehead and neckline.

"He colors his hair." Walt smiled as our conversation came full circle.

Chapter Sixteen

REQUIEM

THE DIVINE CATHEDRAL was completed during a prosperous time for the university about thirty years ago. While the rest of the country wrestled with the Vietnam War and social unrest percolated on most college campuses, Avenell remained an isolated utopia of higher learning. Or, depending on whom you talked to, it cast blind eyes on anything but its own self-interests. I remember it with mixed emotions.

I was a junior that year when the expansion started over on the north side of campus—at first it looked like a bomb had shattered the old church—where unbeknownst then I would one day live in the rectory. I was grateful not to be in Vietnam but suffered the guilt conjured only by a minister's conscience. I knew at that point I would go into the ministry, already had my eye on various seminaries and graduate programs. My brother Tupper, a Marine helicopter pilot, reminded me of what real courage looked like, and my father never let me forget it. I still have not forgotten.

I hadn't thought of Tupper in some time, his absence superseded by my wife's, I suppose. Bea and I rarely discussed him or the way he died, not out of denial so much as out of the privacy of grief, the loneliness of losing a brother. Closer to his age than I was, Bea took his death especially hard. Killed by a sniper's bullet while on leave in Saigon. Not even killed in the line of duty, which, superficially speaking, would have made his death more noble. Just a Vietnamese madman sitting atop the Hotel Tai-Ling looking for American GIs to pick off. He shot three men and a Korean girl before being apprehended. Tupper rested, along with my parents, in the old Avenell Cemetery off Highway 9, next to the Mountain Ridge Methodist Church and the Natural Bridge.

Tupper's death in Vietnam was the main reason I've had such a love-hate relationship with the Divine: it conjures too many personal demons and bittersweet memories. But despite my personal associations with the place and its construction, it definitely captured the essence of God's house and rich Oxfordian tradition of a Christian university. During extraordinary growth and renovations, the board of trustees decided that the previous Church of the Divine was too small. The Martyr's Chapel had long since been abandoned, before World War I, I believe, as too colloquial and confining for the needs of a university the size and stature of Avenell. Thus, the original Divine became the main place of campus worship.

It served well and contained many artifacts, including an altar top—the mensa, it's called—and several pews and relics from its own predecessor, St. Xavier the Martyr's Chapel. However, with the university gaining recognition as a southern Ivy League school, and with the enrollment edging toward two thousand, the old Church of the Divine soon became too small as well.

So in the mid-'60s it was expanded. Five times as big as its predecessor and perhaps ten times the size of the Martyr's Chapel, the new cathedral would have all the modern conveniences—and yet the integrity of style—of the rest of campus. To accomplish this and to further distinguish the large church, architects redesigned it with the deliberate Gothic splendor of Magdalen Chapel at Oxford and Ely Cathedral in Britain's low country.

To elevate it from church to cathedral, political strings were pulled, and the Divine became the central church of the diocese, with the bishop moving diocesan headquarters here while simultaneously overtaking campus ministry. It proved highly impossible, of course, for the bishop to administrate and serve the entire diocese and still minister to the immediate needs of the parish. So in 1972, while I was in New York at Union Seminary, Bishop Hightower moved the diocesan house back to Nashville and the Divine remained a cathedral in name only. At its heart, it was still a small parish church enfleshed in the body of historical artifact.

Perhaps this combination is what I loved most about it. Most students and campus residents similarly shared my affection for the place. With the soaring Avenell campanile—the one photographed for all the catalogs and preview books sent to prospective freshmen—the kaleidoscopic rose window at the east end, the ivy-teased brownstone and patina copper window casings, the Divine Cathedral attracted as many tourists as worshipers. Its cavernous interior and rows and rows of cherrywood pews, Biedermeier chandelier lighting, and geometric marble altar offered a striking exemplar of aesthetic theology.

People liked it but did not always feel comfortable there; it was a bit disorienting in its spaciousness, too Gothic to be taken as anything but a museum or movie set. The Divine was the eccentric old uncle that everyone in the family loved affectionately but did not know how to relate to. My parish of four hundred probably would have moved off campus if the cathedral were not such an icon of Avenell.

Christmas and Easter services were always packed. Commencement ceremonies were also conducted there—which I secretly believed was the main reason the university maintained it. During the last decade the music program had adopted it and used its fine organ for concerts until finally they moved the entire department into new offices over off Ivy Circle. The Divine Cathedral was sepulchral and yet peaceful, a fitting paradox for Gentry Truman's memorial service.

The morning's preview held beautifully, not as warm as the Indian summer day before, but not as overcast and cool as last weekend. I had lingered in the barber shop to have coffee with Walt, Andy McDermott (the eight o'clock appointment), and Red Hollingsworth, our university sports director. Amazingly, no outsiders mobbed the place. But perhaps, I thought to myself, they knew we were talking about them.

"The media's still swarming thick as flies on road kill," said Andy casually from the barber's chair. Walt nodded, and Red and I searched for historical antecedents. The only comparable event we could recall was when President Clinton visited several years back to announce a new arts endowment. Just as then, every hotel, restaurant, and campground over-flowed like a spring flood from a river. Outside Walt's plate-glass window with neat blue-and-white painted letters, it looked like the inside of a Hollywood studio. Cables, cords, and satellite dishes crisscrossed the campus in a manner that reminded me of Gulliver's captivity by the Lil-liputians.

Andy and Red had all the latest gossip, and I indulged myself re-gretfully. Like myself, the young deputy had already been approached by half a dozen reporters, most with irreputable publications or programs, requesting interviews. I shared with them Bea's star watch yesterday, which yielded Diane Sawyer and Tom Brokaw crossing Blanton Lane. The whole town was abuzz. Walt had heard from Trudy at the bakery that gossip columnist Liz Smith had supposedly eaten breakfast this morning at the drugstore counter with opera diva Annetta Fielding. Red had heard from his brother Brent that director Peter Hammond and his latest love, actress Candace Anderson, were staying at the Eagle's Nest Inn off Highway 6. The only cab in Mumford, Bert Rawson's old Ford Thunderbird, had allegedly transported Ralph and Ricky Lauren from the Nashville airport because all the limo services were booked. The larg-est fare he'd ever charged, claimed Bert. Over a hundred dollars.

Now returning from the barber shop a little after nine, I saw the po-lice, county law enforcement, state agents, and National Guard working as busily as ants at a parish picnic to set up a barricade around the church. Rumor had it that mourners would have to show identification, which I did not, but only perhaps because Dan motioned me through.

I entered from the front to get an idea what impressions visiting mourners would gather. Obnoxious reporters already lined the barricade, mingling with law enforcement officers and shouting out questions to me as I marched up the burgundy-carpeted walk. They remained disembodied voices since I refused to dignify their requests with even a look over my shoulder.

"Can you tell us the order of service, Father Reed?" screamed the most polite of them.

"Is it true that you are Marcia's mystery lover?" demanded another.

As the mammoth door closed behind me, the clamor outside seemed no more than the drone of bees or the caw of a passing crow. Inside was like being in a fairy-tale castle, with quiet echoing from the rafters and buttresses. The chancel was bedecked with flowers from one end to another. True to Marcia's good taste, there were no random sprays of red carnations and floral stands of chrysanthemums, potted palms, and the like, the kinds of floral tributes indigenous to small town funerals. No, the church was adorned with the uniform splendor of a royal wedding. The choir loft, the cut-away rood screen, pulpit, slip pews, and side altars wore garlands of waxy green leaves, orchids, and calla lilies like bunting. The place smelled faint and sweet as French perfume and bore the attention to detail that I expected from the widow.

Oversized peace lilies in matte-finish burgundy pots anchored key altar points. Then a sight captured my gaze like a movie screen. In the chancel, centered before the trapezoidal high altar, stood an oil portrait of Gentry Truman by American artist Sinclair Van Reisling. Four feet by five, the legendary playwright, from the waist up, sat facing right, with bifocals held loosely in his left hand. His eyes and jawline were smooth and youthful, yet the silver-streaked hair and posture clearly reflected the older, celebrity Truman, the writer entitled to rest on his laurels. I could imagine Gentry instructing the famous artist on the image he wished to project. The same forethought had gone into the present spectacle. Resting on a golden easel draped with black cloth, it rose from a cloud of several dozen white roses. Lady Astors, if I was not mistaken, or maybe Belgium Snows.

The entire country was focused on little Avenell but would witness none of its true splendor, only the extremes—the image of Gentry the family wished to project or the sensational tabloid tales being fabricated outside the door.

Back home, by ten-thirty I had become more and more nervous about conducting the service. Cameras would not be allowed inside, thankfully, but the cathedral would be filled nonetheless with some of the most powerful and popular people in our country.

"You'll do fine, brother," Bea reassured as we slipped through security clearance at the back door at 11:05.

" 'I can do all things in him who strengthens me,' " I quoted.

"I'll see you after the service. And remember, wait for me before you head over to the Truman house. Security probably won't let me in without you!" Bea traipsed off in her new dark hunter knit, black purse and shoes, and our mother's diamond earrings. Dan Warren was saving her a seat on the fourth row behind the family and close friends.

I had made my own concessions to vanity—besides the haircut first thing this morning, I wore my best dark suit, just back from Tiger's Cleaners, and a new pair of wing tips from the Campus Men's Shop. My vestments were just as crisp and clean as the rest of me thanks to Bea. I figured I would feel more confident to lead the service if I felt good about my appearance. As I looked in the mirror in the vestry, however, Walt's cut could not hide my receding hairline, and my thick blond strands could not camouflage the wisps of silver.

———

At noon the tower bells rang twelve times, and by the last deep peal the din of low voices, coughing, whispering, and even laughing stopped. The string quartet played a selection from Bach, and then I came out in multilayers of black and white—black cassock, white alb, white stole, black biretta.

" 'I am the resurrection and the life; he who believes in me, though he die, yet shall he live, and whoever lives and believes in me shall never die.

" 'For I know that my Redeemer lives, and at last will stand upon the earth; and after my skin has been thus destroyed . . . I shall see God, whom I shall see on my side, and my eyes shall behold, and not another.

" 'For none of us lives to himself, and none of us dies to himself. If we live, we live to the Lord, and if we die, we die to the Lord, so then, whether we live or whether we die, we are the Lord's.'

"The Lord be with you."

"And with thy spirit," replied the multitude.

"Let us pray." In the brief moment I had looked up from my order of service, I counted a half-dozen celebrities surrounding Marcia and Truman's daughters, including a black-turbaned Liz Taylor, Elton John (dressed like a priest himself), and legendary Broadway actress Joan Plowright.

I felt very conscious of playing a part, of having descended into a role as I used my most sonorous tone: "O God, whose mercies cannot be numbered, accept our prayers on behalf of thy servant Gentry, and grant him peace according to thy perfect will. May he know the fellowship of the saints, through Jesus Christ thy Son our Lord, who liveth and reigneth with thee and the Holy Spirit, one God, now and forever. Amen."

The congregation sat, following the cues of those rows in front of them, and it reminded me of students doing the wave at university football games. A sea of fine dark suits, black-veiled ladies' hats, and pale, stoic faces washed up to me.

I climbed the handful of narrow, semicircular stairs to the elevated pulpit, a hand-carved, ancient oak fixture that had always reminded me of a giant chess pawn.

"A reading from the Old Testament, from the book of Isaiah. 'On this mountain the LORD of hosts will make for all peoples a feast of fat things, a feast of wines. . . . And he will destroy on this mountain the covering that is cast over all peoples, the veil that is spread over all nations. He will swallow up death for ever, and the LORD God will wipe away the tears from all faces, and the reproach of his people he will take away from all the earth; for the LORD has spoken.' "

I introduced Gentry's daughters and gave the briefest introduction for the various psalms they would read. The three women rose, dressed conservatively in black and navy high-necked dresses, and stood solemnly in front of the oversized portrait of their father. Jenna began with Psalm 42, her voice a bit shaky, but fluid nonetheless. She passed a large family Bible to her sister Lisa, who read select verses from Psalm 90. Her elegant voice captivated the mourners with its shimmering lilt. Finally, Lucy Truman concluded with verses from Psalm 139. Her words sounded clipped, hurried, but echoed powerfully nonetheless: " 'The darkness is not dark to thee, the night is as bright as the day; for darkness is as light with thee.' "

I stood and announced my readings from the New Testament and then the Gospel.

" 'Love is patient and kind; love is not jealous or boastful; it is not arrogant or rude; love does not insist on its own way; it is not irritable or resentful; it does not rejoice at wrong, but rejoices in the right. Love bears all things, believes all things, hopes all things, endures all things.

" 'Love never ends. . . . When I was a child, I spoke like a child, I thought like a child, I reasoned like a child; when I became a man, I gave up childish ways. For now we see in a mirror dimly, but then face to face. Now I know in part; then I shall understand fully, even as I have been fully understood. So faith, hope, love abide, these three; but the greatest of these is love.' "

"Thanks be to God," responded the congregation.

"A reading from the Gospel according to John."

I read from the eleventh chapter as Jesus traveled to Bethany to console Mary and Martha and to raise their brother Lazarus from the dead. " 'Jesus said, "Take away the stone." Martha, the sister of the dead man, said to him, "Lord, by this time there will be an odor, for he has been dead four days." Jesus said, "Did I not tell you that if you would believe you would see the glory of God?" So they took away the stone.' "

I stopped the story there, before Jesus goes on to call Lazarus forth from the tomb, deliberately. During the reading just then, I had reassembled my notes for the homily I had originally planned and decided to speak spontaneously. I felt God's spirit; it seemed the only thing to do.

"A terrible crime occurred a week ago," I began. "A serious loss that shocks us all, that causes all of us to ask ourselves how something of this kind could happen in our small, peaceful community." Silence, the most quiet the crowd had been for the entire service. A cough, a child's voice. "But I assure you all that our God is still sovereign and that our community and our faith, while shaken, will remain firmly intact."

A flood of words washed from me to this odd assorted audience of family, friends, celebrities, law enforcement, and curiosity seekers. I shared briefly about my own wife's dying, about the kind of grief that ensues, the depth of sorrow. I encouraged forgiveness for those who harbored grudges against Gentry Truman, just as Paul instructed us to endure through love in Corinthians. And I emphasized Jesus' question to Martha: "Did I not tell you that if you have faith you will see the glory of God?"

"Although Gentry is not likely to walk back into our midst right now," I explained, "we trust that through our faith in God's goodness, we will know what led to Gentry's death. Jesus told us that we would know the truth and it would set us free. We may see through a glass darkly now, through opaque glimpses of shadows and smoke, but the truth will come out. And the truth may prove painful. But God will not forsake us, nor abandon us. 'I believe that I shall see the goodness of the LORD in the land of the living!' writes the psalmist. 'Wait for the LORD, be strong, and let your heart take courage, yea, wait for the LORD.'

"Let us pray. Almighty God, grant to all who mourn a sure confidence in thy fatherly care, that, casting their grief on thee, they may know the consolation of thy love. Give courage and faith to those who are bereaved, that they may have strength to meet the days ahead in the comfort of a reasonable and holy hope, in the joyful expectation of eternal life with those they love. Help us, we pray, in the midst of things we cannot understand, to believe and trust in the communion of saints, the forgiveness of sins, and the resurrection to life everlasting. Amen."

"Amen," murmured the congregation.

The service was almost over and had gone remarkably well. I sighed in relief as I seated myself, feeling like a coach awaiting the final victorious moments of the game. Annetta Fielding's rich rendition of "Amazing Grace" and "O! Sweet Freedom" enveloped me in a golden embrace of longing for the final peace of heaven. Perched on the ornate, thronelike sedile, or presider's chair, I wept discreetly, surprised but delighted that the rich music could penetrate my performance mind-set enough to reach me. Amy's lovely face came to mind, dreamlike, far away. It troubled me that I couldn't bring her features into sharp focus in my mental camera. Was I forgetting what she looked like? How odd it felt for such a personal grief to surface in such a public setting.

Although I knew the service like the order of the Beatitudes, I still looked at the parchment program to make sure that nothing had been omitted. Yes, the last order of service; it was time for Marcia's eulogy of her husband. Cale Sanders was still nowhere to be seen. Was he so sick that he could not attend his brother's funeral? Or—the thought darted to mind—sick at conscience that he could not bear the weight of stares and probing eyes?

The Widow Truman rose carefully, as if balancing a book on her head, wearing a smart black dress that, without her black pillbox and lacy veil, would have been stunning at a cocktail party. Lisa Chandler and Lucy Truman watched her attentively with moist eyes. Young Jenna seemed distracted, restless, uncomfortable, fidgeting like a five-year-old. I silently prayed for her relief. Florence Lipton, in a royal purple suit, sat woodenly beside Casey Atwood, who looked particularly despondent. Dylan Klein sat with another young man, presumably about his age, in stern black suits, white shirts, and gray Windsor knots at their throats. Franklin Milford sat with several university trustees alongside Bea, Dan, and several other plainclothes guardians. Numerous movie stars looked oddly out of place, uncomfortable. There were the Laurens. Martin Scorsese. Lauren Bacall.

All were visibly tense as Marcia paused in front of Gentry's portrait. A moment of silence? Inspiration? Respect? After thirty awkward seconds, she ascended the pulpit in her short black dress. She carried a black leather portfolio from which she extracted a single page of typed print. She looked tired, shoulders rounded, defeated by her task.

I continued to scan the packed cathedral for recognizable mourners — either from passing them on the streets here in Avenell, or from their photographs on magazine covers in Walt's barber shop or grocery checkout aisles. Michelle Meadows, fashion diva since Jackie Kennedy's White House days, whispered nervously to Calvin Klein, a second cousin of Marcia Klein Truman's. Various established entertainment reporters, gossip columnists, and news anchors were spiked throughout the throng. Several Broadway directors and producers—there was Neil Simon—and several dozen actresses and actors of stage and screen had all turned out to pay tribute to a man who had died less than two miles away in the intimacy of one of my favorite places in the world.

There was, of course, the unseen presence of the ravenous pack of reporters and the morbidly curious waiting outside the doors. But even the nervous tension they produced paled next to the hold-your-breath moment just prior to Marcia's first word.

"Gentry is pleased that we are all here together to honor his memory." Her lips formed a thin, nervous smile, mirrored by anxious smiles from the rest of us. "What happened a few days ago continues to astound us all. As Father Reed reminded us so eloquently, we hope and pray for justice as much as—or more than—the character of Tenny in Gent's *Breakfast in Birmingham*." She continued by reading that character's impassioned monologue for racial integration, then went on to a passage from his work-in-progress, *Chameleon*.

As Marcia maintained a certain doleful poise, praising her husband's talent, sharing anecdotes of endurance from Gentry's impoverished childhood, of the excesses of success and good fortune, I was struck by the genuine love in her voice.

I reflected on our chats throughout the week, her concern over what I might think of her, of Gentry, even of Cale. Of course, I expected the widow to speak fondly of the deceased today, but that did not necessitate an authentic compassion. Marcia Klein Truman spoke eloquently, lovingly of Gentry Truman with a care lavished only on those securely re-moved from future conflict by death. She daubed her eyes with a corner of white linen at appropriate moments but remained in control of her voice and mournful eyes.

Stealing a glance at my watch, I caught Jenna Truman's expression out of the corner of my vision. Simply put, she writhed. She obviously did not believe a word from her stepmother's mouth. Curiously enough, just at that moment, as Marcia began to draw her praise to an end after twenty minutes, the deceased's youngest daughter stood and screamed, "No! Daddy's alive! I saw him!"

Florence Lipton peeped a tiny scream like a frightened animal.

Marcia froze in mid-sentence.

Just then, lovely Jenna, long, curly tresses pulled back in a sweeping bundle at her neck, faltered and collapsed.

Chapter Seventeen

WAKING THE DEAD

—————

LOW CHATTER DRIFTED through the vast cathedral like reluctant prayers. Just minutes ago, Jenna had read her choice of Psalm 42 quite calmly. She had seemed shaken but sturdier than the other night. What could have prompted her scream and declaration that her father was alive? Her father's ghost again? Her stepmother's fulsome remarks? Her own sense of loss? Lack of medication . . . or perhaps overmedication?

Questions fired like angry flares. My mind scrambled for possible interventions just as Casey Atwood finally stood and demanded, "Doctor! Anyone here a doctor?"

I felt the throb of tension bubble in my temples—my precursor to a migraine. I felt responsible. I should be doing something. I rose and took a wobbly step toward the crumpled Jenna, feeling as weak as she had appeared in those thick moments before collapse. Florence Lipton knelt beside the young woman and cried out. A man in a blue suit with horn-rimmed glasses stood and jostled his way out of his pew row and sprinted down the center aisle.

Marcia stepped down toward the family, now clustered around the young woman and doctor. The murmur of voices rose to a barroom din. Finally Dylan burst out, "She's okay! She's gonna be all right!" With the doctor's help and Ms. Lipton's arm around her, Jenna Truman emerged and was led off through the vestry door behind the right side altar. The bride's room, next to the vestment room, was equipped with a sofa and vanity. Both sisters followed, and it appeared Dylan Klein would, as well, until his mother whispered in his ear and he reseated himself.

Order began to return and eyes focused on me once more, despite continued murmurs and whispers echoing through the lofty church. Suddenly I felt a supernatural sense of clarity and command. Only the committal and the Glasgow Bagpipers remained of the service. I caught sight of Joan Dowinger nestled next to an elderly gentleman who resembled Colonel Harlan Sanders, the fried chicken magnate from years gone by. Presumably, this was Peyton Fentriss, the famous renovation architect. I did not let her piercing eyes, or her own personal quest, deter my focus.

"Please, please. Jenna will be just fine. . . ." I declared as quiet ensued. "Let us conclude our commitment of Gentry Truman into our Father's hands. Amidst the traumatic and disheartening circumstances of his death, we remain confident of the joy and peace that comes from the certainty the Apostle Paul explains in Romans. With him we are 'sure that neither death, nor life, nor angels, nor principalities, nor things present, nor things to come, nor powers, nor height, nor depth, nor anything else in creation, will be able to separate us from the love of God in Christ Jesus our Lord.' It is in this confidence of faith and hope that we lovingly release our brother Gentry into the presence of God. Let us pray."

I prayed mostly for comfort and healing during the grief process for the family. Like my conclusion, I made it brief and to the point. The Glasgow Bagpipers sensed the same urgency and began wailing the mournful postlude immediately on the second syllable of my amen. I did not recognize the rich Scottish tune echoing back and again from the stone arches and high rafters, but the sound was smooth, melancholy, resilient—music the color of dark amber.

As soon as the last note eked from the bagpipes like a dying breath, a cacophony of anxious voices immediately arose. Marcia Truman looked pleased at my restoration of order. Recalling her compliment of my homily in her opening remarks of the eulogy, I exited the side door and was quickly followed by most of the first three rows.

"Father, I apologize for Jenna's behavior. I thought she was feeling up to the service, thought she needed the sense of closure it might bring to this horrible business. I'm sorry she disrupted the service. You handled it very well," whispered the widowed actress. The essence of her perfume quickly filled the small bride's room like incense. I felt dizzy.

"Please, don't apologize. It's perfectly understandable. A daughter's grief, especially in one as young as Jenna—why, it's perfectly normal," I said, instantly annoyed that Mrs. Truman cared more about the performance than her stepdaughter's well-being.

Family members, friends, and a few of the celebrity mourners orbited the bride's room like stray satellites. I found myself in the way and decided I would return to the main vestry and wait. As I slipped away amid the hum of voices and growing throng, I felt a hand at my elbow.

"Dylan? Can I help you? Is there anything I can do for Jenna?" I asked. The widow's son had been blessed with his mother's fine cheekbones and piercing blue eyes. His dark hair, cut stylishly short, framed a square jawed face that seemed bound for the cameras of Hollywood someday.

"Father Reed, Mother wants me to make sure you're coming back to the house—for the reception of family and close friends. You know, a kind of party in honor of Gent. You're coming, right?" He seemed breathless and genuinely eager for my attendance.

"Yes, of course. I accepted your mother's invitation last night. My sister and I will be along shortly. Thank you, Dylan. How is Jenna?" I anticipated getting a straight answer from him, eager to avoid more positive spin generated by Marcia or even Jenna's sisters.

"She seems to be coming around just fine. She's . . . she's had a tough time of it with her father's death and all." He fidgeted with a tuft of dark hair above his ear and smiled up at me.

"And how is your Uncle Cale feeling? I'm sure he was disappointed he couldn't make it to the service." I could still hear voices and the sharp staccato rhythm of high heels and wing tips on the marbled floor out in the chancel.

"He's fine. I don't know what that's all about—he and Mom ar—" He caught himself short, some mental alarm tripped by his disclosure.

He and Mom ar*gued*? I questioned to myself.

Dylan looked over his shoulder and acknowledged the presence of a young blond woman who had just passed us in the hall. "Hey, gotta go! See you at the house!" He bounded after her.

In the main vestry room, Dan Warren and my sister greeted me warmly. I closed the heavy door behind me and began to remove my zebra-layered vestments.

"You were simply marvelous, Grif," gushed Bea, reaching up to hug my shoulder.

"Good job, Padre," Dan chimed in. "You handled that with grace. Grace under pressure."

"Well, Jenna's fainting spell certainly took us all by surprise—things had gone so smoothly until then." I sounded as concerned about appearances as Marcia. "How is she? What do you think prompted her outburst?" My heartbeat was finally returning to stasis, to the even rhythm it employed when not flooded by adrenaline. I lifted a wire hanger from the wardrobe and began to hang my garments.

"Here, let me do that," said Bea. "You never hang things up straight. It leaves pucker marks in the shoulders." I smiled and deferred to my sister's expertise.

"She's fine. The Good Samaritan doc said she checked out fine. Some paramedics are taking her to Carroll County General just to play it safe, though." Dan looked uncomfortable in his gray-pinstripe suit, white shirt, and solid navy tie.

"I hope it's nothing serious," echoed Bea.

"So how did things go on your end?" I asked Dan.

"Pretty smooth. The usual bomb threats and a couple of psycho notes, but nothing that's likely related to Truman's death. Nothing any other celebrity's death wouldn't have attracted," he replied. I smelled mint and noticed he was chewing gum. I was proud of him for not resuming his nicotine habit during the pressures of this case. If there were a case to make one want to smoke, this was certainly it.

"So is there a wake at the house or not?" Bea inquired. "Do you know how handsome you look in a suit and tie, Dan Warren? Absolutely stunning. You should wear one more often."

Dan grinned like a little boy reciting a verse in Sunday school. "Aw, Miss Bea." He shrugged and loosened his collar. "Why do they call it a wake anyway? Gentry Truman won't be waking up for a long time."

"I believe it started as a vigil over the body, a time of grieving, I suppose, before the actual burial. That was before funeral homes and crematoriums like today," Bea informed. "So are we waking the dead or not?"

"Yes, we are—that is, you may still come with me if you promise to be on your best behavior. No questions to anyone about the possibility of murder, no snooping around the house, looking in bedrooms or behind closed doors. Best behavior." My voice stood firm in the windowless room.

"I'll be there, too, for security," said Dan. "It lets me keep an eye on both of you, as well." He winked.

My sister did not seem surprised by my conditions and pleased me by not being coy.

"Of course, Grif. I will be an exceptional guest. No questions, no snooping." She began to smooth a strand of gray hair back into its proper place beneath the elegant chignon above her neck. She tugged at her dark verdant dress, smoothing it, as well, and removed a lipstick from a small black purse, her church purse she called it. It was the antithesis of the large shoulder satchel she carried for everyday use. She moistened her lips together to smooth the pale fuchsia and smiled up at me.

"Waking the dead is a strange custom," I pronounced.

By two o'clock when we arrived, the Truman house looked and

sounded more like a fraternity party than a memorial reception. Bea counted eight limousines and a matchbox-car assortment of Jaguars, Mercedes, BMWs, and a Lexus surrounding the quaint neighborhood more accustomed to ten-year-old Subarus and dented station wagons. The house itself seemed the opposite of the ominous, claustrophobically cozy space I had visited for the past two nights. As we were ushered by Jeanette into the entryway, I realized how large the house really was—probably twice the size of the rectory, which was a generous two thousand square feet including the basement.

I recalled the major renovations that the Trumans had undertaken, even though the writer-in-residence fellowship was only a one-year stint. The search for the house itself had been a quest for the holy grail. According to Bea, Marcia refused to live in our fine collegiate town and voted instead for a Nashville townhouse or one of Atlanta's posh Buckhead estates. Gentry would have neither and commanded a team of realtors to scour the county for the perfect homesite. One of my personal favorites, the old Mayfield place, became his bull's-eye.

Truckloads of renovators—hardwood floor refinishers, plumbers and tilers, electricians and New York interior designers—swarmed the site like a honeycomb for the summer months before the Trumans arrived in August. The finishing touch had been the pink exterior paint with white trim, a bold move causing quite a scandal among the more pedestrian homeowners and campus busybodies, not to mention my sister. I secretly liked the pastel distinction, the gingerbread colors softening the intensity of the large three-story house.

Inside it now we were drafted into the crowded reception, which appeared part cocktail party and part New Orleans jazz funeral. Voices blended and chimed with orchestral rhythm and diversity. Glasses toasted, classical music—Wagner?—played softly, someone's tears subsided in one room while laughter emanated from another. It reminded me of an old-fashioned house party, the kind our parents threw when someone bought a new home or moved into the community. The entire downstairs had been opened up, and the midafternoon sun flourished golden auras around us all. Fresh flowers—more orchids, lilies, and roses in arrangements matching those at the service—adorned most tables and pedestals. A buffet had been set out in the formal dining room, and I found myself in line behind Casey Atwood, who was talking to director Robert Altman.

Bea's mouth vacillated between an O of awestruck wonder and a tight line of disapproval at such extravagant furnishings.

"Would you look at all this food? Fresh asparagus—in November! Now that's a pretty penny, flown in no doubt from some organic greenhouse in California!" whispered Bea. "Be careful of the meat, Grif—you never know when E. coli may be lurking in food you didn't prepare yourself!"

I rolled my eyes and mouthed a *shh* to my sister. I doubted that these caterers, imported from Atlanta, would not know how to prepare their wares.

The spread was indeed an Epicurean feast—artichoke canapés, fresh shrimp with a cocktail sauce containing lemon rind, roast beef, crudités and dips, fresh fruits, and chocolate fondues.

"I see your concern over the expense isn't keeping you from enjoying the asparagus," I said.

"Hmph," murmured my sister, turning her back to me. I followed her through the dining room to another parlor, one that complemented the masculine plaids and dark rich jewel tones of the room I knew from my prior visits with pastels and paisley, lace and chintz. This must be the room where Jenna had bared her grief to Peter on Monday night.

"Look at those Waverly drapes, Grif—that's several thousand dollars you're looking at."

Various people milled and chatted in small islands of conversation. Some stood and formed a closed circle while others sat discreetly on the cream colored sofas and Windsor chairs brought in from the dining room. I didn't recognize any family and realized that I was probably just as curious as my sister about this household. Only my interests centered on the relationships and personal dynamics, while hers fell on asparagus and the cost of drapes.

I listened to words and phrases float in and around the room. Several conversations referenced the outburst and faint by Jenna Truman, but none seemed to offer sound reasoning as to its cause. Dylan Klein wandered in and lifted his drink in my direction with a smile. Lucy Truman appeared and began chatting with a gray-haired woman in a black chiffon dress. I wondered if the woman could possibly be her mother.

So many curious relationships. My discomfort waned, and I began to realize I would be free to leave shortly. I would make a call later in the week to inquire about the grieving process and general spiritual well-being of the family, but I could not imagine that I could be of further use right now. Young Jenna crossed my mind as the only exception. Perhaps I should try to visit her in the hospital tonight. Or, I hoped, she would be released and be free to come home. It was unlikely, but possible, that she had already returned.

I was just about to inquire after her when I noticed a framed original pen-and-ink sketch above the white enamel mantel. It was a caricature of Gentry Truman, with an exaggerated wide forehead and deep-set eyes, a prominent chin, and scraggly goatee. It was signed by Hirschfield.

"Al did that for Gentry probably twenty years ago," someone said.

I looked up and found myself face-to-face with Casey Atwood, who dripped clam dip from a wheat cracker.

"A fine service, Father. I appreciated your sense of pace, your sensitivity to both Gentry's personality and to the Church. Not an easy balance to create," he said, wiping his mouth.

"Thank you, Mr. Atwood. It's not always easy, but I try to respect the family's wishes as best I can." He was a square, heavyset little man, a solid block of fierce determination with a shock of salt-and-pepper hair tracing the circumference of his otherwise bald head. "Did you know Mr. Truman's spiritual views very well? It's apparent from his work that he certainly wrestled with the great faith questions that plague us all."

"You're being kind, Father," smiled the agent. "You and I both know that Gentry Truman's personal spirituality could be fit on the head of a pin."

"I don't presume such about anyone's faith," I replied.

"He was an angry man, Father, a man full of rage. Between you and me, I don't think he ever got over his childhood—being abandoned by both his father and his mother. Forgive me for speaking ill of the dead, Father Reed, but Gentry Truman was a pathetic egotist most of the time."

"So you two had a difficult working relationship?" I recalled Florence Lipton's comments about her employer.

"Ha! You could say that! You obviously don't read the trade papers . . . no, of course you don't. Gentry fires me about once a month and then begs me to come back and revive his career. We had a marriage of convenience, basically."

"Were the two of you getting along well recently—if I may ask?"

"You workin' with the cops now? No, you can ask. It's coming out sooner than later anyway. Gent showed up for our Friday lunch appointment totally sauced." He swallowed the last of his cracker and wiped crumbs on a cloth napkin. "I've got a publisher and two Broadway producers waitin' on this latest masterpiece of his, not to mention Cale Sanders and the university theater company. They've been rehearsin' on a premise and a handful of unfinished scenes since September."

"Writer's block?" I asked.

"Yeah, you could say that. Gent was one of those prima donna writers who always believed that he could only write when everything in his life was going well. Of course, the best stuff he ever wrote was during the worst periods of his life. Go figure. So he shows up Friday for our meeting and still doesn't have the manuscript finished. I've stalled the publishers and producers beyond the limits—this was the fourth missed deadline. He started blaming me for not getting him a better deal with more time and more money. It degenerated into an ugly name-calling match. It ended with him firing me. I was scheduled to fly back to New York on Saturday afternoon, but then with his death and all . . . here I am."

The short, squat man fidgeted with his napkin, and his energy reminded me of a boxer's—direct, fierce, predictably unexpected. All traits that probably made him the great agent that he was.

"I see. I'm sorry that your last time with Gentry had to end so poorly," I said.

"Yeah, so am I. And now I'm stuck in this burg until at least tomorrow—more questions from the cops. It wasn't hard to find witnesses from the restaurant in Mumford where we had lunch who heard us both say some pretty nasty things to one another," he replied and skewered a shrimp with an hors d'oeuvre pick.

I looked around the room for Bea and found her sitting on a floral print sofa with Florence Lipton. The two of them chatted with an elderly black woman whom I did not recognize.

"You ever do any writing, Father?" asked Atwood.

"Well, yes. Mostly poetry, theological articles, that sort of thing," I replied modestly.

"Think you could write up an account of this thing from your perspective? I could sell it for you in a heartbeat," he said.

"I don't think that's the kind of writing to which I'm called, Mr. Atwood."

"Listen, don't look down on it. True crime sells. John Berendt. Ann Rule. Edna Buchanan. Nothing wrong with you making some money for yourself and the church—"

"If you'll excuse me," I interrupted.

"Think it over. Here's my card. Call me anytime, and we can do lunch and discuss." He flourished a small ivory card from a jacket pocket and placed it in my hand before I could refuse.

"Thank you, I'll do that."

I returned to the dining room for a cup of coffee and a sliver of the New York–style cheesecake that was now being served.

"This was Gentry's absolute favorite," I overhead Marcia tell a man wearing small round sunglasses. "It's from that deli at the corner of

Broadway and 24th—we had them make a dozen last night."

I circled the maze of rooms in hopes of finding Jenna Truman or Cale Sanders and instead found each quarter to have its own unique character of attendants—the front parlor seemed rather somber, the music room lively and jovial, the sun room nostalgic and wistful. I recalled Poe's story "The Masque of the Red Death" and shivered involuntarily.

Back in the sitting room, Mr. Atwood was nowhere to be seen, so I joined my sister on the sofa.

"Grif, there you are. I believe you already know Florence Lipton," she said.

The woman extended her hand and we shook firmly. Florence Lipton looked elegantly stylish in her deep violet suit, yet her rimless spectacles reinforced a professional or academic disposition. The glasses also made her appear older from a distance she was likely a good ten years younger than me. She wore a double strand of pearls with an amethyst clasp.

"It's wonderful to see you, Father Reed," she beamed. "I've enjoyed your services for some time now. I'm sorry we haven't met sooner."

So . . . she had decided not to confess her embezzlement to the police. Bea blushed at her new friend's lie, and I felt uncomfortable myself. But I played along.

"Likewise, Ms. Lipton," I returned. "Where did you move from?"

"New York. I was Gentry's personal assistant—a glorified secretary, you might say." She sipped from a cobalt demitasse. Her voice seemed louder than necessary, as if she wanted to impress or inform those around us of her relationship to the decedent.

My eyes drifted to Bea's once more and then to the third woman.

"And this is Mrs. Delthenia Witherspoon, Griffin. She took care of Gentry Truman and his brother when they were boys. She lived next door to Mrs. Lucy Gail Sanders, Gentry's grandmother," explained my sister.

The small woman looked like a tiny princess seated atop the richly textured cushions. Her crinkled skin was a rich ebony, smooth as a sheet of foil crumpled and then unfolded. Her dark eyes shone behind heavy lids; she appeared quite regal with her crown of foam-white hair. I extended my hand in return to hers. It was as firm as Ms. Lipton's, although she had to be in her nineties.

"My friends call me Miss Del—you do the same. You done a good job with Mr. Gent's service, Father, I'm here to tell you," she said and shook her head. "He was a wild one from the day he was born, but that don't keep none of us from deservin' a proper burial. I sure wish Aunt Olive could've been there."

"Yes, ma'am, I agree. We're all the same in our Lord's eyes," I said. "How long did you know Gentry as a boy, Miss Del?"

"Oh Lawdy. I knew Gentry from the day he's born—I was there with his grandmama when his mama give him life. I lived next door to Miss Lucy all my life. Still live in that house. I helped raise that boy—him and Mr. Cale both."

I beamed encouragement for her to continue. "Were they very close growing up?"

My question halted her pleasant memory, and she turned and faced me squarely.

She leaned forward. "Fought all the time because they was so much alike. Those boys mighty close growin' up. It hit Mr. Cale somethin' hard when Gentry up and left and headed off to the city."

"I read somewhere that it created quite a rift between them—one that never quite healed," said my sister.

"Uh-huh. I suspect Mr. Gent getting all rich and famous didn't help much, either," said the old woman. "Mr. Cale, he stuck here and took care of Miss Lucy till she died 'fore he went off to the city and joined the stage. Fortune ain't smiled on him like it did Mr. Gentry."

Just then a giant of a man entered the room purposefully and approached our group. "Father Reed? I'm James McDonnell, Gentry Truman's attorney. May I speak to you—in private?" He extended his hand.

Ms. Lipton drained the last of her espresso, and Bea looked Mr. McDonnell up and down. Miss Del cast her own shrewd eyes over the lawyer's erect figure.

"Certainly. Is anything wrong, Mr. McDonnell?" I rose and shook his hand.

"No, no, not at all. Forgive me for alarming you. It's simply a brief business matter, that's all." He wore an expensive tailored suit, conservative chalk-stripes, and blue shirt with a red tie. "Please finish your conversation here, then meet me in the library—upstairs, second left—before you depart." He forced his lips upward and exited like a messenger having delivered his only line.

"Ladies, if you'll excuse me," I said. "A pleasure to meet you both."

"I hope to see you again soon, Father," replied Miss Del cryptically.

As I left the room to discover the library, Bea's voice trailed, "We'll have to have you over some Sunday after church, Florence." I wondered what had happened to my sister's wait-and-see-if-she's-a-murderer policy. Anything to get me dating again, I supposed.

Lisa Chandler brushed past me and glanced around the foyer hurriedly before moving on to the dining room. The crowd had thinned slightly, and in the main landing I found several veteran actors regaling one another with apocryphal tales of Gentry Truman's theater days. For some reason I expected Cale Sanders to be among them, but he was not. In fact, no one had seen him all day. I glanced into the parlor, where a superfluous fire burned in the stone hearth, and saw Marcia staring into the eyes of Franklin Milford. They sat a respectable distance apart, but there was no denying the love on her face. There, finally, stood Jenna Truman at the window with Lucy Truman beside her, both equally lost in the late sunlight spilling down the mountain. I was shocked that she was home, let alone that she wasn't lying down. Hoping she would be there when I returned, I checked my watch and couldn't believe it was almost five.

I could not imagine what Truman's attorney could want with me. Perhaps he had questions about the family and didn't feel comfortable asking them. He might be under the impression that I was closer to the family than I actually was. Perhaps he wanted me to assist with the family tensions that would likely arise when Gentry's will would be read. My imagination wandered once again over the chessboard of beneficiaries and the immense legacy they would inherit.

The second door on the left, he'd said, which I presumed to be next to Jenna's room. Although my hearing was impeccable, I could not help but seize the opportunity before me. I turned the knob of the first door on my right—Gentry Truman's room, where his youngest child, like a modern Hamlet, had seen his ghost. Locked. At least I tried.

"In here, Father Reed," said McDonnell sharply.

"I couldn't recall which room you said, Mr. McDonnell," I said while praying for forgiveness simultaneously.

"It will only take a second," he said as he ushered me into a posh room that virtually gleamed with books on black shelves against fluorescent white walls and chrome chairs. The only color leapt from the right wall, which held a floor-to-ceiling matrix of framed magazine covers, theater programs, and book jackets: *Theater Arts, Playbill, Actor's Art, Playwright,* and *Stage,* along with *People, Time, Vanity Fair, GQ, Esquire, Atlantic Monthly, Harper's,* and *The New Yorker.* Photographs and drawings from over four decades in vibrant colors—scarlet, magenta, yellow—as rich and varied as Gentry Truman's career.

I was about to scan the bookshelves, since you can tell so much about a person by what he reads, when the attorney led me to a black leather sofa.

"Sorry to make such a fuss, Father. I simply need to make sure that you can be present on this Monday, November ninth, for the reading of Gentry Truman's last will and testament. My office is located in Atlanta, but the reading will be held in the Trustees Room in the Mary Bartlett Building here on campus."

"I don't understand, Mr. McDonnell. Is there some way I can be of assistance? Did the family request my presence?" I peered into his bloodshot eyes.

"No, Father Reed. I can't disclose more than this, so please don't ask me to. Your presence is necessary because you are one of the beneficiaries in Gentry Truman's will."

Chapter Eighteen

FALSE PRETENSES

———

Saturday morning my body ached, and I awoke with a slight fever. It reminded me of the weary, morning-after effects I'd experienced from all-night youth retreats. Only this morning's ailment brought along congestion and a killer headache. I had averted the migraine I expected after yesterday's traumatic service, but my sense that something was attacking my body's immune system had been right on track.

I had told no one about McDonnell's information and presumed that not even the family knew about my inclusion in Gentry Truman's will. Bea had asked on the way home what the lawyer wanted, and I replied vaguely, "To seek my assistance in a family matter." She did not press my dodge, and I was grateful.

Peter had called last night and asked to borrow my car, which of course he could. I called him first thing this morning and asked if he would drop me off at Doc Graham's on his way to his destination. Bea could pick me up afterward by borrowing Joe Brewer's truck. Our parish sexton would be busy today, cleaning up and taking apart the carefully orchestrated service's remnants. Most of the floral arrangements had been donated to the parish in Gentry's name, eclipsing the decorations the church usually had for Christmas.

When Peter picked me up a little before nine, I still couldn't decide if this was a cold, the flu, or simply my allergies catching up with the waning season. He complimented me again on the service and asked about the reception. I filled him in on the details and concluded with the announcement about Truman's will.

"You'll be rich," he smiled. "Now you and Joan Dowinger can co-lead that country club Bible study she's been trying to get off the ground."

"Very funny. Somehow I can't see Gentry Truman leaving me any money. More likely it's a kind gesture, maybe a signed script or something. It is curious, though, since he had to have amended his will this fall to include me. We had never met before September. Makes me wonder if perhaps he did kill himself, had planned it all along. I wonder what other changes he made."

"You'll find out Monday afternoon," Pete said. "I hope you're feeling better. My guess is you're just stressed out. What a week!"

"That's what Bea said. We'll see what Doc Graham thinks." We were approaching the main intersection of Southern Avenue and Highway 9. Most of the TV crews, celebrity mourners, and tabloid reporters had left last night or were departing today. This morning only a dozen trailers and satellite hook-ups remained on the streets. Crushed flowers, crumpled newspapers, beer cans, and fast-food bags were being collected this morning by various teams of volunteers. A group of students from our own parish, familiar with my big blue Buick, waved to us as we passed by. The town had been stressed, as well, and now the mood reflected the melancholy bittersweetness, as when the carnival has moved on to the next town.

"Where are you off to this morning?" I asked. "Are you still on for tomorrow's service?" My curate had volunteered to celebrate the Eucharist with me tomorrow and deliver the homily.

"Absolutely. You've done enough consoling and preparing and preaching this week. Besides, you're sick." He slowed at the main light and waved to Mr. Spradley setting up baskets of squash, late corn, and winesap apples outside his store.

"Lots of errands today?" I asked for the second time. I didn't usually pry, but I had a growing suspicion of my young friend's destination.

"You could say that." Peter looked over at me and smiled. "I might as well tell you. I'm going down to Tremont to visit Leah Schroeder and her family."

"Ah," I said. "Somehow I thought that might be where you were headed."

"If you'd rather I didn't drive the car that far . . ."

"Don't be ridiculous," I declared. "What's mine is yours. Of course you can take the car."

He pulled into the asphalt parking lot beside the brick building that housed the office of Dr. Harrison G. Graham, M.D., M.E.

"I know you're trying to protect me, but I thought learning more about Amish culture and theology firsthand would make an incredible article for *Avenell Theological Quarterly*." The car idled and I heard a slight miss in the timing—was it due for a tune-up already?

"Yes, it would. But, Peter, you don't have to have a reason. I'm glad you want to see Leah Schroeder again. Just be careful. I can't imagine that her parents approve."

"They don't know I'm coming—yet." He smiled a devilishly playful grin, his blond hair tousled like wheat in a windstorm.

"Be careful and enjoy yourself," I said, letting myself out.

"I should be back by supper, if you won't need the car," Pete replied.

"That's fine. I'll tell Bea to set your place. If you're going to be late, give us a call. Otherwise, I'll see you tonight."

I watched from the large bay window in the waiting area as my curate sped off down the highway trailing a stream of tan dust and dry, brittle leaves.

Marge Johnston checked me off her list and chided me again for not having an appointment. I had bypassed her that morning and spoken directly with Harry, who of course invited me to come on down as a walk-in. The wait was only fifteen minutes, time enough for me to skim a special edition of the *Clarion* as well as the *Tennessean* and *Atlanta Constitution*. All three commented on the Hollywood aura surrounding Gentry's memorial, credited me for its tastefulness and sanctity, and recounted in sensationalist details the youngest Truman daughter's breakdown. "Gentry's Daughter Communes with Departed Daddy Dearest!" screamed the headline of the *National Examiner*, a tabloid being read by a young mother with a sniffling toddler across from me.

"This is supposed to be my coffee break," said Doc Graham as he ushered me back to one of his three examining rooms. "Margie's still pouting because you didn't schedule with her."

"I'm sorry, Harry," I said. "But I was afraid she wouldn't get me in for two weeks if I told her my symptoms."

"I'll bet she wouldn't," my old friend laughed. He looked tired, multiple creases ironed beneath his alert eyes. Worry lines ebbed from his forehead to his bald head like waves on a beach. A long handlebar mustache, which Harry often waxed for special occasions, reinforced his old-fashioned, no-nonsense demeanor.

Since it was a Saturday, his nurse Judy Bishop had the day off, and he took my weight, temperature, and blood pressure himself. I unbuttoned my shirt and he listened to me breathe through the cold metal stethoscope.

"No major congestion," he said. "Blood pressure's a little high. Fever of ninety-nine point five. I'd say you're exhausted from all the prayin' and sleuthin' Sam Claiborne's got you doing."

I chuckled. "What's he been telling you?"

"Only that you're helpin' him out. That you talked to Stinky Baxter and helped make some sense of his ramblings."

"Just trying to help where I can. I'm certainly not trying to play detective."

"Whatever you say." He smiled.

"I heard the body hasn't been released to the family yet," I said, recalling Marcia's urgent tone on Thursday night.

"Nope, probably won't be for at least another week. My part's done, though."

"Meaning? It's up to the state examiner now?" I asked.

"Yep. Dr. Lang from Memphis is officially in charge." He scribbled notes on my chart with his left hand crooked over the clipboard. He then dashed off his signature on a prewritten prescription pad, ripped it free, and placed it in my hand in one fluid motion. "Take these twice a day, drink a half-gallon of mountain spring water each day, and you'll feel like a teenager in a week."

"Looks like an antihistamine, vitamin C, and—what's that?"

"Zinc lozenges. There's still controversy over their effectiveness, but the wife swears by 'em. You got a cold is all, Father Grif."

Fumbling with the buttons on my denim shirt, I felt embarrassed for inconveniencing him for such a minor ailment. "Anything interesting turn up in Truman's autopsy?" I tried to sound casual.

He looked at me over the top of his bifocals. "You know I can't talk about it. . . . 'Course, you have been helpin' Sam out."

I tried to seem unconcerned. "Of course, Harry. Forgive me for asking."

"Well," he drawled, "time of death was probably somewhere between midnight and six A.M. There was a fancy watch quit runnin' about two A.M., but that don't mean much."

"Because the killer could have stopped the watch on purpose, or it could be coincidental," I conjectured based on my past conversations with Sam and Dan.

He cleared his throat. "Right. Single gunshot to the deceased's right temple, .45 caliber Colt, clean entry, about the size of a dime, starring around the entry, powder burns from point-blank range. Messy exit caused by an incredibly steep angle impacted from the frontal lobe and cerebral cortex."

"Not that I have much to compare, but it sounds like what you'd expect," I said.

"Yep. Minuscule powder residue on the victim's right thumb and index finger. Though I expected more if he pulled the trigger himself." He looked at me curiously, a teacher responding to a bright pupil. "His liver was shot, a few scars from liposuction and a facelift, ancillary bruises, minor lacerations, high blood pressure, clogged aorta."

I stood and leaned against the door of the closet-sized room shelved with tongue depressors, swabs, needles, and alcohol wipes. "Anything to indicate a struggle or fight prior to the gunshot wounds?"

"Not necessarily. Like I said, a few bruises and cuts, but nothing that's not uncommon for a man of sixty-eight who drinks hard and doesn't take care of himself. Although he wasn't in as bad a shape as you'd think to look at him. He was thinner than he looked in those baggy sweaters and tweed blazers."

"No fingerprints on the body and personal effects that can't be accounted for—the wife's, the brother's, the youngest daughter's. There was something odd—took Dr. Lang to identify it."

I raised my eyebrows, fully engaged with his delivery.

"There was a minuscule trace of a chemical compound—methoxycinnamate dioxide behind the victim's left ear and hairline above the neck."

"Layman's terms?"

"Cosmetic foundation, makeup—probably face powder. Or else some kind of grease paint, pancake makeup, or food color. All in the same category. The compound is used in cosmetics and dyes to bind pigment coloration together. It's what holds together that 'natural' glow most women wear on their faces."

"So this implicates a woman?" I speculated. "Marcia Truman or one of the daughters, even the personal assistant."

"That was my first thought, but the sheriff and Dr. Lang discovered that this compound turns up in everything from fertilizer and lime powder to waterproof ink. We're doing soil analysis to see if there's any around the grounds of the chapel. . . . Sam also pointed out that since we're dealing with a bunch of actors and theater folk, even the men wear makeup, both onstage and off, in some cases. A man vain enough to have a facelift probably wouldn't have any qualms about a little face powder." He closed my chart, and I realized my briefing was at its close. "What do you think?"

His question surprised me, but I thought aloud. "Gentry Truman was vain enough to use makeup, I think. Who knows, you and I may be covering up our wrinkles before it's over with."

We chuckled, and he patted my back as he escorted me into the hall. "What about Mrs. Truman and the womenfolk? Any of them look a little heavy on the war paint?"

"That kind of talk would get you in trouble with my sister and her lady friends. Probably with your wife, as well. No, I wouldn't say any of them look particularly made up. Even if they did . . ."

Harry lowered his voice. "I know, I know. A dumb, sexist question from a cranky old doctor. But never overlook the obvious. First rule in medical school—even hundreds of years ago when I attended."

We laughed again, shook hands, and I was on my way. Marge completed my paper work, took my check, and made me promise to have an advance appointment next time. I nodded, remembering that I didn't have a car. Bea or Joe Brewer would be glad to come and get me, but it was such a lovely day that I decided to stroll down to the diner for lunch. Suddenly I had an idea, made a quick phone call, and then wished Margie a good day.

The diner was less than a half mile from Doc Graham's, but there was no sidewalk, only a well-worn roadside path strewn with Mountain Dew cans and cigarette butts. The litter looked fresh, more leftover sawdust from the media circus's exit, and by the time I reached the diner, I had collected over a dozen cans in a Dairy Queen bag. Already things seemed to be returning to normal. It was only eleven, so there was hardly anyone in the Avenell Diner—too late for breakfast, too early for lunch. The place smelled of onions and peppers, hot grease, maple syrup, and coffee. An Asian student with a ponytail and corduroy overalls was annotating a Norton's anthology with a bright, Day-Glo neon marker. A middle-aged man in jeans and a long-sleeved polo shirt sat writing furiously in a notebook beside the remnants of blueberry pancakes. I took him for a reporter and sat with my back to him. Trudy from the bakery three doors down, next to Walt's and Spradley's Market, sat in animated discussion with Willadean Carisol, the diner's only full-time waitress and fill-in cook when her husband, Willie, took a notion to go off on a moonshine run to the other side of the mountain. It was hard to believe, sometimes, that the twenty-first century would ever dawn on small towns like ours.

I had a cup of coffee—perfectly brewed, rich but not bitter, dark but not thick—and adjusted it with sugar while I waited. Familiar faces drifted to mind as I prayed and watched the sunlight glisten off the sidewalk. Twenty minutes later my guest arrived, and I stood to greet her.

"I'm glad you could make it on such short notice," I said.

Caroline Barr beamed back at me. "I was only changing the cat's box and doing Saturday chores around the office. Lunch with you is a wonderful diversion."

She seemed visibly lighter than the last time we'd met, her eyes bright with their sapphire sheen, her straight auburn hair still damp on the underside. She smelled clean, like soap and fresh lavender and springtime, at ease and youthful in her cotton blouse and Irish-knit cardigan and jeans.

"I'm just glad to see you're not in jail," I said as we were seated.

"Me too," she said. "Your friend Dan Warren was very kind. He took my statement and added it to the case file, but he didn't seem to think my story terribly incriminating at all. Made me think everyone had it in for Truman. Do you have a cold?"

"Yes, I'm afraid so. Just came from Doc Graham's—how inconsiderate of me! I hope you don't catch it."

"I'll be fine. I just hope you feel better soon."

Willadean shuffled over to us, her frosted hair piled on top of her head. "We got open roast beef sandwiches for the special today, with mashed potatoes and gravy. How y'all doing? Father Grif, I don't believe I've met your friend."

I awkwardly introduced Caroline to the oldest waitress in the county.

"Since it's you, Father Grif, and it's such a gorgeous day outside—did you hear it's supposed to turn cold this week? Yep, low pressure front up from the Gulf. Oh yeah, as I was saying, I got my last two Hanover tomatoes out of my garden last week before the big frost. I'll have Willie fix up a Tiger Club if y'all would like."

I nodded and Caroline said, "Make it two—and I'll have a ginger ale, please." Willadean seemed pleased with her influence and returned to the kitchen to set bacon frying, bread toasting, and tomatoes slicing.

"I'm glad it went so well at the sheriff's. See, you had nothing to fear after all."

"Perhaps. I think I'm being watched, though. I wonder if the state agents think I'm as benign as your friend Dan. Or maybe everybody who knew Gentry and has a motive is being followed."

I thought of the odd dynamics within the Truman family. "Or maybe everyone who knew Gentry *has* a motive."

She smiled and brushed her bangs back off her forehead. "Anyway, I'm glad I was up-front about my connection to him. Like I told you before, I'm through giving Gentry Truman any power whatsoever in my life." She wiped a speck of ketchup Willadean had missed from the edge of the table with a small rectangular napkin. "I saw you coming out of church on TV—very dignified and pastoral. The service went well?"

I recounted the order of service, the numerous big names in attendance, and Jenna's fainting spell. "Did you know her mother when you were at Columbia?" I asked.

"Yes," she swallowed. "Elisabeth Downing was a wonderful psychology professor—intelligent, articulate, dry wit. By the time I took her mother's class, Jenna was probably in her early teens. I saw her on campus—Jenna—but I don't think we ever met. As I think about it now, Professor Downing seemed depressed, too self-deprecating, embittered. She was very down on men."

"Is she still teaching?" I asked.

"No, I read in an alumni bulletin that she had retired about five years ago."

Willadean refilled my coffee cup and placed a sparkling ginger ale in front of Caroline. She returned to a red vinyl counter stool, mounted into the floor on a chrome beam, and made plans with Trudy to attend a Pampered Chef party on Tuesday night at Carol Wilhoit's home. It was difficult not to hear their loud, gum-popping conversation, despite my attempts not to.

"What about Cale Sanders? Ever meet him?" I asked, wondering if Caroline would think I asked her here to interrogate her at the sheriff's request.

She sipped the golden-tinged soda. "No, I only saw him from a distance a few times. I hear he's an aspiring playwright himself."

"Did you hear any rumors about a graduate student Gentry was seeing? Someone young and beautiful . . . perhaps to spite his wife?" My eyes were watery, and I remembered that I needed to stop at the drugstore on the way home.

"Yes. Chelsea West. She was cast in the new play, *Chameleon*—oh, remind me to tell you something about the play in a moment. I have Chelsea as a student this semester. Bright woman. Very attractive in a blond actress kind of way."

"So she and Gentry were having an affair? It was common knowledge to most people in the department?" I pushed my coffee cup aside and switched to water.

"She implied to me once in my office that she was only using Gentry to get auditions in New York after graduation. She said that she found him repulsive and that he seemed much more interested in people thinking they were sleeping together than actually doing it." She blushed, like a morning glory infused with a deeper pink. "I hope I'm not offending you."

"No, I asked, after all. So you don't think the two of them *were* sleeping together?"

Willadean walked over and looked at me oddly—probably hearing my last question—as she placed two large white plates before us. Large, top-heavy club sandwiches towered in triangular quarters, held together by toothpicks and surrounded by a bird's nest of thin potato sticks. What a gift of grace to have yet one more garden tomato; the one at the Corner House this week had not been my last after all.

Caroline giggled, and I found it delightful. "I think our waitress overheard you."

"She needs something new to gossip about," I said.

"Referring to your last question, no, I don't think Chelsea would stoop that low. In fact, I overheard her tell another student in class that she'd never sleep with 'the old buzzard.' Chelsea said that she doesn't care what people are thinking as long as she knows otherwise. Like I said, she's a shrewd girl. Plus, I warned her about Gentry in so many words." She bit into the triple-decker sandwich, and tomato juice dribbled down the corner of her mouth and onto her chin. "Oh my, this is good."

"Yes, I love a good vine-ripened tomato." I was well into my third bite.

"What I mentioned a moment ago, about the play—there's some intriguing news making its way around the office. I had to stop in this morning to get a book from my office, and I ran into Loretta Langton, our department secretary. It seems that Truman's personal assistant, Florence Lipton you probably met her at the service was there bright and early this morning to clean out her boss's office. It seems she found a disk."

I stopped midbite and leaned over the table as if to swallow her words. She relished the disclosure. "You know how Truman was supposedly suffering writer's block and wasn't even half-finished with this new great play? Well, it seems this disk has a complete manuscript on it. The disk had been erased, but Lipton was double-checking to make sure it was clean before she tossed it and this huge text file came up in her recovery program. *Chameleon, a Tragedy in Two Acts*, all there. Unless, of course, it belongs to one of Truman's students."

I embraced the hurt in her tone. "I know it's still hard."

"That was uncalled for. The man's dead, for heaven's sake. I'm trying to forgive—I really am."

"I know you are. Forgiveness is a process. If you didn't forgive him, I don't believe you would've gone to the police," I said, resuming my sandwich. "So we may have a world premiere here after all? Wasn't it scheduled for the weekend after Homecoming?"

"Yes, two weeks from today. We'll see. Loretta said that Ms. Lipton was delivering it to Truman's agent in Mumford first thing Monday morning. Remember—you didn't hear it from me." She smiled and dipped potato straws in her ketchup.

So why would Gentry fake writer's block if he had actually completed the play? And why would he want to take his own life if he was still able to write? Or who knew he had completed the play and would kill him for it? Perhaps Cale was going to claim it as his own?

More questions, which I didn't need. I deliberately tried to change the subject, and we began discussing the latest films we'd seen. Her presence brightened the place much more than the single peach rosebuds adorning each table. Her lightheartedness took my mind off my runny nose and dull headache. She reminded me of Amy so much that I ached inside.

Several other diners had arrived shortly after noon, some students at the counter, an older couple across the room from us. I was wondering what had possessed me to call up Dr. Caroline Barr from the Avenell University English Department and ask her to lunch in such a public place as the diner. Was this a date? Did I want to see her, or did I merely want her information on Truman's death?

Just then Andy McDermott burst in the door, the little bell rattling off its hook above the frame. He came right over to my table without even looking around the place, and I could see the tension in his dark eyes and tight-set jaw.

He lowered himself to my ear before I could greet him or introduce my companion. His words were low and forceful. "Miss Bea is in trouble. A state agent picked her up for questioning about half an hour ago. She's down at the station now—Dan sent me looking for you."

"What's she done? Is she hurt?" I leaned into his shoulder and smelled his aftershave, like spiced fruit, even through my congested nose.

"She's fine. The agent brought her in on suspicion of conspiracy to commit murder."

Chapter Nineteen

THE COLOR OF NIGHT

I SNEEZED—and then lapsed into a coughing fit. "Bea," I wheezed. "Brought in on suspicion of conspiracy to murder? You've got to be kidding. That's absurd!"

People were staring at me, at the three of us. Caroline's eyes went wide with fear.

"Let me take you to her right now. Dan said you might want to call your attorney," replied Andy.

I wiped my mouth, pulled out a few bills for our lunch, and rose from the booth. "Caroline, forgive me for running off—my sister, she—"

"Yes," she said. "I heard. Please, go—I understand. Perhaps we can do it again sometime." Regret, concern, and a hint of disappointment laced her tone.

"I'm sorry," I said over my shoulder as Andy guided me out to his squad car.

Ten minutes later I was in the tiny receptionist's area, remarkably uncrowded today, blowing my nose while I waited for my sister. I couldn't imagine what in the world was going on. Shortly, Maria Alvarez picked up her phone, her chocolate eyes meeting mine, and then ushered me back to Sam Claiborne's office.

There sat Beatrice, looking rather dowdy and exasperated, in jeans and one of my old sweat shirts that she often used for gardening. She wore no makeup and her hair was coming undone from the clasp at the back of her head, with wisps trailing like silver strands of a spider web along her ears and forehead. She locked eyes with me the moment I entered the room.

"Well, I have never—never in a million years—seen the likes of today. Griffin, prepare to be shocked. Prepare to pray to our Savior that this is not a sign of the end times," she began as I took a seat. Dan Warren looked up at me from behind a file folder.

"What's going on? Bea, are you okay? Dan, what's the meaning of this?" My indignation and sore throat were getting the best of me.

"Miss Bea was picked up by a state agent in the woods behind the Martyr's Chapel. She was delivering this"—he pointed to a large box on the sheriff's desk—"to Charlie Baxter, who was under surveillance, as you know."

My sister chortled, clearly incensed.

"Bea, is this true? You were meeting Charlie Baxter behind the Martyr's Chapel? What's in that box?" This all seemed like a bad dream—Gentry's murder, the strange confessions I'd been privy to, the uncomfortable attraction to Caroline, and now my sister's part in it. I longed to be in my own bed at home with two shots of NyQuil.

"Yes, yes, yes," she snapped. "I'm a hardened criminal's moll—Bonnie they call me—and I was meeting Clyde Barrows out at the crime scene to exchange some counterfeit bills and bootleg liquor when the G-men got wind of it."

Her sarcasm almost peeled the industrial-white paint off the cinder-block walls.

"Beatrice. Calm down this instant and tell me what really happened. It's clear to everyone that you feel misunderstood," I said.

She exhaled slowly, an exercise from her stress management class at the university last spring. "I was simply trying to do a good deed. Trying to be a Good Samaritan for someone in need. Poor Charlie doesn't take good care of himself; he's too proud to go down to the shelter in Mumford. I was trying to keep it secret simply out of respect to him and my Lord. 'Do not let your left hand know what your right hand is doing.' Since everyone must know everything, I've been leaving him food and old clothes of yours for the past few months."

Dan Warren opened the brown cardboard box and excavated the items one by one: a bag of Jonathan apples, a thermos of homemade stew—we could smell it as soon as he unscrewed the vacuum-sealed cap—instant coffee, a loaf of bread, peanut butter, white tube socks, a bar of Dial soap, deodorant, an old pair of my khakis that I used to paint in, and a torn flannel shirt that I'd never seen before.

"Is Charlie back in custody, too?" I asked.

Dan nodded. "Yep. Afraid so. The sheriff will be back later this afternoon, but until then the state boys are pressin' to keep him locked up."

"What about Bea?" I continued. "Has she really been charged with conspiracy? Has she done anything illegal?"

"No. Special Agent Brown was a bit overzealous at first. After he questioned her and realized the situation, he said she could be released as long as she doesn't leave town for forty-eight hours."

"There goes the bank job in Vegas," quipped my sister.

"So you were the one Charlie was talking about." Suddenly the obvious pieces fit together in my fatigued thinking. "You left food for him the night Gentry Truman was shot. Bea, tell me you were not out at the Martyr's Chapel that night!"

"I can take care of myself!" she exclaimed. "But no, I had dropped off Charlie's things behind the chapel late that afternoon. I saw no one. It was around four-thirty, I'd guess."

"I don't know what I would've done if you were out there when his death occurred. I know you meant well, Bea, but why didn't you tell us this before now?"

"Like I said, it was nobody's business. My fears have come to pass— poor Charlie is downstairs in a holding cell and probably will not be released this time. If Agent Brown had a lick of sense—"

"He's just trying to do his job, Miss Bea," Dan interrupted.

"Well, he at least needs to learn some manners. Why, he didn't even apologize! Can you believe humanity!"

"Bea, please," I said sternly. "So she can go now?"

"Yes. I'm really sorry about all this, Miss Bea. I know you were only doing a good deed," Dan said sympathetically. He extended a legal form for her signature, and she quickly grabbed the pen from his hand and scrawled her name.

I sneezed again, and we left with Bea planning to make homemade chicken soup for me for supper.

———————

"Do you believe in love at first sight?" asked Peter that night as we sat in the backyard and sipped hot tea. I had spent the rest of the afternoon in bed, drowsing my cares away. Doc Graham's medication helped me breathe, and the zinc lozenges, which tasted like peppermint wrapped in tinfoil, soothed my throat. Bea had turned her inner frustrations into maternal sympathy for me. She was having fits now because I was outside in the cool night air, but I felt better than I had all day, and I could tell that Peter wanted to talk. The sky was opaque, a dull, dark blue like milk infused with ink, but several constellations pierced through the gauze.

" 'I do, I do believe in love at first sight. But I also believe in the rights of colored people to sit anywhere they want to on the bus, to drink water from any fountain they choose. I believe in the rights of a man to love a woman the way God intended. I believe in slow, passionate kisses underneath starlight, in the rights of children to play make believe and not have their fantasy shattered because Daddy don't live at home. I believe in the right of women to know "Jolting" Joe DiMaggio's batting average and a man's right to cook himself a nice crème brulée. I believe in life, liberty, and the pursuit of happiness. And I've lived long enough to know that sometimes you got to help God help yourself!' " My attempted falsetto cracked like fine gravel across my raw throat.

"Kevin Costner's speech to Susan Sarandon in *Bull Durham?*" he guessed.

"No, long before that. Rachel Harper's speech to Tucker Primrose in *The Color of Night*. That was my best Vivian Leigh imitation."

"Oh, that's who that was." Peter grinned. "So is that a yes or a no?"

"Love at first sight, eh? As in theory or practice?" I smiled and loosened the polar fleece scarf Bea had insisted I wear like a noose. "As in a romantic ideal to be exposited by Plato and Gentry Truman, or a personal matter between Father Peter Abernathy and Miss Leah Schroeder?"

"I'm serious, Grif. I can't describe to you how wonderful my day was today. I got there right before lunch and she met me in the bakery, the one whose owner first identified Leah in the magazine picture. We had the best vegetable soup and homemade bread I've ever tasted—don't tell Miss Bea—and sat at a small drop leaf table with a handful of tourists and visitors at the other small tables around us. She told me all about her family. She has four brothers, both sets of grandparents living with them, and ten cousins in the area!

"She explained how the founders had moved from Lancaster County after World War II. Obviously, Tremont is not an old order Amish community—they believe in maintaining the principles of godly living amongst themselves, but they believe God wants them to be shrewd in practicing those principles. So they cater to tourists, sell baked goods, produce, arts and crafts. . . . It's really an amazing little place." My curate was almost out of breath from his animated recollection of his day.

I sipped from a mountain-clay mug, one of a pair that Amy and I had bought at the New Morning Gallery in Asheville, North Carolina, during our honeymoon trip. "So it wasn't awkward with her family?" I asked as the warm concoction of lemon, honey, and chamomile embraced my insides.

"Well, they don't exactly know what to make of me. . . . I think Mrs. Schroeder knows that I came down mostly to see her daughter. She answered my questions about Amish lifestyle, as did Mr. Schroeder, but she seemed more concerned with the way I looked at Leah's artwork. She's so talented, Grif! It's amazing—her sensitivity to nature and light, and the way she uses different brush strokes to capture visual texture. . . . I offered to buy one from her, but she said they're not for sale, at least not yet."

We remained silent for a few moments, captivated by twinkling stars as if we were boys. "And you think you could love her already?"

He looked at me in the darkness, shifted to cross his leg, and bumped my knee. "I don't know—it's foolish, I guess. I've never been one to act on first impressions or people's appearances . . . but Leah's different. She's the exception to my usual way of doing things. There was a moment, Grif, right before I left. We were sitting on the front porch, watching the sun set across the pasture, with the hickory and apple trees all ablaze. And there was quiet, just the faint sound of the creek behind the barn, the howl of a dog somewhere . . . but Leah and I were quiet, all talked out. But it wasn't awkward at all. We were comfortable, familiar. I swear I could've asked her to marry me right then."

"Don't swear, but I know what you mean. And there are exceptions. One of the things I always hated about being single, Pete, was the way married men would talk to me about how they decided to ask their wives to marry them. They either made it sound like a mystical, sublime experience from God—they simply knew and just had to sit back and let it happen to them—or else, on the other hand, some men make marriage sound like a dice game. 'Well, it felt like love, so we decided to give it a shot,' they say.

"What I discovered," I turned toward him, "is that love cannot be formulized or entirely explained. It's the same way with God's love. We try to systematize our theology and devise a checklist of rules and formulas for being Christians. But God asks us to obey Him because we love Him. He invites us into a deeper relationship with His Son, His Spirit, and delights in surprising us with His goodness. And one of the ways He surprises us most with His love is through other people. I believe that if we're really blessed, we'll meet a handful of people who love us unconditionally, gracefully. Our families certainly provided that sometimes, maybe a best friend or mentor . . . but for some of us there's someone of the opposite sex, a lover, a medium of transcendent love. . . . I'm rambling, Peter, forgive me." I coughed and took another drink of tea.

"No, no," he said. "I like what you're saying. I know what it was like for you and Amy. Knew that you didn't waste any time after you met."

I chuckled. "Yes, that's true. But we were older, Peter, and looking back it's a gift that we didn't waste any time. You're still a young man, and Leah's even younger still . . . and forgive me once more, but I'm concerned about the differences in your beliefs and culture. Why, if you married her, one of you would have to leave your world and join the other's. You'd either join her family's household in Tremont, or else she'd have to join you up here."

"I know," he said. "And for all her talk about being frustrated with the constraints on her art, I can tell she loves the Amish people and their way of life. I can see it in her paintings. I don't know that I could ever ask her to leave it behind, but I don't think God is calling me to become Amish."

"That is the key, Peter. Trust that our Father will reveal His will to you. Don't rely just on your feelings. Pay attention to His Word, to everyday events. Listen to your life, and you will hear Him speak. Just take it slowly."

"Can I use that in my homily tomorrow?" he asked. "Which reminds me that I better get home and finish it up."

"Of course," I replied.

"Before we go in, Grif," he continued, "tell me more about your lunch with Caroline Barr. In all the excitement over your sister's 'arrest,' you didn't say much about your date."

"It wasn't a date," I explained, trying not to sound defensive. "I simply wanted to check up on her. She had shared some . . . personal concerns when I talked to her earlier in the week. So I combined my follow-up with a spontaneous impulse for a sandwich at the diner."

"You really are sick if you're craving Willadean's cooking," he joked.

"Our time was very pleasant. Dr. Barr is a very intelligent, likable young woman." My tone sounded artificially avuncular and Pete caught me.

"You're not her father, for heaven's sake. You're what—maybe ten years older? So it was a purely professional call?"

I stood and pulled my flannel-lined field jacket around my neck, tucking the red scarf back into its prior position. "No, it was—I honestly don't know what it was, Peter." I collapsed my lawn chair and began to head to the back porch. Peter followed suit and added my chair to his inside the garage. The night shone clearer now, the murky cloud cover lifting, and stars multiplied like the view in a diamond kaleidoscope.

———

I did not go to church for Sunday morning services. Peter would celebrate the Eucharist and deliver a thoughtful, impassioned homily, assisted by two of our deacons, Jack Sheridan and Dwight Taylor. Sleeping late was a luxury, and I could hear Bea scurrying around to prepare herself. Guilt wormed its way into my consciousness as the bell tower pealed out nine chimes, and I watched from the window as familiar figures filed into my church.

Cognitively, I accepted my need for rest and recovery much easier than I did emotionally. Even if sick, I should be right up there beside Peter, smiling, praying, worshiping—and likely spreading a cold to celebrants at the altar rail. Yes, it was clearly a wise decision for me to stay in and rest, but I struggled to relax until after I'd taken a wonderfully hot shower. Back in bed with Buechner's *A Room Called Remember*, an old favorite, I found myself thinking of getting older and living alone for the rest of my life.

Perhaps it was the medication or my restless mood, but many of the same feelings surfaced from the first year after Amy died. Not just the grief, anger, and sorrow—no, there was a frustration, a confusion over my identity and my new role. I was barely adjusted to my status as husband, still a newlywed in many ways, having struggled to relinquish my bachelorhood. Then I was thrust in the role of caretaker, grieving spouse, the recipient of prayers, food, the lovingkindness of others. Another blink and I was the widower, the object of sympathy cards and sidelong glances, awkward attempts at condolence. And perhaps that was the role I resented the most, the pitiful Father Grif, married late in life and, oh-how-cruel, now his lovely bride has been claimed by cancer.

I quit counting how many copies of Lewis's *A Grief Observed* I received. I knew people meant well, didn't know what else to do, but I resented the insinuation that I could learn, as Lewis did, to count it all joy. I don't think Lewis's reconciliation with grief and with God occurred to him as he read a book in one sitting.

No, I did not know who to be. Beatrice moved in shortly after Amy's death and my decision to stay on here as rector. I taught a course at the seminary, which I had done a few times before, and was asked to speak at the commencement that May. I was honored, yet repulsed that we only give the highest credibility to another's faith amid devastating loss and suffering. I spoke on hope, and I preached foremost to myself.

I listened that day, but I did not hear. It took me at least another year to become reacquainted with my own loneliness, with what to do with myself on a rainy afternoon or in the middle of the night when I rolled over to an empty pillow. Who was Griffin Reed?

Perhaps it was a mid-life crisis that would have occurred naturally even if Amy had lived and we had parented a handful of fine children. Perhaps my grieving only interrupted the inevitable as I redefined myself and speculated on how I wanted to spend the last few decades of my life.

John Greenwood and I had talked at some length about this existential identity crisis, and as I thought back over prior conversations, I recalled him saying, "Don't make this too much of a priority. In many ways, Grif, I know you better than you know yourself. Just as Amy knew you in another way better than you know yourself. The same with Beatrice or with Peter. Those we love often know us better because they're not looking up a definition of Father Griffin Reed in the dictionary. No, they're experiencing who we are by the way we love them, by the way God uses us to love them. Why, it's the difference between reading a travel book about the beach and tasting saltwater at high tide."

"But what happens after you return from the beach? Who are you then?" I had asked, pressing his metaphor.

"Why, you're a beachcomber for life!" he laughed. "You cannot pretend that you haven't been there, any more than you can pretend you never loved Amy. It would be convenient if that were the case because then you wouldn't hurt so much. Or you could rush out and try to visit every beach in the world—you could live on the beach! Yet no other relationship or pleasure can replace the intimacy you've known with Amy."

His wisdom and warm embrace as I left that day reverberated inside my cold-fogged head. Somehow his words had something to do with Gentry Truman's murder—and it was murder, I was sure of that—but I could not articulate the connection. Something was being processed in my subconscious and the Holy Spirit was leading me somewhere . . . perhaps somewhere I did not wish to go.

If only I had put things together sooner. Perhaps if I hadn't caught a cold and were more clearheaded . . . perhaps if the weather hadn't turned cold enough to snow. Perhaps then another life could have been saved.

Chapter Twenty

ALL THAT REMAINS

———

". . . UNIVERSITY CLASSES ARE canceled, and operations will open one hour late with only necessary personnel. An Avenell woman was critically injured early this morning at the base of Eaglehead Mountain. Her name has not been released. . . ." The WAVE announcer drifted in from the ancient stereo atop my office bookshelf.

The cold front from the northeast that began rolling in on Sunday afternoon anchored itself squarely over our part of the state by early Monday, bringing with it a fine powdery mist which seemed to freeze on contact. Avenell and Eaglehead Mountain became encased in a silver layer that gave every tree trunk and branch, every telephone wire, every car windshield, every blade of grass a cold, dull pewter sheen.

Dan Warren called shortly after eight to inform me that Florence Lipton had crashed off the side of Eaglehead Mountain as she turned the seventh curve of Highway 19 early that morning. She was found by a trucker from the Tyson Chicken plant over in Lewiston ascending the steep vertical six percent grade on his way to the interstate. Dan told me the paramedics arrived about ten minutes later, climbed down the sheer, rocky face of the mountainside, and with the aid of a fire truck's pulley, hoisted her in a gurney back up to the roadside ambulance. She was conscious briefly and murmured "Gentry" twice before fading on the way to Carroll County General.

She was apparently on her way to meet Casey Atwood, who had driven down from Nashville to meet her at the Mumford Diner. When she failed to show, Atwood had phoned the sheriff's office. According to Dan, Truman's agent confirmed the rumor Caroline Barr had heard in the English department. Florence Lipton *had* recovered a deleted computer file of Truman's last work in its entirety. The disk remained locked in a safe in the university registrar's office until this morning at six A.M. when Ms. Lipton retrieved it from a security guard.

Dan and I agreed that Florence Lipton should never have attempted to make it down the mountain, although it seemed that she was not going fast at all when she lost control and went over the side. It was one of the last few curves, and as such, did not have a guardrail to contain it. Nevertheless, on a dark, foggy, ice-coated morning, the chances of making it down Eaglehead were slim. Plus, she didn't know the road that well, Dan pointed out. Perhaps an animal darted in front of her, or maybe she simply couldn't see the turn through the viscid mist.

Whatever the cause, she now had a severe concussion, internal hemorrhaging, broken ribs, a cracked pelvis, and a severed femur. Doctors lost her heartbeat momentarily during the operation to stop the internal bleeding but resuscitated her. She remained in a coma in the intensive care unit and was not out of danger yet.

The first priority, of course, had been getting Ms. Lipton to the emergency room. Only then had the deputies and fire fighters turned their attention to the recovery of her vehicle and its contents. But the ice-sheathed mountainside yielded neither car nor disk. And if a hard copy had been made, its whereabouts were unknown.

I prayed fervently for her all morning as I shuffled around my office in sweats and my shearling-lined slippers. Ordinarily I'd be keeping a vigil at the hospital, but between the ice storm and my cold, Bea wouldn't hear of it. And there really wasn't anything for me to do there that I couldn't do at home.

Florence's daughter had been called in New Haven and would be fly-ing in that afternoon. I would try to visit tomorrow, perhaps meet with the daughter and offer whatever hope could be mustered. My cold was better, I supposed, which meant that I had slept for several hours at a stretch last night and could breathe through my nose this morning. The zinc did seem to help, and I was getting used to the odd metallic taste that coated my tongue and throat.

My only commitment this day was the reading of Truman's will at two. Other than calling to confirm, I had not thought much more about it until lunchtime, when I reluctantly told Bea about my inclusion over tomato soup and grilled cheese.

"What if Gentry Truman left you a million dollars?" she speculated. "What would you do with it?"

A yellow-orange band stretched from my mouth back to the edge of my sandwich, giving me a moment to consider. "Well, I'm sure he didn't, for one thing. And if he did, I'm not sure that I'd change much at all. I'd be able to support more missionaries and donate to Dawn Orwell's Chris-tian school down in Harpertown. But you know me well enough, Bea. I don't think I want a new Lexus or a condo on Hilton Head. I might travel more, I suppose. Buy more books, maybe a new watercolor or shaker table." I dipped my crust into the warm, hearty soup.

My sister knew that I had inherited a sizable estate when Amy died. I was no millionaire, but some shrewd investments and a liberal insurance policy had basically secured my retirement years. One of the few luxuries I had indulged in was a new mountain bike, one that Peter helped me select. Although I had been thinking of trading in the LeSabre for a sport utility vehicle. *But what would my parishioners think?*

I would postpone that decision at least until the spring, and even then, if I decided to proceed, I could not justify a new one. I wrestled with materialism as much as the next person, suddenly curious to know who would stand to inherit the most from Truman's will. Somehow, the timing of Florence's accident and the reading of the will seemed too close to be coincidence. Yet I couldn't see any apparent connection.

"Joan Dowinger called to ask after you," Bea said. "She's concerned that your illness may interfere with the meeting you scheduled tomorrow at her house. She said she'd be happy to come here if that would be more convenient."

"That's all I need in the midst of everything else," I groaned.

"She said she had some exciting news from Fentriss Peyton . . . or was it the other way around? Some man with two very southern first names . . ."

"Please call her, or ask Roberta at the church office—did she make it in today?—and tell her I'll be at her house at four as promised. . . ." My head felt lined with cotton, insulating itself from the rest of my body.

———

I showered and shaved and bundled up to walk the three blocks over to the Mary Bartlett Administrative Building behind the university center. Bea gave repeated warnings about correct walking procedures on icy terrain. "That's all you need right now, Griffin Reed—a broken bone," she said.

Even though it was normally a ten-minute walk, I figured to allow a good twenty on the miserable cold-choked sidewalks. In fact, I ended up trudging across the lawns with greater success. It was like walking across fields of broken glass, shards of ice crunching like shark's teeth beneath my boots.

Inside the Romanesque building, recently remodeled with white paint, dark burgundy carpet, and a bold mural of the university's history in the front lobby, only a skeleton crew maintained operations. I saw lights in the president's office, in the graduate admissions office, and in the testing and assessment office. It occurred to me, as I trudged up the circular staircase leading to the second floor, that perhaps the reading had been postponed after all, but then I saw Casey Atwood at the top of the landing smoking a walnut-burl pipe and chatting with McDonnell, the attorney.

Atwood nodded, and James McDonnell turned to greet me.

"Thank you for coming, Father Reed, especially on such a nasty day. We're still waiting on some of the family. Please go on in and have some coffee." His voice was low and unctuous, soothingly southern in an educated cadence that neither hid his accent nor relied on it. He turned back to Gentry's former agent.

Inside, a twenty-foot-long conference table spanned the length of the dimly lit room. Illumined by discreet sconces along the heavy, richly paneled walls, the golden ambiance seemed more conducive to a romantic dinner party than official business. The fine woods represented—oak, mahogany, cherry, walnut, hickory—gleamed, each in its own way. Oil portraits of founding fathers Bishop Otey and President Bartlett loomed ominously above the far end of the table. Beneath them sat a silver serving cart laden with carafes of coffee and steaming pots of tea.

Jenna Truman stood with her half sister Lucy while two men I did not know were stirring coffee in fine white china cups. The room smelled faintly of lemon oil, beeswax polish, and cherrywood pipe tobacco. It was a hearty, comforting smell, harkening back to my father's study when I was a boy or the old vestry room beneath James Chapel at Union Seminary.

My boots echoed wet thuds on the highly polished marble floor as I removed my coat, scarf, and hat and hung them from an oak peg behind a large elephant-ears plant in an oversized Chinese vase. When I turned to move toward the gathering, Jenna stood before me, pale and nervous-looking in the shadowy light, a ghost of vibrancy.

"Father Reed, I want to apologize for the disruption I caused at Daddy's memorial," she began.

I could not believe my ears. "Dear girl, no apology necessary. Are you all right? I've been worried about you. It's good to see you up and about."

She smiled demurely, her curly tresses laced in a thick braid down her back. "I'm fine. Just fatigue, the doctor said, and the shock of everything. He adjusted my medication, and I've been getting lots of sleep. Thank you for caring. Lucy told me that you called Sunday afternoon to see how I was doing."

"Jenna, do you remember what you said before you fainted during the service?" My nose tickled as it defrosted from the raw cold outside to the humid warmth of this room.

She looked up at me curiously. I could tell by her eyes that she was unaccustomed to direct questions. "Yes." She smiled. "I do. For ever so slight a second, I thought I saw my father peering around the corner of the archway on my right. You know—over in front of the walkway below the stained-glass gallery? I'm sure it was just stress and my medication."

"Perhaps you saw someone who resembled your father?" I suggested.

"Yes, that's what Marcia and Cale think." She fidgeted with her hands before pulling out a handkerchief from her velveteen jumper, a deep violet color that made her look paler still.

"Where are Marcia and Cale?"

"We left right before them. They were going to stop by the dorm and pick up Dylan; they should be here any minute."

"Is your uncle feeling better? I've been concerned about him, as well," I said.

"Cale seems fine to me—I'm not sure I ever knew exactly what was wrong with him." She paused as Franklin Milford entered the room before continuing in a throaty whisper. "Forgive me for saying it, but I suspect he was drunk the whole weekend. He has a . . . problem."

I nodded complicitly. "Has he always drunk so much?" I whispered back just as the object of our discussion entered with Marcia at his side.

"No, I don't think so. I guess it runs in the family, though," she said.

The others had arrived. Lisa Chandler and Dylan Klein entered like a prom king and queen, followed by Atwood and James McDonnell. The low thrum of voices echoed throughout the cavernous room. Marcia looked markedly tired since I saw her last, gray circles shadowing her eyes. Her drab olive suit did not complement her coloring, either. She wore a black-and-green scarf and none of the elegant jewelry I had come to expect. She nodded my way with a nervous smile as she seated herself next to McDonnell, who was asking us to please join him at the table.

Cale Sanders gave me a snide grin. He, too, looked tired and uncomfortable, but nonetheless dapper in his black cashmere sweater and tweed pants. His black Italian boots tapped a sharp staccato as he approached the table and took a seat next to his sister-in-law. Upon closer inspection, Dylan looked tense, more visibly shaken than I had seen him before, and I wondered if grief were catching up to him, or if, perhaps, a more immediate concern pressed him.

The three sisters arranged themselves on McDonnell's left, from oldest to youngest, and I took the heavy mahogany-and-leather chair next to Jenna. Truman's former agent sat next to me. The tall, thin attorney stood, looking quite birdlike with half bifocals perched atop his sharp, patrician nose.

"Thank you for coming. I believe we're all here—everyone except Florence Lipton, who, as most of you probably know, was in a serious car accident this morning at the base of Eaglehead Mountain. I talked to the hospital administrator around noon, and he stated that she is still unconscious and in critical condition. I'm sure we'll all want to keep her in our prayers." His words were carefully chosen, well-spoken and crisp, like those of a disk jockey or television reporter, people who maintained ordered, calm demeanors under pressure. Outside the heavily draped windows, tree branches stood frozen, silver-black branches guarding us like the barrels of sentinels' guns. I slipped a zinc lozenge in my mouth and returned my attention to McDonnell.

"My assistant here, Michael Levine, will be scheduling individual appointments with each of the beneficiaries and trustees of the estate after the reading." One of the men I had not recognized, in round tortoise-rimmed glasses and pin-striped suit, nodded and held up a sleek Waterman ballpoint to identify himself. His boss continued. "My law clerk, Michael Petrovski, who helped prepare and amend the documents we are about to read, will also be recording our proceedings here." The clerk smiled grimly behind a sheaf of collated papers and three black leather portfolios. He stood and began passing out the first stack of stapled documents to each of us.

"Here is a copy of the last will and testament for each of you—you're welcome to consult your own personal attorneys, but under no circumstances may you disclose any of its contents, or the proceedings today, to anyone outside this room. Failure to comply will result in immediate forfeiture of any inherited assets, benefits, fiduciary holdings, or appointments. If you agree to said terms, please sign the top page of your packet and pass it down to Michael."

I signed quickly, watching the others around the table do the same. Only Cale Sanders hesitated as if relishing the moment. Petrovski collected the agreements quickly, shuffling the fine parchment-bond sheets like oversized playing cards.

James McDonnell continued. "It will be necessary for me to read the following preamble and then the list of beneficiaries and trustees. 'I, Gentry Dunlap Truman, of New York, New York, being of full age, sound mind and memory, and under no restraint, do make, publish, and declare this instrument to be my last will and testament and hereby revoke all wills and codicils ever before made by me. . . . ' "

The attorney droned on through the names of spouse, children, and then came to name the executor of the estate: Cale Spencer Truman. Both the new executor and the widow nodded their approval. It struck me odd, however, that Marcia had not been named executor. I wondered, too, how long ago this will had been made and amended. *Patience*, I told myself and tried to listen while scrutinizing the responses of those in front of me. Only Casey Atwood escaped my line of vision.

The soothing monotone of McDonnell's legalese combined with the room's wet-mitten warmth made me drowsy. The dull lighting from both within and without only contributed to the effect. Finally, however, we were getting to the specified legacies.

" 'To each of my three daughters, I leave a joint trust to be formed from the copyright annuities, including film, stage, and foreign subsidiary rights of my works, *General Store, The Ghettos of Heaven, Breakfast in Birmingham*, and *The Color of Night*. The trust will be governed by a board executed by Father Griffin Reed, rector of Avenell Parish, whose parish shall be entitled to a stipend of $25,000 annually for compensation

of Father Reed's discretion.' " Low murmur of whispered voices. Mc-
Donnell paused to sip water from a tea glass before continuing.

" 'To my wife, Marcia Klein Truman, I leave $100,000 annual stipend
in trust to be forfeited, along with all rights and claims to the estate, upon
remarriage.' "

"You—he—I!" Little rodent squeaks of disbelief from the widow.
Cale patted her shoulder as if to console her.

"Finally, all that remains of my estate, including scripts, books, plays,
poems, stage and screen rights, any written works, use of my name or
likeness, along with the remainder of the Federal Colony life insurance
policy after probate shall go solely to my brother, Cale Spencer Sanders,
esquire, executor of the estate."

The whispers rose to a cocktail-party chatter of desperate voices. The
three sisters huddled, and Lucy Truman looked up to smile at me, as if
we were winners in the perversely parceled Monopoly game that was her
father's estate.

"So why were the rest of us even asked here?" demanded Atwood.

The two Michaels looked up at their boss, who remained calm and
seemed to enjoy the chaos caused by his monologue. "I'm just following
the instructions of the deceased," McDonnell barked, implying by his
tone "don't be a sore loser."

Marcia looked paler than the wan sunlight diffused through the afternoon fog. She looked betrayed, angry, foolish, and vengeful all in a
convergence of the most honest emotions I had seen from her yet. Cale
smoothed the back of his head, plucked a white thread from his fine black
sweater, and lowered his eyes to the floor. A certain smug superiority pervaded his motions. I did not have to be an attorney to know that he was
the big winner here today.

"So how much is the estate worth? How much insurance did he
have?" asked Franklin Milford, vicariously wounded for Marcia.

"At the close of business on the day Gentry Truman was discovered—
which is the date on the death certificate—the estate was appraised at
$16,200,043.10. Ten million of that is the proceeds from two life insur-

ance policies. The rest is from real estate, royalties, and subsidiary rights."

A low wave like a seismic tremor crept through more murmurs and stares.

"And outstanding debts?" asked Cale.

"Approximately $6,572,000. Before his death Gentry Truman was about to declare bankruptcy." McDonnell drained the last of his water and closed his portfolio.

"This is absurd," said Marcia. "When was this will drafted? This is *not* the contract that we drew up together last year." Her voice simmered with rage.

"It was authorized on October first of this year, signed and notarized on October fifth. It's a valid will. If you have prior claims, you're welcome to have your attorney file to contest." James McDonnell clearly did not care about prior claims, probably why Gentry liked him so much. He buttoned his dark gray suit jacket and arranged the largest of the black portfolios. "Thank you all for coming out today, and please drive safely. My card is included in your packet; please call if I can be of assistance. Those of you named as heir or trustees, please schedule with Michael before you leave."

The starched attorney exited the room, leaving behind the stale smoke of contempt for his client. His leather soles echoed rapid-fire clicks across the landing and down the stairs.

"Well, it looks like brother dearest wasn't in a very giving mood this year," smirked Cale. "I suppose we should be lucky he didn't leave everything to his good friend Father Reed, here."

My headache returned as my last dose of aspirin wore off. I ignored Cale's remark and began collecting my coat and scarf. The daughters were lined up before Michael, the personal assistant who perused a leather appointment book. Franklin Milford was trying to comfort Marcia, who seemed stoic and impassive, staring out into the gray void of the afternoon. Dylan stood awkwardly with his hands in his pockets. Casey Atwood left without saying a word.

"What's the matter, Father? Cat got your tongue?" Sanders goaded me.

"I'm glad to see you're back to your old self. We missed your caustic wit at the memorial service." I hated to stoop to his level.

"Ah yes. Feeling a tad under the weather I was, a bit like yourself now. It seems that young Jenna"—he raised his voice—"provided all the excitement required. I do hate that I missed the dear, sweet sentiments shared by all those people for poor brother."

"I'm sure you do. Look, I'm sorry that I couldn't persuade the police to release the body to you and the family for cremation. There's nothing I can do."

"I understand. The authorities are not convinced of what we all know—that old Gentry finally toppled over the edge and did himself in. But who knows? Maybe one of these disgruntled beneficiaries wanted her pittance sooner than later." He lowered his voice to squeeze it out the side of his thin mouth. "You do know, don't you, that if Marcia had divorced Gentry she would have been a pauper? Prenuptial agreement. She was wealthy enough at the time they married, but a lifestyle like hers doesn't come cheap."

"Why are you telling me this?" My head was throbbing now and my voice burned with exasperation.

"I thought you and Deputy Dawg were playing at detective. I just thought you'd want to keep score for your little game of Clue. 'I'll pick Miss Marcia with the revolver in the chapel.' "

His sister-in-law turned at the sound of her name and marched over to us. She locked eyes with Cale before speaking through clenched teeth. "You and I have to talk. Now." Franklin was close on her heels.

Cale turned casually and grinned. "Good to see you again, Father Reed. I hope we can get together like this again some time. Y'all come back now." His black silhouette disappeared into echoed footsteps.

Michael the personal assistant was now free, so I approached to discuss dates. We found a time in December, although I told him I might have to reschedule depending on Advent services.

I turned to bid good-bye to Jenna, Lisa, and Lucy, who seemed rather unaffected in comparison to their stepmother's angry siege.

"It looks like we'll be working together," said Lisa.

Lucy smiled at me kindly. "I'm sorry you've been dragged into all this. I suppose you should be flattered that Pop trusted you—at least more than Marcia and Cale. I still can't believe the settlement—I expected the legacies to be reversed, Cale with a small stipend and Marcia with the bulk of the estate. My father loved surprise endings."

"He loved hurting people," said Jenna. "I'm sorry, but you both know it's true."

"Do you have any idea how much your trust will accrue?" I asked, trying to sound businesslike.

"The legal aid guessed that royalties from those four plays bring in several hundred thousand dollars a year. We're not going to be as rich as Uncle Cale, but we should all be comfortable for the rest of our lives. It's more than I expected," said Lucy.

"Me too," Lisa confirmed.

"I was surprised to hear that Gentry was about to declare bankruptcy," I continued.

"So were we! But Daddy was far too proud to ever admit that he was insolvent. All that shame from his poor upbringing, I guess," replied Lucy.

"I think he would have preferred to die than to admit he was broke and washed up," said Gentry Truman's youngest daughter. I wondered if Cale felt the same way.

"Jenna!" exclaimed Lisa Chandler, "I can't believe you'd say that!"

"You know it's true, Lisa," replied her younger sister. "Daddy may have indeed been driven to suicide by his financial problems."

"Do you think your father killed himself?" I asked, adjusting my scarf and buttoning my wool trench coat.

The three of them looked at each other as if they shared the secret of their father's death. "No," said Jenna finally. "We don't."

Chapter Twenty-one

HOMECOMING

———

GENTRY TRUMAN'S DAUGHTERS did not elaborate on why they believed their father had not taken his own life. And I puzzled over the contradictory information they had provided. On one hand, they believed Gentry would rather die than declare bankruptcy, yet on the other, did not believe he shot himself in the Martyr's Chapel. I could not decipher the paradoxical nature of their father's character.

By Tuesday my cold was definitely waning. I was relieved but wished I did not have to tax my system by meeting with Joan Dowinger for afternoon tea. I half expected the entire diaconate to be assembled, along with the vestry, the bishop, Frank Milford, Peyton Fentriss, and anyone else the lonely empress deemed necessary for my conversion. I had prayed about it. I had walked through the lovely cathedral that very morning, now back to normal except for a few remaining lilies in the narthex. I tried to see the Gothic arches with their raised marble brows through fresh eyes, to view the place as a student, then as a congregant, to imagine what Joan had in mind. Painting over the stone? Knocking down the rood screen and creating portable altars? Replacing the color scheme with earth tones and sleek metals?

I had to admit the drapes along the low, mullioned windows looked shabby, dust-covered, and frayed along the edges. The faded burgundy pew cushions and prie-dieu needlepoint kneelers were seeded and even bald in some spots. But it was what one expected in an old cathedral. Perhaps it just needed a good cleaning.

These were the thoughts assembling themselves in neat defensive formations as I rang the Dowinger doorbell promptly at four. The house, a lovely Georgian antebellum home, was built in 1824 by State Senator Claude Boyett as a summer home. It had been restored in the early 1920s by a bootlegger catering to fraternity boys at Avenell. Shortly thereafter, Henry Dowinger had bought it and brought his wealthy family to live there. His son, Joan's husband, had inherited it. As I heard padded steps approaching me from the other side of the New Orleans–style grilled door, I wondered how previous owners would have responded to the renovations Joan had completed last year.

If she were a young faculty wife or a bachelor professor of modern art, the renovations might have made sense. But for an older, distinguished Daughter of the American Revolution like Joan Dowinger, they only seemed trendy, a last swim in the tide of commercial aesthetics. The white-washed, handmade bricks had been covered with aluminum siding, the fieldstone chimney had been painted black, and the gardens alongside the graceful fish ponds and grape vineyards were xeroscaped. The effect looked like a postmodern tornado had just whipped through a schizophrenic artist's home.

A college student in a black skirt and white blouse greeted me. "Mrs. Dowinger will be right with you, Father Reed. Please have a seat in the front parlor." She ushered me into an open-ended, spacious sitting room decorated in an ornate Oriental motif. A lovely Japanese watercolor of snow-kissed mountains over the chrome mantel was the only thing I liked in the room. Most of the other objets d'art competed: origami swans, silver candelabras, bamboo rugs, silk tapestries. I chuckled, imagining the cathedral in a similar Oriental motif.

"Griffin, how in the world are you feeling? Forgive me for not offering my hand, but I absolutely must stay healthy. My herbalist has made me promise not to touch anyone's hands this flu season. Remind me to give you some fresh echinacea before you leave. Please, take your seat. Karen? We're ready for our tea now, dear." Joan wore a bronze-colored sweater and matching straight skirt, which fit snugly over her wide hips. A large topaz dangled from a golden lasso of a chain around her neck.

"I'm feeling much better, thank you, Joan. I appreciate your concern." I seated myself on the silk champagne-colored divan, rearranging cushions with Kabuki masks embroidered on them. The young brunette maid appeared with a silver serving cart bearing a Wedgwood tea service.

"Forgive me for not using the Nagasaki tea service like I'd planned—but Trudy down at the bakery had a fresh tiramisu this morning. It's absolutely divine! So then I decided to use the demitasse set from Venice, but then I really just wanted a good cup of Earl Grey."

No wonder her house looked like an explosion at a furniture store.

"Joan, I've given your suggestion considerable thought and prayer and . . . oh, thank you." Karen served me a steaming cup of rich, dark tea. I adjusted raw sugar and fresh cream into it.

"And?" Joan asked impatiently. "Before you tell me, let me share what Peyton Fentriss said last Friday. The man's an absolute artistic genius! His idea is to close off the front entrance and build a facade onto the side where the vestry door is located. Of course, that means we'd have to move the altar to what's now the left side, below the stained gallery of the miracles. . . ."

Thank goodness she paused for a bite of Trudy's lovely dessert. "Oh, this is delicious!" she praised. At least we agreed on something today. The layers of golden cake, chocolate, and custard melted effortlessly in my mouth.

Perhaps it was my cold, but I had no patience. "Joan, before you go on, I'm afraid that a renovation of that kind is out of the question. We're talking about a beautiful Gothic cathedral here—not someone's dollhouse. I'm all for a good spring cleaning, but rearranging the doors and altar—next you'll be telling me that you want to move the organ and put in an orchestra pit."

"Well, I had talked to Dr. Forsythe in the music department about—"

"Joan, please tell me you didn't. You must slow down. As I promised you last week, I will bring this before the vestry and our diaconate, but I am not in favor of it."

She pouted and sipped her tea. I finished my tiramisu but all enjoyment had been deferred.

"Well, I see. I don't want to fight you on this, Griffin, but if I have to, I will."

"And I don't want to fight you on this, Joan, but if you force me to, I will. The entire parish appreciates your immense generosity—you know that. But I believe there are worthier causes, greater needs in our community than playing Rubik's cube with our perfectly beautiful-as-it-is cathedral." I wiped moist crumbs from my mouth and felt a sneeze approaching.

"Gesundheit!" she said.

"Thank you. I'll be going now, Joan. Thank you for the lovely tea. I can show myself out."

"Good day, Father Reed. Thank you for coming."

Karen emerged with my coat and hat.

Outside the brisk air restored my sense of proportion and sanity. Daylight savings time had ended a few weeks ago and the sun was trying to beat its new curfew amidst a dazzling array of shimmering frozen branches. Much of the ice, especially on the sidewalks and streets, had melted today, the temperature just above freezing. Yet many trees had been lost, power lines downed, and bones broken by the remaining layers of ice. The large tulip poplar in Joan's yard was especially lovely, a handful of yellow leaves encased in ice like beetles in fossilized amber.

I did not like conflict, and I secretly believed Joan was hoping to capitalize on that knowledge, but I would leave the parish before I would see the cathedral restructured as if it were nothing more than a child's Lego set.

After supper that night John Greenwood called to see how I was getting along. We talked about Gentry's memorial service and about Bea's involvement with Charlie Baxter.

"Perhaps it's a way for Bea to grieve your brother, Grif. Wasn't he a Vietnam vet? Maybe it helps her to help someone like Charlie," offered John.

The humble chaplain's insight might seem merely psychodynamic speculation to some, but it felt like divinely inspired wisdom to me. Finally I shared the situation with Joan and my strong resistance to her plan.

"Wow, you've really got your hands full," he said sympathetically. "I remember her from the picnic this summer—a large woman in seersucker and a straw hat with fresh roses on it."

"Yes, that's the one. She means well, John, but she's gone overboard. I can't imagine that anyone else will agree with her, but she's so used to getting her own way. She has too much money and too much time on her hands." I shuffled papers on my desk and switched the phone to my right ear.

"Grif, have you tried to compromise? You said yourself, the Divine could use a good cleaning."

"I suggested that to her, but she has blinders on to anything except a renovation."

"What about a *restor*ation?" he asked.

"What's the difference? I don't see what you're getting at."

"Well, the two words are often used synonymously. But there is a difference. Renovation is a reinvention, to go back to the original concept and do it again. It might mean destroying or replacing the original. A restoration, on the other hand, is an affirmation of the original. You're not trying to reinvent something, to change it so much as you are trying to bring out more of its original purpose. It's the difference between plastic surgery versus exercise to alter one's appearance. Both make a person look different, but only the natural way tends to bring out a person's true features."

"So how do I apply this to Joan's crusade to change the Divine?" I asked, distracted by his explanation.

"You agree with her that the church needs to be cleaned and modernized. But call it a restoration—new paint, new cushions and drapes,
clean the organ pipes, wash the windows, polish the marble. Give her
something new to buy, and stick a plaque with her name on it, and she'll
be happy."

I mulled over his suggestion. I liked the implications of his semantic
distinction. "Would I be stretching your point too far to say that renovation compares to when we try to change ourselves, to reinvent ourselves, to live by our own efforts. And restoration is about redemption,
the way God restores us to holiness, to Christlikeness?"

"You could say that." John chuckled. "Everything is sermon material
for you, isn't it?"

I laughed. "And what if it is?" We exchanged our good-byes, but my
mind continued to explore the power of language to shape our percep-
tions. My mind settled on Gentry Truman's death.

A new line formed, connecting various points within the plane of
possibility. A web of suspicions was converging in my mind, growing,
connecting, forming a pattern that was insidiously and unbelievably evil.

The rest of the week returned to normal temperatures and seasonable
pursuits, chiefly, Avenell University Homecoming weekend. Storefront
windows were painted with caricatures and cartoon scenes of our mascot
the Tiger defeating our opponent's mascot, which this year happened to
be the Cumberland University Falcon. Consequently, the bakery window
depicted a ravenous tiger with a Tweety Bird in his large orange paws.
Below it a caption read, *I tawt I saw a Tiger Cat!* Another scene, this one
gracing Spradley's Market, showed the tiger dressed as a pilgrim and sitting down to a Thanksgiving meal of roast falcon instead of turkey. *A
traditional meal of roast bird with all the trimmings!* Avenell posters with
Go Tigers! were plastered everywhere, along with an oversized banner
hanging across the main intersection reading, *Avenell—"Burning Bright
in the Forests of the Night!"* The line, taken from Blake's "Tyger, Tyger"

poem, had become a traditional university slogan after a mural depicting the poem was painted in the athletic center back in the '50s. Most fraternities required iniates to memorize the entire work. That, and the university's Latin motto, "*Semper Veritas.*"

The decorations were silly and exuberant with the enthusiasm that only undergraduates experience for their new home-away-from-home. Avenell colors, royal blue and white, adorned lampposts and streetlights. This year seemed more jubilant than recent years past, as if the students needed to shrug off the tragedy in the Martyr's Chapel and the malaise of this week's weather.

However, the rest of us could not escape the pall of suspicions and fears of imminent violence lingering in the aftermath of Florence Lipton's crash and Gentry Truman's will. My cold had now dwindled to a minor inconvenience, so I visited the hospital for a few hours on Wednesday morning. Truman's personal assistant showed no change, still critically comatose. She might never regain consciousness.

I met her daughter, Valerie, a lovely long-limbed, athletic-looking young woman with her mother's eyes and nose. She clearly idolized her mother and seemed to know nothing about her mother's relationship with Truman or her embezzlement from him. It was certainly not a responsibility I was called to. After considerable prayer about the matter, I had decided that I would only mention Florence's confession to Sheriff Claiborne if she died.

I took Valerie a gift basket assembled by Bea that included everything from homemade brownies to a paperback *Perelandra* to bubble bath. She asked me to pray for her mother with her in the tiny closet-sized chapel up on the hospital's third floor, and I was relieved to be useful. I left her with my phone number, and she promised to call if she needed to talk or if there were any changes in her mother's condition.

Dan stopped by that afternoon brimming with information, as usual, in his uniquely efficient yet laid-back manner. I related my visit to the hospital, and he informed me of details from the scene.

"Strange thing is, Florence Lipton stopped her car approximately a hundred yards from where it left the highway. We have a clear tire print match taken from the shoulder. Why would she stop the car and then two minutes later lose control?" he asked, pouring himself a glass of milk as we sat at the breakfast table in Bea's blue-and-white kitchen.

"If she were pushed?" I ventured.

"Exactly," he said, wiping a white mustache from his dark upper lip. "Doc Graham called the attending physician for us at the hospital. There's a head wound on the side of the head that doesn't match anything she could have hit in the car on impact. It seems likely that she was flagged down, knocked in the head, then pushed down the mountainside."

"Then she's lucky to even be alive," I said. "Let's just pray she makes it. Her daughter has no one else in the world."

Dan nodded as he munched on one of Bea's peanut butter cookies fresh from the oven. Peter's Next Generation group was hosting a bake sale during Friday's Homecoming parade in order to raise money for a missions trip to Mexico.

"Check this out," said Dan, wiping greasy cookie crumbs on the side of his pant leg before thrusting a sheaf of notarized papers my way. It was a copy of the report from a Vanderbilt professor of art appraising *The Walls of Paradise.* I thumbed through the five pages signed by Dr. Geoffrey R. Lindendorf and occasionally recognized a word or phrase—pigmentation, authentic composition, oil concentration, Hudson Valley School, highly Romantic. In my naïveté I was looking for a dollar amount, but found none. "So is it a Bierstadt or Frederick Church? Is it worth a lot of money? Any connection to Gentry Truman?"

"No, as best I can tell," replied Dan, licking his lips and debating on another cookie. "Professor Lindendorf said at most it's worth a few hundred dollars—basically whatever one could get someone else to pay. If you read the report carefully, you'll see that he advises us to have second opinions because he's made some close calls. But he's also made it clear that even if this were an unknown work by a famous artist, it would be extremely difficult to verify. Miss Bea's idea to raffle it off might not be such a bad one."

"And no connection to Gentry's play of the same name?" I asked.

"Not that we can tell. It seems purely coincidental," Dan replied. "Lindendorf thinks 'Walls of Paradise' is an old nickname for Eaglehead Valley. He thinks the framer likely named the painting, not the artist."

"You know, in my business, Dan, nothing is purely coincidental. I can't help but think it means something," I said.

"I'll bet you're one of those people who hears messages from God through songs on the radio," teased Dan.

"Maybe I am." I laughed along with him. If indeed this lovely landscape portrait had nothing to do with Gentry Truman or his death and if it were not worth more than a few hundred dollars, I knew the perfect place for it. But it would be a while before the recipients of the gift would be ready for it, if they ever were.

I phoned to speak to Marcia Truman on Thursday, purely a courtesy call, just to follow up and let her know that my prayers for her and the family continued. Jenna answered the phone and seemed genuinely pleased to hear my voice.

"It's been rather tense," she whispered after we exchanged greetings. "Marcia's upset and has fought with Cale quite a bit. I overhead her say that she's thinking of contesting the will."

"Is she there now?" I asked, imagining the ugly court battle that could ensue.

"No, she's off with Franklin. I think something's up with them, too," she continued in her lowest voice.

"Why do you say that?"

"I'm not sure. I've just never seen Milford wound so tight. I heard him tell Marcia that he's afraid she will leave him now." I could hear jazz playing in the background.

"How are you feeling, Jenna? Are your sisters still there?" I asked.

"I'm feeling pretty good, actually. Thank you for asking, Father. Lisa flew out yesterday and Lucy will be here until this weekend when she flies back to Prague."

"Is there anything I can do for you?" I imagined the way this sensitive young woman was likely absorbing the many tensions, spoken and unspoken, in her father's house.

"No, just keep praying like you do. Thanks for calling."

I stood at my desk, looking off into the blunted blue of the Cumberland Plateau, and wondered when it would all end—the secrets, the lies, the jealousies and fears spawned by one man's death.

Inside my bedroom is a framed cross-stitch reading *All Shall Be Most Well.* Amy stitched it shortly after we were married, and it proved an ironic harbinger of her disease and our loss. It was a quote from Julian of Norwich and figures centrally in another popular gift for grieving widowers, Sheldon van Auken's *A Severe Mercy.* Just then I went and stood in front of the sign, as if waiting for it to speak an oracle of hope. Would everything really be "most well" for Jenna and the remnants of Gentry Truman's family?

Friday shone as bright and winsome as a spring day, the antithesis of Monday. While the university was officially open and Franklin Milford sent out a memo stressing the necessity of maintaining classes, most professors were out with their students after lunch working on parade floats or lining Southern Avenue for a choice viewing spot. Most of the sororities and fraternities collaborated on Homecoming activities, especially the floats. Built on flat trailers pulled by trucks, cars, or golf carts, floats usually depicted scenes similar to those in storefront windows downtown. This year the Phi Kap and Tri Delt float had been suspended for poor taste: a church scene, crudely resembling the Martyr's Chapel, in which a Cumberland University football player, who bore an uncanny likeness to Gentry Truman, was being shot by the Avenell Tiger.

The temperature was in the mid-fifties, and it was difficult to believe the campus had been a living ice-sculpture only days before. Bea and I settled in front of the cathedral with lawn chairs and cameras. She wanted a shot of the Next Generation's float for the parish newsletter.

The marching band played, students threw handfuls of hard candy and toy whistles to faculty and neighborhood children clamoring alongside them, and the Tiger football team waved and growled from an open trailer, the same one that would be used for the hayride Saturday night after the game. It was all wonderfully small-townish and sincerely heartwarming, a celebration of the school, what it stood for, future hopes and dreams. Many alumni, identifiable by their expensive sweaters and kiltie loafers, pompons, and cups of beer, mingled with their children and former professors along the parade route.

The parade was just about over when Peter came sprinting his way to where Bea and I perched, his wind-tossed hair like blond feathers in a blender. "Enjoying the parade?" I asked before decoding the urgency in his eyes.

"President Milford would like to see you in his office right now," Pete said in winded breaths.

"What's wrong?" I asked, folding my chair and handing my camera to Bea.

"I don't know, but something's up. His secretary sent a work-study student to find you—she happens to be in our youth group and found me first. You want me to go with you?"

"No, I'll be fine. Just pray it's nothing serious."

I was dressed casually in khakis and a plaid twill shirt and was mistaken for an alumnus by more than one inebriated student—"Go Tigers! Yee-ha! Semper Veritas!" topped by a high five—as I made my way upstream to the Mary Bartlett Building and the office of the president.

Inside, the building seemed just as deserted as it had on Monday when I was there. Two university legends, Velma Whitehall and Mary Alice Taylor, both in the admissions office, made their way down the hall and smiled a greeting to me as they passed. The president's office was on the ground floor, encompassing an entire suite at the west end of the building. Inside its white double doors, Sarah Atkins' greeting telegraphed panic and relief amid the tasteful, masculine oak panels, hunting prints, and university portraits. "Go right in—he's waiting on you. Coffee?"

"No, thank you," I said and knocked on the stately oak door before turning the brass knob.

"Come in," he replied in a flat, officious tone. I shut the door behind me.

Franklin Milford stood at the window, which commanded a lovely view of the bowling green commons and the dull tips of hill-sized mountains behind the university center. With his back still to me, he said, "Grif, it's over."

"What's over?" I asked, waiting at the corner of his massive antebellum plantation desk. The despair in his voice seeped through his handful of syllables.

"My life. My career. Marcia. It's all over. Sow the wind, reap the whirlwind."

"Frank, tell me what this is all about. Why is everything over?"

"Here, take a look at the latest copy of the *Midnight Star*. It's dated Monday but hits the stands tomorrow." He turned and tossed a copy of the glossy tabloid on his desktop. It smacked his leather desk blotter like a dead fish.

And its headline smelled just as bad. *Marcia's Old Flame Univ. Pres. Helps Murder Gentry*. Alongside it ran a black-and-white photograph, grainy and magnified but clearly identifiable, of Marcia and Franklin kissing passionately.

Chapter Twenty-two

THE BIG GAME

I TURNED TO the article in the center of the slick sensationalist periodical. More still frames taken from a hotel parking lot surveillance video showed the widow and the university president embracing, kissing, and in the last shot, a color photo, passing what appeared to be a gun. The electronic date recorded on each frame was 10-30, the night Truman presumably died. I skimmed the text, assembled by a slimy private-eye-turned-reporter, and realized the allegations, if true, could indeed bring an end to many facets of Franklin Milford's life.

"I thought Marcia was at the ballet with her son the night Gentry was murdered," I stated matter of factly.

"They drove down to Nashville that afternoon, but she impulsively decided to drive back with me. Obviously a big mistake." His voice sounded pitiable, drained of its usual sonorous authority.

"This kind of sensationalism is despicable, Franklin. Reprehensible. I'm sure there's an explanation for these photographs. No one who knows you or Marcia will believe this article." I slapped the tabloid shut and turned it facedown, an advertisement for press-on nails clawing at me from the back cover.

Milford chuckled. "Even if some of it is true? Grif, that's what I love about you. You're always willing to give any man the benefit of the doubt. Yes," he laughed harder, almost hysterically, "there's a perfectly good explanation for those photos. I was kissing my mistress, another man's wife, in the parking lot at the Nashville Hilton. Later, in the driveway of her home, I'm seen slipping her a nine-millimeter Beretta for protection against a psychopathic, emotionally abusive, alcoholic husband. It's just a coincidence that said husband dies later that same night—in a place where the lovers used to leave messages for one another." His laughter subsided, but the wild flame in his eyes did not.

"You and Marcia left messages for one another in the Martyr's Chapel?" I stammered.

"Don't worry, we didn't violate the place. For heaven's sake, we haven't lost all sense of decorum. We'd simply meet there or leave notes in the pew rack on the back wall. It was perfectly harmless—until Gentry decided to die there."

"Is that why Gentry went there the night of his death?"

"I don't think so. Marcia believes it's the reason, but I don't think there's any way he could have known. No one ever saw us there."

The fact that no such rumor or speculation had made the rounds in a small town reinforced, but did not assure, his disclosure.

"It gets worse," he continued, trying to bridle his outburst. "I had a verbal argument in which I threatened Gentry just days before his death. And his lovely secretary, Florence Lipton, heard me. Although she seemed preoccupied when I came out of Truman's office, I'm sure she overheard me. Truman was drunk, taunting me, coyly implying that his wife would never leave him for me. I lost my temper, said things I regret."

"Did Lipton tell the police what she overheard?"

"Not to my knowledge. It's one of the few things they didn't ask about in the two interrogations. Unless they're simply sitting and waiting for something like this to break." He jabbed the magazine. "I acknowledged the affair to Sam Claiborne, and he said he'd try to keep it under wraps. But he warned me that something like this could happen." He looked boyish, unrepentant but remorseful for getting caught.

"Franklin, I . . . I'm sorry. This does look grim. Marcia had told me that you and she had been involved for several months. That she had asked Gentry for a divorce at the party the night before he died." I shifted my feet and felt the weight of my silver cross on a sterling chain, a gift from my own wife, resting heavily against my breast inside my shirt. Somehow my awareness of it seemed awkwardly comforting.

The president seated himself stiffly in the burgundy leather wingback behind his desk, his dark suit, white shirt, and striped tie immaculate. "An idle threat," he said, removing his oval glasses and massaging his eyes with thumb and forefinger. "She had no intention of divorcing him, although I'd begged her to for months."

"What do you mean? She told me she had threatened before, but that both she and Gentry knew she meant it this time."

"If she divorced Gentry Truman, Marcia would get nothing in the settlement. She signed a prenuptial agreement that states irrevocably, undeniably that she would leave the marriage only with what she brought into it. Which was very little. That's what Truman taunted me with on the Tuesday before his death. I've never said as much to her, but I think she married Gentry for his money—that and the 'legendary star' mystique. A humble university administrator cannot compete."

"The two of you knew each other in college, correct?" From a neat front corner of his desk I picked up a crystal globe paperweight that captured the stained-glass pattern of the Divine Cathedral's rose window.

"Yes, we both attended Wake Forest as undergraduates. We were an item for over two years until her infatuation with the stage set in. After that, no man could hold her. We had lost contact for many years—she became an actress, I attended grad school—but then we met up at a fundraiser in New York a year ago last spring. Her son Dylan was interested in Avenell, and, of course, Gentry was from the area. . . ."

"How long had he known about you and Marcia?" I asked, holding the paperweight loosely, assessing its weight.

"Oh, at least since this past summer when they moved here. Evidently, I was not the first dalliance she's had during their marriage. That alone should have told me something, but it didn't. I was different, of course. We were meant to be together. I felt little guilt, Griffin. My job is so lonely . . . and it wasn't like Marcia was happily married to Gentry."

"I know how lonely single life can be," I whispered, looking out beyond the window, temporarily blinded by the falling orb of golden afternoon light, the vermilion shimmer of scarlet maples in the treeline beside the green. Outside, excited shouts and animated voices made plans for the Homecoming dance that night in the university ballroom, oblivious to their leader's plight.

"It's well and fine for you to play the lonely widower, Grif, but I needed someone. Someone full of life and beauty and intellect, someone who respects me and cares about what I do each day." He had replaced his glasses and sat swiveling in his chair, arms extended with fingers pressed together palm to palm, his voice effusing control once more.

"Is that how you see me, Frank?" I asked. "The lonely widower relishing his grief?"

"I'm sorry, Grif, I didn't mean anything by that. You have your faith, and perhaps that's enough for you. But all I have is the university and Marcia, and now I'm likely to lose them both."

"Has Marcia seen the tabloid yet?" I let my hurt slide into the weighted glass in my hand and replaced it on Milford's desk.

"No. We were scheduled to have lunch together, but she never showed. She's terribly upset with Cale right now—thinks he had something to do with Gentry's will being changed right before he died. She doesn't see how she can survive on what he left her. I expect she's off somewhere trying to hire a lawyer or butter up Cale. I'm no longer a priority."

"Now that she's free to marry you, she doesn't want to?"

"Yes. She says she's not sure what she wants, but I can tell by her tone of voice that she wants out. Although she does seem confused, very distracted—which is unusual for her. She's usually such a control freak—that's why I bought her the gun, she was afraid of Gentry when he was drunk." His tone changed, registering an octave lower. "Or perhaps the actress is simply refining a role. She's grown tired of me and has more urgent concerns."

"Do you know Cale Sanders well?" I asked.

"No, not really. Mostly through Marcia. It's funny, really. She and Cale have tended to be allies these past few months. He's covered for her a few times with Gentry when she was with me. Why?"

"Do you think she and Cale are involved?"

"No. Although she told me they had a fling back when she first landed in L.A., probably twenty-five years ago. Do you believe Cale shot his brother?"

"No, actually, I don't. Do you know who shot Gentry?" The words formed a lead-weight volley, almost accusatory.

He smirked. "Yes, that's why I arranged to have these pictures of me smeared all over the tabloids! No, I don't know who shot the man! I'm tempted to believe he killed himself and arranged for it to look like a murder—that would be such a Truman thing to do!" His anger corroded the integrity of my question. "Do you know who killed Gentry Truman?"

"Yes, I believe I do," I replied calmly. "But I want to be sure before I make any accusations."

His eyes braced themselves against his narrow sockets. "Grif, if you know something, don't sit on it." He jumped to his feet again and faced the window, pulled the sheer fabric back from the window. "Don't endanger yourself."

More fading sunlight spilled mottled shadows across the room. A pair of blue and white balloons drifted across the horizon from the direction of the parade and Fraternity Row, beautifully ephemeral in their helium-induced escape from earth. How had Robert Frost described his longing in "Birches"? Something about climbing away from the ground until the branches cannot support him further. The poet's insistence on going *toward* heaven instead of *to* heaven had always intrigued me. What is it about us as humans that insists on remaining earthbound? Fear of judgment? Of the unknown?

I turned to go. "How can I help you, Franklin? Is there anything I can do?"

"You can remain my friend. That's all I ask. Do you think I should resign?"

"I don't know what I think right now. Franklin, you wouldn't . . . do anything rash, would you? Even if you are forced to resign, even if Marcia should leave you—"

"Would I take my own life? Is that what you're asking so diplomatically?" He yanked the brass pull on a green-globed desk lamp. "No, Grif. I'm not that desperate yet. I can always go back to teaching. . . ." The diffused emerald-toned light gave his face odd shadows around his eyes and mouth.

"Will you do me an extraordinary favor, Frank? Will you call me when you hear from Marcia again?"

"Yes, I'll let you know as soon as I hear anything."

I went home, called Dan Warren, and asked him to beef up security around Florence Lipton's hospital room.

———

By Saturday, copies of the tabloid spread like a brush fire along the mountainside. I would later learn the board of trustees called a special meeting for Monday morning to discuss the situation. In the meantime, Franklin Milford was forced to make a public appearance at Jensen Field with the Homecoming king and queen to flip the coin for the football game.

My sleep the prior night had been restless, filled with dreams of Charlie Baxter and my brother Tupper, Gentry Truman with gunpowder and blood on his hands explaining the meaning behind the Petrarchan sonnet, and my sister trying to warn me about the pot roast. Next, I followed strange tunnels to the Martyr's Chapel where it had become a stage, complete with actors, an audience, props. Backstage, Marcia argued with Franklin Milford over where they should bury Gentry. It was very ominous, and I awoke with the sun, struggling vainly to form a narrative from the discordant, surreal scenes.

Our university president had not called me with news of his beloved, so I called the Truman house myself and spoke with Jeanette, who informed me that Mrs. Truman and Mr. Sanders had not been seen since Thursday evening. Dylan and Jenna had left shortly after eight to drive Lisa Chandler to the airport in Nashville. She would have one of them call me when any of them returned.

I was worried but prayed for patience and God's sovereign timing as I took my shower. I did not want my anxiety or my film noir dreams to deter my course of action for the day. After breakfast, I debated on wearing clericals or not, but decided to dress for the game in a white shirt, Avenell-blue cotton sweater, and gray corduroys. I carefully folded my rabat, a black shirt-front with clerical collar attached, to replace my sweater later in the afternoon. My sister found the rabat comparable to a dickey, the faux-collars women often wore beneath sweaters or jackets, and teased Peter and me about pulling "rabats from our hats."

Next, I dialed Caroline Barr, and with the same spontaneity as my call the previous Saturday, I asked if I might drop by that morning.

"Of course," she replied. "I was just debating on whether to attend the big game this afternoon." Her sarcasm betrayed her lack of athletic enthusiasm, and I smiled to myself.

"I tell you what. If you help me with some rather strange favors this morning, I would love to take you to the Homecoming game—I believe kick-off's at one?"

She agreed, and I was gathering my notebook to be on my way when Beatrice appeared in the door of my study. "May I have a word with you?" she asked gently.

"Of course. Is everything all right? Florence Lipton hasn't . . ."

"No, no. I assume her condition is the same as it was yesterday when you were there. No, I just wanted to tell you—I know that you had lunch with Dr. Barr from the English department last Saturday. And I think it's a wonderful thing. I know I'm rather possessive of you sometimes—one minute planning a blind date, the next forbidding you to go—but I want you to know that I think it's time for you to move on. I believe Amy would want it that way. Who knows what our God has in store for you? I guess I'm saying that I don't want you to worry about me if you should ever . . . if Dr. Barr turns out to be . . ." She nervously wove a tissue through the lace of her fingers.

"Beatrice, you constantly surprise me," I said sincerely. "I appreciate your blessing. And if the time ever comes when I'm considering a new roommate in the rectory, you'll be the first to know."

"So . . . does that mean you do or you don't like Dr. Barr?" she asked, bouncing back to her usual forthrightness.

"I like her just fine. We're becoming friends, I suppose. Actually, I'm quite curious about her. You don't have any hair color, do you?"

"*What?* What's Miss Clairol got to do with anything? You know I don't use the stuff. I thought we were talking about Caroline Barr?" My sister shifted her stance in her sensible Clark walking shoes. She wore royal blue knit pants and an Avenell Tiger sweat shirt. She and Roberta Montoya had tickets on the fifty-yard line.

"Oh, nothing. Just wondering. Yes, I'm fine. Look, I'll see you at the game." So many considerations spun like plates above the dowels of my mind.

At Caroline's neat cottage, as she offered steaming chicory with milk, I told her that I was going to ask several strange questions and would appreciate her honest response unless they proved too personal.

"Does this have anything to do with Gentry's death?" she asked, and I nodded.

"Ask away, then."

"I need to see pictures of you at Columbia—photos when you were Carol Tyson-Burks. And then I would like a current photo of you." She looked at me curiously, a bit wounded at first, her eyes tracing mine for unspoken communication but shifting to tentative trust.

She marched sock-footed down the golden hardwood hall into her bedroom. I heard a file cabinet rake and close, boxes shuffle, bureau drawers slide, and a cedar chest creak before she said to herself, "Yes, here you are." She hurried back into the room and sat close enough to me on the blue sofa that our knees touched.

"Almost twelve years ago. This was taken just before Truman stole my scenes." She pointed to a short, weight-burdened woman in a navy double-breasted pea coat posed stiffly before one of the famous lions guarding the New York Public Library at Fifth Avenue. Her hair was curly and dark, a listless, mousy brown color forming a claustrophobic helmet around her lovely face, which was further obscured by large octagonal glasses guarding the beautiful blue eyes. She looked to be in her late thirties in the picture instead of a decade younger. "Pretty sad, isn't it?" she said, biting her lower lip as if awaiting my judgment.

"No, not at all. It's only sad that you struggled to love yourself. You look shorter here   have you grown since?"

Tears brimmed her eyes, and she smiled. A whisper of perfume caught me with soft lavender notes. This was more painful for both of us than I had realized.

"No, it's simply the extra weight I carried—almost forty pounds. And poor posture—I didn't carry myself very well."

"You've certainly changed."

"Here—this was taken this past summer at new student orientation." This snapshot exuded color and more favorable lighting, as well as a happier subject. She wore trim khaki trousers, a short-sleeved white linen blouse, and looked radiant with straight, shoulder-length auburn hair, a genuine smile, and piercing eyes. She looked taller, but her explanation bore out the illusive reality of weight and posture in the first photograph.

"Other than the internal transformation, how did you go about restoring yourself? Did your training as a dramatist help you make this transformation? If I didn't know better, I'd say you were older in this picture instead of this one from last summer."

She blushed, accentuating the strawberry flecks of freckles across her nose and cheeks. "Yes, I suppose my writer's self-consciousness finally helped me. And I did have a friend who was a makeup artist for the traveling company of *Les Miserables*. We were undergrads together, and she was always dying to get her hands on me for a make-over. When I was finally ready to change, I gave her a call and went to visit her in San Francisco. She helped me shop, pick out clothes, the whole bit. It wasn't instantaneous, but Teresa's loving expertise sure made a difference."

"So if I were an actor preparing for a part, how would you coach me to get into character?"

"Well, it depends on the role, of course. Method actors are notorious for getting inside their characters and holding on to them for the show's run. There's an actor on Broadway in the show *Capeman* who played a convicted murderer. He was the star of the show but insisted on having the smallest dressing room available—no bigger than a broom closet—just to know how it felt in a confined jail cell."

"If I were going to be playing Gentry Truman on stage, how would you go about transforming me?"

"Well, you're at a great disadvantage to play scum like him—you're much better looking, several inches taller, and kinder in disposition." Intrigue fueled her animated compliment.

"Thank you. But let's say that I'm roughly the same height, with similar features. Then what?"

"I would apply makeup to give you the same-shaped face—high cheekbones, deeper-set eyes, older, more wrinkles around the eyes. Your hair—well, we'd probably need a wig, and if we had an unlimited budget, we could dye the wig Truman's salt-and-pepper color to a perfect match. After that, we'd work on wardrobe—relatively easy in this case. The last part's the hardest—teaching you his mannerisms, stance, walking patterns, voice modulations."

"Do you color your hair?" I asked abruptly.

"Well, yes, I highlight it. As you can see in the picture, I'm naturally a bit darker, so I highlight."

"Do you have any hair color here?" I continued.

"Hmm, I usually have it done by my stylist, but wait a second . . ." She scurried to the bathroom and the echo of banging drawers resumed.

"Here—will this do? It's probably a couple of years old—I moved here with it. It's not really my shade—or yours." She laughed and I joined her.

The dark amber bottle was smudged around the cap with dried color like mud. I scanned the label, read directions and ingredients.

"So simple, really," I said. "So blatant that it's frightening."

"What?" she asked.

"The murderer," I replied.

———

That afternoon in the cool autumn sunshine, as a crowd of almost four thousand watched the Avenell Tigers defeat the Cumberland Falcons by two touchdowns, I sat with Caroline Barr and discussed the finer points of the I-formation and the crucial role of the running game. We sipped Cokes from plastic Tiger's Paw tumblers, ate two hot dogs with spicy gold mustard apiece, and discussed our lives as if we had never heard of Gentry Truman. Many parishioners saw us, waved, and seemed genuinely pleased that I was enjoying the company of a lovely woman, even if she was twelve years my junior. If Joan Dowinger was looking for ammo, I knew I was opening up a foothold in my willingness to be seen with Caroline in such a public venue.

Nonetheless, I thoroughly enjoyed myself. We discussed recent books we'd read and more we were hoping to tackle over the upcoming Christmas break. The Pride of Avenell Marching Band performed a stirring tribute to disco and the 1970s, complete with bell bottoms and halter tops on the majorettes and tie-dye streamers on batons. Caroline and I laughed, swapping stories about our own undergraduate years, even as we surveyed the sweater-and-tie young men with their dates in blue plaid skirts and white blouses, cream colored pompons and blue-ribboned corsages bulging from their shoulders. The afternoon air shimmered with the golden breakdown of autumn, like a dark walnut about to be cracked by azure skies, the wind lingering with remnants of hickory-wood smoke from the bonfire the night before.

Near the end of the fourth quarter, as four o'clock approached, I asked Caroline if she'd be interested in driving down to the valley with me. There was one more detail I wanted to verify.

"I'm game—besides, I think you need a bodyguard." She smiled.

We beat the crowd, although some students were already heading back to their dorms or the Tiger Bay Pub for post-game cocktails. I quickly checked messages at the rectory, but no one had called. My adrenaline percolated nonetheless. I left Bea a note telling her where I was going.

As we drove down the mountainside, the hills and treeline eclipsed the last planes of sunlight and it suddenly seemed much later than it was. I had donned my rabat before assuming the driver's seat while my companion looked on curiously. Caroline seemed to enjoy our air of shared adventure, seemed implicitly comfortable with my odd behavior and nervous tension. Finally, however, as we leaned into a narrow curve halfway down Eaglehead, she could contain herself no longer.

"May I ask where we're going?"

"Down in the valley, on the other side of Mumford. The Eagle's Nest Retirement Home."

Chapter Twenty-three

THY KINGDOM COME

THE EAGLE'S NEST RETIREMENT Home was located off Highway 88, about five miles from the Mumford square, on the way out of the county toward Lewiston. A sprawling, single-story network of brick wings with shuttered windows, it looked like a suburban miniature of the Pentagon, despite the care that had been taken to blend into the rolling farmland and neighborhoods of new redbrick homes growing around it.

The place was one of the most cheerful of such institutions I had ever been in privately owned and highly resistant to eager advances by HMOs and home health care companies. Despite the open windows and natural lighting, vases of fresh flowers and potted mums, the smell could not be eradicated, the poignant blend of urine, menthol liniment, mildew, and ammonia that pervaded such places where many awaited death and others fought him at the door.

Miss Olive Merriweather's room was 4-C, and the receptionist reminded us that visiting hours were over at six, even as she regarded my clerical collar. Our heels left muffled echoes down the tiled corridors as we made our way to the fourth and final wing. We heard a variety of voices and gentle laughter as I knocked sharply on the oversized veneered door.

"Come on in, honey," came a high, sweet voice.

We entered and found not the hospital bed and metal rails I had expected, but a large suite with antique furnishings, a cotton-rag rug, numerous photographs, and a large, cheerful watercolor of Eaglehead Mountain in springtime. This room smelled faintly of gardenias and was clearly someone's home, not an institutional cell.

"Miss Merriweather?" I asked. "I'm Father Griffin Reed, from Avenell Parish up on the mountain. This is my friend, Dr. Caroline Barr. May we come in?"

"Sure thing, Father. I thought you were Nurse Nancy with my medication—it's about time for her to come round. Y'all come on in, we got plenty of room." She smiled up at us from a full, round face ponderous with pink, wrinkled flesh. Alert blue eyes regarded us curiously. Her hair was curled in waves of white-gray smoke that sat atop her head like meringue. She wore a loose cotton housedress of green flannel that disguised her large-boned frame even as she sat on the edge of a quilted full-sized bed. She extended a long-fingered hand and shook mine firmly.

"This is my friend, Delthenia Witherspoon."

"Oh, Father Reed, how nice to see you again—we met last week at Gentry's house!" The small black woman looked like a life-size doll compared to her companion.

"Yes—Miss Del, how nice to see you, too. This is Caroline." A delicate clasp of feminine hands among the three women.

"Oh, I wished I could have made it to the service. Del has told me all about it, but I just didn't think I was up to it. The girls—Jenna and Lucy—offered to come and get me, but I wasn't sure I could bear the trip and my grief at the same time. Did you know my Gentry, Father Reed?" the old woman continued excitedly.

"Yes, in a limited capacity. I've always been a fan of his works. I'm sure you're very proud of him."

"Oh my, yes. I made an entire scrapbook once tracing Gent's fabulous career. I still can't believe that I've outlived him—I would never have thought it."

I leaned against a cherry sideboard cluttered with metal-rimmed photographs—a few I recognized as Gentry and his daughters and Cale. A large playbill for *The Color of Night* signed by the cast and dedicated to Aunt Olive was framed on the wall behind the door. Caroline settled in the only remaining chair, a Boston rocker draped with a white, crocheted lap blanket.

"And what about you, dear?" Miss Del motioned toward Caroline. "Are you helping Father Reed find out how Gentry died?"

The question took me by surprise, but Dr. Barr seized the opportunity. "Yes, you could say that. Did you know him growing up?"

The two old women cackled like witches auditioning for *Macbeth*. "We lived next door to each other for over forty years!" shrieked Olive. "After my sister Ellen died, I moved in with Mama—my husband was killed in the service—and helped her raise Cale and Gent. Del, here, lived next door to us out at the sand plant in a house bought from the Sears and Roebuck catalog. I remember when Mr. Abe—that was Miss Del's husband—assembled that house all by himself with only little Adam to help him!" The two women shared memories back and forth with their eyes.

"What were Cale and Gentry like as boys? Did they look alike?" I asked.

"Oh, honey, I never seen two nuts off the same tree look alike the way those boys did. Most everybody thought they's twins, even though they were fourteen months apart."

"But Cale had a different father," I verified.

The wizened old faces exchanged another intimate look. A long, uncomfortable pause. "I don't see why it matters none now," said Miss Del. "Tell this Father the truth, Ollie."

"They had the same Daddy, Father Reed. Cale and Gentry was true blood brothers. They both found out after they were grown. Mr. Spencer Dunlap Truman fathered two sons by my sister Ellen." She opened up a nightstand next to her bedside and raised a cracked red-leather album to her lap. She thumbed slowly through a stack of loose photos inside the cover. "Here it is—this is Cale and Gentry's parents."

The yellowed black-and-white was almost brittle but still as smooth to my fingers as the finest porcelain. A woman with a short, flapper-style haircut and a low-cut dress laughed next to a handsome, suited gentleman with a familiar bemused smirk on his oval face. His hair was combed back away from his forehead, and he held a brimmed felt hat in his hand.

"Why do the biographies say that Gentry and Cale are only half brothers?" asked Caroline, looking over my shoulder.

"Well, when Ellen got pregnant with Cale, Spencer was engaged to someone else, a young society woman back in Savannah. He didn't love her, obviously, but he couldn't bring himself to tell his parents—or his fiancée—the truth. So he supported Ellen, promised to marry her some-day, and she had Cale out of wedlock. She fabricated some story about a fling with a passing salesman to save her lover's family name. Mama was against it the whole way. . . .

"Later, when she became pregnant with Gentry, Ellen tried to force his hand. They broke up but couldn't stay away from each other. Finally, when Cale was about two and a half—so Gentry would have been about a year old—Spence married her despite his family's objections. We Sand-ers have always been proud, even if we were brought up as poor country folk. Nothin' wrong with simple livin', is there, Del?"

Her old friend made a clucking sound like a mother hen. "Oh my goodness, no. The good Lord watch over poor people as well as he watch over the rich—more so, I think to myself sometimes. Ain't that right, Father?"

"Yes, ma'am." I smiled. "The good Lord does watch over us all." I turned back to Gentry Truman's aunt.

"Do you have any pictures of Cale and Gentry together? Maybe as teenagers?" I asked. The old woman immediately started spidering her long fingers through the black pages of the album.

"This was taken right before Gentry left us and hitchhiked to New York," she said. "This was his sixteenth birthday party." She handed over another snapshot, this one more ivoried than yellowed. In the portrait two young men in white shirts and dark cardigan sweaters leaned on each other in front of a tiny, clapboard house. Each had short, dark wavy hair, broad smiles that hung like quarter-moons above defiant chins, and long limbs. I was speechless.

Caroline voiced my question: "Which one is Gentry?"

"See what I mean about them boys lookin' like two peas in a pod? That's Gentry on the right. Cale was about a quarter-inch taller."

"Was there a copy of this photograph in the scrapbook you put together for the Harpertown Library?" I asked, finding my voice.

"Sure enough—did you see it?" She seemed pleased.

"No, unfortunately, it was missing. But this photograph is very helpful—would you be willing to let me borrow it for a little while? I'd like to show it to the police."

She seemed confused, reluctant. "Well, all right, if you promise to take good care of it."

"Yes, I promise."

"Did Gentry and Cale get along as closely as they resembled?" Caroline asked.

Miss Del guffawed and held her knee through the gray wool knit of her skirt. "They fought like Cain and Abel—one trying to outdo the other. It was always a toss-up who was the smartest."

"How did Cale feel after his brother ran away to New York? He must have been lonely," I suggested.

"Oh, he was. Poor Cale felt totally abandoned after that. Their father was never there, then Ellen died in that horrible fire, then his only brother left—I'm not sure he ever forgave Gentry," said Miss Olive.

"When was the last time you saw either of them?" I asked, glancing at a porcelain clock hand-painted in roses and violets on the nightstand. Visiting hours were almost up.

"Well, usually at holidays, they'd try to make it down, but since they've been up in your neck of the woods, they come to see me every few weeks, I reckon. Cale more than Gentry. Cale was always such a sweet boy, always made time for me. Gentry was always busy, busy—then restless if he did come. I've been wondering why Cale hasn't been down since the . . . accident," she said.

"You haven't seen your nephew since Gentry's death?" I repeated.

"No, he promised to come by this next week. I know he's taking it hard."

"Miss Olive, you've been most kind. I hope that the reason I'm here won't result in further heartache for you."

She looked at me with owl-eyed intensity. "I appreciate your kindness, Father. But I done seen enough trials and tribulations to last a lifetime—almost two," she chuckled. "When I'm hurtin' or in trouble, I just pray, 'Lord, thy kingdom come.' "

"Amen," said Miss Del. And we left the two old friends to eat their supper together, which arrived just as we were leaving.

———————

"I don't know what plan you're concocting in your mind, but you must let me help you. I'm afraid that something else is going to happen," said Caroline as we sliced through the crisp night air driving up the dark mountain. Stars were sprinkled like platinum filings above us.

"Most of the pieces are just about in place," I said. "I think I need to call Dan Warren as soon as we get home. It may be his job from here on out."

We remained comfortably silent for the remaining ride home until we reached the neon-frazzled outskirts of Avenell. My mind drifted to Peter and his infatuation with Leah Schroeder. He had not asked for the car this week, but I suspected he had found a way for the two of them to see each other.

Along the intersection of Southern and Highway 9, Homecoming revelers peppered the streets, many with beers in hand. I prayed that none would be driving tonight.

Pulling into the narrow driveway to Caroline's home, the dark Pine Woods crowding either side, I didn't know how to thank her for spending the day with me. Once again, she found words first.

"I've thoroughly enjoyed your company today. I hope you find the justice you're looking for." An edge of sarcasm creeping in? Had I misjudged her?

"And I've enjoyed yours. I can't thank you enough for your help, especially this morning. And I hope you have a new appreciation for the sport of college football."

She laughed as I walked her to her door in the early evening darkness. "Call me if I can help you. I'll do anything I can."

"You are a very courageous woman, Caroline. But promise me that you'll lock your doors and stay in tonight."

"I can take care of myself."

"I don't mean to insult you. I know the sheriff's squad is still patrolling the area, but since they removed the detail from the Martyr's Chapel . . ." I wondered if she knew this already.

"Like I said before, I can take care of myself. I have a weapon—a holdover from my New York days. I know how to use it if necessary," she said, clearly annoyed at me now.

"I'll call you in a day or so. After this mess is all over. . . ." I headed back to the car, guided by the interior light flooding from the open driver's door. Had I been wrong to trust her?

———

Back at home, dark possibilities circled through my mind, a flow chart of tragic contingencies, even as I prayed a prayer of protection. I was restless for resolution to the suspicions that had plagued me for the past few days. Greater still, I was anxious for a criminal to be stopped before any more lives were ruined.

Despite the tension building inside me, roiling like storm clouds, I found the hall lamp on at home amid the comforting souvenirs of normalcy. Bea was playing canasta at Roberta's tonight—they had invited Doris Montgomery and Janice Phillips. My note had been amended with Bea's scrawled message: *Call Dan. I may be late—don't wait up. Love, B—*

I realized that I hadn't eaten since lunch and rummaged around in the fridge for sandwich fixings. I hoped Caroline didn't think me rude for not taking her to dinner.

Maria Alvarez picked up on the first ring at the sheriff's office, catching me with a mouthful of ham and swiss on wheat. "I'm sorry, Father Reed," she said. "Dan and Sam are over on the other side of the mountain. A trucker jack-knifed and the state boys called us for back-up. They'll probably be back in a couple of hours. Is it urgent? Should I radio them?"

I chewed thoughtfully for a moment. "No, don't radio them. But ask Dan or Sam to call me as soon as they check in, please."

"Will do," she said efficiently and hung up.

I tried Franklin Milford, both at home and office, and machines discharged similar official sounding messages each time. An answering machine also picked up at the Trumans with Marcia's patronizing voice asking callers to leave a message.

There was little I could do but wait. I finished my sandwich, flipped on the television, and channel surfed until I found a familiar black-and-white movie just starting. Brando and Leigh in *The Color of Night*, directed by George Cukor, screenplay by Gentry Truman, based on his stage play, winner of four Academy Awards. I hit the remote's Off button sharply and sat alone in the lamp-lit shadows of my den.

The phone rang shortly before midnight, and I bolted upright from a tenuous sleep, momentarily entangled in my recliner's extended ottoman. I picked up on the third ring. "Grif?" It was Franklin Milford. "Marcia just called me. She sounded tired, said she couldn't talk just then. She asked me to meet her at our usual spot in twenty minutes. I'm about to leave, but I'm calling you as I promised."

"Frank, I'd like you to do me a favor. Let me meet Marcia first—give me a chance to talk to her before you arrive. Just fifteen minutes—that's all I ask."

He hesitated just as I heard a car door slam.

"Griffin, I don't think that's a good idea. I've honored your request to know that Marcia's okay. She and I have a lot to talk about . . . it's rather personal despite how public our relationship's become. I appreciate your concern."

"Frank, for Marcia's safety as well as your own, give me a fifteen-minute head start, and then you two can talk all you want."

He paused again. "All right, Grif. I'll meet you there shortly. But I want to know what's going on."

"Thanks," I said and hung up just as Bea walked into the house.

"What's going on?" she asked.

"I can't explain right now," I said quickly, buttoning my field jacket. "But call Sam and Dan and have them meet me at the Martyr's Chapel. Better safe than sorry. I'm not taking any chances."

"Griffin Reed, I know that tone in your voice. Something's terribly wrong. I'm not going to let you leave this house without Sam or Dan accompanying you."

"Sis, I love you. But there's no time to lose. Please do as I ask and call the sheriff's office right now. If you get Maria, have her radio them in their cars. It's urgent." I tried to remain calm but could feel adrenaline spasming through my system. Bea had already picked up the phone as I closed and locked the door behind me.

Frost was beginning to blanket the outside world, leaving a thin crystal pattern across my windshield. Music blared in the distance, from the Sig Ep house it sounded like, and somewhere a dog barked.

I parked on the narrow, gravel roadside shoulder behind a grove of cedars. There were no other cars around, but I expected that one was hidden in some nearby barn or pine grove. I climbed over the flimsy fence and trudged across the dark hillside toward the chapel. Up above me the moon shone a half-faced candle's glow of pale light; clouds had rolled in to blot the inky night.

At first it appeared that no other lights were visible, no signs of life from within the church, but as I approached, I could see dim candlelight and hear low, angry voices. I debated on whether or not I should wait on Milford, and more important, on law enforcement, but recognized my caution as fear. If I were going to wait, then why had I come ahead of them in the first place? I crept slowly toward the narrow, four-paned windows and peered in. The glass was opaque, however, obscured by time and woodland pine needles. I could distinguish only that all the candles were lit, sending cold droplets of sweat down the sides of my body. I felt a gnawing fear, as if some perverse ritual were about to take place.

I would have to get inside the chapel to be of any use. I crouched along the base of the fieldstone structure, bracing myself against smooth rock like a mountain climber until I turned the corner and felt the heavy iron door-pull in my hand. Praying it wouldn't creak, I gently, carefully pulled the unlocked door toward me. I crawled on hands and knees inside the tiny narthex and lowered myself behind an oak pew. Strange shadows leapt and flickered like fiery tongues from the odd angles of candlelight. Yet as I slowly peered above the pew toward the front of the chapel, a scene far more sacrilegious than I could have imagined assaulted me.

Kneeling before the marble altar was Marcia Klein Truman, positioned loosely like a rag doll with ankles and wrists secured with silver-gray duct tape. And there in the dark, candle-lit shadows, a familiar figure, a taunting voice.

"Did you really think I would let you ride off into the sunset with your beloved Franklin?" His insidious laughter. He was dressed all in black and wan shadows bounced off his face, yet there was no doubt about who he was. It was like staring at one of those optical illusions or 3-D puzzles and suddenly seeing what had been there all along, disguised as something else.

In front of me, brandishing a handgun at his next victim, stood Gentry Truman, back from the dead.

Chapter Twenty-four

THY WILL BE DONE

ALL DOUBTS ABOUT IMPLAUSIBLE details quickly evaporated. The man standing before me was indeed Gentry Truman, with a calm smirk on his face that could have belonged to his dead brother, but, in fact, did not. The chapel seemed what the playwright wanted it to be, not a holy place, a sanctuary for those hungering and thirsting for righteousness, for solitude with their Creator, for a place of worship. Instead, the rustic church had become a stage, a setting for the final obstacles to be overcome in the perfect denouement of his twisted little drama.

It appeared that he was about to shoot his wife in the head and then frame her lover. I prayed that Bea had reached the sheriff and was taken seriously. What if they assumed she was simply overreacting? I could just hear Sam Claiborne's sincere dismissal of my sister's request. *"Yes, ma'am, Miss Reed, I'll send a squad car by when I've got a free man."* If she reached Dan Warren, he'd take her seriously, but would he come right then? Or what if Franklin walked in early and got us all killed? Why in the world had I come here without a weapon of any kind, especially when my worst fears were being transcended before my very eyes? Seconds passed and these fears ricocheted through my mind like emotional shrapnel. Gentry Truman placed the barrel beside Marcia's head. I heard him release the safety—there was no time to charge him.

"Stop! By all that's holy!" I shouted. Marcia screamed, high-pitched, theatrical.

The man masquerading as Cale Sanders for the past two weeks jerked the weapon back as if it controlled him. He thrust the gun in front of himself and stepped cautiously down the narrow chancel. "Who's there?" he snarled. His prisoner tried to turn, as well, but seemed unable to move against her bindings.

I stood up and squared my shoulders, strode forward into the flickering lights cast by the offertory votives and altar candles. Even the small candle fronting the aumbry, a small carved recess where the sacrament was stored when the church was in use, had been lit. Oddly, it glowed white, usually meaning it contained the holy Eucharist, instead of red, signaling its absence. I silently prayed Christ was present in the place.

I regained composure, had to buy time. " 'Hold your hand, my lord!' " I recited. " 'I have serv'd you ever since I was a child; But better service have I never done you Than now to bid you hold!' "

"Bravo, Father Reed! You can join your Gloucester as she's about to die! I'm impressed with your memory of *King Lear*, but you'll recall what happens to your noble First Servant! He dies in vain!" He motioned me forward with the sleek gun barrel.

"Then you missed the whole point of the scene, Gentry. The servant upbraids his master's cruelty to Gloucester simply because of his intolerance for injustice. He'd rather die for what's right than sit idly by and let an innocent man be tortured. Of course, you don't have a moral conscience any longer, do you?" I had to engage him, buy more time.

"You're really quite clever, Reed," said Gentry Truman. "Nosing around here, asking questions there. Always pretending to help, the dutiful priest offering his godly services." He moved behind me and shoved the Beretta between my shoulder blades, directing me to the same altar chair where he had murdered his brother Cale less than two weeks ago.

"I'll have to improvise my little drama now. It was going to be a crime of passion, the staid university president losing control and killing the lovely young widow who refused to marry him now that she was free. You see, Franklin and Marcia conspired to murder her husband, the legendary playwright Gentry Truman.

"But this is much more plausible—the heroic priest has deduced their terrible crime and followed them to the chapel, where he confronts them. There's a fight for the gun between the two of you before you're both shot. Marcia lands a stray bullet and voilà, a happy ending!" I sat stiffly in the straight-back wooden celebrant's chair, its thin faded cushion no comfort.

"Here's another possibility! You appear so holier-than-thou, when really you're just as fallible as the rest of us, more so as it turns out. You were having an affair with the seductive actress, of all things, and *you* helped her murder her husband. Shame on you! You became so remorseful that you decided the only way out is to end her life as well as your own. Fearless Franklin follows you here to fight for dear Marcia in vain. Last performance, final curtain. You were really not so holy, after all." He grinned, and I could see yellowed teeth bared like fangs.

Marcia found her voice and begged, "Gent, no, don't even think it. I'll help you, you need me, we can leave this pathetic little place and start over somewhere else—Europe or South America." I watched her wrestle the duct tape binding her ankles and wrists without success.

"Don't be a fool, Marcia. Did you really think I trusted you? I simply *needed* you. I needed a washed-up actress for the performance of her lifetime. None of my other wives were available, so I settled for you." He turned the gun barrel back to me.

"How would you like to die, Father? Would you like the authorities to find you embracing Marcia's half-clothed body with a bullet through your head? Maybe Milford walked in on you together and shot you both before doing himself in."

Marcia whimpered, tears spilling like water from a cracked vase.

" 'Our Father,' " I stammered automatically, " 'who art in heaven, Hallowed be thy name.' "

"Shut up!" Gentry screamed. "Don't try that holy abracadabra on me!

You don't get it, do you? I have *nothing* to lose. I killed my brother! Do you really think hearing the Lord's Prayer is going to make any difference?"

" 'Thy kingdom come. Thy will be done, On earth as it is in heaven.' " My breath was shallower and shallower. It reminded me of the first time I officiated the Eucharist at a service and thought I would hyperventilate. I stifled laughter then that I knew might quickly lead to hysterics. I had to keep my head. I had to buy time, leave room for Dan to arrive, for something to happen, for God to work. *Oh, Lord, please.*

Inspired, I asked, "And why, Gentry, why did you think you could get away with it? Not just one crime, but two. You not only murdered your brother, but you thought you could become him, assume his identity like it was one of your new suits from a London tailor."

"Why, I simply borrowed one of your Sunday school lessons—Jacob and Esau, remember? I was literally inspired! The usurper, the trickster, is the one who got his father's blessing by disguising himself as his brother. It suddenly seemed so clear. I had a face-lift, just like Cale, began losing weight—it's amazing how motivated one becomes when he's about to 'kill' himself! The resemblance was there all along—why, as boys people used to think we were twins. Our voices sounded alike, many of our mannerisms were the same. If I kept a low profile, stayed out of direct light and public scrutiny, I knew it would work.

"Cale was always jealous of me, but he never believed that I envied him, as well. He and I both knew that he had more talent than I did. And now it looks like his ship is finally coming in. He has a new play set to open on Broadway after Christmas. It's a shame he won't be here to enjoy it!"

"You're truly insane if you thought I wouldn't notice the difference! As if I wouldn't recognize my own husband," Marcia taunted.

"Ah yes, you were the wild card. As distant as we'd become, sleeping in separate bedrooms, I wasn't sure you'd notice! But then, you do have an eye for detail. Yes, you were the only obstacle, dear. So I made a contingency plan—and see, it worked!"

"I had no choice," she whined. "You threatened to implicate me in the murder! It was the only way I could get my share of the insurance money."

"You were on the verge of bankruptcy and your prenuptial agreement would have left you penniless if you'd divorced him," I added.

"Yes, my dear wife needs her fine things," snarled Gentry. "All those jewels and designer dresses don't come cheap for a has-been! Hardly on a university president's salary!"

"Leave Franklin out of this!" ordered Marcia.

"If only I could. He's the only one you seemed to care about. The only one who I couldn't explain away—he's not younger than me or better looking or richer. And he's certainly not as talented as I am. I never figured it out."

"You don't have the capacity to love anyone but yourself," she returned.

"Love," he snarled. "As dear Rachel says so eloquently in *The Color of Night,* 'All we have is ourselves in this life, and those fleeting moments where we delude ourselves with the illusion of love.' You fail the quiz— we must read our lines more carefully!"

"So let me see if I've got this straight," I began, my heart ticking like a stopwatch. "You got your brother drunk, drove him out here, dressed him in your clothes and then shot him in the head with your old .45. You then called me to foreshadow a suicide, as if you were distraught and depressed. You set the stage, planted the gun, and changed into your brother's wardrobe and began your act.

"But then God throws you a curve ball. Good old Charlie Baxter shows up to pick up the food my sister left for him behind the church. He wanders in to eat his supper and finds a dead man. He checks Cale's pulse, picks up the .45, and then panics when he realizes he could be implicated."

Marcia was breathing more deeply, and her mascara ran down her cheeks like giant whiskers. She nodded at my attempt to piece together the narrative.

"Suddenly the perfect suicide has gone awry. Now it looks like murder, only your new identity is one of the chief suspects. Once Marcia discovered your little secret, you blackmail her into compliance. The next fire to put out is Florence Lipton's discovery of a disk you thought you erased with your pathetic script. The world would find out after all that Gentry Truman really was washed up!" I relished my words.

"Shut up! You think you're so smart. Prepare to meet your maker, Padre." He came closer, and I thought he would shoot.

"So you follow Lipton down the mountain, run her onto the shoulder, and then knock her out. Then you retrieve the disk, start her car again, and push her over the side. Only one obstacle left. Marcia. But what a lucky break for you. You've decided to frame Franklin Milford for Cale's murder as well as Marcia's just as news of their affair breaks in the tabloids. But you didn't count on me showing up instead of Milford. You know the police are on their way, don't you?"

"You're bluffing! And you're the least of my worries, Reed. It's all over but the altar call. 'Softly and tenderly, Jesus is waiting!' " He fingered the trigger and hummed in a shrill falsetto.

"No matter how many people you fool, you will always be Gentry Truman. You cannot fool God—He made you and knows you! You can pretend to be Cale Sanders or the Duke of Windsor, but you will always be the same man in the eyes of God." My legs twitched, the kind of weak flutter I used to feel before a track meet in high school.

"No! I am Cale Sanders now. You pathetic losers are the only ones who know the truth, and you're about to die." He paused intently.

"You can't possibly understand," he began again. "You have no idea what it's like to be at the absolute top and look down on the rest of the world like it's a garbage heap of glittering toys. I was king of the hill! I had four—count them out loud, boys and girls—four plays running simultaneously on Broadway! I had millions and millions of dollars stashed in dozens of banks around the world—I was richer than God! I had beautiful actresses begging for me to sleep with them—to even look at them! I had it all!" His voice became hoarse, enervated, almost hysterical. "Do

you think I would give all that up without a fight? Do you?" He bore
down upon my temple with the pistol.

"But you haven't had any of those things in *years*!" whispered Marcia.
What strange allies she and I had become, prolonging our mortality, begging time for some cavalry that might never come.

He turned like a shadow back to his wife. "How dare you! You un-
grateful little tramp! I gave you the best of everything—and what did you
give me in return? At least half a dozen affairs, more credit card bills than
the national debt, and a life of sheer misery most of the time!"

His body seemed to shift back and forth between the slumped posture
of Gentry Truman and the straight backbone of Cale Sanders. Even his
face and eyes seemed to transform in the dim light, like a living Dr. Jekyll
and Mr. Hyde morphing back and forth before me, an actor who can no
longer discern his role from reality.

"Let her go, Truman. Or at least kill me first."

"I don't know who's the bigger fool—you or me. You think I'm a
terrible person for wanting to survive, wanting to begin again, for fighting
for what's rightfully mine. I think you're a fool for piddling your life away
on parish potlucks and white-knight delusions of grandeur."

" 'For whoever would save his life will lose it,' " I whispered, " 'and
whoever loses his life for My sake shall find it.' "

"Just shut up! I'm sick of your self-righteous verses and platitudes!"
He took a step up the altar. "It's show time! Say good-bye, Marcia!" He
aimed the pistol at his wife's head, point-blank range.

I reacted in a single fluid motion without thinking. I charged around
the altar and clipped his arms straight up. He fired, and we wrestled for
possession. He was stronger than I would have guessed, wiry, flexible,
meeting me turn for turn with a determined ferocity. Marcia cried out
like a wounded animal.

"Freeze!" came a strong feminine voice from the shadows at the back
of the church. Gentry and I held fast to one another's wrists but all motion ceased.

Caroline Barr burst forward from the darkness with a revolver extended.

"It's over, Truman! You're finally going to get your due," she said. Her hands were shaking delicately, as if the weapon were too heavy for her slender fingers.

Gentry suddenly wrenched free of my grasp and backed away two steps. "Well, well. If it isn't time to add another cast member to our casualty list. Little Carol Tyson-Burks. Still struggling with that writer's block, honey? Afraid someone will steal your precious words?"

"The game is over. Police are on their way." Her voice was steely and poised, electric with determination.

I could tell Truman was wavering, weighing his alternatives. I prayed that Caroline wasn't bluffing, that Dan and a cadre of law enforcement officers were on their way. If only we could hold out for a few more minutes. Would he kill us just for spite, just to punish others for loving goodness, for caring about justice?

"Drop it! Drop your weapon!" Caroline ordered.

"What? This little thing?" giggled Gentry fiendishly. "I'm afraid I can't do that. I've gone to a heap of trouble to keep my role in this farce we call life. I'm not sure I'm ready to play a bit-part as a death-row convict." He held the gun to his own head.

Suddenly, animated shadows consumed the chapel.

"Drop the gun, Truman! We have you surrounded!" Dan Warren's bass voice commanded like a giant stereo speaker. Dark-clad figures, a surreal Greek chorus of justice, inched forward slowly, slowly.

Marcia whimpered behind me while my eyes darted from the barrel at Gentry's temple to the revolver in Caroline's pale hands.

And then it was all over, like a dam bursting in a mammoth flood of release. Gentry laughed, a hopeless chortle like a dog choking that sent a cold current down my spine, then pulled the trigger. His head recoiled from the blast like broken statuary, as he escaped the defeated body he had schemed so desperately to protect. He collapsed like a scarecrow in a field that had been harvested long ago.

His wife sobbed hysterically in loud choking sobs. Caroline remained stationary, with her arms extended and the gun still in her hands, even as a dozen law enforcers shifted like mercury to control the scene and restore order.

Caroline began to shake, rocking her arms, along with the revolver, back down to her sides. Her shaking became violent, tremulous as a leaf in a hailstorm, and I rushed to hold her. My own heart had finally started beating again.

THANKSGIVING

————

MORE THAN A WEEK LATER I stood in the Avenell Cemetery on a cold autumn morning before a gravestone marked with Amy's name on it. I placed a dozen white roses in the marble vase built into the marker and knelt on the frosty carpet of manicured lawn. I prayed and thanked the Father for such a wonderful woman's presence in my life. I stood there for almost an hour, pacing alongside the many other markers and stone angels, the marble and granite guardians of the dead. It's silly, I know, but I wanted to talk to Amy about all that had happened to me in the past month. I wanted to tell her that I liked Caroline Barr very much.

There was no answer, of course; nor did I expect there to be. Only the cawing of three crows wired to a telephone line across the field. Only the wind rustling the remaining handfuls of shriveled leaves clinging to the large beech and oak trees overhead. But there was peace.

————

Back at home near mid-morning, I helped Bea slice onion and celery, crumble corn bread and stale white bread for the dressing. We were expecting nine—maybe ten—for Thanksgiving dinner later in the afternoon. My sister was busy chopping fresh celery with a determined vigor.

The large bird roasting in our oven already infused the cozy kitchen, indeed the entire rectory, with its golden aroma. We had much to be thankful for.

"Do you really think he thought he could get away with it?" asked Bea, halting her rhythmic chopping for a moment. She had only asked me this three times before, and I thought I had made her promise that we wouldn't mention Gentry Truman's name all day today.

"Yes," I said, a bit exasperated. "I think that vanity coupled with wealth, selfishness, and hatred is a potent formula."

"But really," said Bea, resuming her knife blade to a celery stalk, "trying to impersonate someone else? I can't believe he lasted as long as he did. And even though she didn't murder poor Mr. Sanders herself, Marcia Truman was just as guilty as I suspected. Didn't I tell you she was dangerous?"

I brushed my cutting board's worth of onion into an oversized aluminum bowl with the various bread crumbs. My eyes were misting from the potent root. "Marcia was caught in a difficult situation. She felt she didn't have any choices. I'm not excusing her, but I ultimately hold her husband responsible for the misery of all involved."

"It's wonderful, though, that Florence is doing so well," she said. "I called yesterday and talked to her. She thinks she'll be out of the hospital in another week. Said she's thinking of moving up north, close to her daughter. She's very grateful to you, you know."

"I'm just glad that she survived an ordeal that was intended to kill her."

" 'You meant evil against me, but God meant it for good, to bring it about that many people should be kept alive . . .' " she said quietly.

I looked at her curiously, marveling that any redemption whatsoever could emerge from one man's perverse selfishness.

"When did you know that Gentry was really alive, Grif?" my sister asked. "When did you even suspect such a thing as him killing Cale and assuming his identity?"

"Believe it or not, I think it was that Tuesday afternoon when I talked to John on the phone, complaining about this renovation business with Joan. It was his idea to distinguish between renovation and restoration. It got me thinking about how change occurs . . . how people change most of all. By the end of the week, I managed to make most of the pieces fit, although it sounded ludicrous. Talking with Caroline about her own changes and the accompanying make-over helped.

"When I discovered that the trace chemical found on the deceased's neck was also found in hair color, it seemed logical that hair color had been washed out of his hair. Gentry had gray; Cale did not, even though he was older. After Cale passed out drunk and before he shot him, Gentry had washed his brother's hair with a professional hair solution to remove the color. He even trimmed it to match his own cut, even though theirs were very similar. Then Gentry colored his own hair to match the shade Cale had used. Add a false mustache like his brother's, and Truman was all set. So much of the transformation, as Caroline informed me, was attitude and acting, and Gentry was a master at both. The physical resemblance and clothing were merely props."

"So young Jenna really did see her father in his bedroom that night you were there," observed Bea.

"Yes," I said. "Gentry had forgotten to destroy a letter he'd received from Cale that expressed his unwillingness to forgive his brother for abandoning him. Gentry was afraid the letter would provide additional motive for his new identity. Jenna walked in on him, and even though he was disguised as Cale, in the dark she instinctively knew it was her father."

"Same thing at the memorial service?" asked Bea.

"Yes. Marcia admitted that Gentry couldn't bear to miss this outpouring of warm wishes and fond memories for himself. Who hasn't fantasized about witnessing his own funeral? So he hid in the bride's room and peeped around the corner when he dared. Jenna once more was the victim of her own acute sensitivity and her father's deception. . . . Apparently, no one else noticed."

"How are the girls handling all this?" She emptied her minced celery into the mixing bowl and began adding more sage.

"They're still in a difficult place. It's one thing to accept your father's death; quite another to realize the depths of his selfishness. They're going to invalidate the will and reach a new settlement that includes Marcia more proportionately. They've asked me to be the executor and I've agreed, although I'm not looking forward to it."

"One more reason to stage his own death and assume his main beneficiary's identity. He went from bankruptcy to multimillionaire in one black second. . . . I still can't believe it. And I still can't believe that you could've easily ended up another of his victims. Griffin Reed, you promise me that you'll never put yourself in that kind of danger again!"

"I'm thankful for our Lord's protection, Bea. But I'd do the same thing again if I had to. Besides, I'm safe as long as Caroline's around . . . and Dan Warren." I chuckled but sincerely admired the courage of my friends.

"What time did you tell her to come over?" asked Bea, suddenly keen to change the subject.

"I told her around noon, although I made it clear we wouldn't be eating until two. She insisted on bringing the cranberry relish—her grandmother's recipe."

"She's a lovely woman, Grif. Remember what I told you before. Be open to what God's up to." With a large wooden spoon, my sister mixed chopped hard-boiled eggs and chicken broth into the dressing. "Taste this, please. More salt?"

"It tastes just fine, Beatrice. Just fine."

Around our table a few hours later I was surrounded by faces I loved: My sister sat on my right, and then Dan Warren and his wife, Diane, along with their twin girls, followed by Jenna Truman in a lovely navy dress. Next, Charlie Baxter sat upright in a clean shirt and new jeans, alongside Joan Dowinger, of all people, looking regal as always in a white blouse, black skirt, and cardigan. "I came as a pilgrim!" she'd said at the door. My curate, Peter, sat next to her, discussing plans for the new restoration project in the Cathedral of the Divine beginning in January. Between him and myself sat Caroline Barr, who had canceled her plans to fly to her mother's house in Albany because of the flu. She had confessed to me the day before that she was feeling much better but was glad to have an excuse to stay in Avenell for the holiday. Her hand felt warm and comfortable inside mine as we all held hands around the table and gave God thanks.

I was overwhelmed with the many blessings in my life. I was grateful for the way the Father had chosen to use me to bring about His justice and to spare other people's lives. Most of all, I was grateful for the presence of my extended family around me, especially the new woman to my left.

After the overwhelming meal—the turkey juicy and the dressing perfect—Bea and Caroline served coffee, and Jenna offered us our choices of pumpkin pie or coconut cake. I turned to Peter. "Have you talked to Leah this week?" I asked.

"Yes," he replied with a mysterious gleam in his eye. "Once everyone is seated again, I have an announcement to make."

I didn't know what to think, and fortunately, I was not kept waiting long as the others placed the last desserts on the table and rejoined us at table.

"I want you all to be the first to know. I asked Leah to marry me this morning. That's why I was late—I drove down to Tremont and back."

"Peter, that's wonderful!" exclaimed Bea.

"Congratulations, Pete!" Dan and I said in unison.

"Has she responded yet?" I asked.

Pete's voice shifted. "Not yet. She has to discuss it with her parents."

I heard Bea whisper to Joan and Charlie across the table, "She's Amish."

"I talked with her father first," Pete continued. "But he wasn't very excited about it. He didn't forbid it, but he didn't give me his blessing, either. He only said that he wished to talk to Leah after I proposed. I told her to take as much time as she needs to decide, but I feel like I'm about to burst having to wait!"

As I bit into pumpkin pie, little did I know then that Leah's surprising response—and the ensuing consequences—would lead me once more into a web of secrets, hidden motives, and murder in her unique community. But that's another story.

In the meantime, after the dishes had been cleared and the leftovers wrapped, we gathered around the upright piano that had been my mother's, and Bea played for us. As my heart flooded with gratitude, I stood alongside my hopeful curate, clasped my arm around his shoulder, and raised my voice with the others:

> *All creatures of our God and King,*
> *Lift up your voice and with us sing,*
> *Alleluia! Alleluia!*
> *Thou burning sun with golden beam,*
> *Thou silver moon with softer gleam,*
> *O praise Him! O praise Him!*
> *Alleluia! Alleluia! Alleluia!*

The Judas Tree
D. J. Delffs

Father Grif gets unwittingly wrapped up in another murder mystery when Leah Schroeder, the Amish woman engaged to curate Peter Abernathy, stumbles upon a grisly hanging. As Father Grif investigates, layers of secrets come together like the strands of an Amish quilt: a secret affair that split the community and ended in death more than twenty-five years ago, an unexpected rejection of values, and a young victim carrying the blame for his father's death. Amid the spring splendor of Avenell University, Father Grif unravels the consequences of betrayal and the power of a community united in faith.

Watch for *The Judas Tree*, to be released during the summer of 1999.